LURES

SUE GOYETTE

Lures

a novel

Harper*Flamingo*Canada

Lures: A Novel
Copyright © 2002 by Sue Goyette.
All rights reserved. No part of this book may be
used or reproduced in any manner whatsoever
without prior written permission except in the
case of brief quotations embodied in reviews.
For information address
HarperCollins Publishers Ltd,
55 Avenue Road, Suite 2900,
Toronto, Ontario, Canada M 5 R 3 L 2

www.harpercanada.com

HarperCollins books may be purchased for
educational, business, or sales promotional use.
For information please write:
Special Markets Department,
HarperCollins Canada,
55 Avenue Road, Suite 2900,
Toronto, Ontario, Canada M 5 R 3 L 2

First edition

Canadian Cataloguing in Publication Data

Goyette, Sue
Lures : a novel

I S B N 0-00-200506-9

1. Title.

PS8563.0934L87 2002   C813'.54   C2001-902517-3
PR9199.3.G659L87 2002

HC 9 8 7 6 5 4 3 2 1

Printed and bound in the United States
Set in Monotype Garamond

*for my mother, Carolyn,
and for my sisters, Pam and Lori*

I know,
I know and you know, we knew,
we did not know, we
were there, after all, and not there
and at times when
only the void stood between us we got
all the way to each other.

PAUL CELAN

Autumn

Slowly the trees gave up their green, surrendering to yellow, to red and orange, and then the leaves of Beaumont turned brown and fell from their branches. The streets that made up the town became lined with them gathered along the curbs and at the base of lampposts. The seasons were shifting, and for one day the light teetered, balanced itself evenly with the dark and then slowly began to recede. Equinox. The weekends were spent raking the leaves into huge piles that kids and the wind destroyed, whipping the leaves back up to the sky and sending them blowing down driveways, across streets and into other yards. People tried bagging them, burning them. They opened their arms wide to them and tried carrying them, lifting them and putting them away. But they couldn't hold them all and had to keep bending, raking, gathering. Autumn had come to the town overnight, it seemed, and all of a sudden it was everywhere. Just the way the stop signs had disappeared in the town, replaced now with signs that said *Arrêt*. Overnight. It took days for people to notice that all the street signs now said *rue*. *Rue* Hillside, *rue* Maple, *rue* Oak.

The town workers in their orange coveralls drove around in pickup trucks, clearing sewers and dragging away picnic tables to store until spring. They collected all the flower baskets that hung from the lampposts on the main streets; they rolled the barrels that still had snapdragons, the last daisies flowering limply in a tangle of dying stems and leaves, into the back of their trucks. It was their job to prepare the town for the next season, to keep it running smoothly.

Beyond the town, surrounding it, were highways, service roads, narrow dirt paths tracked down by kids on their bikes, who rode through brush, ducking under low branches until they got to the edge of the town. Train tracks bordered the southern edge, and beyond them the highway ran east and west towards the south shore of Montreal. There were buildings at the town's centre, hardware stores, a fire station, boulevards with medians that had colour-coordinated petunias blooming only weeks ago—white and pink with dusty miller planted in between, patterned—that were now just stalks, browned and finished. Surrounding the stores were apartment buildings, cedars planted beside the entrances, their tips yellow. There was always a mattress in one of the garbage bins, stained and collapsed over itself, always bags of garbage, a broken chair or a lamp waiting at the curb, always a car with its hood open and someone bent into it, a cigarette like a small chimney wafting smoke over his shoulder. Young families lived there, retired couples, students. You could read the buildings by the balconies: small flags, wind chimes, an old bleach bottle with the top cut off full of clothespins, lawn chairs and a Hibachi all crammed together on one balcony or empty cases of beer stacked by the door, a kitchen chair and a can full of cigarette butts on another. The parking lots beside the buildings were filled with aging cars, rusting Novas, Malibus, and polished new Buicks with fuzzy steering wheel covers. *Je me souviens*, each licence plate declared. *Je me souviens*.

Rippling farther out were semi-detached houses, duplexes as well. Signs on the doors that said *Bienvenue*, the occasional Welcome, and smaller signs in windows that said *Oui* or *Non* for the milkman. These houses had small, well-tended yards with hedges dividing the property, small wooden fences. The doors and shutters were painted mostly to match each other, although there was an occasional building painted two wildly different colours, and you'd wonder whether it was a showdown somehow, a dispute between shutters and doors.

Even farther from the town's centre were the houses with big backyards and swimming pools, winding stone paths that led from back door to patio, around gardens, and to pools above or in ground. The farther from its centre, the greener the town got. The yards were well maintained, the leaves raked, the trees almost blending, matching in colours as if planned. Reds and yellows with the occasional brilliance that a maple could contain, that fevered orange that seemed pure fire, the canary yellow of birch twittering in the soft breeze.

Before the town exhausted itself, gave up to the mountain along its eastern shoulder, the train tracks, there were smaller houses again, older houses, bungalows with big living room windows without sheer curtains. Houses you could look into that seemed part apartment, with mops drying on their porches and the occasional kitchen chair dragged out, and part backyard, with small, well-tended garden plots, stubborn goldenrod still growing between gladiolus and peony stalks.

And after those streets, the town ended and the grass grew high, trees bunched, gulleys ran. It was a border of bulrushes and dogwood, slim-trunked birches and poplars, between the last street of houses and the highway. The trees and bushes were dense enough that when kids did bike through them on narrow, single-file paths, they could hear the highway without seeing it, and the traffic, pushing the hundred-kilometre speed limit, sounded like the roar of ocean. Always they felt a small pang of disappointment when they finally did clear the trees, the grass, and saw it for themselves: the highway, four lanes across, the cars a blur driving by the town's welcome sign, *Bien-venue à Beaumont*. And there was the thundering of the train they tried to yell through, screaming into the sound of it. They were always surprised when it was gone, surprised at the enormous wake of its silence, startled into silence themselves.

The last bus out of town stopped running just after midnight. There was only one twenty-four-hour dépanneur; the rest closed at eleven. The last train before morning went by at about two, year round, in all seasons. The lights along the road to the mountain had burnt out or had been turned off, and now at night the mountain looked like a long beast lying on its side, the one light left on at the parking lot near the apple orchard positioned where an eye would be. If you looked northeast out of town, you'd see the beast watching the town sleep with its one eye open, never blinking. It watched the stop signs being exchanged with signs that said *Arrêt* on every corner, it saw the last bus's headlights wind their way up its side and then back down its tail, and it watched fall creep up on summer, secretly pinching the tips of leaves, the clover and asters, and turning them brown. It watched the cold peer into windows and leave them frosted by morning.

And if you couldn't sleep, the train's long, low whistle would lament with you, pulling out your troubles, your worries, along the track that ran on the southern edge of the town. The sound of it commiserated with you, understood the sinking feeling you had in the pit of your stomach, and took it, weaving it between the woods and the highway where the tracks ran. It was a sound that everyone in the town knew, that everyone heard awake or in dreams. And in dreams, it would transform from train whistle into a thin dog howling at the end of its chain or a woman lying down, her arm extended the width of the empty double bed, lonely. Lonely. It was a sound that left a taste in everyone's mouth, that reached into homes and whispered *homesick* and *sadness* and *leaving* and *arriving*. But most of the time no one heard it because the people in the town had heard it too often. They took the sound of it for granted, just as they had begun to take summer and its heat, its sky full of stars and its goldenrod, for granted. And now when they woke, the people of Beaumont, they woke to autumn. The trees that had once engulfed street lamps, the maples, the birches, the branches that had glowed with swallowed light, now surrendered their green, now began to give up their leaves and stand bare against the low sky. Already it seemed colder, the colours that were left lingering brilliantly. The wild asters, the thistle, vivid and stubborn in the pale premonition of winter. Almost daring.

*   *   *

Grace was locked out of her house again. She noticed the cold now, but not the bare trees. Her yard didn't have any trees. Just one dwarfed crabapple in the backyard that her father had pruned too severely and kept teetering between life and death, and menaced by caterpillars.

Her older brother was home but was sleeping in his basement bedroom. Grace imagined him lying there, still in the clothes he had come home in, under his Pink Floyd and Zeppelin posters, hung over, dried up, passed out. He wouldn't hear her. She kicked at his window anyway and then went back to the door. No one ever remembered that she didn't have a key, that she was outside when they locked the door.

Her father had bought one of those fake rocks that hid house keys for this exact situation. But he kept it inside because he didn't want anyone to steal it.

She kicked the door again. If Sharon still lived around the corner, she could go there to wait for her mother to come home, but Sharon had moved. Like half the town, Grace thought glumly, half the town that had joined the exodus from Quebec to somewhere "out west." Calgary. Edmonton. Cities where there were jobs that didn't require French, cities that were far away from the politics of French signs, from the talk of separating from the rest of the country, from René Lévesque.

Her family had stayed. Her mother worked downtown, taking the bus every day, and her father worked all night at an oil company. He was in charge of parts, he'd tell anyone who'd listen, and parts were parts, no matter what Mr. Lévesque spouted off.

Tools, Grace would say to herself silently every time he bragged. He was in charge of tools. And she wished she could be French, to say words like *peut-être* and *pouvoir* and to wear black eyeliner and tight Lois jeans the way the French girls she watched at McDonald's did. They seemed so confident, flirting with the boys working at the counter, teasing them, making them blush. The guys they were with never took their cigarettes from their mouths and watched their girlfriends talk, squinting through the smoke smouldering between them. No one ever watched Grace like that.

She imagined sitting at the supper table asking for the *sel*, the *poivre*. She could just hear her father ask her what the hell she was doing talking like those goddamn Frenchmen at work. Didn't he have enough of them to put up with, he'd say, jabbing the air between them with his fork, without his own daughter speaking like one of those Pepsis?

Clé, she thought, she coaxed, looking again through her pockets. She kicked the door again and decided to walk over to Lily's house. She'd already done that twice this month for the same reason, and Lily was always home, copying the *World Book of Knowledge* into Hilroy copybooks. She had told Grace in French class that she'd been doing it since she was fifteen, for two years now, and was almost finished the letter *c*. "Knowledge is key," she had said, "a way out." This impressed Grace. She'd watch Lily in French class neatly underline the word she was on and then write out the entry under it. She was doing it for the knowledge, Lily told her, and so her younger brother and sister would have the encyclopedia as well. Grace envied Lily. Even when they hadn't been friends, Lily had always been on the edge, not fitting in but always busy, happily engrossed in her work. Grace envied her not just for the copybooks already filled and piled on a bookshelf in her room, but for the smell of supper cooking in her house, the music that played in the living room, her mother who had smiled at Grace when she had first visited, for the way the lights were turned on before it got completely dark. Grace's house was always empty, and when it wasn't, she wished it was. She was alone in a different way from Lily. And the door was always locked when she came home from school. Her father was afraid she'd lose a key and then every Tom, Dick and Harry would find it and let themselves in and rob him blind. She was seventeen, she had replied, and he had just shrugged. She kicked the door once more and then headed towards the train tracks, to Lily's house.

*   *   *

Curtis, Lily's younger brother, opened the door when Grace knocked. He peered at her through toy binoculars.

"Hello. Is Lily home?"

Curtis nodded yes with the binoculars and then looked up at Grace's face before running off down the hallway. A younger girl followed him. She looked back at Grace curiously, sucking hard on the soother in her mouth. Grace smiled and the girl smiled back, the soother slipping out of her mouth until she slurped it noisily back in.

"Hey, Grace." Lily had come down from her room and was holding her copybook to her chest. "Are you locked out?"

"Yeah. I can't believe I forgot my key again." Grace shook her head. She couldn't tell her friend that her father had forgotten her again when he had left for work, that he had turned before leaving, put his key in the deadbolt and without one thought of her locked the door. She hadn't been hanging around Lily long enough to admit that the fake rock was kept inside so it wouldn't be stolen. *Restez calme*, Grace thought. She had read that in the metro once, on a sign that explained what to do in case of an emergency. *Étage 1: Restez calme*.

"Well, come on in. Are you hungry? My mom just made some muffins."

Grace followed Lily into the kitchen, stepping over a stuffed bear and a line of wooden blocks that had been placed meticulously in a straight line all the way down the hall. Curtis watched them through his binoculars, ignoring Dellie who was skipping and hopping and making smacking noises with her soother.

Lily's mother was sitting in the kitchen with a sketch pad on the table in front of her. She was peering closely at a glass bowl full of eggs and barely looked up when they all came in.

"Can we have a muffin, Mom?"

Lily's mother, Eliza, nodded without looking away from the eggs. Grace watched her while Lily handed out muffins to Curtis and Dellie. Eliza had started drawing the bowl and then stopped. She looked up at Grace and smiled.

"Hello, Grace. I didn't know you were here."

Grace smiled shyly.

"These eggs are giving me a hard time. Or rather the weight of them. They're hard-boiled and I'm trying to draw them heavy, if you know what I mean."

Grace smiled as if she did, as if drawing hard-boiled eggs was something her mother did as well and she was used to it being a problem.

The only time Grace ever saw her mother holding a pencil was when she was making up the grocery list or marking down "pay" on the calendar or "milkman" or "period." She couldn't even remember her mother hard-boiling eggs. She made pasta for supper, tuna casserole, macaroni and cheese. And Grace made her own sandwiches for lunch. Peanut butter and jam, peanut butter and banana, sometimes just peanut butter. Her mother said sandwich meat was too expensive and her brother Gary ate it all up in a day. It wasn't worth buying, her mother had replied when Grace had asked her to. Chop up a hot dog, she had suggested, if you want sandwich meat.

Grace took the muffin that Lily was holding out to her and bit into it hungrily and looked around the kitchen. Cupboards were opened, the light over the stove was on. The flour canister was still out and a dusting of flour had covered the measuring cups, the spatula, the counter. Winter, Grace thought, with the sky outside a deep blue that made bare trees a work of art. She realized that she thought of art when she was in Lily's house; at home they were just bare trees and a sky full of dark, heavy clouds. Curtis and Dellie followed the girls to Lily's room and stood lingering in the doorway, watching Grace and Lily sit down on her bed.

"You guys go play now. Grace and I are going to talk."

Curtis pretended not to hear, engrossed with looking at his muffin through his binoculars. Dellie pulled out her soother and took a bite of hers, smiling widely while she chewed.

"Go on. Go finish making your road with blocks, Curtis. Dellie will help, won't you, Dellie?"

Dellie nodded eagerly, her curls bouncing like tightly coiled springs on her head.

"Oh yeah, Lily. I'm the best helper in the world," she exclaimed, holding her soother in one hand and putting her muffin down on the floor. "I am this many," she told Grace, holding up four fingers. Curtis swung his binoculars to look dubiously at his younger sister. He looked back at Lily, clearly dismayed.

"Go on, Curtis, she just might surprise you."

"Yeah, c'mon, Curtis." Dellie meowed at her brother. "Did you know that I'm a pussycat, Curtis? Cats like building roads." She plugged her soother back into her mouth triumphantly and then went downstairs to help build the road that was lined up in the hallway, Curtis following her reluctantly. Lily closed her door.

Grace had leaned against the wall, watching. Her house was so different from this one. Hers was cleaner but barer. Her mother liked things tidy and kept all the living room furniture covered in plastic. The carpet down the hallway had a plastic runner over it and so did the carpet up the stairs. Even the kitchen table had plastic over it, with the placemats underneath. Easier to wipe, her mother had told her, taking the cloth from Grace and wiping the table herself.

"Your mother doesn't mind you eating in your bedroom?" Grace was trying to pick all the crumbs off her shirt. "My mother would kill me if she even found a plate upstairs."

Lily looked surprised. "She doesn't really care about stuff like that," she said.

"Gary keeps his door locked, but my mother goes into my room all the time. To put away the laundry, she says."

Lily shook her head sympathetically. "My mother is pretty laid-back about food. My father complains if we leave stuff around. I think it bothers him more than her."

Grace stayed until she knew her mother would be home and then she got up from Lily's bed and went downstairs, exclaiming over the length the wooden block road was before she left.

She looked into the kitchen where Eliza was still drawing the eggs, shading in the bottom of the bowl now. Lily's father, Stan, was at the stove, stirring something in a pot, stew, Grace thought. They both smiled at her when she said goodbye. Lily's father made her blush with his wink.

Grace walked across town towards home, past houses with lit windows and families in living rooms, in kitchens talking about their day, how good it was or how bad. Store windows advertised *ventes* and *prix réduit, bière froide*. She crossed intersections where cars were forced to slow down to let her by. The traffic was heavy now with cars full of people coming home, rush hour. Rushing to get home, she thought, to take their shoes off, to relax.

The front of her house was still dark. She walked up slowly to the plain semi-detached, thinking about the word *semi-detached*, thinking there wasn't anything "semi" about it. Even though her house was attached to the one beside it, it felt completely detached from everything on the street. It didn't have a garden under the living room window as the other houses did, it didn't have any window boxes. The lawn went right up to the house, the walkway was crumbling and the grass that had sprouted between the cracks was dead now, dull and brown. Detached. The neighbour had painted his door twice since her father had used up some leftover paint to paint theirs. Their door was once a bright red and now was fading into a colour Grace couldn't even name. Rusty blood, maybe, or scab.

She went up to the side door and turned the handle. The door was still locked. She knocked on it and heard someone inside turn the deadbolt. Her mother opened the door and looked out suspiciously.

"Where have you been?" she asked when she saw Grace.

"The door was locked again. I couldn't get in."

Sheila looked at her daughter, still holding the door only partway open. "Why didn't you wake your brother?"

Grace looked at her incredulously. "You're joking, right?"

Sheila shook her head and let go of the door. Grace went in, hanging her jacket on one of the hooks. Gary was up and peering sleepily into the fridge. His plaid shirt looked crumpled and his jeans were saggy and stained. Thin whiskers grew along his chin and his eyes looked red and washed out.

"Didn't you hear me pounding on your window, Gary?"

"Huh?" He looked groggily at his sister as if she was familiar but he couldn't place her face, couldn't remember who she was. "Oh, sorry, man. I was crashed. Hey, Grace, you owe me ten bucks."

Grace looked quickly at their mother, who was dumping macaroni in a pot of boiling water. The steam from the pot fogged up the window and made the ceiling glisten. Was he crazy bringing that up in front of her? She looked at him; he was looking into the fridge again, oblivious to her glare. He was stoned, she thought. Again. Ever since he had started dealing grass for Ralph Harris, he was smoking all the time. Stupid. And moronic for mentioning in front of their mother the money Grace owed him for the weed she had fronted last weekend. She grabbed her knapsack and quickly headed up to her room before he could say anything else.

She went by the living room, seeing the plastic-covered sofa, the chairs, the lampshades differently now after being in Lily's house. The only thing hanging on the wall here was her father's barometer, which he'd tap nightly, standing up on his toes to read it as if he knew what atmospheric pressure was, as if he could forecast the weather. There were doilies on the back of the chairs, the sofa, under each lamp, each ashtray on the tables. It looked as if huge identical snowflakes had fallen in the room, landing everywhere, the furniture iced over in slippery plastic. Grace breathed out, half expecting to see her breath. Her living room was more like winter, she thought. Lily's house was summer, warm and inviting. There were drawings on the walls, faces smiling down, trees. Grace's father had put labels with his name and social insurance number on the television and stereo. If she looked closely, she could see those tags on practically everything that plugged in.

Even when her parents weren't at home, Grace could hear her mother with her plastic couch saying, "This is mine." And her father, his name marked carefully in capital letters on the side of the TV, answering, "Well, this is mine." Even Gary's room in the basement had a big Keep Out sign he had stolen from some construction site. The only room she liked was her own, she thought, closing the door behind her. She liked her posters and the small poems that she had copied out and hung on her wall, the African violets, the ivy she had bought at the school fair and kept on her dresser. She liked her books columning crookedly against the wall and the dust that swirled under her bed, the fine blanket of it on her night table and lampshade. She liked the cobweb hanging in the corner from the ceiling. And she especially liked the lock on the door that had been moved several times, leaving holes in the frame and the door itself. Eight holes. Eight times her father had broken down the door. It was his house, he had bellowed, and he'd be damned if he was going to be locked out of it.

Curtis liked quiet. He wanted to build his road, lining the edges of the blocks together so there wouldn't be a space between them, and he wanted to do it quietly so he could count them. He was up to thirteen. But he had to count them over and over because Dellie kept humming and singing about roads and teddy bears and mommies and daddies and cats. He hardly ever talked, and when he did, he spoke quietly. His sister, he thought, was his *opposite*, sounding out to himself the new word he had learned in school. He looked over at Dellie, who was squatting over the road, one hand straightening a block and the other taking out her soother to sing and then putting it back into her mouth. They were opposites, all right. She was faster than he was and ran all the time. That was why he loved his binoculars, that was why he wore them around his neck all the time, even to school. He could look at things really closely with them on. He also liked to count. He liked numbers way better than words. Numbers were important, he thought. He liked knowing that he had twelve red Hot Wheels cars and sixteen blue ones. He liked knowing that he had five feathers from his older brother, Jerry, and eight rocks.

Curtis smiled to himself, thinking about Jerry. He didn't live with them any more because there had been too much yelling. Well, he did live with them, Curtis corrected himself, but only sometimes. Jerry liked being outside, his father had explained to him when he had asked. He liked the sky better than ceilings.

"Curtis, watch me hopping."

Curtis looked up and saw Dellie trying to jump over the blocks he had set up. She was really good at talking, he thought, but not very good at hopping, and he sighed heavily, getting up to fix the blocks she had knocked out of place. Cats weren't supposed to hop, he thought, didn't she know anything?

Their father came into the hallway wiping his hands on a towel.

"Hey, cowboy, hey, Dellie, how does supper sound?"

"Yummy in my tummy!" yelled Dellie, running over to her father and throwing her arms around his legs. He laughed and swung her up over his shoulders.

"Who wants to buy a bag of potatoes?" he asked.

"Hey," Dellie shrieked, "I'm not a bag of potatoes, Daddy!"

Stan carried his daughter to the foot of the stairs. "Lily, supper's ready." He put Dellie down and tousled Curtis's hair when he went by. "Come and get it, Curtis."

Eliza moved the bowl of eggs and her sketchbook and sat back down with her family, kissing Dellie's finger where she had knocked it on the table. Stan pushed Curtis's chair closer to the table and then passed the potatoes to Lily, who had just come down, sliding onto her chair beside Eliza. He turned to get the salt and pepper shakers from the counter and banged his head on the corner of the open cupboard door.

"Jesus Christ," he said fiercely, rubbing his head, and then sat down.

They all caught their breath and held it, watching him, waiting. No one exhaled until he motioned for them to start, to fill their plates before he served himself, and then they all talked at once. Relieved that his anger had blown over this time.

Jerry watched his father move from the kitchen counter to the table through the window facing their backyard. He was standing behind his house in the woods that grew between the town and the railway tracks. Behind him, beyond the tracks, was the highway. He could hear the traffic speeding by the town.

He watched his family come into the kitchen, the light from the window spilling out into the yard, yellow, golden. Every window in the back of the house was lit; there was a tricycle in the pool of light from the kitchen. He could take about forty steps and be at the side door. The handle turned to the right, the screen door would squeak, the solid one wouldn't. He could pull the extra chair from the living room into the kitchen and sit with them, dip his fork into whatever they were eating, and he could eat with them. His family was that close. Seventy-five steps to the front door, where both doors creaked, the knobs turned left and the inside door would sometimes stick. It frightened him sometimes, how close they were and how far away. He was the same, they were the same, but in a matter of a few moments—his father pushing him, his head hitting the wall, his shoulders, Jerry pushing back, his mother holding his arm—in the moments when his father pushed him away and his mother held him there, something stepped between him and his father and created a distance that couldn't be measured by anything now except "before" and "after." It became his point of reference when he thought about his life. In the backyard, forty steps from the back door, from dragging the chair to the kitchen table and sitting down with his family, was "after." "After" was that afternoon of being pushed too hard, of leaving and then watching the way back home cave into itself, disappear.

He blew into his hands and leaned against a birch. Watching them made him feel warm. He waited until they had all sat down to eat and then walked into his yard to the back porch and opened the clothespin box quietly. He took out the sandwiches Lily had left for him and then went back into the woods.

The town slowed down on weekends. Cars drove to the grocery store in no hurry to get there, in no hurry to park. Side streets were filled with kids playing; street hockey nets barricaded some streets, and though it was cold, bikes were still around, basketballs. When the sun did come out, it came out abruptly and shone on only some of the cars, only some of the yards, before another cloud skidded along in front of it. It was then that people would look up at the sky and wonder what had happened to the light, only after it had gone.

Sheila had spent the morning refolding the towels in the linen closet. She liked them folded three times and piled neatly. Every time Gary or Grace went in for a fresh towel, they'd leave a mess. So did her husband, Les.

Just thinking about Les and the mess he always left made Sheila purse her lips. She went into her bedroom to look out the window to see what he was up to now. Whatever he was doing, he would prove she was right. He was only capable of making a mess. That was the one thing she could count on. And then she'd have to fix it. That was why she had to watch him. Always. God knew what would happen to him without her.

Through the window Sheila watched him uncoil an orange extension cord and plug it into the outlet at the back of the house. He couldn't be mowing, she thought, looking at the grass that was dull and brown. He bent over something he had put on the ground and soon the backyard was filled with the sound of his new electric hedge trimmer. She watched him carry it in front of him to the cedar hedge that bordered their yard with their neighbour's. Technically it wasn't their hedge.

Les knew that. Their neighbour had trimmed the hedge the weekend before, making Les haul out his file folder labelled Household and unroll the deed to their property. The hedge was marked clearly on their neighbour's land, Sheila had pointed out. A mistake, Les had hissed. Any numbskull could draw up plans, but it took a specially trained draftsman like himself to do it properly, and was she, he had asked, inches from her face, calling him a liar?

She watched him slice branches off the side of the shrub, waving the hedge trimmer in front of him like a flag sema-phoring the message that he was Les McIntyre and if he wanted to trim the hedge, he'd damn well trim it.

She picked at the windowsill nervously, watching their neighbour come out on his back porch still in his bathrobe and gesture wildly with his cigarette at Les, who ignored him and worked his way to the top of the shrub.

The cedars looked bare now. Sheila could see through them into the next yard. She could almost smell them as the pale moons of their cut branches glistened in the sun. She heard her husband's voice over the whirr of the trimmer's motor and backed away from the window, not wanting to be seen, not wanting the neighbour to look up and see her, connect her to Les as his wife. She went into the bathroom and opened the medicine cabinet, taking out the small pill bottles with Les's name typed on them, pills for his heart, for his blood pressure; she took down the blue Vicks bottle, the ointment that he'd rub slowly onto his chest and nose before bed; she took down his bandages that he wrapped his knee up with and the eye drops he used when his eyes felt dry. She took down his nose drops. When they first were married, there had been room in the cabinet for her Avon facial scrub, for the razors she used to shave her legs, even for her face cream. He was charming then, singing to her, wooing her, luring her in. And the way he used to dress, always in a suit, a tie with a matching handker-chief. If she complained about the pile of clothes in the bedroom, the wet towels behind the door, he'd promise to try harder. He needed her, he'd tell her, and then he'd rub his chest and wince at the effort of it all. His heart always ached. Sheila rolled her eyes.

At first she had felt needed, and she had thought being needed meant being loved, but slowly she had realized that he never really listened to her, that he just waited for her to finish talking so he could talk some more. "Would you let me put in my two cents?" he'd ask impatiently and she'd indulge him. But by then it was too late to walk away; they had a mortgage, a car payment, a daily routine. She was stuck. She snorted and opened the medicine cabinet wider, careful not to catch sight of herself in the mirror. Her eyes were her daughter Grace's eyes looking back at her, bewildered at how she left herself behind, went to work every day, how she made supper, crocheted until bedtime, how each day rolled into another until her life had become a clump of days she couldn't tell apart. Just thinking about them all exhausted her. Sheila couldn't stand looking into her eyes and seeing them question her beseechingly. Grace's eyes and her small voice as a young girl asking Sheila to read to her, the same book every night. She had carted it around with her everywhere and would sit next to anyone and demand to be read to. "Are you my mother?" Grace would ask along with the baby bird in the book. She'd ask the fridge, the couch, the front door: "Are you my mother?" It drove Les mad. "Take your nose out of that book, for God's sake. Your mother is sitting right over there, she's not the goddamn television set." Sheila remembered the relief she had felt when Grace stopped asking, when she learned to read on her own. "No," she used to want to answer, "I'm not really your mother." She was too tired most nights to sit with her daughter and read. She was glad when Grace could finally do it on her own.

Never mind, she thought, and returned to the job at hand. Les had taken over the medicine cabinet shelves and she couldn't remember when it had happened. He had taken over slowly, she supposed, pill bottle by pill bottle. First his angina medicine for the heart pains he felt when they talked about money, and then his nose drops, his special drops for his ears so he could hear better, hear himself talking. Sheila emptied the cabinet and began scrubbing the shelves vigorously as if she could scrub the sound of him and his hedge trimmer, of his voice, sarcastic and needling, from her life. "No, I'm not your mother. No, I'm not your wife."

Grace lay in bed thinking she needed a job, just a part-time job to keep Gary off her back. She hated owing him money, but when she stood in his room waiting for him to pull out his stash from under his mattress, the black light on his night table casting small purple dots all over her arms, Pink Floyd moving from speaker to speaker from one then the other corner of his room, it was hypnotizing. "How much cannabis do you want?" he'd ask, holding out a little plastic bag of plumply rolled joints. "They're all flower tops," he'd say, holding them out closer. "Really mellow. They're going to go fast, I probably won't get any more for a few weeks." He'd look at her and smile sweetly, raggedy and stoned, and then tell her that he was doing her a favour, selling them so cheaply to her, and he never fronted. No coin, no candy was his policy, but since she was special, he had said, since she was his sister, his little sister, he'd do it for her. And then he waited.

It was easier when Sharon lived in town. They had been best friends until last year when Sharon's father had got a job in Winnipeg and moved them away. Sharon used to get an allowance and would pay half. But Grace was on her own now and Lily didn't seem the type to smoke. Her mother had scoffed at Grace's suggestion of an allowance. For what? she had asked. We get you everything you need.

Smoking took the edge off things. Smoking was spring. It made her hungry and then even peanut butter tasted good.

And she could always count on Gary to have some dope or to buy her a mickey of rum or Southern Comfort. That was the one thing she could count on him for. "I'm your personal candyman," he'd tell her whenever she asked him for anything.

The Crémerie was looking for part-time help. She had seen the sign on her way home from Lily's. Grace swung out of bed. She'd get dressed and go down and apply. Serving ice cream couldn't be that hard, she figured. *Crème glacée. Voulez-vous de la crème glacée?* Easy.

She pulled up her blind and looked out the window. Her father was waving a hedge trimmer in their neighbour's face, yelling so hard he was standing on his tiptoes. She watched incredulously as the neighbour took a pair of shears and began savagely attacking the hedge that stood between them. Her father did the same on his side. The hedge shrank quickly between them; its cut branches, thrown over the men's shoulders, soon covered the lawn. Grace backed away in disbelief.

Les leaned the hedge trimmer up against the house and came in, red-faced, throwing his work gloves on the floor.

"Goddamn Frenchman, couldn't understand a word he was saying."

Grace watched him, holding her toast between the plate and her mouth. Les looked over at her.

"Did you see what that maniac did to my hedge?"

Grace shook her head.

"That Mr. Pepsi cut the goddamn hedge down to my ankles. I said to him, 'Listen here, Mr. Frenchie, you are not acting like a Christian,' and do you know what he said to me?"

He sat down at the table beside Grace. She could smell the cedar on him; small green branches stuck out of his hair. She shook her head.

"No. You don't know what he said to me." Les drummed his fingers on the table. His nails were dirty, his hands small and strong-looking. Thick veins grew like roots over his knuckles. Grace looked away.

"I don't even know what the Jesus he said. I told him to calm down. 'Calm down, buddy boy, I can't understand a word of what you're saying.' But that crazy SOB started trimming away. I tried reasoning with him, I tried to keep my composure and hear him out, but he doesn't even speak English. What could I do? I'm a reasonable man, right?"

She nodded.

"I can keep my temper under control, can't I?"

She nodded, chewing her toast and watching him.

"Didn't I teach you kids to think before you act?"

She nodded again.

"I'm a good Christian, Grace and he's one of those goddamn separatistes."

"You taught us to step on toes under the basket where the referee couldn't see."

He looked at her.

"Well, you scored a basket, didn't you, in that game against Châteauguay. Where would you have been without your old man that day, eh, Grace?"

She didn't return his smile.

"And you told us how to drive a bird crazy by putting salt on its tail and the best way to cut open a deer and gut it."

He leaned back and smiled modestly. Grace watched him for a minute and then got up. She needed a job, needed money, and maybe then she could get away. Be on her own and take care of herself. She was seventeen.

Les got up and opened the fridge.

"Sheila!" he hollered at the ceiling. "What do I have to do to get some lunch around here?" He picked up a bowl of leftover macaroni, looked at it closely and then put it back.

"That'll teach the bugger to mess with Les McIntyre," he said into the fridge full of leftovers and milk. "Mr. High-and-Mighty with the three-piece suit and the brand-new Mustang, and he's got himself a hand trimmer. A hand trimmer. He doesn't know who he's dealing with," he said, smirking into the fridge.

Grace snuck by him, not wanting to have to agree with him again.

There were two grocery stores in downtown Beaumont about three blocks apart. One was new with a large fresh produce section, an aisle of wines with different kinds of cheese to accompany them and a car pickup lane where young men wheeled out groceries in any weather and piled them expertly into trunks or onto back seats. It was one of a chain of stores opening all over the province. Provigo, people would say to themselves, wondering what the word meant. The cashiers, even the ones who had been at the store before, seemed different, more efficient, as if they had been trained to whip bills out of their registers, touch their fingers to their tongues and flip back each dollar while counting out loud: *vingt, quarante, soixante.* The other grocery store hadn't changed since it opened. IGA. The aisles were narrow and the pyramids of canned goods always seemed to sway when a cart turned from one aisle to the next. The specials were handwritten on cardboard, not printed with small illustrations of fruit or T-bones the way they were at Provigo. In IGA the cashiers wore cardigans over their uniforms, called to each other for price checks and change. Some spoke French with an English accent and the French cashiers spoke English haltingly, but they spoke English.

In between the two grocery stores were strip malls that used to be filled with bookstores, stationery stores, but now were housed with new boutiques that sold everything from expensive wool and complicated sweater patterns to designer children's clothing embroidered with sailboats and ladybugs. A new McDonald's and a pizzeria had been built, with signs boasting a patio and specials every day. The shoe store that had been there for years had been painted and given a new name:

23

Chez Michel. The shoes were displayed on glass counters now, and well-dressed salespeople, young and smiling, waited to measure feet, to watch customers walk slowly in front of mirrors looking at their feet. *Fantastique*, they would say, *superbe*. The legion hall was behind the IGA. Grace still half believed that the FLQ hid in the legion because the huge FLQ logo was still spray-painted on the wall beside the door. She would look closely at men who stumbled out of the building unsure of their footing in the wash of bright daylight.

The Crémerie was between the bakery and the pet store. A long bench was pushed against its window and above it, taped to the inside, was a poster of a small child going cross-eyed at how high her cone was.

Grace opened the door and went in. A bell rang and a big woman in a pink-striped uniform came out from a room behind the counter. Grace couldn't take her eyes off the woman. She was tall, close to six feet, and was wearing a baseball cap with an embroidered cone on the front.

"Est-ce que je peux vous aider?" The woman's voice was hoarse, raunchy. She coughed and then remembered to smile at her customer. She smiled quickly and then stopped. It was more of a glare with her teeth, Grace thought, stepping back.

"Um, I've come about the job."

"Ah, *oui*, *oui*. Come 'ere and tell me your name." She spoke English haltingly, each word sounding like a piece of gravel she had found in her mouth and had to spit out.

Grace followed her into the small office at the back of the store. The woman sat down at a cluttered desk and picked up the cigarette she had left burning in the ashtray. Grace noticed that the ashtray was shaped like a cone as well; the cigarette burned in a pink ceramic scoop of ice cream.

The woman inhaled deeply and looked over the smoke at her.

"Do you speak French?"

Grace thought quickly of all the ice cream words she knew. *Fraise, chocolat, vanille, cornet*. Enough, she thought.

"Yes."

The woman nodded and stood up, nearly banging her head on the shelf above the desk. It was full of baseball trophies and team pictures. Grace looked closer and saw that the teams were made up of older women and they all wore uniforms with "La Crémerie" written across their chests.

She handed Grace an application form and a pen. Grace tried not to stare at the woman's hands, at how thick her fingers were and at the black hair that sprouted above each knuckle, the bitten nails. She watched the woman squash the cigarette in the ashtray, splitting the butt apart.

"You fill that in." She motioned for Grace to sit in the chair and cleared some papers off the desk to make room, and then she went out into the store, leaving Grace under the supervision of her smiling teammates, holding baseball bats and looking victorious.

It took Grace only a few minutes to fill out the form. She brought it out to the woman, who read it, saying the words softly to herself, and then motioned Grace to follow her back into the office. She lit another cigarette and, with it clenched in her teeth, rifled through the uniforms that were hanging on a hook behind the door. She picked one and handed it to Grace. And then with the cigarette still in place she said something about *la salle de bain* and *à gauche* that Grace didn't understand. She waited and then motioned with her head and Grace realized that she was supposed to put it on, to change into the uniform in the *salle de bain*.

"Okay, okay, *oui, oui*," Grace replied, smiling to show she understood.

À gauche, she said to herself, *à gauche*, left, she said left. She held the uniform out as if it could lead her in the right direction. She opened the first door she came up on and stepped inside. The door closed quickly behind her. All around Grace were big tubs of ice cream. *Pacane au beurre, banane, menthe au chocolat fondant.* Towers of tubs were stacked from floor to ceiling; her breath came out in spurts of frost. This was not the *gauche* the woman was talking about, Grace realized, burning with embarrassment. She thought of going back out and finding the bathroom but the woman might hear her, might find out that she couldn't really speak French, so she changed in the freezer, careful not to lean against a tub. She opened the door and walked out as if nothing had gone wrong. *Restez calme*, she thought, first step in an emergency.

The woman's name was Ann. Ann shook Grace's hand with such a grip that Grace nearly cried out. She showed Grace how to scoop ice cream properly, making an S with the scoop in the middle of the tub. She showed her how to wrap the cones with napkins and how much hot fudge she was allowed to use. She got Grace to peel a banana and slice it in a banana split dish without ever touching the banana, just the peel.

"How do you say 'scoop' in French, Ann? Like 'how many scoops?'"

Ann had told Grace that she had hired her because Ann couldn't speak English and needed someone to help her.

"*Boules. Combien de boules voulez-vous?*"

"*Boules?* Like balls? How many balls do you want?"

"*Oui, on dit boules.*"

The bell rang over the door and both Ann and Grace looked up. Ann wiped her hands and disappeared into the office. An older man came up to the counter. He pulled at his moustache as he peered into the glass, reciting each flavour he saw. And then he straightened and spoke, looking up at the price chart.

"*Je voudrais un cornet, s'il vous plaît, à la vanille—non, non, à la menthe.*"

Grace waited, her scoop poised, ready.

"*Oui, à la menthe, s'il vous plaît.*"

"*Une boule où deux?*"

"*Pardon?*"

She cleared her throat. Her voice had sounded loud and clumsy. *Boule* had rolled out of her mouth like a dropped bowling ball heading determinedly for the gutter.

"*Une boule où deux?*"

He looked at her strangely for a minute.

"*Une, s'il vous plaît.*"

She nodded and scooped, then handed him his cone. She counted quickly in her head. *Cinquante* was fifty, *soixante* was sixty, *soixante-dix* was seventy, so seventy-five was *soixante-quinze*. The man had his hand in his pocket, waiting.

"*Soixante-quinze sous, s'il vous plaît.*"

He handed her three quarters and left. She felt exhausted. Counting and waiting and scooping, hearing herself speak French, sounding so English. She wasn't used to making eye contact with someone who spoke French. Her instincts were to look down, to hope to be ignored, because she couldn't understand much of it. It was like being in French class and not knowing the answer, the teacher scanning all the faces for the one most filled with doubt. She had learned to let herself sink into her surroundings, chameleon-like, so she wouldn't be expected to answer. But it was going to be different here. She closed the cash drawer and leaned against the counter.

She hated owing Gary money.

Lily wrote out the word *Cyclone* and then underlined it neatly with a red pen. *A system of winds*, she wrote, *or a storm, that rotates inwards, around a centre of low atmospheric pressure (depression)*. A system of winds, she repeated to herself. It sounded both magical and technical. She imagined strands of wind swirling down trees and telephone poles, meeting together, weaving and twirling, a herd of winds taking a town by storm. And everything, she realized, when she thought about it, was a system, a part of something larger.

Some entries snagged her attention, got caught and stayed with her long after she wrote them down. She could feel the word *cyclone* rotate inwards and settle with the other entries she still thought about. She put her pen down, lingering, not wanting to go on to *Cyclops* yet. Curtis opened her door and peeked in. Dellie pushed the door open wider and pranced inside.

"Are you ever gonna wake up or what, Lily?" Dellie jumped up on her sister's bed. "Curtis and I thought you'd sleep all day!"

Curtis walked over to the side of the bed as well. Lily smiled at him and closed her copybook.

"What have you two been doing all morning?"

"Well—" Dellie took a deep breath. "First I woke up and then I got out of bed and then I opened my door—"

Lily could hear her father singing downstairs now that her door was open. She could smell coffee and hear the radio beneath his voice. She listened to him sing, deep and rumbling, until Dellie yanked at her sleeve.

"And then Curtis poured milk onto the Rice Krispies and then—" She stopped and tapped her finger on her cheek, looking at the ceiling. "What did we do after we ate our cereal again, Curtis?"

Curtis thought for a minute.

"We played cars," he whispered solemnly.

"Yeah, we played cars. I had that blue car, the really fast one, faster than Curtis's green car, and we raced them down the hall and then we got dressed and I put on this shirt with the pretty little flowers." She bent over her belly to examine the flowers on her T-shirt again.

Curtis put his hand on the encyclopedia, running his fingers along the gold edge of pages. His sister read really big books. He looked at her, wishing he had brought his binoculars up from downstairs. She looked really smart with her glasses on. Lily smiled at him and he smiled back shyly. Maybe one day he could copy out the encyclopedia too, he thought. Maybe one day he could be smart like Lily and work hard at his own books.

Dellie was jumping on the bed.

"Check me, Curtis. I'm bouncing."

Lily caught her in a hug and then put her down on the floor.

"I'll be down in a few minutes, okay? I've got to get dressed."

"Okay, Lily." Dellie ran to the door and stopped quickly, almost skidding into the wall. "Did you see that, Curtis?"

Curtis nodded and followed her out of Lily's room, closing the door quietly behind him.

A cyclone of sister, Lily thought, getting out of bed. A system of people. A family.

It began raining during the night. Grace had heard it hit the roof; the eaves dripped on the other side of her bedroom wall. And it was still raining when she woke up. She was lying on her bed reading, but the dark clouds that moved across her window were distracting her. They were taking over the sky, sliding and rolling across what could have been a pale, grey day. She got up and looked out her window. The rain had persuaded the drab out in everything. The shed in the back-yard looked browner than it was and the trees in the neigh-bour's yard still had leaves that were shivering and holding on tightly in the wind. Grace could see the long garden and picnic table next door as well, now that the cedars were cropped so close to the ground. Trimmed? she thought. More like butchered.

She got the Crémerie uniform out of her closet. We all scream, she said to herself, her head stuck in the striped top, her arms over her head, for ice cream.

Ann turned from the counter when the bell over the door tinkled.

"*Salut, Grace. Ça va?*"

"Um, *oui*. Hi." She tied the apron around her waist and went behind the counter. She was right on time. "I guess it'll be pretty slow because of the rain, eh?"

Ann gave the icing tube a final squirt on the side of the cake she'd been decorating and then looked out the window.

"*Les anglais aiment la crème glacée quand il pleut.* The English will come."

"The English?"

"*Oui, oui.* When the—*comment dit-on 'temps'?*"

Grace looked at her boss helplessly. She had no idea what Ann was trying to say.

"You know, the sun, the, um, *la neige*, the temperature." Ann began speaking louder as if raising the volume of her voice would help translate what she was trying to say.

"The sun—" Grace repeated dubiously.

"*Oui*, the sun, the rain, *le temps! Le temps.*" Ann gestured out the window with her icing tube.

"*Le temps,*" Grace repeated. "*Le temps.*"

"*Oui, le temps. Quand il fait mauvais, les clients anglais viennent.*"

Ann spoke quickly, not at all like Grace's French teacher, who sounded out the words, pronouncing them slowly so the students would hear them. *Le chat. Le chien. La fenêtre.* Ann talked so fast that Grace couldn't hear when one word ended and another began. Ann watched her and tried again. "*Le temps,*" she said loudly, her voice echoing in the empty shop. The clock ticked in the silence.

"The *temps*, the time?" Grace guessed, looking up at the clock, each number a small cone.

"*Non, dehors. Le temps est dehors.*"

"*Dehors?*"

"Houtside, *dehors.*" Ann's face was getting red. She put down the icing tube she'd been gesturing with and went into the office. She came back, exhaling, leaving a trail of cigarette smoke behind her.

Outside, Grace thought, the sun, the rain, as if the words were numbers she could add up for the answer.

"The weather?" she said dubiously.

"*Oui, oui,* the weather! *C'est ça,* the weather." They both sighed deeply. Neither could remember what they'd been talking about, but it didn't seem to matter any more. They were exhausted, trying to understand each other. Ann turned back to the cake, swirling pink roses along its edge. The freezer and the fluorescent lights hummed. Grace felt a small pain behind her right eye that she knew would later expand into a headache. She hated this job. She hated how stupid it made her feel.

Ann gestured with her head for Grace to answer the phone when it rang. Maybe that was how it would be, Grace thought to herself, going into the office. Maybe they'd end up communicating with nods and shakes and claps.

The phone call was for Ann. Ann hung up after grumbling something and came out of the office undoing her apron.

"Five minutes. I'll be back."

Grace nodded and watched her leave.

The grey sky made the neon ice cream cone in the store window look brighter than usual. The front of the store was all windows that the rain drummed on. A wall of rain, Grace thought, leaning against the counter. It was raining harder now. She watched people hurry by on the sidewalk getting drenched as they went. Five minutes, she'd be alone for only five minutes. The clock ticked each second loudly. She got a plastic spoon and began picking out some of the chunks of fudge in the fudge brownie ice cream. She turned her back when the bell on the door jingled, wiping the chocolate from her mouth.

The people who had been passing by the store looked soaked; their hair was plastered to their heads, their clothes hung wetly from them. The guy standing on the other side of the counter, rain rolling off his beard, off his leather jacket, seemed gigantic, as if he had expanded with the rain, filled himself up with grey sky and downpours. Ralph Harris. The guy Gary sold his weed for. He smiled languidly at Grace and let his eyes wander slowly down her body, lingering on her breasts, and then back up to her face.

"Hey there, Grace. I didn't know you worked here," he drawled.

His voice, his eyes, were like a tongue that slowly tasted her, licked her up and then down, hot breath and panting. She stepped back from the counter. Gary had told her about

Ralph—how he had knifed a guy who owed him money. He had taken out his switchblade and stuck it into the guy's leg and then kept on talking like nothing had happened.

He liked that she was afraid, she could tell. He licked his lips as if he could taste something in the air and stepped up closer to the counter.

"Well, aren't you going to ask me what I want?" The pause between his words was heavy, like cement.

"What can I get you?"

"What do you have?"

Grace recited the flavours, feeling as if she was back in elementary school naming the capitals of the provinces, but instead of twenty-four pairs of eyes on her, there was just one, and while she was naming the ice cream flavours, she felt like she was watching a type of geography lesson. The geography of her body. His eyes pawed at the buttons of her uniform, the capital of, the population of, the borders blurred and hot. Goosebumps shivered down her arms. Her hatred fuelled an anger that allowed her to look into his eyes. He had small, reptilian eyes. Flat and ungiving. She thought of a snake Lily had told her about. Brown Pacific. How it had no natural enemies and could eat all the small birds and insects on an island. An environmental nightmare, Lily had said.

"Cherry," he said. "I want cherry."

"One scoop or two?"

"Two scoops. Two scoops of your cherry."

She ignored his sneer and scooped the ice cream. He took it from her, brushing his fingers against the inside of her wrist, and laughed when she recoiled. His fingernails were black with grease and all the lines on his palms were black too. Even his lifeline, Grace noticed when he held out his hand for his change, was one long black line.

She scrubbed her hands under hot water until she thought he had left. Drying them on her apron, she turned and he was sitting at the small table in the corner, licking his ice cream and watching her. When he finished the cone, he took out a long knife and began cleaning his nails, his eyes never leaving her. She turned her back on him, rather than show him how much he had unnerved her. It wasn't the kind of knife you'd use to whittle or cut a rope, it was the kind of knife that could carve skin. It was the kind of knife that made people dance or sing or anything else you wanted them to do.

As she turned to go into the office, he stood up and took a step towards her. Their eyes locked.

"Your brother owes me money."

Grace's heart was all the birds that made up the island of her, fluttering in her throat, knowing what they faced. An environmental nightmare. He took another step. His legs were massive, each one the width of her waist. His hair had dried wild. She backed up to the wall. The only place to run would be inside the freezer. *Dehors*, the sun, the rain, weather. Her brain was filled. He could block the way to the bathroom if she tried that. She remembered the phone. He took another step, a baby step, a giant step. He was close enough for her to see his eyebrows—they joined in a V above his nose. He had a gold chain around his neck. Hanging from it was a small gold fist giving the world the finger.

"Tell him that I want it."

She nodded and the door opened to a bunch of wet kids all wearing the same jackets. A team, Grace thought, a team had come to save her. Ralph folded the blade up against his leg, his eyes still not leaving her, and then he laughed and turned and left. Grace had no time to think. Fourteen or fifteen kids were all yelling what kind of ice cream they wanted. They had just won their basketball game thirty-six to two, they told her, and they wanted to celebrate.

When Grace had started work that afternoon, there were still some leaves on the trees, but when she left, the trees were all bare. In one afternoon the rain had driven the last of autumn to the ground and continued to rain long after the leaves had fallen. The sky was low with a hint of winter in it, the grey, bleak winter that iced up windows and devoured light, feasting on it at either end of the day, chewing at its edges until there was more dark left than light. In one afternoon, she thought to herself on the way home, everything had changed.

Gary was in the kitchen warming up some soup when Grace came in the back door.

"Can I have some, Gar? I'm starved."

He looked up from stirring, his eyes red and heavy. For a moment, Grace wasn't sure whether he knew where he was or who he was talking to.

"What?"

"Can I have some soup? I'm starved, I haven't had supper yet."

He looked at the pot he was stirring. There was mountain time, Grace thought to herself, and standard time, Atlantic time, and there was Gary's time. He had a way of slowing everything down. He looked at the ladle he was holding.

"You want some soup?"

"Yep."

He opened the cupboard and got another bowl. He tore open the crackers he had put on the counter and took a handful. Grace watched him eat them, one at a time, with his eyes closed, rocking back and forth on his heels.

"I'm just going to help myself, okay?" she said.

He opened his eyes, startled, and looked around in confusion. Then he moved out of her way.

She thought of telling Gary about Ralph but decided to wait until he ate. He bit his tongue and squinted at his soup, walking as if balancing on a high wire. Grace got up and turned off the stove; the element coiled a bright orange. She wiped the counter and put the crackers back and then sat down. He ate in silence, slurping and paying far too much attention to the vegetables, she thought.

"So, how've you been, Gar? What's new?"

He stared at the wall below the clock.

"Um, not too much, Grace. Business is good, really good." He wiped his hands on his jeans, then drummed a little on his legs.

"Do you owe Ralph a lot of money?"

Gary chased a pea around in the bottom of his bowl with his spoon. He finally slid it on with his finger and then looked up at her suspiciously.

"Why?"

"Well, he came into the store today and told me you owed him some money."

Gary looked at her for a minute.

"He said that to you?"

She nodded.

"Well, I'm going to pay him back tonight. I've got it all except for that ten you owe me."

She dug into her pocket and pulled out some bills.

"I've only got a few dollars but you can have them. I'll have the rest next week."

He smiled brightly at her. He was like that, a cloudy day with the odd moment of sunshine, but when the sun did shine, the rays were direct, warm. She loved it when he actually looked at her with his eyes focused. He left the kitchen whistling and drumming on his legs.

After Grace had finished cleaning up, she turned to go to her room and nearly walked into her mother.

"There was a five-dollar bill on my dresser." Sheila's hair was so permed, the curls seemed to be moving. Medusa, Grace thought, and looked away. "I want it back now."

Grace looked at her mother's feet. Pink satin slippers like ballet shoes. She tried picturing her mother pirouetting, standing on her tiptoes and dancing around the kitchen. She couldn't.

"I want that money back," Sheila said, looking at her daughter.

Grace couldn't imagine how her mother had named her, how she could have looked down at her baby and mouthed the name Grace. You were born on a Tuesday, Sheila had told Grace in explanation and shrugged. Tuesday's child, full of Grace.

Gary must have taken the money; he always did. But she couldn't tell on him because he was the one who had to face Ralph. He had enough trouble. And her mother would never believe her. She never blamed Gary for anything.

Grace nodded and wondered if he'd cover for her. It would never occur to him, she thought. He kept himself so far away from them all that even if he wanted to, even if he tried, he'd never reach her in time to help. He helped her by keeping her in grass. "You need anything for tonight?" he'd ask generously. He could've been saying, "you want to get numb too, you want to shut them all out?" He knew about that, wanting to shut them all out. He was a pro. Grace hurried past her mother.

She went into her room and closed the door, turning on the small radio her father had given her when he bought the new one. She'd written "Grace" with red nail polish where the label with his name and social insurance number had been. After a few seconds she turned off the radio and decided to go out, to ride over to Lily's. Downstairs, she pulled on her jacket and closed the door as quietly as she could behind her. The rain had stopped but the air still held its dampness. She pulled her sleeves down over her knuckles. The night smelled smoky and cold, the metal handlebars reflected each street light she rode under. Lily lived on the outskirts of town near the railroad tracks and Le Bertin, the bar on the highway. Grace turned onto *rue* Mapleside and headed out of town.

Lily's house needed painting. The porch light shone on peeling paint and bare wood. Even in the dark Grace could see a car up on blocks in the front yard. Someone had put dirt in the opened trunk and planted a small shrub. She leaned her bike against the side of the house. A cat came around the corner and rubbed against her leg. She bent to pet it before going to the front door, stepping over a wagon and pieces of wood. When she didn't hear the doorbell ring inside, she knocked. A small face looked out the living room window at her, then shrieked and disappeared. Dellie. Grace was about to knock again when she heard a train whistle. Her feet felt it coming down the tracks first. Even the trees seemed to shake with it as it rushed and thundered by, and then it was gone. In its wake the silence caved into a siren, a horn and cars, and then the front door opened.

Lily's father looked so much like Elvis Presley that Grace nearly gasped out loud. A youngish Elvis with sideburns and thick black hair. The top three buttons were opened on his bowling shirt, and his name—Stan—was embroidered above the breast pocket. Grace blushed. She had never seen Lily's father up close. She could smell cigarette smoke on him, could see a tattoo snaking out from his sleeve.

"Hi. Is Lily here?"

"She sure is. Come on in." He turned into the hallway. "Lily, you've got company."

Grace followed him in. She stepped over the shoes and boots that lined the entrance. Curtis was watching her through his binoculars at the bottom of the stairs. His hair was parted and neatly combed behind his ears. There were cowboys and tumbleweeds all over his pyjamas. Dellie came running downstairs naked and screeching with laughter. Lily's father scooped her up with one hand and carried her back upstairs.

"Dellie, I told you to wait. Let's get you a nightie."

Curtis was studying Grace's shoes with his binoculars. She moved her feet so he could get a better look. After a few moments he lowered the binoculars and looked at her.

"Hi, Curtis. How are you?"

"Fine," he answered in a soft, serious voice.

Grace smiled and looked up at Lily coming down the stairs.

"Hey, Grace. Do you want to come up? I was just finishing my English homework."

Grace followed her up the stairs. Each step had something

on it that she had to step over. *Hot Rod* magazines, plastic teacups with Mickey Mouse decalled on them, a soother. The wall going up the stairs had two framed pictures, one of a clown and the other of a ship. When Grace looked at them closely, she saw that they were made with string wound around tiny nails.

"Who did the string art?"

Lily looked back to see what Grace was talking about.

"Oh, my brother did."

"Curtis?"

"No, my older brother did them at camp." Lily stepped aside to let Dellie go by. The little girl had on a nightgown now and her curly blond hair had been combed and was now full of static electricity. She thumped down each step on her bum, grabbing the soother as she went by and sticking it into her mouth.

"You have an older brother? Does he go to our school?"

"No, he quit a couple of years ago, but you've probably seen him around. He's outside a lot. I think everyone calls him Rave but his real name is Jerry." Lily opened her door and closed it behind them.

"Rave is your brother?" Grace couldn't believe it. Everyone knew Rave or at least knew of him. He was always outside on the mountain or at the lake in the centre of town. And he was beautiful. Long, straight black hair and intense eyes. The name Jerry didn't seem to suit him, she thought. She'd always known him as Rave and he was wild. Almost the opposite of Lily. Grace had always considered Lily to be one of those girls who studied, who read extensively, who was good at school and at following instructions. They went to a big high school and Grace had learned to read people at first glance; she could tell the way they dressed, who they ate their lunch with, everything about them. Lily was always alone, always reading from an encyclopedia, so Grace figured she was shy, far from wild. Lily would be a salve, she thought, after the erratic behaviour of her house, the empty house that Sharon had left behind.

Rave didn't fit into Grace's picture of who Lily was. He was unexpected.

Lily sighed and sat down on her bed. "Yeah, he's my brother and I know everyone thinks he's crazy, but he just likes being outside. My mother says he has fewer layers of skin than everyone else does so he feels things more. And he's got my father's temper. I guess he feels more at home on a mountain."

Grace could see the resemblance now that she knew they were related. Lily had the same dark eyes behind her glasses, but hers were quieter, gentler. Rave's eyes were electric, smouldering, the times she had seen him.

"What are you working on for English?"

"We had to write a poem so I'm writing about Curtis and his binoculars. It's not going too well. I was tempted to just forget it and get back to work."

"Are you still on c?"

"Yeah, it'll probably take a couple more weeks. I used to think I'd have it all done in five years but I don't know any more."

Grace didn't know what to say. She didn't even know where she'd be in five years. Curtis opened the door and began studying her face, his binoculars pressed to his eyes. She wasn't used to being looked at so closely and stood up quickly, self-consciously.

"I've really got to go. I just dropped by to say hi."

She went downstairs, navigating each step in the dark. Outside, her bike was cold and her breath burst from her in clouds. She stood for a while in Lily's driveway before riding off in the opposite direction she had come from.

Le Bertin was only a ten-minute ride from Lily's. Years ago a lighthouse had been attached to the front, along with a neon sign of a naked woman sitting in a cocktail glass. The town had petitioned city hall about the nudity and now Le Bertin was just a rundown bar on the highway with an empty neon martini glass tipped against its side. Behind it was a neglected mini-putt. Grass had grown over most of the holes and the big, grinning clown face at the eighteenth was faded and leaning to one side. Grace remembered aiming her ball at its mouth when she was young, hoping to get it in with one stroke. A free game. She never did. But she did collect the beer bottles thrown onto the course every weekend, and she'd cash them in at Snow White, the candy store, for Popeye cigarettes and Sweet Tarts, jawbreakers.

Grace hid her bike in the bush beside the bar. She straightened her jacket and tucked some hair that had gotten loose from her braid behind her ears. Then she decided to pull off the elastic and shake her hair free. She wished she had put on some makeup. Breathing deeply she walked into the bar as if she was balancing Lily's encyclopedias on her head. She didn't look anywhere but straight ahead. The letter *c*, she thought: confident, cool, casual. Gary always hung out in the back, near the pool tables. She walked to his table and sat down beside him. Capable. He looked at her, surprised.

"Hey, Gracie, what are you doing here?"

Grace looked around the table. There was a pale blond girl sitting across from Gary. Ralph was over at the pool table with a few other guys. She gritted her teeth and made herself return his gaze without looking away first. A couple of older men slouched at the bar holding onto their glasses of draft, and a woman sat at the other end dressed in a tight red skirt that kept riding up her legs. She was smoking a long cigarette and blew the smoke out slowly, seductively, into the almost empty room. At the far end of the bar was a table full of bikers in black leather. Grace had seen their motorcycles outside. They rode over from the next town down the highway. Gary had told her that they rented a house and just hung out, drinking and smoking. She remembered how impressed he had been that there was no furniture in their house, that they had constructed chairs out of empty beer cases. He'd been asked over with Ralph, he had told her.

The woman behind the bar came over and emptied their ashtray and wiped the table with a dingy cloth.

"Who's your friend, Gary?"

Gary lifted his bottle to his lips and took a long swig before he answered.

"This is my sister, Grace. Grace, this is Jackie."

Grace smiled at her, but Jackie kept wiping without looking up.

"Is she eighteen?"

"Oh yeah, she's eighteen all right." Gary winked at Grace.

"Does she want something to drink?"

Gary looked at his sister.

"Yeah, she'll have a Fifty and bring me another too, all right?"

Jackie looked around the table.

"Do you want another beer, Sandy?"

Sandy shook her head and continued peeling off the label on the bottle in front of her. Grace had never seen anyone so skinny. She tried not to stare and was glad when Jackie came back with the beer. She watched Gary pay for them and waited until Jackie left to thank him.

"No problem, but if you get caught, you're on your own."

Grace nodded. She leaned over to him and whispered, "Did you pay Ralph?"

"Yeah. Don't worry about that shit, okay?" He looked around nervously.

Grace watched Ralph lean over and line up his cue. He moved his arm back and forth slowly, closing one eye before hitting the white ball. She watched a striped ball roll and sink into a corner pocket. Ralph straightened, leaning on his cue, and winked at her. She took a sip of beer, watching him defiantly over the bottle. His wink was brazen. "You see?" he seemed to be saying. "I knew you'd be here sooner or later." Fuck you, she thought.

He walked over to the table and stood behind Sandy. She began to fidget and squirm, turning to look up at him and then turning back around.

"Hey, Grace, what are you doing here?" he asked her smoothly, putting his hand on Sandy's neck, rubbing her skin with his thumb.

"Just having a beer with my brother."

He laughed and sat down, taking a cigarette from his pack and lighting it, his eyes on her the whole time. His thumb had left a bright red medallion on Sandy's neck. She rubbed at it. Grace watched Ralph through his smoke until Jackie came and put a beer down in front of him.

"This is from your friends over there. They said to say thank you for the trip."

Ralph laughed and raised the bottle in the direction of the bikers' table.

"Cheers," he yelled and they all did the same, lifting their bottles and then drinking. "I sold the dumb fuckers some of Peter's homemade acid and told them it was red microdot. Bon voyage, assholes." He stood up and went back to the pool table.

It made Grace sick the way Gary laughed at everything Ralph said, the way he nodded in agreement. He had mumbled "dumb fuckers" right after Ralph had. She watched her brother but he didn't look over at her. He kept his eyes down, looking intently at the table.

"Can you spare a smoke?" Sandy slid her hand across the table. Her fingers, Grace noticed, were long and thin, the index and middle fingers stained a deep yellow, ochre. The mark Ralph had left on her neck was brighter now and had blotched bigger after she had rubbed at it. It looked like the shape of a country, or a continent. The continent of Ralph. She took two cigarettes from Gary's pack and handed one to Sandy, holding the lighter out and waiting until the cigarette lit.

"So how long have you been going out with Ralph?"

Sandy exhaled. "I don't know, a couple of months I guess. He's so sweet, he's really good to me, you know? He never means anything bad, and if I want any shit or anything, he always gives me some. Like he'd give me anything I want.

Look, he gave me this ring." Sandy held out her hand to Grace.

"Is that an emerald? That means your birthday is in May, right?"

"Nah." Sandy examined the ring herself now. "I just like green."

"Yeah, green's nice." Grace looked up at the Labatt clock. It was later than she realized. She put out her cigarette and stood up. "It was good meeting you, Sandy. Take care of yourself."

Sandy nodded, engrossed by the lit end of her cigarette, rolling it on the side of the ashtray, and then she inhaled from the cigarette deeply, watching the end burn brighter. Grace waved to Gary and left.

Lily couldn't see anything without her glasses. Before bed she leaned over the sink and lathered up her face with the oatmeal soap her mother had bought her. She traced the line of pimples along her jaw with her fingers. Mountains. The Andes, a chain of mountains in South America, extending along the whole length of her chin. A system of pimples. She surprised herself, the way information came back to her in pieces. Somewhere inside, Lily knew she'd never finish the entire alphabet, but she also knew that just the idea of one day owning a complete set of encyclopedias made the range of mountains on her face seem more bearable. She erected that goal between her and the world: a barbed wire, an electric fence, a dizzying column of words that she lovingly transcribed into dozens of Hilroy copybooks. And it had to make her smart, she figured, all that reading, all that copying. University was important, her mother always told her. Education is the key, she'd say, don't do what I did and rush into marriage.

Lily knew how expensive university was. She could see by the way her father grimaced when the furnace came on. She could tell by the way his face creased when he was sitting at the kitchen table paying the bills and the way the memory of those creases stayed now, fine lines that furrowed his forehead, bracketed his mouth. The strands of black hair that had turned white and couldn't blend in. Money made his shoulders sag. And it made him mad. He'd snap at them, snarl unexpectedly. Even when he was quiet, he smouldered, his silence filled with small sparks waiting to burst into flame. A forest fire of a father, Lily thought. He breathed at the worry deeply, like wet wood, coaxing it, sighing and shaking his head, reaching into his pockets as if somewhere he could find relief or help. He needed things easier. If she was going to go to university and study, the way she dreamt of doing, she'd need good grades, she'd need reference books, she'd need to keep copying. And she needed to do it without asking him for anything more.

She rinsed off her face and patted it dry, then put her glasses back on. Curtis opened the door slowly, peeking in at her.

"Come on in, Curtis. I'm finished." He walked half asleep to the toilet. Lily waited for him in the hall and then followed him to his room where she tucked him back into bed.

Later, lying in bed, Lily added Grace's name to her list of people she worried about. Jerry was first; she always worried about him outside. At least he was coming home more often at night now that it was getting cold. She'd sometimes hear him come in late though he'd always be gone by morning. And she worried about Curtis because he hardly ever talked. Whenever she dreamt of him, he was always screaming and she'd wake up with a headache. And now there was Grace. Lily had never met anyone like Grace before. She was the strongest and weakest person Lily had ever encountered. She was a paradox, and it seemed to Lily that of all the people she had to worry about, Grace was the closest to catastrophe. At least Jerry had his mountain and Curtis had his binoculars. Grace didn't seem to have anything. She never had her house key, she never even had much lunch. Lily fell asleep thinking about Grace locked out of her house. She had set her glasses on the night table beside her and the lenses caught the hall light, reflecting it long and thin into her darkened room.

*   *   *

Gary finished his beer and ordered another one. Ralph had gone over to talk to the bikers with his girlfriend and Grace had left. He was alone. He felt his smile slide from his face and land somewhere around his feet. He was exhausted. Being with anyone lately was like climbing an escalator that was going down. Even with Grace; especially with Grace. Had he paid Ralph yet? She had no idea. And she was always watching him. Even when they were just eating soup, she watched him, expecting him to whip out a superhero's cape and rescue her from the evil jaws of their house. Fuck. He had enough to deal with. He couldn't save her.

And Ralph. Gary looked over at the bikers' table and Ralph was waiting to meet his gaze. He lifted his beer in Gary's direction and then chugged it back. Ever since Gary had bought his first dime bag off Ralph, he had been in Ralph's radar. It was like a form of torture, a continual dripping of water, needles under his fingernails, Ralph's watchful eye always knowing where he was, what he was doing, how much money he owed him. Gary owed him a lot. More than that guy Ralph had stabbed in the leg. More than Gary would ever hope to make. He didn't like thinking about it. Being stoned was easier; it turned the volume down on everything. Smoking untied the knot of him and set him free from his family. He could watch his mother with her poodle hair nag his father as if they were a bad TV show. He couldn't hear his mother scream at Grace. When he was stoned they were all like mimes, acting in the exaggerated way that mimes did, and all he had to do was watch.

And it wasn't so bad. So Grace got yelled at a lot. Sticks and stones. She was mouthy anyway. And as he thought that, he knew what he was doing. He knew that he was steering clear of a path in his mind, and the entrance to that path always started with the word *but*. *But Grace didn't know everything.* And that was when he'd skid and swerve to avoid hitting the end of that thought, when he'd imagine nailing another board across its entrance: Keep Out. Danger. That was when he'd light up a joint and lie back, pull the smoke down deep into his lungs. Then he didn't give a shit about anything.

He watched Ralph cross the room, leaving his girlfriend at the table with the bikers, and approach the two women at the table next to his. After a few minutes one of them got up and followed Ralph to the pool table. Gary watched as Ralph showed her how to hold the cue; he stood behind her, raised one of her elbows and talked into her ear. They both laughed and she straightened up. One of her bra straps slipped; it was deep purple. Gary watched her hitch it back up with her thumb. Ralph looked over at him and winked. Gary smiled back, disgusted at how eager he must seem. Like a fucking puppy, he thought to himself, taking a long swig of beer. I'm just his fucking dog. He got up to leave and caught Ralph's eye, nodded and then turned towards the door. He didn't see Ralph motion to one of the French guys; he didn't even see the biker stand up or notice that he was following him out to the parking lot. When he turned around outside, he was surprised to see the biker, and was surprised to feel the first punch, surprised when he fell over and surprised still by the taste of gravel. Chalky almost.

He waited until he heard the bar door close before he got up and stayed on all fours a while, catching his breath, swaying and fighting the urge to puke. He spat out some blood and a strand of it hung from his mouth. He wiped it on his sleeve and then lurched upright. Through the small window of the door, he could see Ralph talking to the guy who had hit him; the guy was laughing and Ralph was holding his lighter out for him. Before Ralph could look over, Gary picked himself up and left the parking lot, walking along the railway tracks. Far off he heard a train whistle. It was about two o'clock in the morning and there was only one car on the road, waiting at the intersection for the red light to turn green. "Fuck waiting," Gary muttered, his jaw throbbing. He didn't want to know what Ralph was thinking, what he was planning next. He looked back at the car, still waiting at the red light.

"What the fuck are you waiting for, asshole?" Gary screamed at the driver. "Why don't you just go through? Just drive through!" His throat felt raw from screaming and he wondered why he had yelled so hard, so furiously. And he wondered who it was that he was yelling at.

Curtis talked to Jerry more than anyone else. He waited for Lily, who smelled like soap, to tuck him in and then he closed his eyes and pretended to sleep. He thought of *Stuart Little*, the book his mom had read to him and Dellie, and he wished he was as small as that mouse. Then people wouldn't always notice him and wonder why he was so quiet. He could sneak around and do what he loved to do, and that was just to watch. He could hear his father snoring; he always snored like a big bear growling. Lily said that bears snore too, she was the smartest girl in the world. She had shown him how to make a bird feeder with a milk carton and it had worked until the wind blew it away.

Dellie was sleeping too, with her arms straight up over her head like Supergirl. She always slept that way. Their mom said Dellie had been like that in her belly too and that's why the doctor had cut Dellie out of her. But it hadn't hurt her and her scar was like a big smile under her tummy.

Jerry always came in just when Curtis didn't think he could stay awake for another minute. Just as everything started to get fuzzy and his arms felt heavy and stuck to the bed, the door would open and Jerry would come in smelling like outside, the way trees smelled. Curtis knew because one day he had smelled a tree and it smelled just like Jerry. Then Curtis had looked around to make sure no one was watching and had pressed his nose into the bark, taking deep sniffs of his brother, his big brother, Jerry. Jerry the tree.

Jerry always brought Curtis something—a rock with a bit of fool's gold in it or a feather. Once he brought him a turquoise piece of shell. Jerry said it was a piece of a robin's egg and that the baby bird had probably used Curtis's milk carton bird feeder. Curtis kept everything Jerry gave him in a big tin box that had once held Christmas cookies. Except for the eggshell. He had taped that to a piece of paper and had then drawn a picture of himself and Jerry. He had that drawing on the wall near his bed.

Tonight Jerry brought him a pine cone. Curtis rolled it in his hands the way his teacher had shown him to when he wanted to make a round ball with the orange clay. Tomorrow, he promised himself, he'd look at it with his binoculars. That was the best way of seeing things.

"There was a girl here tonight visiting Lily. She was sad. Her shoes were a little muddy too." Jerry nodded. He seemed to enjoy listening to Curtis so much that Curtis truly believed Jerry's favourite thing to do was listen. And since he loved his brother, he talked and talked to him, hoping he was making the listening part of Jerry happy.

"Lily's writing a poem about me and my binoculars. I think Lily's worried about her friend because she stayed at the top of the stairs for a long time after the girl left, just thinking. Lily thinks a lot."

Jerry looked at Curtis and waited for him to go on.

"Miss Leduc told me on Friday that taking away is the same as subtraction and another word for that is minus. Oh yeah, Daddy made hamburgers for supper and forgot to watch them because Dellie needed a bandage and the hamburgers got all burnt, but Mommy said she liked them that way, but he said it was a waste of good meat and hit the counter with the frying pan. I put on a lot of ketchup and pretended to like them but they tasted gross and then Daddy got really mad because Dellie spit hers out."

Jerry waited, lulled by his younger brother's voice. And when Curtis didn't have any more to say, Jerry leaned over him and hugged him tightly. Curtis hugged him back. With his eyes closed, he could imagine that he was hugging a tree again. He buried his nose in his brother's neck and smelled the mountain, the night air, the green moss on bark, leaves.

"Good night, Curtis. I'll see you soon."

Jerry left and soon Curtis fell asleep, the deep sleep of contentment, thoughts of his brother wafting over him like a cloud, snagging on branches, covering the moon and then leaving it bare. He nuzzled up to the thought of Jerry the way he nuzzled up to his blanket, his special blanket that he couldn't bear to be without, especially during the long wait of the washing machine. When Jerry came, Curtis felt the same way he did when his blanket was finally washed and out of the dryer, still warm. Content.

Curtis had a notebook. Lily had given it to him to keep him occupied while she worked on hers in the afternoons. At first he had filled it with the curly lines and shapes he thought letters should look like. He made groups of these shapes he thought were words, and with these words he made up stories. Then he tore all those pages out and ripped them up. They weren't words, he now knew, but just baby scribbles. He couldn't write all the words he wanted to so he decided to turn the book into a train notebook. Every time he heard a train, he marked a line in his notebook. Lily was in charge of words and their letters and he was in charge of counting the trains that went by behind his house. No one knew this was his job, except his mother. And he hardly missed a train when he was home. If he heard one during supper, he'd run up to his room to mark it down, and when he came back, his mother would wink at him. That wink made him feel like the peacock he saw once at Granby Zoo. He felt bigger after that wink, taller and capable.

He worried though, when he was at school. While he coloured in squares and triangles, he thought about all the trains he was missing. If he thought about it long enough, his stomach would start hurting and he'd have to put his head down on his desk. Once he threw up and his dad had to come and get him and bring him home. As soon as he was home, he felt better. His mother was sitting in the living room in a long nightgown, smoking a thin cigar and reading from a big book. She didn't get off the couch but called him over and felt his forehead. The smoke made him cough so she shooed him away, and after his dad went back to work, the house was quiet. Dellie was napping, his mom turned the pages of her book quietly, everything seemed to be holding its breath waiting. He got a piece of paper from the desk in the dining room, lay on his floor and drew tracks. Thin, wobbly lines that crossed each other and travelled from one corner of the page to the other. They reminded him of the scar on Jerry's leg.

When Curtis woke up in the morning now, there was frost on his window. The grass was white-tipped and the puddles had islands of ice in them that reflected the big clouds rushing by. He hoped Jerry wasn't too cold outside. Lily's friend Grace had come back again after school. He heard her telling Lily that she had seen Jerry near the highway, that he had watched her ride up to their house. Curtis went back to his window, this time with his binoculars, and waited for whichever came first, his brother or a train.

Stan scrubbed his hands at the kitchen sink before peeling the potatoes for supper. Through the window he watched his son lean against a pine a few yards behind their property line. The window could have been a time portal and he could have been watching himself twenty-five years ago. The same dark hair, the shoulders slouched, wiry. He remembered standing like that, hands in pockets, cigarette clamped, coiled, ready to pounce. He remembered the rage that had filled him then, the fights he'd picked, grabbing his beer bottle by the neck and cracking it against the bar, offering to slice anyone who came near. It still returned, swift and sure in the middle of an argument with Jerry or when the kids got too loud, and he'd wonder afterwards if he had been screaming at his kids or at himself. It returned in words he could recall his own father yelling at him. After, exhausted by it as if the rage had been a storm that had whipped through him, leaving bits of him scattered and torn, he wondered if anger was genetic, passed down from generation to generation like the colour of hair or freckles.

It would be so easy to open up the back door now and call Jerry's name, the way he'd done for years when he put supper on the table. It would be so easy to cup his mouth with his hands and offer his voice to the space between his son and him, fill it with an invitation to come in, to sit down, to finally come home. But something always happened to the words he spoke to Jerry; as soon as they left his mouth they sounded different than he had intended. They changed mid-air between them and he always ended up watching them land nowhere near where he had meant them to. And though his rage hadn't devoured him, it still sometimes charged ahead of his thoughts, and sometimes, without thinking, he yelled, he exploded, he struck out, and too often Jerry, who had been within range, was the target. Too often. And then Jerry had begun firing back. Their anger ricocheted off each other, leaving shrapnel and scars. They were too much alike for Stan to do anything but watch through the window as his son leaned against the tree.

He dried his hands on a tea towel, folded it and hung it back on the rack. He was tired. Dellie had been up every couple of hours last night stuffed up with a cold; Lily had cried out in her sleep. When he had dozed off, he had dreamt of an airplane flying low over his house, the whole yard in its shadow. He remembered the sound of it more than anything, how wrong the engine sounded. He heard himself call for his kids, heard his wife frantically trying to clear everyone out the house, and then he heard the plane crash, sliding across the backyard and stopping just where Jerry was standing now.

Stan shook his head to get rid of the image and got the bag of potatoes from the pantry. Everything he did in the house was his way of apologizing to Eliza. After he'd curse or bang a pot onto the stove, he'd look at her and immediately feel sorry that he was who he was. She deserved better. She had left him the night he had fought with Jerry. That last night. Something in her eyes, in her touch, had left him then; he had felt part of her go and he didn't know when she would come back. So he cooked, he'd fill the tub and bathe the kids so she could read, so she could sketch. It was the least he could do. He could hear his wife move around upstairs. Lily had a friend over and Curtis was in his bedroom. Dellie sat in the hallway with a muffin tin, busy taking her soother out of her mouth and putting it in different parts of the pan. She sang a song about Mr. Golden Sun, clapping her hands and then grabbing the soother quickly and popping it back in her mouth. He could still see Jerry too, though the sun had started to go down. And for a minute he let that secure feeling wash over him, when everyone was under the same roof. He stood there in its embrace until the darkness forced the window back onto itself and all he could see in it was himself.

Grace's father, Les, knew that silence had the same properties as water, that it could fill your ears and nose and lungs and drown you. And it held the weather the way water did and it also held God. That is what his father had taught him. Looking over the rowboat into the lake, where the weeds grew right to the surface, his father had said that they were closer to God than in any church. It had been quiet then, so quiet that Les could hear the sun hit the water and disappear beneath it, melting in cloudy shafts through the weeds, so quiet his breath began to match his father's and soon they were breathing together, sitting in a boat in the middle of the lake.

And at first it had been an easy silence. Les baited his hook with worms that looked lucky, cast his line in and then waited. It was a simple silence, the shadows of birds crossing over it, dragonflies skimming its surface, but then it deepened and grew more complicated.

Les's mother thought God could only be found in a church, that the lake didn't hold God, it held fish: minnows and perch and bottom-feeders, suckers, she called them. Jesus, Les's father would snort, Jesus was a fisherman.

His mother would roll her eyes to the ceiling and point at the two of them standing in the doorway and tell them how sinful they were to be fishing on a Sunday. She had broken her pointing finger and had refused to go to a doctor; it had healed crooked, and curved down from the knuckle as if she was divining sin. Sin, she told Les when she tucked him in that night, could rot a human soul faster than that mouse that had gone through their pantry. And once a soul was rotted, it was forever damned to burn in hell. She tucked the blankets in all around him so he couldn't move and then she turned off the light. Les had become an altar boy that year. And if he were to pick the time when the silences became harder, it would be then, that summer he was nine. The summer his mother set out to save his soul and his father taught him to be quiet and not scare all the fish away.

Les had become an expert at not scaring the fish away, at staying afloat in the quiet it took to lure one in. He became patient and could wait all afternoon for a catch without complaining. He backed into his driveway, his eyes in the rear-view mirror. And then he sat in his car for a minute before turning off the ignition. The engine was warm and sounded smooth. He leaned over and locked the passenger door and then looked into the mirror. He could just see his eyes. They were blue, like a lake or the sky. He slowed his heart to his breathing and felt the silence enter him, calming him like water lapping against a boat. He could wait for weeks before he got a catch, he had grown to be a patient man. A man who had come to understand the ways of God.

Gary lay in bed with his eyes closed and listened to his father's steps overhead in the kitchen. He felt his stomach turn and leaned over the garbage can just in time. His eyes were still closed. He touched his lip gently and remembered what had happened. Then he threw up again. The memory of last night felt like it was right behind him, projected on a wall. He heard his father's footsteps moving from the fridge to the table above and felt the ceiling lower with the weight of him. He opened an eye and squinted at his room; the smell of puke hung in the air. One of his teeth was loose and he moved it with his tongue, then checked the rest of his mouth. He didn't want to go back to sleep but he didn't want to go upstairs and see his father either. Gary felt his stomach turn again. He groped for his wooden box on the floor and with one hand opened it and got out a joint. As he lit it and pulled the harsh smoke deep into his lungs and held it, Gary could hear his father's footsteps leaving the kitchen and moving farther away into the living room. Exhaling, he felt his shoulders loosen and stretched his neck sideways. When the joint began to burn close to his fingers, he found his clip and smoked it until it was just paper. His body had stopped hurting and his stomach had calmed. Ralph had just been showing off, Gary figured. Showing those bikers how tough he was so they wouldn't try to fuck him over. He lit a cigarette and balanced the ashtray on his chest. He had to get some cash fast. The smoke rose and moved with the heavier marijuana smoke until Gary couldn't see his ceiling. It hung there moving so slowly, it hardly moved at all.

Night solidified the mountain. It sat on the edge of town, a sullen shape that seemed to absorb the darkness. The sky drained into its coniferous trees. The pines, the spruce, the balsam on the mountain seemed to grow thicker, blending into the shadow of the trees at dusk and overtaking the paths beneath them. The limbs of the bare trees were coaxed out, defined by the night, thin, pale semblances of their daylight selves as if X-rayed, the silver bones of them pointed and fine.

From the town though, the mountain seemed whole, a mass of night. But for Rave, who walked up the mountain almost nightly, it was a clan of trees, a genealogy he had memorized. Each combination led him to a different destination. A clump of pines, the grove of birches, sugar maples, Douglas firs, eastern red cedars led him to the smallest of the five lakes on the mountain, where once he found a lime green tree frog. Black ash, white pines, spruce after spruce led him to the apple orchard that the monks from the monastery on the southwest side of the mountain took care of. Some nights he walked beneath the gnarled apple tree limbs and was awestruck by their arthritic knots and the long, straight rows of them, how the moonlight lit the aisles of grass between them as if inviting him to the small tool shed at the edge of the orchard. He sometimes spent nights in the shed, warmed by its wood stove and the blankets a brother had thoughtfully left. Sometimes he slept at home. Warmer nights he spent under trees, in lean-tos he had woven together with pine boughs and spruce or in the small cave high up on the cliff that overlooked the orchard and, farther out, the town with its street lights and chimney smoke.

Beneath the night, amid the dark-needled branches, the mountain broke back down into trees. Rave knew the mountain by them, by sight or touch, even by smell: the clear, green smell of pine, the birchbark smell, peeled and pale. One of the monks from the nearby monastery had harvested trees from his travels, had planted them and had mounted their names on metal plates hammered onto posts. Rave had these memorized and would recite them as he walked through: Norway spruce, Vancouver fir, Japanese yew, butternut. His favourite tree, the one he walked towards with intent, the one he planned on seeing, thinking of it midday and in the middle of town, was an old pine that stood alone in a clearing, the grass beneath it sloping towards woods and then a lake. He had stood under this tree with one hand on its trunk more times than he could remember. This tree, he often thought to himself, was the one he'd be if he could be a tree. Lightning had struck it years ago, stripping all of its branches off one side. They never grew back but the side with branches thrived. And the top of the tree, when Rave craned his head back to look up at it, flourished, arrowed itself straight to the moon, the stars, the whole night sky. Walking towards it, seeing its silhouette in the distance, took his breath away, made his heart hammer as if he were walking towards someone he hadn't seen for a long while, someone he truly had missed. When he finally reached it, stood under it, half under branch, half under sky, his father, his house and all the expectations of him fell effortlessly to his feet. He'd breathe in, smelling the night, the Big Dipper, the smudge of Milky Way, and he'd breathe in the pine, its bark and branches, its needles, and he'd feel how long ago the lightning was, the crookedness of healing, how close the sky had become, and it made him feel right, connected to something, at home and welcomed in a way he didn't feel anywhere else but here, on the mountain, under his tree. He trusted that feeling more than anything else. It had never wavered, had never changed.

Sheila was dreaming. She knew she was dreaming when she watched herself walk down the basement stairs, holding onto the railing with one hand, the other hand reaching out in the dark ahead of her, navigating. Les was standing in the middle of the basement, sawing a long piece of lumber. He had a pencil stuck behind his ear and a ledger book lay open on the piece of wood he was cutting. Her grandmother was standing beside a chair facing him; she beckoned to Sheila to come and sit down. Sheila watched herself manoeuvre around the board Les was cutting, stepping into the sawdust on the floor all around him. She looked back over her shoulder, saw her footprints and felt a pull of anxiety about trailing the wood bits through the house. Her grandmother tapped the chair.

"Sit down, Sheila."

Sheila sat, and as soon as she sat, looking up at her grandmother, the line between the dream and her conscious mind blurred and she let go of the idea that she was dreaming. She was sitting in the basement with her grandmother and with Les, who had begun to saw so forcefully that she couldn't hear what her grandmother was saying. He stopped finally to write something in the book, taking the pencil from behind his ear and licking the tip before writing.

"I'm going to show you how to crochet. You'll need a hook. Here, I brought you one." Her grandmother placed a slim white hook in Sheila's hand. "It's from your grandfather's hand, his ring finger, but he won't even notice." She leaned closer to Sheila and whispered, "He's a drinker, your grandfather," then stood and looked at her triumphantly. "Bet you didn't know that, eh?" She sighed. "What are you going to do with lemons but make lemonade? You make the best of what God gives you, Sheila. You crochet."

Sheila watched her grandmother undo her bun and unwind her scraggly, thin hair. She took a small pair of scissors from her pocket and cut the hair off.

"We'll use this. It's just a nuisance anyway, having to put it up every morning." She looped her hair around Sheila's hook and then hooked another strand through it.

"That's a chain stitch. If you want to crochet anything, you have to know how to chain. Now you try."

She watched Sheila hook the hair and nodded. "That's it, keep practising. Loop it through. That's it, chain."

Sheila continued, the long strand beginning to coil on her lap. She concentrated, with her grandmother urging her on, chanting *chain, chain*. And it was like a chain, she thought. Her grandmother's hair was the soft grey of chain-link fences. The hair began to feel heavy; the coiled strand in her lap felt weighted.

"Sheila."

She looked up from her hook. Les was standing in front of her holding an armful of blocks of wood that he dumped at her feet.

"I've finished my calculations."

She waited for him to go on, trying to shrug off her grandmother's hand on her shoulder, ignore her grandmother's hissed order to chain.

"We owe ten times the worth of this wood multiplied with interest, with a ten percent discount knocked off by my buddy down at the skate factory."

Sheila was perplexed. "What does that mean?" She felt her stomach knot, hook into itself.

"Chain, Sheila, for the love of sweet Mary, chain."

"It means that if I did my calculations right based on this here wood and that pile of screws over there, I have just enough time, if you put down whatever you're doing, to get to Canadian Tire before it closes and buy that router I need."

"Don't you listen to him, Sheila. Keep chaining."

Sheila looked up at Les. His face was red, the pencil back behind his ear. She could feel her grandmother leaning on the chair behind her, she could smell the talc her grandmother used, hear a faint whistle in her breathing. She looked into her lap. Chain. She straightened the chain she had made and wrapped it around her. She felt a small pleasure at having made such a long chain. They were arguing over her but their voices sounded faint and far away. The chain bent into place, like barbed wire, and she realized, looking up at them, that she was safe from them, she had saved herself. And then she woke up.

It was Thursday, Grace thought, pulling on her socks. Payday. She had worked only three shifts though. Four hours each. Excruciatingly long. It was the same with all the customers who came in. She'd smile, then they would assume she'd understand them and would speak to her in French so fast that she had to learn to listen for the flavour they were ordering. Just that, the familiar *érable* or *fraise* bobbing in the wash of rolled r's and nods. Sometimes they wanted to talk first and would smile after saying something, waiting for her to answer, to converse. She'd shrug and smile back. *Je ne comprends pas.* I don't understand. They'd frown and then the conversation would turn into a straight business exchange. Here's your cone, *voilà, merci, bonjour.* It was exhausting. The highlight so far had been when Bob, the town crazy guy, had come in. He had sat down and taken off his shoes and then carefully put each sock on the opposite foot, put his shoes back on, stood up slowly, testing his feet, and then smiled broadly at her. She watched him leave, whispering urgently into his watch. Bob was the highlight only because she didn't have to talk. She didn't even have to understand. She was relieved when Ann had told her that this would be her last week until the spring.

Thursday, she thought again, leaning over the bathroom counter to get close to the mirror to put on her mascara. Payday, her father used to yell when he worked days and they'd all pile into the car and drive to Miracle Mart to shop and then eat supper in the diner at the back of the store. Grilled cheese and coke. She cringed, thinking of how her father would tell anyone who'd listen how Grace always used to get lost, wander away from them. "She used to ask the goddamn television set if it was her mother," he'd roar, slapping his knee. "Oh, Grace, I'm just joking, for God's sake. Can't you take a joke?" Family history. They finally safety-pinned a large index card to her snowsuit before their trips to Miracle Mart. It had her name printed in black marker and her father's name. "So they know who they're dealing with." It became part of their routine of leaving. Turn off the lights, turn down the heat, pin on Grace's card.

She could remember being lost. Standing in an aisle of light pink makeup sponges and hairnets and her mother, her father, her brother all gone, disappeared. The first time it happened, she had sat down and cried, afraid they had forgotten her and gone home. A woman with a shopping cart full of disposable diapers had found her, told her to hold her cart while she picked out a pair of eyelash curlers and then took her to customer service where they made a loudspeaker announcement.

Her father had been furious, which had made her mother's lips disappear and Gary sneer at her. After the first time, she became quite good at getting lost. She'd look up at the big signs hanging from the ceiling and use them as a sort of map to the customer service desk. Customer service was near jewellery, jewellery was next to bathroom accessories and next to that was kitchen utensils. But why hadn't they been watching her? she thought now. She had been only seven. "You wander," her father had explained. "You've got to learn to stop wandering." She had been only seven and she had been left wandering around Miracle Mart by herself. *Je ne comprends pas.* I don't understand. One by one they would arrive at the customer service desk, Gary with a Hot Wheels car that he'd beg for later and get, her mother with a big jug of Mr. Clean or Javex. Her father always came last, red-faced and irritated. Later, when her mother stopped going, Les would pull money out of his pocket. "Go pick out a record or something and meet me back here in an hour." But that was much later and after that they stopped going altogether. Miracle Mart. She shook her head and ran downstairs. She didn't want to miss her bus.

Grace looked for Lily in the school library. She found her sitting in her usual seat at the big table by the window. Grace pulled a chair over to her and sat down.

"Hey, Lil, what are you on now?"

"Oh hi, Grace, umm, Daedalus. He was this architect in Greek mythology. It says he built a labyrinth and had to make wings of wax and feathers to escape the island of Crete. How are you? Are you okay? You look mad."

"Oh, I'm all right. That is so cool that he made wings to escape his island." Grace sat for a minute and watched Lily write. "Well, I guess I should go and let you concentrate." She waited but Lily kept writing. She pushed her chair back.

"Are you leaving? Sorry, I just want to get through this. I'm almost finished this notebook and I want to change to a new one before lunch is over. Why don't you come over after supper? It's my dad's night to bowl."

"Okay, I'll see you later."

Grace nodded and then turned away, hoping the crowd would swallow her up. She walked past the library and down the hall towards the gym. She read every bulletin board she passed, trying to appear as if she was looking for something and not just wasting time before the bell rang. This was when she missed Sharon the most, when time dragged its heels, scuffed its way to the next bell, when she was alone. She took the long way back to her locker and then opened her combination lock slowly. She hung up her coat, which had fallen down, then closed her locker and went into the girls' washroom. Looking in the mirror, she unbraided her hair and then braided it again. She went into a stall, came out, washed her hands and then dried them. She tied her shoe. Unlocked her locker again. Five minutes left before the bell rang. She sat on the bench near her locker and waited. A group of kids walked by pushing each other and laughing. Grace pulled into herself, hoping no one would notice she was sitting there alone. She began to doodle on her math copybook, absentmindedly drawing feathers and then wings, making columns of them as if they could be added, as if the sum of them held an answer she needed to know. When the bell rang, she made her way to her math class and sat down. She was the second person to arrive. She kept drawing until the teacher rushed in late, his arms full of books, apologizing.

Jerry waited until Lily had come out of the house. She left last. He waited until her bus came and she got on before going into the backyard. And then he waited a few more minutes to be sure, checking the yard next door. It was empty. He looked into the woods—forty steps, just forty steps. Rave began with one, and before he knew it, he was at the kitchen door.

His mother was waiting for him at the table. She had set it with placemats for each of them. She had brushed her hair up into a ponytail and had made tea. This was their second visit. The first was brief, in the doorway. Eliza had pressed food into her son's hands, had given him a pair of mittens and thick socks. They had barely spoken, not sure how to in this new territory of "after," as if they were somewhere foreign now, in the new territory of Jerry just visiting instead of staying. Eliza wanted to press words into her son's hands like warm stones. Words he could take out later, wherever it was he slept, wherever it was he lay down. She wanted to give her son something solid so that he'd know even when she wasn't with him that she was. But she still didn't know how.

This time there were soup bowls and spoons, a pot sitting on the stove filling the house with the smell of soup. Jerry breathed deeply. Turkey soup, she had made him turkey soup.

It was different being in the house without his father there. The air was easier to breathe. It didn't have the current that sparked between the two of them, that dried, tindered feeling of something about to ignite. He leaned back into his chair. His mother had told him once, before he had left, that his father meant well, that he just wanted Jerry to turn out better than he had. And that his anger was old and had nothing to do with Jerry, that Stan had been hurt, wounded by his own father, and to be patient with him, that he was a good man underneath. Jerry remembered shrugging her off, still blistered by the rage that had enflamed his father earlier, the scalding reprimand about coming home too late, or leaving for work too late, or whatever it had been about that time— that time the rage had spread quickly, like a brush fire, and joined forces with all the other times his father had got angry at him for his own good, until the space between them burned out of control.

The sun came through the window and landed on the table between him and his mother. Jerry watched her lift up the teapot. The weight of it bent her wrist and made her hand shake. She poured a little in her cup, decided it wasn't steeped enough and set the pot down. Reaching for the plate beside her, she handed him the sandwich that was already made. He took it wordlessly and set it before him. Then she got up and ladled soup into a bowl for him and put it down in front of him, placing her hand on his shoulder. He closed his eyes at her touch. When was the last time she had touched him? he wondered. Curtis was the only person who ever came near him now, and having his mother this close, breathing in the smell of her, hearing her hum under her breath, it awoke a hunger for his family. For that easy bantering after supper, the shrieking upstairs at bathtime, Dellie, Lily. She gestured for him to eat. Neither of them had broken the silence yet. Jerry ate his soup and then the tuna sandwich. He followed her into the living room with his mug of tea and lay down on the couch and watched his mother sit in the rocking chair and begin to rock slowly, sipping her tea. His eyes closed and he felt a blanket being pulled over him, her hand pushing back his hair, lingering on his face.

"Your father is trying," she whispered, and then he slept without dreams until she gently shook his shoulder a couple of hours later.

The school bus would be dropping Curtis off soon, soon Lily would be home, Dellie would be back from the babysitter. Jerry looked around the living room, drank in the mess and warmth for later and then got up and left. With his mother watching him, he crossed the yard and disappeared into the woods.

The night was cold and clear. The moon had freed itself from the hydro wires and pine trees and rose untangled in the sky, lighting paths and puddles with silver light. Rave walked towards the mountain. He wanted to go by the orchard and planned to spend the night in the shed. He wondered if there was any wood left for the stove and was trying to remember if he had chopped enough. Coming from the opposite direction, Gary was walking down from the mountain with his hands in his pockets, hunched and deep in thought. He'd been sitting on a rock watching Ralph drink with a couple of French guys who had wanted to buy a quarter ounce.

The street Rave was crossing and Gary was on was being dug up. Long concrete pipes lined the curb and made the road narrow. Their sleeves almost touched when they passed each other, and each, lost in his own thoughts, had jumped to see someone so close by. They nodded at each other and kept walking. When Gary looked back, Rave had disappeared and he was alone on the street. He noticed the pipes for the first time. They were long and came up to his thigh and looked strange in the moonlight, not like pipes at all but like something out of a science fiction novel, the kind of books he used to read when he was a kid. Tubular transport systems or something. Without thinking, he climbed into one. Inside smelled of wet cement. And though it was dark, the moon lit up one end and cast a pale light inside. He sat, his back curved to the side of the pipe, and walked his feet up the side facing him until he was almost in a fetal position, letting his head lean back and rest against the concrete. Sound was amplified and a car passing sounded thunderous. He took his cigarettes out and lit one, blowing the smoke to the side. Ordinarily, closed places freaked him out. He remembered hiding in the front closet once to scare Grace. His face had been pressed into coats, and he had become overwhelmed by the smell of shoes and wool, the darkness and the need to stretch his legs. He had to get out before she even came close, he needed to move. But this pipe felt good. Its cold sides penetrated through his jacket and made him feel more awake than he had in weeks. He was hidden from the street, from anyone walking by, and was cocooned in cement. Transported. Slowly the muscles in his body relaxed, his legs, his neck, though he hadn't even realized they'd been tight. He felt himself breathe and with each exhalation felt tension leave his body.

Outside something began tapping the pipe. He opened his eyes, startled by the scraping sound along the top as if something was being dragged against the cement. Gary held his breath and sat up, trying to hear voices or footsteps, anything that would indicate what was making that sound. For a moment he thought it might be an animal but quickly dismissed the idea—the sound was almost metallic. He waited, hoping whoever it was would continue walking, and was surprised at how afraid he felt. The sound of his heart seemed to slide from his ears and mouth into the pipe, where it echoed and kept an ominous beat. It was like a bad horror movie, he thought, the killer taking one slow step at a time. The sound stopped as abruptly as it had begun, but then he saw legs standing at either end of the pipe. Jeans and construction boots; jeans and running shoes. He knew the boots, recognized the way they were scuffed and turned outwards as if each leg wanted to go in the opposite direction of the other. Ralph leaned down and looked into the pipe, laughing. Then Gary heard something being dragged at the other end of the pipe, and the opening darkened and was blocked. Ralph stood and stepped back, and then that end was blocked too. Gary heard him kick whatever they had used to block the pipe and heard him laugh again. The laugh grew fainter and fainter until all that was left was an echo that wound itself around the beating of his heart like cigarette smoke. The pipe filled with those two sounds. He heard breathing and realized he was close to panting.

It took Gary a while to slow his breathing down. He had to stop himself from remembering Ralph's face looking at him, sneering. Had Ralph really seen him sitting there? He slid over to the closest end and used his lighter to see what was blocking it. It looked like a board, but when he put his feet up to it, it didn't move. His heart leapt up to his tongue and for the first time he could actually taste fear. It tasted of cigarette smoke and cement. He remembered how the gravel had tasted in the parking lot the night he'd been beaten. It tasted like that.

He moved to the other end of the pipe, sliding down on his stomach using his elbows and knees. They had used the same kind of board and it didn't move either. He began kicking at it and yelling for help, imagining Ralph and those French guys leaning on the next pipe, laughing at him. He thought if he stayed quiet, they'd get bored of watching and would let him out. His kicking and yelling had filled the pipe, and as the echoes died down, silence filled the space. The cement felt colder now, clammier.

Rave sat on a cold aluminum lawn chair that had been left out under a deck and he waited. He had seen the three guys walking down the path off the mountain and had doubled back to wait until they had passed. He had watched Ralph drag the handle of his knife down the pipe as if he were slitting it open, skinning it, and then he dragged boards over and wedged them in place with pieces of wood. Rave waited until they had turned the corner, then waited a few more minutes in case they changed their minds and came back. Clouds had moved over the moon and the street was left with just the street lights to illuminate it. A couple of lights had burned out and the one closest to the pipe that Gary was in stuttered like a strobe. Rave kicked the pieces of wood away and then walked quickly back up the driveway and under the deck.

Gary came out head first and tentatively looked around before pulling the rest of himself out. He straightened his body while cautiously looking around for Ralph. The street was dark in places and the street light above him faltered a final time. For a moment it lit up the street and then went out. He walked home slowly, looking behind him every few steps, listening hard for any sound that he was being followed. Everything about him listened and heard nothing but night sounds, cars on the highway, somewhere a siren and his heart, his breathing. He was alone.

Rave sat back in the chair for a long while after Gary left. The sky cleared finally and the moon, which had been holding in its light, let it go in one long sigh, the slow breath of it finding small surfaces to hold it, slivered and separate.

On the outskirts of town, past the highway and closer to the service road, the old power plant sat in darkness. Graffiti covered its bricks, and in the field behind it tall hydro towers stood like long-legged insects grazing in the moonlight. In the shadow of the building was a cement pit about ten feet long and four feet across. It was over eight feet deep and had once been used as a reservoir but now held only cigarette butts and a damp darkness. The moon had climbed higher and pushed the evening's clouds close down to the horizon. The occasional plane with blinking red lights pulled long, wispy trails from the clouds up into the sky like ropes of a net, of a ladder, that hung there, lingered and then eventually settled, gave way and faded back down into the dark band of clouded horizon.

Ralph sat on the edge of the pit with Mike, a skinny, pimply guy who had picked them up and driven them there. Below them in the pit were the two French guys Ralph had been drinking with earlier on the mountain. They were bruised, their shirts ripped. Ralph talked to Mike without looking down at them, ignoring their pleas for a hand up. And he didn't stop talking when he stood and pulled down his zipper, continued talking as the high arc of piss got caught in the moonlight before landing on them. He drank his beer and looked over intently at the highway as Mike dragged over boards and rocks and threw them down into the pit. He was bored. When he finished his beer, he stood and threw the bottle like a knife. It cartwheeled, the amber glass briefly caught in the light, then fell with a dull clunk. There was a scurrying, swearing, and then Ralph left without looking back. Mike hurried to catch up, then ran to the old Impala that had been hidden in the shadow of the building. He started the engine, waited for Ralph to get in and close the door and then drove slowly out towards the highway, not turning on the headlights until the car reached pavement.

Grace came down the stairs still tired. She went into the kitchen and put two pieces of bread in the toaster. She jumped when she turned and saw her father sitting at the table. He was usually at work by now.

"What are you looking at?"

"Nothing. I just didn't see you when I came in, that's all."

He was sitting with his boots still on. He looked away from her when she spoke.

"Aren't you going to work?"

"That's none of your business."

At first Grace was surprised by the force of his anger but not for long. She could feel her stomach clench, her movements quicken, the cogs of her own anger gripped, blazing. "I'm not telling you to go to work. I was just asking why you hadn't, that's all."

"Don't you talk to me like that, do you hear me?" He bent and untied his boots and then slid out of them. "If you get lippy with me, you'll be sorry. Do you understand? Pardon me? I didn't hear you."

Grace felt her teeth clench, her molars grind together. "Yes, I understand."

He nodded. "Your problem is that you don't enunciate. If you don't speak clearly, no one will listen to you. You have to speak up. Pronounce your words. Enunciate and for God's sake it wouldn't kill you to smile, would it? Do you have to be in a snit all the time? Do you think I'd be where I am in the world if I didn't smile and win people over? Lure them in, be charming and speak up. Stop slouching and don't look at me like that!"

Grace was dumbfounded.

"Are you out of your mind?" She turned and buttered her toast, hoping that he'd go away. When she turned, the chair was empty, his boots still there, as if he had disintegrated or had been yanked right out of them.

She caught the reflection of her eyes in the knife she was using. They looked back at her unsmiling, steely, each a blade that cut into her. Her father was an asshole and she needed a flock of feathers, she needed to escape. His voice replayed in her head as if she couldn't let herself forget who he was, couldn't let herself get used to him. *Je me souviens.* "Get your nose out of that bloody book," he'd always snarl. "I'm in charge of parts, missy." Les of the tool department, Les of the grey sweatsuit. Grace's eyes watched her so intently that she had to blink and look away. She knew that *Restez calme* was the first step in an emergency but she couldn't remember the next steps. There were three, she thought, maybe four listed on the panel in each metro car, with illustrations. They were more complicated and used words she had never heard of, words she couldn't decode, words that didn't help her in her own personal emergency. Breathe, she ordered herself, think.

Curtis went to his usual spot under the slide. While he waited for his friend, Jeremy, he fished his binoculars out from under his jacket and scanned the playground. He found the teacher who was on duty and then turned back to the schoolyard to look for Jeremy.

He focused on each group of walking children, moving his binoculars slowly from face to face. He took a step back when he saw the car behind one of the groups he had been watching. His mind raced in confusion. It was never parked there in the morning. He looked again, moving the thin plastic dial until he could see the driver. Curtis dropped his binoculars quickly; the man had been looking right at him. Shivers crept up his arms the way they did when Lily tickled him slowly, only these shivers didn't make him laugh—they made him afraid.

69

He turned his back to the street and counted the windows on the side of the school. He pictured each number as he said it quietly to himself. The number two was always purple and bendy as if it was made out of playdough. Three was glittery. The hair on the back of his neck prickled and itched. Curtis took off his mitt and scratched at it and then turned quickly to make sure the man was still in the car. Four windows, five windows. Jeremy came running over, his mitts hanging from his sleeves and his hands tucked up.

"Look, Curtis, my hands are cut off." He flapped his mitts and raised his arms.

Curtis laughed and ran reluctantly after him, his binoculars bumping into his chest as he ran. When the bell rang, they both headed for their lineup, pushing to be first, to be picked to hold the door open for everyone.

The seagulls descended onto the playground as soon as the last of the kids disappeared into the building. The gulls squawked territorially at the crows perched atop the swing sets, watching. They pecked hard at the ground looking for apple cores and cracker bits, anything left behind for them to eat. They strutted bossily around the garbage cans amid the crows, fighting each other over old crusts, shiny wrappers. Then they left, leaving the schoolyard empty, the windows full of movement.

Les didn't even think. He just signalled left, pulled into the street and drove to the French elementary school that started recess twenty minutes later than the English school. He drove urgently, rolling through stop signs and nudging pedestrians to cross faster by creeping up to their legs. When he got to the school, he parked facing the playground and sighed deeply. There were children everywhere, running and swinging, shinnying up and sliding down poles. He shivered and felt his cock pull. A child walked near the car, brushing it with his sleeve. Les inhaled deeply from his pipe, clamping its stem in his teeth. The windows fogged with his breathing and he turned the fan on higher.

The summer he was eight, Les was touched by the hand of God. At first he thought that it was Father Robert touching him, but God moved in mysterious ways, he was told, and Father Robert was acting on God's command. Every Thursday, after choir practice, Les would collect the hymn books and return them to their shelf, and every Thursday Father Robert was commanded by God to touch Les and make him feel the burning of the power of God on his penis. Les offered to pray instead, to kneel before the altar and offer up his service in another way, but Father Robert was sure God wanted to be served his way. At first this had puzzled Les. Why his penis, he wondered, why not his heart or his head? What good did it do God to touch his penis?

Father Robert filled with the Holy Spirit when he obeyed the command of the Lord. His eyes bulged with it, his cheeks turned red. He panted and sweated as if the Holy Spirit was giving him a good chase. He told Les he wanted him to feel the Holy Spirit too, to be filled with the glory of it, and then he took the boy's hand and put it on his own cock and there they stood, holding each other's cocks, their arms extended like transmitters for this spirit to volt through. Les felt it surge under the priest's cassock and felt afraid and tried to take his hand back, but the priest's eyes flew open, his nostrils flared, his face blazed red and shiny. Later he walked Les through the pews to the front door. They stood in front of the holy water and he talked to Les about sin and souls and the will of God and about hell. Les walked home with God on his shoulders, all of Him perched there like a giant parrot repeating what Father Robert had said, and tied to God were heaven and hell and they dragged behind him as well.

And God didn't climb off when Les got home. He felt Him settle on his shoulders, holding him under his chin. Even while he ate his grilled cheese, drank his milk, God whispered in his ear. He pointed to the calendar Les's mother kept tacked by the window and made Les look at it. "That's my son there, dying on the cross for you. My son died for your sins." Les thought that God sounded mad at him, that somehow he had angered Him. He prayed harder at night before bed; he hardly ever sat with his dad. His dad thought God was a lake and now Les knew better than that.

Lily was copying out the entry for damselfly. It was a good entry. She liked when the information sounded poetic with no population or longitude and latitude numbers. *A slender, elongated, blue abdomen and one pair of membranous wings.* Membranous wings sounded so much more hopeful than wings of wax and stuck feathers. She should tell Grace, she thought. She looked out her window at the greying sky. She could hear Dellie running around, screeching and laughing. Curtis must be chasing her. Lily got up and went downstairs, half thinking of making them all a snack and half lingering with the damselfly. *Membranous wings that are held vertically over the body when at rest.* She put her arms out and imagined the metallic blue of its stomach.

"Plane, Curtis. Lily is a plane." Dellie ran from Lily back into the living room with Curtis right behind her. Lily flew behind them, swooping close enough to tickle them, and then swerved away into the kitchen. Her mother was sitting at the table, holding an empty cup and staring into it as if looking for something.

"Would you like more tea, Mom?"

Eliza looked up slowly from the cup and smiled at her daughter. "Yes, Lil, that would be wonderful." And then she looked back down at the cup in her hands.

Lily plugged in the kettle and took down some crackers, then spread peanut butter on them for Curtis and Dellie. She rinsed the teapot, which was still on the table, and cleared the dishes that had been left. She briefly wondered who had eaten lunch with her mother but didn't think more about it. The kettle came to a boil and she poured the water into the pot, the steam fogging the window. After she placed the pot back in front of Eliza, she carried out a plate of crackers and a couple of tumblers of juice into the living room. She wasn't used to seeing her mother in the kitchen after school. She was usually drawing or reading.

Dellie and Curtis sat around the coffee table making each other laugh and spraying cracker crumbs across the table. Lily heard her mother's chair scrape the kitchen floor and then watched as Eliza walked slowly into the living room, balancing her full cup. She made her way to the big reading chair and set the cup down on the table beside it. There was a blanket folded on the back of the chair and she pulled it off and wrapped herself in it before sitting down. Dellie ran over and climbed into her lap. Eliza opened the blanket to the little girl and buried her nose into Dellie's fine, curly hair, breathing deeply as if committing the smell to memory. Dellie smiled and snuggled in closer. When Curtis saw his sister cocooned, he ran over too, and again Eliza opened her blanket up. The three of them sat there, covered warmly in the dark green blanket, their heads leaning into each other, until Eliza fell asleep. Lily helped the kids down without waking her. She brought out the markers and papers and got them colouring pictures of bugs.

She drew them damselflies, turquoise and thin. Dellie covered her paper with black dots and skinny legs.

"Spiders," she screeched and stuck them in Curtis's face. Curtis ignored her, pressing hard on his brown marker, making it squeak as he drew a tiny beetle in the lower right-hand corner of his paper. Beetles, Lily had told him, had hard shells and didn't squash easily.

When they finished drawing, Lily let them turn the TV on low and left them sitting on the floor. She was late making Jerry's sandwich and had to get it outside before her father came home. He had said that Jerry would come home when he was hungry, and would be angry if he knew she'd been feeding him. She went into the kitchen and took out the ham slices and mustard from the fridge. Three slices of bread was all she dared to take and she made him a triple-decker sandwich, cutting it diagonally the way Curtis and Dellie insisted their sandwiches be cut. She wrapped it in plastic, put it in an I G A bag and stuck it in the clothespin container on the back porch. When she had first started leaving Jerry food, she had left it on the railing, double-bagging it, but after a wet and windy night she had put it in the wooden box and he must have found it because when she checked the next morning, the sandwich was gone. That was weeks ago, after the first frost. She had worried about him in the cold and this was all she could think to do to help him.

Every day when she was making these sandwiches she thought of how unfair it was that she couldn't talk to her brother because of her father. She thought of leaving Jerry notes in the bag. Small pieces of paper with cheerful messages about having a good day, with happy faces drawn into each round letter, but he didn't need wishes for a good day, he needed his own warm bed. When she had asked her father why Jerry didn't want to come home, her father had just shaken his head. "He just doesn't like ceilings, Lily, that's all. And this house is too small. It's as simple as that." He had looked up above him as if trying to read the ceiling for more clues, then looked back at her and smiled. "Some days," he had added, "I'm not too fond of them myself."

Lily knew there was more to it than that. She had heard them fight, heard them scream at each other about all kinds of things. She had seen her father's face after Jerry had left once, the rage making him look like a stranger. Stan had always been two fathers, one for Jerry and one for her. The memory of a crooked shaft of sunlight through the small basement window, the dusty Mason jars, the spiderwebs and his belt being whipped out of its loops, cracking towards Jerry's leg. What was it that time, a broken window? A muttered retort?

Jerry, always Jerry, fighting, holding back the tears, and the sound of leather hitting flesh. He was a different father for Curtis and Dellie, growling on the floor as they climbed all over him, tyrannosaurus, all of them laughing, rolling into tables, the cats watching sleepily from the chairs. Her mother was the age Lily was now when she had got married, when they'd had Jerry. Seventeen. A lifetime ago, Eliza would sigh.

A few years ago Eliza had slowly stopped making the meals and the beds. One night supper wasn't made. It was after a night of one of Stan's rages, the night Jerry had left. Something in Eliza had simply said *Enough* and she had sat down. Lily had watched her parents exchange a look, a significant look, she thought at the time, though she didn't know what it had meant. Eliza decided then not to yell back at Stan but to move back instead, to retreat. Lily's father took over without ever complaining. He stepped into the space Eliza had left empty, explaining to Lily that her mom was just tired of being the chief cook and bottle washer and he was going to take over for a while, that they were a team. But once in a while, when he was tired, he would slip into the father Lily remembered him being, clenched and enraged. Then the house did seem smaller, bulging with his voice, and Lily would think of Jerry and remember why he had wanted to leave.

"He's like a seahorse," Grace commented that night. "The male seahorse takes care of its young, like your dad." She had come to the door as Lily and Stan were doing the dishes. Eliza had been in the living room on the couch, drawing, while Dellie sat behind her, brushing her hair.

"My mom takes care of us too, she just does it differently, that's all. She draws us all the time and she sketches things around the house. She always reads to Curtis and Dellie too. She always sits with them." Her family managed fine until someone came into the house and pointed out everything that seemed odd. Lily hated being reminded how strange her mother seemed. It was the way their family worked, she told herself in quiet defence. And she hated that the town knew her brother as "Rave" as if he were a lunatic. He had lost his temper, he had told her, and yelled at some kid for carving his name into a tree. Stark raving mad, someone had said and it stuck. Rave. They didn't even know him.

"Oh, your mom is great, Lil, I didn't mean that she isn't. Your house is just way different from mine. My house is filled with furniture that's covered in doilies and plastic and most things have my dad's name stuck on them. Your house seems like it's one big room. Even Jerry feels a part of it. It's weird. Like when we watch TV?" She paused to make sure Lily was still listening and then went on. "When we watch TV, it's like it's my mom and dad and me. If someone came in, they'd see us sitting there all apart. Your family seems more connected."

"Why is your dad's name on everything?"

"Oh, he's paranoid that someone's going to take something. I tried to tell him that if they did, they could just peel the label off, but he got all pissed off and told me I didn't know what I was talking about. He loves putting those labels on. It's almost as if he buys things just to put another label on something. He wants to buy a cassette player and tape all of his records. Weird. Sometimes he uses this electric etcher thing too, so the back of the TV has his name and social insurance number carved in skinny little crooked letters. It's like all his possessions make him important. He's always been like that, always wants to know what kind of car someone's driving. He always thinks everyone else is a loser."

"Is he afraid of being robbed?"

"Sort of. I think he thinks we're going to take them. I don't know. He's really strange. Maybe he thinks he'd be less important without his cassette player. And he doesn't make sense. He thinks he's this celebrity, that everyone wants to be like him, but all he does is hand out tools all day. Parts, I mean, for the refinery, oil stuff. Jesus. King of his domain."

Lily couldn't imagine living with someone like that.

"What about your mom? She must be nice, right?"

Grace snorted. "She's into covering everything with plastic

so we don't spoil things. She's just as fucked and she crochets these doilies so they're everywhere, doilies on the chairs, on the tables. It's like a blizzard of doilies." She didn't look at Lily but picked at her sock, engrossed suddenly with a thread that had become loose.

Lily wasn't sure what to say. She thought about saying that she was sorry but she didn't think Grace wanted her to be sorry. She was about to tell her about the damselflies, their membranous wings, when she looked at the doorway and saw Curtis's binoculars peeking in. "Curtis, are you going to bed now?" The binoculars nodded. "C'mon and give me a hug." He pushed the door open and walked shyly to the bed, giving Grace a wide berth. He let Lily hug him and then looked back into his binoculars at Grace. Grace waved and smiled gently.

"Hey, Curtis, buddy. Have a good sleep, okay?"

The binoculars nodded and Lily got up off the bed. "I'll be right back, Grace, I'm just going to tuck him in." She put her arm around her brother and led him out to the hall. Grace stayed on the bed, picking at the thread. She kept pulling at it and the sock began to unravel. She worried she had told Lily too much and felt shame burning hot in the pit of her stomach. Plastic on the furniture usually seemed normal to her, and most of the time she forgot that it wasn't. She felt shocked to hear herself talk about it out loud as if she was seeing her family through Lily's eyes. She felt alone sitting there, listening to Lily sing softly to Curtis in the next room. She realized, hearing herself talk about her parents, that they treated her like furniture too, that a part of her was covered in plastic, that her father's name was engraved on her somewhere, her mother's doilies were lying on her back to protect it, Sheila would say, from wear and tear. The idea made her want to run. She got up when Lily came back in.

"Hey, Lily, I've got to go. Homework and stuff. I'll see you tomorrow."

Lily nodded and got Grace's coat.

"See you tomorrow, Grace." She watched her friend run

down the stairs and waited while she put her shoes on. Grace straightened and said good night into the living room, opened the door and quickly left. Lily stood at the bottom of the stairs chewing a piece of her hair. She wondered what she could do for Grace. She thought again of damselflies, of their delicate wings, opened and ready for flight. Their slender, elongated bodies sounded part girl. Even wings of feathers and wax got Daedalus off his island.

Grace ran through Lily's backyard, hurdling over tricycles and small gardens. She ran as if she could run fast enough to win, to break the finish-line ribbon, the umbilical cord connecting her to her family, connecting her to the shame that cartwheeled through her always. She could almost imagine her father etching his name on her heart. She wanted to scour herself clean of him, of her mother, she wanted to run from the whole idea of them and break through the finish line that connected them all. But she had no idea how long the race was, no clue how she should pace herself. She ran as if they were right behind her and didn't stop at the woods on the edge of Lily's yard, didn't slow down when branches whipped her face and tried to trip her. She could feel them breathing, her father's nasal, heavy breath, her mother's lighter one sighing right behind her, catching up, reaching out to stop her from running too far or too fast. She wanted to get lost, to lose them. Through the trees she saw the light of the highway and headed towards it. Her eyes stinging, her heart pounding, full of her parents. She didn't see Rave sitting above her in one of the maples, eating his sandwich, didn't feel his eyes follow her through the trees until he couldn't see her. She was far enough away that when he jumped down, she didn't hear him land.

Ralph sat on the hood of the Impala with a beer between his legs. It had been a slow night and he was bored. He hated being bored. He took out his knife and began carving his name on the car. Mike protested but then shut up when Ralph stopped, his knife mid-air, glinting with the lights that lit up the side of Le Bertin. He continued, the sound of metal scraping metal filling the parking lot, and when he finished, he brushed aside the paint that had flaked off and admired his handiwork. Neither he nor Mike heard Grace until she stood in front of them, out of breath, her hair full of twigs and dead leaves.

"Whoa, Gracie, you look great. What are you running from?"

"Have you seen Gary? I really need to find him."

"Gary, eh?" Ralph pulled at his beard, his eyes sparking, looking down at his friend. "Gary. Have we seen Gary, Mike?"

Mike shook his head.

"Wait a minute," Ralph continued, still pulling at his beard. He took a long gulp of his beer. "Didn't Gary say he was going to hang out at the power plant, Mike? Yeah, yeah, that's where he is, at the power plant."

Mike looked confused for a second and then sneered.

"Oh yeah, Gary's at the power plant."

"Where's the power plant, is it far?" Grace looked from one to the other, her voice high and hurried. She had hoped he'd be at the bar.

"Oh, it's not that far, Gracie-poo. Mike here has wheels. We could drive her, eh, Mike?" Mike nodded quickly and got into the car. Ralph slid off the hood and stood in front of Grace.

"Sociable," he said, tipping the bottle to her and then guzzling the rest of the beer back. He tossed the bottle over the car and grinned when it smashed. "Hop in."

Grace looked back to the bar, uncertainly. The last thing she wanted to do was get into a car with Ralph but she also didn't want him to know how much he scared her. And finding Gary was important, she needed to see him. She needed to know that she wasn't alone in her fucked-up family.

"C'mon, Grace, it really isn't that far." Ralph opened the door and waited.

She looked dubiously from Ralph to Mike. If anyone knew where Gary was, it would be Ralph, she reasoned to herself, trying to calm the panic that clawed at her throat. Every instinct told her not to get in the car, not to go anywhere with Ralph. *Restez calme*, she thought. This was an emergency.

She climbed into the back seat and watched Ralph slide in the front. He hit the naked doll that was hanging from the rear-view mirror and looked at Mike, then back at Grace, smiling.

"Dance," he muttered, smirking at the swaying doll. The sweat that had been rolling down Grace's back turned icy. She shivered and pulled her coat closer. Mike turned and looked at her before he started to back up. His face was lit green by the sign for Le Bertin; when he smiled, his teeth looked black and pointy. Reptilian, Grace thought, he looked part lizard.

"It's okay, Ralph, I'll just wait for him here." Grace started to slide towards the door.

Ralph turned around to face her. "It isn't far, Grace." Then Mike gunned the engine and the car moved to the highway and headed out of town.

Rave ran through the woods after Grace, wondering what she was running from. He ducked under the branches that were still swinging in her wake and kept her in sight, breathing evenly and quietly. His mother had given him his green winter parka but he wished he was still wearing his jean jacket and sweater as sweat rolled down his spine and his shirt began to stick to him. He stopped when he got to the parking lot and watched Grace talk to Ralph. Rave knew Ralph; he had watched him many times on the mountain. He'd seen him beat up a few guys and had been at the lake when Ralph had stabbed Steve in the leg. And he had watched him trap Grace's brother in that cement pipe a few nights ago.

Seeing Grace talk to Ralph made Rave nervous and he flinched when he heard the beer bottle break. Ralph was in one of his moods, he could tell. When he saw Grace climb into the car, Rave ran without thinking, without a plan—he just ran to the highway and stood on the side of the road, willing the car to turn towards him. And when it did, he stuck out his thumb and waited for it, not blinking in the glare of its headlights but willing it, his eyes on the dark shape of the driver, to stop.

"Hey, hey, Rave, what are you doing out here, looking for a drive?"

Rave shrugged and looked down the highway.

"Well, where ya heading, buddy?"

Rave cleared his throat and shrugged again. Ralph looked over to Mike and shook his head.

"The more the merrier, right, Mike? Get in back there beside Grace."

Grace slid over and Rave got in, slamming the door behind him.

"Do you know Grace, Rave? Grace, this is Rave."

Grace smiled a small smile. "Hi."

Rave looked at her; he had never seen her this close. He'd watched her leave his house and often followed her home, but he would see only her back, sometimes her profile and her long braid or ponytail. Even in the dark car he could see her eyes. She'd been crying and her cheeks were scratched. He had seen her leave his house, seen her stand in his lit kitchen talking to Lily, seen her looking over her shoulder as she biked down his street. Now, beside her, he saw her in a different way. He felt her the way he felt landscape and he knew her in that moment the way he knew his tree, the way he could read the sky for weather. He felt her leg along his; his breath quickened and he could feel his cheeks flush. She seemed part birch, thin and silvery, pale, and she seemed part lake, not any lake but the one between the cliff and pines, the lake that seemed clear and deep at once. He was surprised how all the times he'd seen her came flooding back now, how all the times he had thought about her seemed to have been polished and made clear. This recognition was like rocks that caught the sun or the moon and sent a glimmer back in reply. He knew her in a way he knew no one else. It came to him that he'd been watching her. Closely from across yards, from behind trees. He looked over at her again and found her looking back; they both smiled and looked away quickly. Her eyes were deep, he thought, eyes he could dive into. Rave felt his heart stand up. He knew in that instant that he had no choice but to dive in.

Ralph spoke low to Mike and then Mike pulled the car back onto the road and continued towards the power plant.

"Grace wants to see her brother so we're taking her to the power plant. Okay with you, boss?" Ralph grinned at Rave and blew smoke into the back seat. Mike laughed and looked at Ralph. He sat hunched over the steering wheel and every once in a while his eyes would meet Grace's in the rear-view mirror and he'd lick his lips and shift in his seat. Grace felt fear paw at her stomach. She looked over at Rave but he was just sitting, staring at the back of Ralph's head. His face was paler than she had remembered, his hair so black it almost looked blue. He sat uncomfortably, moving his legs often. His hands were on either knee; his fingers, she noticed, were long and thin. She looked away quickly when he turned to her. The car slowed. Mike peered out the dark window looking for the old service road and turned onto it, the wheels spinning for a moment, gravel and dirt flinging up behind them.

Grace moved to the edge of her seat trying to see Gary in the dark. The car pulled up to an old brick building. She couldn't see anyone there but it was dark, she figured, and he could be sitting beyond the reach of headlights.

They got out of the car. Mike opened the trunk and took out a beer for Ralph and himself. Ralph looked at Grace and opened the beer with his molars, spitting the cap out beside him.

"Uh-oh, Gracie, I don't see Gary."

Grace felt the fear that had been pawing her stomach jump up on her, nosing her face. She swallowed hard.

"You knew he wasn't going to be here, didn't you, Ralph. What the fuck are you up to?"

"Nothing Gracie, just having a little fun."

Mike's laugh punctuated everything Ralph said. Grace looked over at him in disgust.

"Fuck off, Mike."

Ralph laughed. "Mike, now you've pissed Gracie off."

Grace knew that Rave was behind her. She sensed him and was tempted to lean back on him. He felt solid, as if he could handle the weight of her if he had to. She wondered briefly if what she felt for him was trust. She tried pushing off her fear, and beneath it anger sat ready to be lit and stoked. She could hear Ralph breathe, could hear his tongue slide across his lips. His eyes were like hot, sweaty hands.

"Now, Gracie, how can we make you happy to be here?"

Mike leaned back on the hood of the car drinking and watched them both steadily. She was about to tell him to fuck himself when she felt a movement, and before she could turn, Mike cried out.

"Fuck, he threw a fucking knife at me. Fuck, get it outta me, Ralph. Jesus."

A knife handle was sticking out of his leg and around it his jeans darkened with blood. Before anyone could say anything, Rave grabbed Grace's hand and began running with her into the darkness. Grace tried to look back to see if they were being followed but she almost tripped and had to stop looking. She let Rave run in front of her, guiding her behind the building and down through a ditch. They kept running, over iced puddles and long grass, moving quickly from the road. She stopped when Rave did and they both bent over and took hard, fast breaths, the air cold in her lungs, her eyes tearing.

"They didn't follow us," Grace panted.

Rave shook his head. "Ralph's too fat to run anywhere and Mike can't."

For a while neither of them spoke. Grace felt her heart slowly sink back down into her chest.

"That was so amazing. You moved so fast I wasn't sure what was going on."

Rave nodded and pulled her to the ground. They lay down, flattening the grass, the sound of the hollow stalks breaking, giving way to their weight, the length of their bodies. The car drove past them on the far side of the field, creeping along the road. It was the only car in sight. They watched it up speed then and head towards town.

"We can't stay here long, they might come back. Are you ready to go?" Rave looked over at Grace. She nodded, and when they both stood up, the grass stayed flattened where their bodies had been. They jogged towards the road, cutting across more fields and ditches until they could see the town edged in trees. They moved quickly and didn't stop until they reached a clearing in the woods just out of town. There was a lean-to built around a few pines. A big rock sat near its opening and the moon sent slender columns of its light down, catching patches of frost and ice.

Grace's legs felt part rock and part flame. She leaned on the rock and let it support her. Her toes tingled with cold. Rave stood under one of the trees that surrounded the clearing and watched her. The silence was deep; only the occasional car could be heard out on the highway. The trees moved in the wind, creaking and knocking branches.

Grace felt her anger thaw and with its melting came the image of Ralph and Mike looking at her, Mike snickering and Ralph's eyes intent on her face. She shuddered, realizing how stupid she had been, getting in the car with them. No one would have heard her yell or scream way out there. Her body began to shake, her teeth clattered.

"C'mon, I'll walk you home." Rave went into the lean-to and pulled out a blanket and then put it awkwardly over her shoulders. "Walking will warm you up and you need to get home."

Grace could only nod.

He realized suddenly that she was the first person he had spoken to in months besides Curtis and his mother. And

Grace was the first person he had wanted to talk to, the only person.

He took her through his backyard. She moved around a tricycle without wheels that looked as if it were growing up from the ground. There was a rusted wheelbarrow resting against the house. The clothesline sagged and swayed in the wind. She followed him through more backyards, paths between houses across streets she'd hardly noticed before. Rave moved quickly and silently, his arms close to his body. She lost sight of him in the shadows a couple of times and had to squint to keep him in view; he wasn't used to having someone with him, she could tell by the way he made himself slow down and wait for her. She was surprised by his sense of direction—after a dozen backyards she had given up trying to figure out where they were. He knew the town by its land, she figured. He used the streets only when he had to cross them to get back on grass and out of the street lights' glow. Although he waited for her, he didn't have to turn back to look at her to know where she was. Grace made more noise walking; even her breathing sounded louder to her. Her coat rustled and she could hear her braid sweep back and forth across her back. He could easily slip ahead into the darkness and disappear, but she could tell he was checking his pace to match hers and she was walking slowly, her legs tired and sore from running. She felt as if she'd been running for days. She tripped over a bare root and Rave stopped to steady her with his hand. He held branches for her to duck under. He made it easy for her to follow him.

Every time a car passed, her heart thundered into her skull. She hated being afraid but she wasn't afraid for herself any more, she was afraid for Rave. Ralph would never let him off that easily. He might have tonight but there would be other nights, many other nights. Soon it would be December, she thought, and nights would be even longer, giving Ralph more time. She shuddered. He'd want revenge; he'd hunt Rave in the woods at night until he got him. Ahead of her Rave nimbly jumped a low gate. A porch light caught him in its glare and for a moment he seemed stilled by the light, hovering almost, and then he moved from it back into the darkness. Easily.

Gary lit another cigarette and looked back up at his ceiling. He couldn't get out of bed. His body felt filled with wet sand, cement that was slowly hardening. He imagined a long, rickety flight of stairs in his body instead of veins and bones, and deep at the bottom of them, in the cellar, was a fence with a gate. All day he'd sat at the bottom of these stairs and had imagined opening the gate. He knew that once he did, everything he had kept inside of himself would come stampeding out. What he needed to do was to keep it shut, use everything he had to keep it closed, tightly tethered. He couldn't start thinking, couldn't let his thoughts assemble, become a mob, an army of angry, urgent thoughts, demanding freedom, justice. He kept everything in its separate corner, herding each thought like an unbroken horse, rearing, into a separate corral. Ralph and the money he owed him in one. His parents in another. Grace. Soon, he felt, these thoughts would break out and run wild.

Even though he sat up slowly, his head still buzzed with a rush of blood, and for a moment he felt as if he was going to black out. He steadied himself on the side of the bed. He needed to eat, he needed to piss. Digging into his pocket, he pulled out a small ball of foil that he opened, and with his pocket knife carved off a chunk from the dark brown hash that had been wrapped up. He knocked over the ashtray on his table looking for the straight pin he had slid under it. Cursing, he bent, trying to stay balanced on his bed and pick up the ashtray at the same time. Nothing was easy. He righted himself, placing the ashtray on his chest, and skewered the piece of hash onto the pin. He was exhausted from lying in bed and not thinking. He watched his thumb flick his lighter and held the flame just under the hash until it lit, flambéed, then holding the pin to his mouth, he breathed in, inhaling the smoke, feeling his thoughts unmoor and float away. He kept lighting the hash, softly blowing out the flame until nothing was left and his head felt soft and cushioned, his mouth dry. He was hungry and headed upstairs to the kitchen, shoulders hunched in the old grey cardigan he had got for Christmas a few years ago. The sleeves were too short now and his wrists were bare and bony. He wondered how long he had been asleep.

He was spreading Cheez Whiz on crackers and dropping chocolate chips slowly onto the cheese spread when Grace opened the back door. He turned slowly and looked at her, his eyes taking time to adjust to the darkened doorway.

"What happened to your face? It's all scratched up."

Grace looked at him long and hard without saying anything. The tears that she had run from, the need to find him, engulfed her. Her eyes filled.

"I was looking for you. Ralph told me you were at the power plant and he got Mike to drive—"

"Ralph took you to the power plant? Are you okay, did he do anything to you?" Gary seemed uncomfortable with the questions. Uncomfortable about having to ask them without really wanting to hear the answers. He held a cracker up to the light, nudged one of the chocolate chips deeper into the cheese.

"No, Jerry, I mean Rave—they picked up Rave hitchhiking and he threw a knife at Mike and we got away." She continued looking at him, hardly blinking, waiting.

He wanted her to stop looking at him that way, to stop expecting something from him. He chewed slowly, savouring the salt of the cheese and the small bursts of sugar. He was too tired for this, for her. He felt her eyes burn into him, descend inside him one stair at a time until she was looking right at him. He felt the panic of fence slats giving way, the pushing mob of thoughts, and beneath that sound, the quiet knowing. If she hadn't escaped, if Rave hadn't saved her, Ralph would've had her, would've held her down for Mike to have her too. He felt bile rise in his throat and turned to the sink and threw up.

When he finished wiping his mouth, he turned and Grace was gone.

Outside, Mike turned the headlights on after Grace went into the house. Ralph motioned for him to pull out and start driving again.

Curtis didn't recognize the lunch lady. She was taller than Mrs. Sears, her face was pointier. And she didn't know him the way Mrs. Sears did, didn't know that he liked staying under the slide, watching the other kids play on the playground equipment. He needed his binoculars to see them closer. She had shooed him out from under there, had told him to go and play, to get some exercise, and now he was standing in the open where everyone could see him, even the man in the car. The slide kept him hidden; it was like having a beetle shell over him. He didn't like standing in the middle of the playground feeling all soft and skin. He didn't want the man in the car to watch him, to see him getting tingly and scared.

It wasn't that he didn't play; he did, with Jeremy, but they played under the slide. Sometimes they'd stand next to it and send small rocks sliding down onto a green plastic soldier that Jeremy had in his pocket. Sometimes one of them would place a cookie at the bottom and roll an apple over it. They played all kinds of games but Curtis liked playing under the slide best. The big boys didn't bother them, didn't grab their hats and run, passing them back and forth high above their heads. If anyone stood and made fun of them, they could just turn and keep playing, the long plastic tube above their heads protecting them like a hard hat from thrown rocks.

Mrs. Sears knew that; she never made them exercise. Curtis stood between the swings. Jeremy had gone and joined a bunch of boys who were being chased by girls. He watched them screech and run between the other kids in excitement.

"C'mon, Curtis, Mandy's got Devon's hat, we've got to get it before she gets her germs all over it." Jeremy ran by Curtis, shouting back to him over his shoulder.

"Yeah, Curtis, we need your help. Ashley says she's going to kiss it."

Curtis let himself be pulled into the current of running bodies. He ran back and forth across the playground, helping Devon get his hat back. When the bell rang, they all ran to their lines. Curtis stopped for a moment and stood by himself. The first lineup was heading towards the door. His neck felt prickly from running and getting sweaty. He wiped it with his mitt and turned. He remembered the other reason he liked to play under the slide—it blocked the view of the street, and Curtis figured if he couldn't see the man, then the man couldn't see him. The car's headlights caught the sun and glinted like two eyes. He held his binoculars up and then turned around abruptly. The car was empty. He hurried over to his line; the boys were in the front, pushing each other and laughing. He stood at the end by himself. Even with his back to them, he felt the car's headlights send spikes of sunlight right through him, and he nearly tripped in his hurry to go into the school. Inside he stumbled again. Without the sun the hallway seemed extra dark, and for a moment Curtis could hardly see.

Les felt blessed. Wednesdays had always been lucky for him. He walked in the opposite direction from the kids who were returning to school after lunch. He didn't move out of their way and felt them brush against him in their hurry to get to the schoolyard. He felt joyous. The boys reminded him of himself at that age, busy and full of plans. He looked into their faces wistfully, wanting to see some recognition, wanting to be included in their jokes, their teasing. He walked slowly to stay surrounded by them for as long as he could. Every hair on his body stood at attention. He stopped himself from laughing out loud and said a small prayer of thanks when he saw one little boy approaching with his head bent, trying to figure out the zipper on his coat.

"Hey, there, fella." Les reminded himself not to sound too anxious, too eager. That would scare the boy away. He'd read books, had studied how to be charming. "I hate those zippers. Do you need some help?"

The little boy stopped and looked at Les. Les smiled gently and took another step towards him. The boy nodded and Les quickly dropped to one knee.

"Let's see how this fits. Oh, this is a hard one, it's stuck, no wonder you're having trouble." He let his eyes slide down over the boy while he tugged at the zipper. He was so small, so sweet—Les could feel his heart melt hot and slide along his limbs. Butter in a frying pan, fish floured, salt and pepper. His mouth watered. He made himself smile reassuringly.

"There we go, I got it." He zipped the zipper and left his hand on the boy's shoulder for a moment, squeezing it softly. The boy twisted from his hand and ran ahead to catch up to his friends. Slowly Les straightened and then quickly looked around. No one had even noticed him. He continued walking, whistling quietly to himself, and when there were no more kids on the sidewalk, he stood at the far end of the playground and watched them run. He stood still the way his father had taught him all those years ago. Don't even move, his father used to tell him, or you'll scare the fish. Les had to learn to move slowly and deliberately. On those long August afternoons, watching the water for a ripple, for movement, watching his line for the slightest tug, Les had learned patience. He was good at waiting.

When the bell rang, he watched them run in a frenzy to their lines. One boy lingered. Les saw him look towards his car and then run to the school. Les felt his line tug, watching him run. He was the kind of boy Les remembered being, smaller than the rest of the boys, quiet. Perfect. He smiled and waited until the boy had disappeared into the building.

*   *   *

When Les got home, Gary was at the kitchen table pouring maple syrup onto toast. They briefly looked at one another and then looked away. Gary winced as if he'd been cuffed. Les felt the joy that had filled him dissolve.

"Why don't you get off your lazy ass and get a job?" he snarled at his son.

Gary picked up a book of matches that he had tossed on the table and began tearing it up into little pieces. He continued tearing while his father stood there glaring at him. The maple syrup pooled on the bread and then started soaking into it.

"Answer me. I said, why don't you get off your lazy ass and get yourself a job? Do you think I enjoy supporting you? I've worked for twenty-three years. For twenty-three years I bust my ass and all you do is lie around, for Chrissakes, and eat me out of house and home and you can't even eat right. Syrup and bread in the middle of the day."

After all of the cover of the matchbook was torn off, Gary pushed his plate away and began lighting the matches one by one, letting them burn as close to his fingers as he could. It disgusted him how cowardly he was, he couldn't even burn a whole match. It hurt too much. He sat there dumbly, barely listening to his father.

"—respect. Is that too much to ask for? When I was your age, there was no way I'd ever treat my father the way you treat me. He would've killed me. This is my house, and when you are in my house, you have to obey my rules." Les felt his speech gaining momentum. "Listen here, mister, I've studied enough child psychology to know what you need. Bet you didn't know your old man had studied anything. Well, for your information I know plenty about psychology and the human condition. I've read Dale Carnegie, ever heard of him?"

Gary was down to the last match. He dragged it, striking it slowly, surprised that it ignited so quickly. He watched the plump flame burn quickly to his thumb and finger. He willed himself to continue holding it, no matter how much it burned. He bit down on his tongue when it got closer to flesh, trying to ignore the heat, the thought of flesh meeting the flame and burning. He dropped it into the ashtray, still burning. He was such a loser. He looked up at his father, looking at him for the first time in months. Les's ears stuck out, red from being outside.

"Fuck off, Les. Why don't you just fuck yourself, asshole."

Les looked at him, his lips pulled back, disappearing. "Don't you talk to me that way, you ungrateful son of a bitch."

Gary glared at him as he got up from the table. He shouldered his father out of the way and went downstairs to his bedroom, slamming the door. He heard his father upstairs turning on the faucet and getting a glass of water. Gary knew he was cornered. He couldn't go upstairs without facing Les again and he couldn't go outside without running into Ralph. He lay on his bed, and when he couldn't sleep, he pulled a plastic bag from under his pillow and picked out a clear capsule. THC, horse tranquilizer, just what he needed. He broke the capsule open and carefully tapped the powder onto his cigarette case. He still had a five-dollar bill left, he remembered, and got it out of his pocket and rolled it into a straw. Dale Carnegie this, he thought, snorting the powder up into his nose. He did it in two deep pulls and then lay back and felt the powder melt sour down the back of his throat. "Child psychology, my ass, Les," he said out loud, coughing at first and then swallowing hard. He had to get up, had to pace his small room from one wall to the other, not thinking, just walking—walking and turning and walking and waiting to be tranquilized. Comfortably numb, he thought. And cold.

Jerry's mother had a bowl of chili waiting for him. He left on his boots and jacket. He was exhausted and still chilled from the night before. After bringing Grace home, he had stayed and watched the house until Mike's car had slunk off. Then he had gone up to the mountain and tried to sleep in the tool shed by the orchard. He had lit a fire in the wood stove but ran out of wood before he could fall asleep. Everywhere he looked he could see Grace, could hear her voice. He breathed deeply and could almost imagine how her hair would smell. Like apple maybe, or cedar, the small seeds bunched at the end of a branch peeled apart. He breathed then as if she were there, as if she were lingering near him. He wished that he had listened more closely to Curtis when his brother had told him about Grace; he wished he had kept every little detail about her for later, to take out and savour. He wished he had had the courage to reach up and trace the scratch that ran under her eye and down to her lip when she was thanking him. He almost did, his arm started to rise, started to reach for her, but he thought maybe she wouldn't want him touching her, maybe she'd back up, alarmed. She had warmed him, the way she had looked at him when she thought he wasn't looking, the shy way she had taken him in. Those quick glances returned to him after she had gone into her house, and later as he lay under the small window in the shed, those glances warmed him still, made his stomach flutter like an aspen, he thought, smiling; a poplar in the wind, that's how she made him feel, like dragon-flies flitting after each other over the lake, swooping and lacing themselves closer, that's how he imagined her with him. It was cold and he knew he faced a whole season of snow and wind, but she had given him a little April in the small looks and smiles she had for him. The month of May and melting. She melted him. He had lain beneath the window, watching clouds and stars move by it, and then the moon appeared, centred in the pane. Barely a crescent. He had never felt happier and more alive. Small electric charges beat out of his heart.

Jerry took a spoonful of the hot chili and then dipped a piece of buttered bread into the bowl. He smiled up at Eliza, fingering the stone he had picked up for Curtis the night before. After he ate, he'd put it on Curtis's pillow for him to find. His mother didn't sit with him; this time she stood by the kitchen sink, looking out the window. He could still remember how when he was young and she got that look in her eyes, all dreamy and far away, he'd do something by himself and leave her alone. She never got angry if he talked to her then, she just didn't seem to hear him, engrossed in whatever she was drawing or reading. She used to get that way after a fight, after one of his father's outbursts.

He scraped up the last of the chili and sat for a minute, wondering if she was going to make tea or whether he should put the kettle on for both of them. He decided instead to butter another piece of bread and then go up to leave Curtis his moon rock.

Upstairs he sat on Curtis's bed and looked around. This room used to be his until he had moved downstairs and then outside. He opened the drawer in the little table by the bed, not to look at its contents but just to move the drawer in and out. It used to stick when he used it. He noticed Curtis's notebook and slid it out, curious about what he'd been writing. On the first page was a small picture of a train in the upper right-hand corner and then the next few pages were filled with lines, like the number one written over and over. Jerry flipped to the back of the book. On the last page on the top was a picture of a car. The headlights had slit pupils and the fender had jagged teeth. Jerry laughed to himself, thinking it looked like a shark. Under the picture were more lines and more pictures of the car, its teeth looking more menacing, pointier. He carefully put the notebook back and closed the drawer. He had meant to put the rock on the pillow and then go back downstairs but instead he lay down for a minute and fell asleep.

When he woke up, he wasn't sure where he was or how long he had slept. He looked up, panicky at seeing a ceiling, and then recognized it as Curtis's ceiling. He heard a rustle and looked over at the floor. Curtis was sitting with his back to him, bent over his notebook. Jerry could tell he was trying to be quiet, and when Curtis started turning a page, slowly and deliberately, Jerry cleared his throat.

"Hey, Curtis, how are you doing?"

"I'm okay, Jerry." Curtis's voice sounded small and serious.

"What are you doing there?"

Curtis loved Jerry's voice. He closed his eyes while his brother spoke. His brother's voice was deep and soothing, like a blanket, Curtis decided. His own voice, he thought, sounded like Dellie's plastic doll when it was squeezed too hard.

"I'm working on my notebook."

Jerry nodded. "Important work."

"Yeah, I had to mark three trains. And one car." He said the word *car* quickly as if just saying it, holding the word in his mouth, burned his tongue.

"You're counting trains, eh?"

"Yeah, remember I told you about that? I got them all down here." He patted the notebook possessively. "I know I've missed a few 'cause Daddy makes me go to bed early and I have to go to school, but I try to remember them and when I get home I mark them down." He was going to say how important it was for him to mark each train, record its passing, as if something big was depending on him. That it mattered.

"What car are you counting?" Jerry thought of Ralph and Mike leaning against the Impala, its headlights glaring at him and Grace, and the straight, sure shot he had taken with his knife. "What car is it, Curtis?" All of sudden Jerry felt uneasy and remembered Curtis's drawing. The shark mouth and slit eyes didn't seem as funny any more, the jagged teeth.

Curtis looked down at his notebook and didn't say anything right away. Jerry waited, an icy finger of fear tapping him on the back. Curtis shrugged. "Just a car, Jerry."

"Why are you counting it?" Jerry sat up, swinging his legs to the floor. He let his body slide off the bed and sat cross-legged beside Curtis. Curtis pulled himself into the space between his brother's legs and snuggled into him. Jerry could hear Dellie and Lily downstairs and hoped they wouldn't come up and find him there, home. For good, they'd think. He breathed in the boy smell of Curtis's head and spoke into his hair. "Why are you counting a car, Curtis? Is it following you?"

Curtis shook his head. He mumbled something, his head bent, his voice muffled in his shirt.

"What? I didn't hear you." Fear was tapping more insistently now, poking him in the back and stomach.

"I said, it parks at my school," Curtis repeated louder.

Jerry didn't know what to ask next. He knew he had only a few minutes until Lily either came up or called Curtis down for supper. He could smell onions frying and the sky had already darkened since he had woken up. The light by the bed had been switched on.

"Are you afraid of this car, is that why you have to watch it?"

Curtis nodded a slow yes and then Lily did call him from the bottom of the stairs. Jerry helped him stand, pulling him close for a second and then turning him around towards the door.

"You go eat now, Curtis. I've got to go anyway. Listen to me though." He waited until Curtis had turned back to him and was looking up at his eyes. "I don't want you to be afraid any more, okay? Where do you see the car? At school?" Curtis nodded again. "Well, you don't have to worry about it any more, okay? I'll do the worrying. That's what big brothers are for, right?"

Curtis nodded and smiled shyly.

"Bye, Jerry."

Lily called again, this time not singing his name but shouting it. Curtis waved from the doorway and then Jerry heard him clumping downstairs. Jerry picked up the notebook left on the floor and turned to the back pages. Curtis had added another line to the page. He had pressed so hard on his pencil that the mark was imprinted on the next blank page like an echo of the car, the sound of its motor driving away. Jerry wondered why Mike and Ralph would be hanging around the schoolyard. He put the book back on the floor, the way Curtis had left it, and then stood at the top of the stairs listening for a moment to the sounds of knives and forks on the plates that he knew were white with a border of blue flowers. He heard Dellie ask for more ackle juice and smiled at her tiny voice. And then he went down the stairs slowly, putting his foot down carefully on each step, stepping over the seventh and ninth stairs that creaked, until he was downstairs in the hallway. He opened the front door quietly and slid out into the night, pulling the zipper of his jacket up to his chin and shoving his hands deep into his pockets, his breath sudden bursts of stored-up warmth from his house. He quickly scanned the sky as if for a navigational clue and then headed north through the yippy terrier's back-yard, over the stone wall, towards Grace's house, leaving a wake of barking dogs behind him.

Grace hadn't seen the fight break out. She had been sitting in the parking lot behind the school, skipping her morning classes. The last time she looked up there were two groups of guys in the parking lot with her, one from the French high school that shared their parking lot and the other, closer to her, from her school, the English one. When she looked up again, they were fighting, each boy paired with another, headlocked or rolling around on the pavement. The fight was still going on when the lunch bell rang, and soon the yard was filled with students from both schools, surrounding the fighters and cheering wildly. Smaller fights erupted around them, like sparks jumping from a fire and staying lit, threatening to burn into bigger flames. One of the guys fighting had insulted the other guy's girlfriend.

Teachers came out from either school waving their arms and trying to instill order. One teacher, a balding middle-aged man with wire-framed glasses, was flapping a clipboard and yelling "People" and "Chill out," which made the boys fighting nearest to him look at him menacingly until he retreated. The parking lot was filled with teenagers now as the word of the fight went through the schools and emptied the students into the yard. Someone turned on a radio and soon the spectators grew bored with the fight. Frisbees were brought out, a football was tossed lazily over the crowd. Clouds of breath and cigarette smoke hung over the small groups huddled together. When the bell rang at the end of the lunch period, students swarmed in the opposite direction from the schools as if they had planned their escape. A walkout, someone yelled, don't go back in.

Beyond the two schools was a drainage ditch between the road and the small town. Herds of kids from both schools headed across it. Grace stood up and walked slowly towards them as kids pushed and shoved all around her in their hurry to leave the school grounds. A television news truck came and a reporter began questioning the students on what he was calling a language war, interrupting them when they tried to explain that someone had called someone's girlfriend a slut. "Tell me more about the hostility between the Francophone and Anglophone students," he'd coax, "and how it's been building up." "She's a fucking whore, that's why he's hostile. She cheated on him in the back of the fucker's car." Grace shook her head. Then she felt her hair being tugged and quickly turned around. Ralph stood behind her, her braid and Jerry's knife in either hand.

"Here's your boyfriend's knife." Ralph smiled at her. "Tell him I sharpened it for him for next time he needs it."

Grace looked down at the braid. Already the blond hair looked dull, lifeless. She sputtered and turned back to Ralph, trying to piece together what had just happened, but he had disappeared in the crowd. She tried moving sideways, against the current, and finally found herself on the edge of the students. She went to a bench and again looked down at her hair and the knife. The handle was metal and she could see the sky behind her reflected in it. She opened her bookbag and slid Jerry's knife and her braid into it and took her time zipping it back up. Only when it was closed and she had sat down on the bench did she allow her hand to move to the back of her head to feel the sharp ends of her cut hair. It had taken her so long to grow.

*　　*　　*

When Grace finally got home, she was surprised to see her father's car still in the driveway; he always left before she got home. Gary had dragged the picnic table from the backyard to the side of the house. He was sitting on it smoking. When she got close, she could smell the sweet pull of hash. He was smoking a joint right outside their house.

"Hey, Grace."

She walked to the bench slowly, trying to figure out what had changed about him. His hair was greasy and hung limply behind his ears. She saw that there were long rips across the legs of his jeans and a fading bruise on his cheekbone.

"Hey, Gar."

He beckoned to her to come closer, and at first she thought that he was going to pull at her hair or whisper something, a secret or advice, but he put the lit end of the joint into his mouth, leaning close to her mouth, and breathed out a long breath of smoke that she inhaled without thinking. A stinger, she thought, swallowing the combination of breath and smoke from her brother's mouth, feeling it burn in her lungs. He leaned back, taking the joint out of his mouth, and watched her, nodding. There, he thought, he had helped Grace.

She exhaled slowly and turned to the house, not knowing what she should say to him. There was something raw about him. His lip, she had noticed when he had leaned in, was swollen, split, his eyes were bloodshot and heavy, the pores of his cheeks black and whiskered. He seemed so far away that she couldn't stand to be so close to him.

The door was unlocked. There were dirty dishes on the counter and a cupboard door ajar. She could hear the TV on in the living room. She thought of going in to see who was watching it but then remembered her hair and went instead into the bathroom. It took her a few seconds to look into the mirror and when she did, she gasped. She'd never had short hair in her life, and now with her braid gone her head felt too light, her neck bare and too exposed to sun and temperature. She hadn't realized how heavy the braid had been, how it had fallen between her shoulder blades and kept her head anchored. She looked at her face with dismay. Her eyes were glassy and red, her lips were torn from biting them, her mouth was dry. It would be too easy, she thought, to cry again, to go upstairs and put on the radio and just not move. She'd have to find Jerry and give the knife back to him; he'd need it when he met up with Ralph again. She straightened her shoulders and faced herself again, pushing her short hair behind her ears.

"What the hell did you do to your hair? If you wanted to look like a boy, I could've taken you to my friend Luigi, the barber. He wouldn't have given you a hack job like that. Or I could've given you a trim. I was good enough to cut your bangs all those years, wasn't I?" Grace's father was sitting reclined in his chair. He was wearing a pair of blue sweatpants and a matching hooded sweatshirt that Grace had never seen before. He hadn't shaved and his hair looked tousled as if he'd been rubbing his hand through it a lot.

She shuddered at the memory of sitting on a kitchen chair with a sheet around her shoulders while her father took more and more off her bangs to straighten them while her neck prickled with cut hair.

"What are you doing home? Shouldn't you be at work?" she asked, hoping he'd forget about her hair.

"They laid me off so I'm on vacation until they realize how lost they are without me. I told them after they gave me my papers, I said, 'Listen, don't call me up when you can't find your own arse.' I told them in no uncertain terms not to call me until they had a job for me. 'Listen here, Mr. Klink,' I said to that goddamn German they've got, I said, 'Between you and me, nobody knows shit about how this place runs and they're making a big goddamn mistake if they think it'll run smoothly without Les McIntyre—'"

"Does Mom know?" Grace interrupted.

"Your mother thinks she knows everything." Les shook his head. "All your mother cares about is money. She doesn't care that after twenty-three years of good service to those bastards,

I'm treated like a piece of shit. All I can say is that they're going to be one bunch of sorry suckers when it dawns on them that they've lost my expertise."

"You're just in charge of tools," Grace said. "I don't think the place will fall apart if you don't turn up to hand out wrenches and pliers."

"I'm in charge of parts, missy, and don't you talk that way to me. I'm in charge of parts—not just tools—and it would be a cold day in hell if the world could get along without them. Parts make up the whole and where would we be without them? What would hold us together? What would make us tick? There'd be no planes without parts, there'd be no buses or cars. Even goddamn can openers have parts, Grace."

Grace could feel her teeth grind into each other, her jaw clamp tight and the muscles of her cheek contract. She ran up the stairs, her hands curled tightly into fists. He was such an asshole. She didn't know what she was going to do with him home all the time. She'd go crazy. Maybe she could stay at Lily's, she thought, but their house was small. If Sharon still lived in Beaumont, Grace could stay there. Her mother had never minded. Grace could hear Les yelling at her from the bottom of the stairs.

Supper that night was horrible. Her father chewed the macaroni and cheese loudly. And her mother pushed the noodles around with her fork, chewing a noodle at a time, fast and furious. Grace sat there, not wanting to eat. Gary emptied his plate after covering the macaroni with ketchup and left within minutes of sitting down.

Les stopped chewing and took his handkerchief out of his back pocket. He blew his nose into it and then motioned with it to Grace's plate. "Aren't you going to eat? That's good food, you better not let it go to waste."

Grace looked at her mother. Her mother didn't look up but continued to push the heap of macaroni around in the middle of her plate. She sighed and shook her head.

"What are you heaving and hoing about over there?"

Sheila looked up at her husband with contempt. "Are you talking to me?" she said icily.

"Yes, I am, I asked you why you were heaving and hoing."

Grace looked back and forth between her parents. She could feel the tension coil up and then leap across the table. She pushed her chair back.

"You sit yourself down, Grace, and eat your supper."

Sheila stared into her plate as if it were a crystal ball showing her the future. Hard noodles and dried-up cheese. Grace picked up her fork and moved around clumps of macaroni so some would look eaten. The silence was peppered and burnt; it was a tough and withered silence that had been left too long on its own and had dried out. She played with her food for a while and then pushed back her chair again; and when Les didn't seem to notice, she got up and quickly went to her room.

It was harder to sneak out of the house with her father home. He sat in his chair, the television set on and turned low. Every time a car drove by he raised himself half out of the seat, pulled back the curtain and looked out the window to see who it was. Her mother, on the couch, would look too, only she craned her neck rather than moving her body, her hands stilled, holding her crochet hook and cotton thread. Grace stood halfway up the stairs in shadow and watched them. The scene looked choreographed: a passing car, her father moving up, pulling the curtain over, her mother twisting her head. They'd stay motionless, poised like that for a couple of seconds mid-air, hovering and watching, until the car passed, and then they'd settle back into their seats, her father grunting with the effort of holding himself up, her mother stabbing at the doily she was making, hooking the thread around and through. During commercials her father would get up and pull back the curtain even farther and take long looks up and down the street.

"Frenchie there across the street must've gone to the hard-ware store—he's fixed his porch light."

"Hmm," Sheila replied.

"'Course, if he knew what he was doing, he wouldn't have used that kind of light, they're too easy for kids to take out with a rock." Les paused and waited for Sheila to indicate she'd been listening. He continued after she muttered something to herself.

"Serves him right. I'll bet he paid twice what my buddy at Canadian Tire would've charged him. He would've given him a discount if he had mentioned my name. Fifteen per cent at least." Les shook his head and sat back down.

Grace looked at the striped wallpaper on the wall going up the stairs. The olive green stripes seemed to turn to steel, like alchemy, she thought, only paper to metal. The stripes could easily be bars, and with the railing on the other side of her, Grace felt the narrow space on the stairs tighten and compress. She had to get out.

"I'm going to Lily's to get some homework," she called over her shoulder, hurrying to the side door. She wanted to get out before her father called her back, before her mother spoke up and said she couldn't. As she closed the door behind her, the night air awoke the cold of Jerry's knife in her pocket . She didn't know where to start looking for him. Looking up at the sky, she saw that the night was clear. She headed towards the highway, to the woods he had brought her to the evening before.

Grace thought about retracing the route they had taken but figured it was too early; she could still see people through the windows, washing dishes, reading. And she wasn't sure she could head in the right direction without getting lost. She didn't know the sky well enough for it to guide her. She stayed on the road, choosing the long way rather than risking the main streets. Even though she had the knife, she didn't want to see Ralph again.

She walked along, looking into the windows of the houses in her neighbourhood. She could see paintings on people's walls, photographs. And the light in most living rooms was warm, welcoming. Every house she looked into gave her a view of what her own house wasn't.

Some houses had For Sale signs, *À vendre* signs swinging from their posts in the wind, all of them lifting with the same gust, orchestrated by the wind, a symphony of sales. The sound of traffic grew when she got closer to the town centre. The street lights glowed amber and the dépanneurs were still busy, people standing in line with newspapers and cartons of milk, pointing to Export A packs, Players, behind the counter. A couple of souped-up cars revved in the parking lot. Guys in jean jackets and leather lounged against them, dragging hard on their cigarettes and blowing the smoke down and away from their faces. Grace saw herself reflected in one of the store windows, collaged with a *Prix réduit* sign, and hurried on. She hated the feeling of not being good enough, of always comparing herself to everyone else and falling short. By the time she got a pair of jeans like the ones everyone else was wearing, the other kids had stopped wearing them. She could never catch up and always seemed to be on the outside. A group of French girls her age stood clumped at the corner as she walked by. They were laughing and shoving one, who had long brown hair and that smooth skin they all seemed to have, skin without freckles, maybe one or two moles, dark, sexy moles that said "beauty mark" not sunburn or fair skin the way her freckles did, blotchy.

A guy in a car yelled something in French as he drove by and the girls turned, responding. One of them winked and blew a kiss. Grace had no idea what he had said, no idea what the girls had replied. If he had yelled at her, she would have been perplexed at how to respond to something she didn't understand. Was it an insult? a come-on? She had no idea and even now felt baffled. She wondered briefly when the last time was that she hadn't felt confused.

When she got to Lily's house, the living room curtains were still open but the lamps were turned on. She stood for a minute watching Lily's dad talk to someone on the couch. He still had his blue uniform on from work and a tea towel hung over his shoulder. Grace looked up to Lily's room. Curtis was looking back at her with his binoculars. She waved and he returned the wave by moving them up and down. She thought about going in but then decided that returning the knife was more important.

The path leading into the woods was smooth from use and there was enough light in the sky for her to see the twisted roots growing up from the ground. The trees were old here and mostly pines with the odd spruce and birch. The branches stretched out over her head like long, thin limbs and she walked within the columns of tree trunks, listening to how the wind gently shivered down the branches through the needles and then down the trunks. She had never smelled the colour green so strongly and was surprised at how the moss seemed to glow between the tree roots. No wonder Jerry liked it in here, she thought, looking back. The trees seemed to be following her, leaning along the path and breathing her in as deeply as she was drinking them in. Grace felt her father and mother fall from her as if they were skin she could shed, skin that would dry out, fill with raspy wind and tumble into the dark, rusted needles beneath the trees. Her step quickened and her shoulders straightened. The air seemed medicinal; it cleared her head and sharpened her focus. She wondered if Jerry was watching her and felt herself grow warm.

The blanket he had draped over her was back, folded inside the lean-to. She thought about going in, sitting under the dried pine boughs and seeing what he looked at when he slept, but she felt she'd be imposing. Instead, she placed the knife far enough back in the lean-to so its blade wouldn't catch the moonlight and give itself away. He needed to find it, no one else. Then she leaned against a big pine and waited, hoping he'd appear. The bark seemed to absorb the cold part of the darkness, and the darker the woods got, the colder its surface became. Rougher. Eventually she had to stand up and move. She stayed, still hoping to hear movement, a rustle, and then Jerry, but the woods were still. The only sound was a train pulling the night apart with its long mournful whistle: alone, alone. She headed back to the path and walked through the trees, slowly going back home.

It bothered Sheila that Grace had gone out. It bothered her when Les got up and put on his coat. Gary was out as well. It bothered her that she didn't know where they went. She slipped the thin crochet hook into the next stitch and pulled the thread through. This quieted her, this hooking and pulling, working in circles around and around as the doily got bigger. It also bothered her that the casserole dish had to soak; the cheese was dark and hard along the edges, impossible to scrub off, even though she had tried with her fingernails. She didn't like going to bed with dirty dishes in the sink and she didn't like it when everyone was out and she didn't know where they were. Grace was at Lily's. But Les and Gary, where could they be going? Gary had his gang of friends and Sheila imagined he was with them somewhere. But Les, Les was usually at work; where would he have gone? If she wasn't so tired, she would go out and look for him, make sure he was staying out of trouble.

She felt a sinking in her stomach and soothed it by reciting each stitch as she hooked it. Chain five, skip first double crochet, double crochet in next eleven stitches. Her fingers worked quickly, looping the cotton over the hook and catching it, pulling it through each stitch. There was something about working in circles that calmed her; her thoughts matched the rhythm of her hands. She'd leave the porch light on—chain five—she'd try scrubbing that casserole dish before she went to bed—single crochet in next chain four loop—and dry it and put it away. She was surrounded by doilies. Each one represented the small catastrophes of her life in twenty-one rounds of mercerized crochet cotton. The doily on the back of the recliner was the first time the mortgage had bounced, the doily under the lamp was when they had to take out a loan to pay their Chargex card, the doily under the other lamp was when Les had driven that brand-new Malibu home, the day after he got laid off a few years ago. Every ashtray, every figurine had a doily under it; the drawers of the china cabinet were full of the daily mishaps, disasters she kept at bay with her hook. Slip stitch into next double crochet. She'd have to talk to Les about money and to Grace about a curfew. Chain three. And she'd have to talk to Gary about his life. Double crochet in next nine stitches. She crocheted fast, going quickly in circles, like her life, she thought, spiralling, chain five, skip first stitch.

She had tried teaching Grace to crochet a few years ago, had surprised herself by how patient she was explaining the chain stitch to her. Grace had watched and then taken the wool and shown her mother that she already knew how to make a chain with her fingers, nimbly looping the yarn and slipping it through. "Who needs a hook?" she had asked her mother. Sheila could have sworn Grace had said: "Who needs you?" She had taken the wool from her daughter and gone back upstairs, adding Grace's comment to the pile she'd been collecting over the years directed at her. The pile was immense now, an island she'd visit when she felt a new indignation. She had added it to the top of the heap, hoisting this new but inevitable disappointment in her life up with the rest of them, and she'd stayed there, perched on the top, the vantage point from which she watched her life drag on. She hoarded these comments for proof in case anyone ever asked how bad it had been for her, whether all her patience and care ever paid off. Oh, it paid off, all right, she thought, looping the cotton thread even faster. She was paid back over and over again by not being appreciated. She'd never been treated fairly, she reminded herself, picking up the stitch she had missed with her hook. Why would that change now?

*   *   *

Lily carried her notebook and encyclopedia down from her bedroom. She couldn't resist. Everyone was sitting in the living room and she had spent the past few minutes upstairs listening to them laugh and talk. She stood for a minute at the entrance to the room and looked around. The coffee table was cluttered with Curtis's homework. Their cat, Pussycat, was curled around the newest addition to the house, a small white kitten that Dellie called Baby. Dellie was sitting behind her father on the back of the couch, brushing his hair and stopping occasionally to cup his face in her tiny hands and sing along behind him to the record their mother must have put on. Curtis was sitting between Eliza and Stan and was outlining their hands on a piece of paper. Dellie was the only one who noticed Lily and stopped brushing.

"Wait, Daddy, wait." She scrambled off the couch and stood before Lily. "Lily, look at my eyes," she said, looking earnestly at her sister, her eyes glaring, not blinking. Lily waited. "Ready, Lily?" Lily nodded, not sure what she was supposed to do.

Dellie continued to stare into her sister's eyes, her brow furrowed with concentration. After a few seconds she smiled and stood back. Lily wasn't sure what had just happened and waited for Dellie to give her a clue.

"My eyes are purple now, I made my eyes turn purple!" Dellie's voice was brimming with joy. She skipped around the coffee table and stopped in front of the two cats. "What's new, Kittycat? Oh, oh, oh, oh," she sang with the record.

"Dellie has learned magic," Stan offered to Lily. "She can turn her eyes purple."

Lily looked from her father back to her little sister, who was standing in front of her again. She nodded slowly.

"It's easy, Lily, I just think of purple things really hard and ta-da." She twirled and nearly lost her balance. Lily reached out and helped her stand. "Tra la la la, I got purple eyes."

"Wow, Dellie, that's amazing. How did you learn to do that?"

Dellie shrugged and spied a soother sticking out from under a chair. She wiped it off on her T-shirt and then stuck it in her mouth, twisting it around with her tongue so it looked as if someone was winding her up. She danced back to the couch, still singing around her soother, "Oh, oh, oh, oh," and climbed up behind Stan, reaching down for the brush he was holding. Stan looked at Lily and winked. Dellie had put plastic barrettes along the front of his hair. Bright orange barrettes with butterflies and flowers that looked neon against his shiny black hair.

Curtis had been oblivious to all the eye colour changing. He was back at the coffee table, intent on the drawing he was working on. Several of his drawings were already taped to the wall. He took his drawing seriously, Lily thought, watching him hunch over his paper intently. He was pressing so hard with his crayon, she was afraid he was going to snap it in two.

Eliza had moved over into the spot Curtis had been in and now let her head lean against her husband's shoulder. She was wearing the bracelets Lily loved. Thin, silver bangles that individually looked unimpressive, but when she wore them all— she had about fifteen—they slid up and down her arm musically. Lily loved when her mother danced with them on; it was as if her arm was part of the song and Eliza moved it like a snake over her head. Lily tried ignoring Tom or Engelbert singing and listened only to her mother's arm, the shimmying silver of her movement, her quiet laugh when the song ended, as if she was delighted by the sound of the bracelets as well.

Curtis pushed himself away from the coffee table and looked down at his picture, squinting. He picked it up and turned to show his parents on the couch and then got up to show Lily. Lily took the drawing from him to look at it more closely. On each of the fingers he had drawn feathers in vibrant crayon colours, purple, sea green, magenta. Each thumb had become a face of the birds facing each other. Around the birds, he had drawn a wobbly heart, and then outside that he had coloured the paper sky blue with thin, wispy clouds and a tiny, sturdy rainbow in the upper corner. He let Lily hold the drawing while he ran upstairs to get his binoculars. She held it up for him as he studied the picture carefully, adjusting the plastic yellow dial between the lenses. When he had finished, he took the picture and ran into the kitchen. Lily could hear a drawer slide open and figured that it was the junk drawer and he was getting the tape to hang his picture up. She watched him try to decide on a place on the wall. Already there were several drawings, mostly his, but lower on the wall Dellie had started to hang drawings too. Lily saw that she had hung up the spider picture that she had drawn a few days ago. Once Curtis picked a spot, he studied it from several angles and even sat for a moment on the end of the couch, checking to see if his picture would be visible from there. Satisfied, he tore off a piece of tape and stuck the paper against the wall, then stood back to admire his work.

The record stopped and the next one fell into place on the turntable. After a few moments of silence Engelbert's deep, crooning voice began to fill the room. Lily leaned back. She heard her mother sigh, a long sweet-sounding sigh. No one but Engelbert made her mother sigh like that. Tom Jones could come close but when Engelbert sang, her mother became immediately transported. If there were such things as out-of-body experiences, Lily knew her mother had one every time he sang. She pictured her mother floating beneath the needle on the arm of the stereo, right into the groove of Engelbert's voice. She pulled him around her like a comforter and held him like a cup of steaming tea, breathing in the Engelbert of him.

Lily always watched her father while Eliza listened. She often worried that he'd be hurt by the attention Engelbert got, but he never seemed to mind. Sometimes, without warning, he'd grab Eliza and begin crooning to her, whirling her around madly, and she'd close her eyes, her bracelets swooning. He'd end the song at her neck, kissing it hard and deep, and Lily would have to look away, her face feeling hot and pink. It hadn't occurred to her that he looked like Elvis until Grace had pointed it out. She knew that cashiers were always teasing him and the lady at the bakery always seemed flustered when he looked right at her. She'd adjust her apron and touch her cheek, leaving a trail of flour where his eyes had been.

And when he talked, he made people feel as if they were in on the secret and that he needed them to be in on the secret. She had also seen his face change, become almost unrecognizable. She'd seen him hold Jerry up to a wall, push him into it with every word he forced out, as if he wanted his son to disappear into the paint, deeper even, into the plaster, the joists, into the very house he was ordering him out of. Lily sighed and looked back down at her book. She was on the word *dandelion. Dents de lion, teeth of the lion. A widespread perennial weed.* Who would have imagined that teeth of the lion were growing in everyone's yards? she thought. For a minute she pictured the leaves hinged, like Venus flytraps snapping at running shoes and cat paws. She yawned, and as if the yawn reminded her father of something, he abruptly sat up.

"All right, Delilah, it's bedtime for you and for you too, Curtis." Before he could stand up, Dellie had slid down behind him and swung herself onto his lap so she was facing him. She took his face in her hands and stared intently at him.

"Dellie, your eyes are turning purple again." He shook his head admiringly.

Dellie jumped off him and strutted around the living room, her eyes opened wider than usual. Eliza grabbed her and pulled her onto her lap. Dellie squirmed, sucking hard on her soother, looking pleased. Eliza kissed her and offered her cheek to her daughter. Dellie pulled out the pacifier with a pop and gave her mother a long, slurpy kiss, then one on her forehead, her cheeks, her nose. Curtis waited his turn and then wrapped his arms around his mother's neck. She pushed his hair from his eyes and they rubbed noses solemnly, looking deep into each other's eyes.

Lily continued writing her entry, half listening to the squeals of laughter coming from upstairs. She wondered if Jerry was okay, and for a minute she wished he was there, sitting where the cats were sleeping, reading a book or just watching as she was. But lately when she thought about her brother outside, she didn't feel that immediate worry she used to feel. She had been thinking about what Grace had said, how he seemed to be in the house, even if he wasn't. It was true. His drawings still hung on the wall, his string art was still framed. A couple of his sweaters still hung on the hooks by the door. Lily realized now why their back door was never locked. She had always thought it was because her parents were being careless, the way they had let the yard go, but she was sure now that they left it unlocked on purpose, so Jerry could come in if he wanted to. The more she thought about it, the more it made sense. Every night her father let the cats in or out and then locked the front door behind them. Then he'd turn down the furnace and check the back door, turning the knob to make sure it was locked, and every night Eliza would follow behind him, turning the back door handle in the opposite direction. She had seen them look at each other as if exchanging something silent between them before going to bed. Unlocking had become part of their ritual of closing up.

Lily leaned back into the chair and let her pen drop. Engelbert tiptoed up to her, and before she knew it, his voice slid through her hair and wrapped around her shoulders like a shawl. She closed her eyes and let him stay there, enjoying the warmth he brought, the soothing stillness he caressed into her thoughts.

Eliza watched her daughter close her eyes and lean back into the chair. She was seventeen. Eliza looked at her with the gentle, probing curiosity of someone sifting through old papers, photographs, for a clue, a hint to a time long gone by. She was Lily's age when she was pregnant with Jerry and couldn't remember ever looking the way her daughter did, smooth skinned and long limbed and totally enraptured by a song. She remembered worrying each day whether the baby had moved or not and lathering her body with cream, hoping to stop or at least slow down the long, purple stretch marks that had begun to slither across her hips and onto her belly. "It's because you're so fair," her doctor had told her, his hand on her stomach. "There's really nothing you can do about it." And she shuddered then, remembering his dark office, its beiges and browns, its worn poster of reproductive organs, the picture of ovaries like ripe apricots hanging from Fallopian tube branches, the cigarette smoke ribbing from the ashtray to the ceiling, his frayed cardigan, and her mother sometimes waiting, her coat buttoned, her purse on her lap, the brass clasp of it shut as tight as her lips, her hands clasped shut, closed as well. Her mother in the waiting room but most times not. "There's really nothing you can do about it" was a phrase Eliza had worn down with wear. In the bathtub with a wash-cloth over her mountainous stomach, bending to try to tie her shoes, the sturdy kicks the baby awakened her with, the dull ache of her back. Stan was older than she was, sheepish when she had told him. They were lucky, he had said, holding her tightly to him, that they loved each other so much.

Eliza watched her daughter whenever she could, without even realizing that she was taking note. Every time Lily threw herself on the couch, balancing a bowl of chips and a book, every time she'd race to the phone when it rang or laugh uproariously upstairs with her friend Grace, Eliza was saying quietly to herself: That's what it would've been like. That's what being seventeen should be. And the seventeen-year-old girl in her, the girl who counted out change for the taxi, pant-ing out directions to the hospital, the seventeen-year-old girl in her who envied the older woman she had shared a hospital room with, almost inaudibly would reply, Oh, and then urge her: keep watching.

Lily opened her eyes when the singing stopped and looked over at her mother, smiling warmly at her, and Eliza smiled back, smiled back at her daughter sitting so lovely and still, and they stayed there in their silence. Eliza wished she could have been the mother to both of those seventeen-year-old girls, wished she could gently soothe the frowning brow of reminiscence, ease the worry from her younger face in a way her own mother had never bothered to do. "It's going to be all right," she said silently to both girls. "Everything will be just fine. Relax, be gentle, you're going to be just fine."

It was different now. She knew more. All the time she had imagined tragedy, imagined loss, she knew now that she had got it wrong. It wasn't that simple. Her life had taken a turn. It had left the path she had planned and so she prepared herself for the certainty of the longing she'd always feel for what she had missed. Her children had surprised her. The capacity she had for love. The unexpected joy they brought had turned out to be simple; the sadness was more complicated. Jerry filled her with a ferocious hope and an aching loss at the same time. Her son who could no longer be in his own home. It took her breath away sometimes, when she articulated his leaving. Not setting a plate for him at supper, not finding him asleep on the couch in the morning, bathed by the blue light of the television set. If he had slept on the couch, he was always gone before any of them were up. "Of course they're going to grow up, that's what they do," Stan would say to her. And she knew that. She knew that. But in watching Jerry go, his boots so big, his back so broad, she watched a part of herself leave as well and that wasn't easy. There was nothing simple about that kind of loss.

And there wasn't anything simple about what she felt for her husband. She deeply loved the Stan she had first known, the Stan who would bring her cups of tea, drink from them and warm her stomach with his hot breath, the Stan who would get out of bed and shut the window or open the window, who would bring home candy necklaces when they were so broke and who'd later slide one up her leg like a garter and slowly bite it off her. That was the man she remembered, that was the man she stayed true to when she'd watch him slide into the pit of his bottomless anger. She'd lose him then, lose her grasp of him, and that was when she felt the muscle of her marriage, that was when she had to hold on harder than she had ever had to before.

He'd come back, sometimes taking longer than ever, but he always came back as surprised at himself as she was. And then he'd feel miserable, would say he was sorry over and over again, would tell her that he didn't know what had come over him. And then he'd apologize by making supper, bathing the kids. Those apologies were important to him, he needed, he told her, to make amends. And so she let him, hearing the "I'm sorry, I'm sorry" in every made bed, in every place setting, in every clean pot. And somehow it worked. Except when she thought of Jerry. Stan couldn't dust enough, couldn't hang out enough clothes, scrub at the bathtub, he couldn't tuck in each of their children enough times for her to forgive him for what he did to Jerry. And he knew it. She wasn't sure what to do and so she drew, she drew to record, to mark down like a kind of charting, a mapping of her children, her home, because they were the quickest way, she realized, the most direct route, to her own heart. She'd show him her sketches and he'd look at them long and hard, and slowly he'd nod as if he understood something else about her. Daily she tried to capture what it meant to her, her children, their growing up, their leaving in the small ways they did every day. And Stan kept trying to read her drawings, as if they held not just a clue to Eliza's heart but a code that might somehow help him to figure himself out. It was the best way to love him, Eliza believed, to love them all, and so she drew.

Les held out the car vacuum like a gun. Sheila clutched her purse facing him. They stood there without saying anything. She felt her anger seep from her as if he had already plugged the vacuum cleaner into the cigarette lighter in the car and it was sucking her out of herself. She almost forgot what she was angry about.

Her purse straps felt heavy hanging from her wrists. It was an old purse, the leather cracked and scruffed. She had lost it once, left it on the bus, and had panicked until the bus company phoned her. Everything was in it. Everything that mattered. Her wallet, her lipstick. A collapsible cup she used when she had to take Aspirin for her headaches. Keys.

She didn't go anywhere without it. It was a part of her, another organ, like a heart. Its straps, the ventricles that silently pumped all the information the purse held back into her, reminding her of who she was.

She had just come in from work. Behind Les she could see the dirty dishes he had left all over the counter. The kitchen table was covered with newspapers and the box and instructions for his new car vacuum.

"We can't afford that," she told him coldly. "You're not working, remember?"

He held it out in front of him like a divining rod. It was compact and black, its cord coiled like a telephone cord.

"I need it," he replied. "The car has to be clean, doesn't it? How can I expect somebody to hire me if they see me getting out of a dirty car?"

Sheila shrugged and took off her coat. "You're out of work. I don't think you should be spending money right now, especially on—" she motioned to the vacuum—"things we don't need."

Les nodded to the counter. "I bought you a colander, didn't I? You can't say I don't buy you things too. And don't try to tell me that you don't use it. That colander drains twice as fast as the cheap ones. I pay the bills, don't I? I put food on the table. If I want to buy a goddamn car vacuum so I can keep my bloody car clean in order for me to get a new job, then I will."

His face was shiny with perspiration as he waved the vacuum in Sheila's face. She backed up and felt the wall behind her. She felt the vacuum drain the energy from her as she watched him pace with it. She just wanted to sit down and put her feet up. She'd had to type the same letter four times this afternoon at work. The phones had never stopped. She looked at Les, at the way he was strutting around, and was reminded of a rooster full of importance and noise. His ears stuck out and the light of the window shone through them. She was too tired to answer him and left him in the kitchen to go to the bedroom and change.

Upstairs, Sheila hung up her blouse and skirt and slid on some sweatpants and a faded pullover that had been bleached too often. She looked at the unmade bed, tempted to lie down, to close her eyes and not go downstairs. Les's pyjamas were thrown across his pillow; a crucifix hung directly above his side of the bed. His night table was covered with pill bottles and an alarm clock. There was a book face down on the mattress. She picked it up, surprised. Les never read. Dale Carnegie. She shuddered and carefully put it back, then went downstairs to start supper.

Les was sitting in his La-Z-Boy watching the news. The newspaper was scattered at his feet; dirty glasses and a potato chip bag were within arm's reach. The rest of the living room was spotless. The plastic on the chesterfield had slipped off one corner though. Sheila hurriedly straightened it and looked around again. The coffee table was in its place, two feet away from the chesterfield and centred perfectly. If she ignored the La-Z-Boy and Les, the room looked just the way she liked it. She let herself look cautiously over at her husband, who was digging in his ear with a matchstick.

He glanced at her briefly and then examined the matchstick.

"I'm hungry. Are you going to make supper?"

Sheila felt rage percolate in her stomach; she felt it begin to boil and whistle furiously in her brain. Les had gone back to watching TV and she turned and went into the kitchen, slamming the pot onto the stove and taking down a can of spaghetti sauce from the pantry. She didn't hear her daughter come in until Grace pulled out a chair and sat down to take off her shoes. She had put her knapsack on the table. Sheila grabbed its strap and threw the bag on the floor in front of her daughter.

"The last thing I want to do," she said hotly, "is to pick up after you."

Grace looked up at her wearily. "Hi, Mother, and how was your day?"

Sheila had turned back to the counter, stacking the dirty dishes into the sink. She threw them in, not caring about chips or cracks. He was a son of a bitch, she thought to herself, and she was stuck here with him. He had made sure her name was on every loan he signed, the mortgage, the credit cards. She had signed her life to him and now she was stuck in the middle of it—the small knot in the centre of one of her doilies. After all she had done for him too, all those nights sitting up with him listening to him go on, dropping everything to take him to the doctor's. She sat on the island of her indignation, stranded, and turned the water on hard and squeezed the bottle of dish detergent, which was almost empty. She shook it and shook it and finally a thin line of soap came dribbling out. Not enough for a full sink. When she turned back to Grace, her daughter was gone. The water for the spaghetti began to boil, steaming up the windows and making the ceiling wet. Sheila pulled out a handful of the pasta and twisted it over the pot. She imagined his neck, the veins that bulged when he screamed. The pasta crunched when it broke and she dumped it into the pot. The boiling water splashed up onto her arm and briefly burned her. She turned on the cold water to soothe the spot that was pulsing with pain and stuck her arm under the faucet. The hot water that came out at first made her jerk her arm back fast.

She used to think she could help him. He'd tell her that she was so smart, and he would listen to her make plans for their future, for how she thought they should live, but then he'd come home with a barbecue starter or a Coleman lamp for when the power was out. Small gadgets at first, engraved butane lighters, special pipe ashtrays, gimmicks he'd marvel over. Then the things he brought home got bigger, more absurd: a revolving tie rack, a metal tree to hold his cufflinks. She had to phone the power company and convince them the cheque was on the way and he had come home with a special bank that magically sorted the coins that were inserted. He had never really listened to her.

Tonight, Les ate loudly as usual, the spaghetti sauce turning his lips a bright red. When he finished, he pushed his plate away and undid the drawstring on his sweatpants. He got up and walked to the sink, examining the colander filled with left-over pasta. He tilted it to see its sides and nodded, satisfied. Grace had left. Gary hadn't even turned up. She was alone with him. The windows were still steamed; long drips began to make their way down the middle of the glass. He coughed and spat into his handkerchief and her supper slid in her stomach. She stayed in her chair until she heard him shuffle into the living room, holding her breath until she heard the TV. The kitchen clock ticked loudly and she got up and started washing the dishes.

Les heard her banging the dishes around and snorted. If a man couldn't buy a goddamn vacuum for his car so he could get a job, then there was a problem, he thought. He changed channels but couldn't find anything that held his attention so he decided to go outside for a walk.

Only lately had he started walking. He used to rely on his car as a sort of armour. If he stayed in it, he'd be safe. No one could sneak up on him, every angle was covered. Walking was different. It was more dangerous. But it was worth it. He sometimes found himself on a sidewalk heading towards a bunch of kids. The agony twisted around excitement with small thorns of heat prickling his body and by the time they passed him, their arms sometimes touching him, he thundered inside. That was why he'd been reading his Dale Carnegie books again. He needed to be reminded how to converse, how to smoothly talk lightning bolts while he was thundering for their limbs so fine and thin—like trees, he thought, long-limbed trees in a thunderstorm. Dale Carnegie was just honey for the bees, worms for the trout. Lures. He felt his lips pull over his teeth in a smile as he put on his coat. He stood for a moment in the doorway, tamping down tobacco in his pipe, and continued smiling like a salesman.

He could talk circles around anyone, he figured. The clattering of Sheila doing the dishes behind him broke his concentration. He frowned and then breathed deeply. Patience, he told himself, and then left the house without even thinking of saying goodbye.

It was a cold night. Les lit his pipe and began walking towards the elementary school where the town's basketball teams practised. Tonight was Wednesday. The bantam boys would be on the court. He knew when the Cubs met, when the soccer team try-outs were, when baseball season started. This town was his lake. He had grown up reading weather and water height and temperature. He still wore his *Field & Stream* pins on his jacket. He spent summers climbing in and out of boats, careful not to tip them, and using his paddle to push off from the wharf and to guide him and his father past the two big rocks before the water deepened. This lake was easy. It had a newspaper announcing events, it had long sidewalks and dark nights. It had bikes that broke and balls to chase. He held the bowl of his pipe in his hand and let the heat warm his palm, then returned it to his mouth. He turned down a side street and away from traffic. He'd walked this path many times in his head, had figured the quickest way to each field, each school. The wind was like water and slowly he let the silence fill him. Already he'd begun to wait, watching the horizon for movement, the slightest shift, the pull.

* * *

Gary was surprised to see his father leave the house. He watched him stop and light his pipe; clouds of smoke puffed over his head, lingering then disappearing into the night air, absorbed by the darkness. Gary had been leaning against the picnic table having a cigarette, not wanting to go in and face supper with his family, when Les had come out. Gary was tired of them and was waiting for the kitchen to clear out so he could go in and boil some water, steep the magic mushrooms he had fronted off some guy named Jean-Claude. Magic mushrooms. It would take a ton of shrooms to make any of this magic, he thought. Abracadabra, turn this man into a mouse. He pictured Les and his big ears, Les sprouting a tail. His father, he knew, was a coward and still Gary couldn't stand up to him, still he couldn't look Les in the eye and tell him what he really wanted to. He imagined it often enough, would watch the scene unfold in his head almost every day. "Les, buddy boy, it's time you listened to me for a change." Oh, Gary could easily imagine what he'd say to his father if he could, but it was like everything, like Ralph staring him down, even like a match burning down to his finger. He thought too much about the flame hitting flesh, thought too much about the burn before-hand. He had inherited his father's eyes and his cowardice. He patted the mushrooms in his pocket. Soon there'd be magic, he promised himself. Soon.

He watched his father walk down the driveway, leaving a wake of tobacco smoke. The smell of it, Old Port, made him feel choked as if he were in a burning room, the door handle too hot to touch, and he knew suddenly that he had to escape, even if it meant crawling on his stomach, breaking a window, cutting himself all up in the process. He had no choice; he had to escape.

Gary didn't know why he was following his father. He didn't even realize he was until he felt himself quicken his pace when Les slipped around a corner faster than he'd been walking before. He was going somewhere, Gary thought. He wasn't walking the way most older people walked after supper, slowly, digesting their meals, looking into windows and commenting on lawns or paint jobs. He was walking as if late for something. Gary thought maybe his father might be going to see a friend, but then he realized with some surprise that his parents didn't have any friends, that they never went out socially. His mother had bowled for a few years, but Les had been so pissed off when she'd go out, insisting that her place was at home, that she had finally quit. And now that Les was home at nights, they both sat and watched TV. Night after night they sat, Les in his chair and Sheila on her plastic couch, entranced by the blue light of the television screen, hypnotized, practically drooling, his mother's hands a blur of hook and thread going round and round.

Gary followed his father to the edge of the schoolyard, perplexed at why his father would be going into an elementary school at night. A meeting, he thought, maybe it was some kind of town meeting. But what would his father be interested enough in to leave his La-Z-Boy and actually walk to? Gary waited while his father tapped his pipe on his heel. Embers sprawled along the parking lot of the school, getting caught up in the wind and then burning out. The smell of his father's pipe lasted longer, staying outside after Les went in, almost like a patient dog waiting for its owner. Gary gave his father a few minutes and then followed him into the school. He was curious now.

The hallway was empty. Paintings of farmhouses and horses filled one bulletin board. Another was filled with hearts and small pictures of children who had been caught doing an act of kindness. Gary read a couple. Sam, for letting Rebecca use his pencil crayons. Rochelle, for sharing her snack with Leo. Stevie, for helping Matt tie his shoes. Gary smiled to himself and continued down the hall. He could hear the sound of basketballs being dribbled, a whistle being blown. He cautiously peered around the corner of the hallway that led to the gym, baffled at why his father would be there. The gym doors were closed and his father was nowhere in sight. He went up to the doors and peeked through the window carefully so no one would see him. He saw a bunch of boys, aged about nine or ten, practising their dribbling and jump shots. Their coach, a short man in a track suit, was watching them with a whistle held between his teeth. A few parents sat on a bench. In the far corner of the gym, watching on his own, stood his father with a look in his eyes that made Gary step back.

Gary turned sharply and ran back to the door, his stomach twisting and his heart an echo of his footsteps, urging him to hurry, to hurry before Les saw him, before he saw Les— His head filled with all the vague rumours that he had heard. He could see Ralph sneering at him, offering him a cigarette, a beer, and calling him a faggot. Smirks and looks between Mike and Ralph made sense now. Everything slid into place without effort, without strain. He looked again at his father, his hands in his pockets, and he had to leave, he had to run.

He found himself back in the parking lot and tried to breathe deeply, inhaling his father's smell that still lingered rather than the crisp air of the November night. Gary could taste the tobacco, smell it on his clothes. It branded him, it twisted into his hair and settled into his ears. And he began to run as if he could lose it, turn a corner fast enough, slip into cedar hedges without its seeing. Escape. He ran from his father's smell and he ran from the school and all those fucking stupid acts of kindness, that wall of hearts and happy little faces, he ran from basketball and from whistles, he ran from Grace. He ran from his pathetic, disgusting, fucked-up life and he didn't look back.

Once Les had left, Sheila let her shoulders sag. She got up from the chair and went back to the sink, leaning her hips against the counter, and felt the warmth from the hot water in the sink on her face. She remembered reading how the steam from hot water was a good way to open up your pores. Maybe that's what she had let happen. Maybe doing the dishes every night had opened her pores to the point where they'd never close again and she was left opened to everything. No wonder she was tired, no wonder she barely had any energy at all. It was coming for her in every direction. She hardly had a chance.

She scoured the pasta stuck on the bottom of the pan, and when she had finally scrubbed it all off, she could see where it had scorched the pan. Great, she thought, getting a new S O S pad from under the sink. Nothing was ever easy. She wished with all her heart for them to go away. "Go away," she said under her breath and then louder in the empty kitchen. "All of you, just go away and leave me alone." She rinsed the pot, turned it upside down in the drainer and pulled the plug in the sink. She watched the water spiral down the drain. "Just leave me alone."

Curtis could hear his mother humming in the bathroom. He knew the song. It was about green grass and home. He hummed with her, lying there in his bed, waiting for his father to come and tuck him in. Finally he heard footsteps heading towards his room. Curtis smiled, waiting.

"Hey there, big guy. Did you get those teeth brushed?"

Curtis nodded.

"Well, let me see."

Curtis smiled as hard as he could, baring all his teeth and wiggling the loose one with his tongue. Stan covered his eyes.

"Easy, Curtis, you could blind a guy with those shiny teeth. I bet you could use them as a flashlight in the middle of the night if you had to pee. Just open your mouth and they'd glow for you."

Curtis nodded and continued wiggling, hoping his father would notice.

"What do you have there? Is that a loose tooth? Let me see."

Stan gently moved the tooth back and forth with his index finger. "By God, Curtis, you're growing up so fast, your teeth are falling out."

Curtis grinned and snuggled deeper into his bed. Stan bent over him, pulled the covers up and waited for Curtis to lift his chin, then tucked in the blankets. "Do you want a song?" Curtis nodded quickly. "All right." Stan sat back down on the bed and cleared his throat. He began to sing to his son in a low voice that made Curtis sleepy.

Curtis lay awake in bed after his father left. In the glow of the night light he counted the stripes on his bedspread. Nineteen blue stripes and twenty white ones. He wondered how many he couldn't count because they were tucked in. He wiggled his tooth some more, anxious for it to fall out and for the tooth fairy to bring him some money. He tried counting all of his teeth with his tongue but kept losing count, counting the same one twice and having to start over. The effort made him tired. For a moment he pictured Dellie's book about counting sheep. He envisioned a sheep hurdling over a fence in the middle of a meadow, not a real sheep but a cartoon one. His mother had always told him that when he couldn't sleep, he should count sheep. He didn't understand how counting could make him sleepy; counting made him a little worried because he was always afraid of missing one. The worry made his eyebrows scrunch together like caterpillars being poked. He felt them now with his finger, felt them smooth back out into lines. His finger found its way to the top of his head and wound its way into his hair. He twirled and twirled it, his hair sliding around until it got stuck, and then he'd unwind it and start again. This made him feel tired. And though he promised his father and Lily he'd try to stop, whirling his hair made him feel like putting his thumb in his mouth. He reasoned with himself: how could they expect him to twirl his hair and not suck his thumb? How was he supposed to fall asleep? Curtis turned over on his side and pulled his knees to his chest, sucking his thumb and twirling, and soon fell asleep, his thumb slipping from his mouth and resting on his lips.

Grace listened for sound from the top of the stairs. Her mother was still in the kitchen, putting dishes away. And not gently, the way she told Grace to do it. Sheila was slamming them away as if they were exclamation marks that punctuated her thoughts. She was still mad. Grace would have to wait to go out. Once Sheila was sitting down watching TV, Grace figured she was safe. Nothing would move her mother from the TV then. And Grace needed to go out. She could feel the air in the house ready to boil over, and she wasn't sure why. Ever since her father had been laid off, things had changed. He had cut out a picture of a snow blower from the Canadian Tire catalogue and had stuck it to the fridge. Her mother nearly combusted when she saw it, screaming about long-distance bills and the oil. Grace had never seen her so wild. And Les didn't even seem to hear her. He had looked right past her and opened the fridge, searching for some gherkins to go with the sandwich he was making. He was boiling two eggs in a small pot on the stove. Supper hadn't filled him, he had complained, rubbing his stomach. The water had been boiling for several minutes and the eggs kept bumping into each other, the water splashing and sizzling onto the red-hot burner. Gherkins, Sheila had screamed. Grace had been mesmerized by the thick cords of veins pulsing on her mother's neck; even Sheila's hair, coiled into tightly permed curls, seemed ready to spring. Her lipstick had bled into the wrinkles that crackled from her lips.

Grace had been dismayed, not by the anger but by how it had transformed her mother's face. It worried her because she thought maybe she was getting a glimpse of herself in a few years. Her fingers went up to her mouth even now, in the dark at the top of the stairs, away from her mother, and she slowly traced her lips for wrinkles. She pulled at her hair, which was now short and straight. Her parents had stopped caring that she was around, listening. Or they had forgotten she was there.

Gary hadn't been home for a couple of nights. He had sensed the storm, Grace thought. He must've known what was coming, abandoned ship. Who could blame him? She heard her mother Frisbee a plate into the sink. It clattered but didn't break, which seemed to make Sheila all the angrier because there was more slamming. Grace heard her father get up; there was a shuffling noise and then the door closed. She waited for the sound of his car but never heard it. She sat on the top stair and waited. She could hear the cupboards being slammed closed and the faucet being turned on and then off. She heard kitchen chairs being shoved back into the table. Finally she heard the TV and then the creak of her mother settling onto the sofa. Grace stood up and went down the stairs slowly, calmly. She would just tell Sheila she was going out to help Lily with her homework, that's all, and then she'd put on her shoes and leave without waiting for an answer.

Sheila didn't even look up, didn't even seem to hear her walk by. Grace just kept walking and got her jacket and shoes. She wondered how she thought her mother could stop her and realized she couldn't. No one in this house could.

No one in this house could stop anything now. Grace left her house, left her mother sitting in the living room with her lap full of doily and left the dim light of the kitchen. Dim because one of the light bulbs had burned out and no one had bothered to change it. Dim because the house sat on the edge of winter, facing the inevitablity of it, and already the windows let in drafts, the doorways had halos of cold air around them. The pantry had only a couple of cans of beets from years ago, bought by mistake.

Grace left her house, vaguely thinking of how dismal it seemed, her mother in her bleach-splattered track pants, sprawled on the living room couch like she'd been flung there, and the kitchen light, yellow and thick, trying to follow Grace through the door and out into the night. She closed the door harder than she had to, as if the light was sticky, made from a substance that could keep her glued to the walls, stuck to her house. She ran down the driveway and decided to walk to Le Bertin and find Gary.

Sheila heard the door and turned off the TV. She sat back down and waited for the silence of the house to fill her like water. She thought of how she liked lying back in the bathtub and letting her head submerge underwater, how distant the house sounds were then, the dripping of the tap loud and soothing, a heartbeat of water. But beneath the heartbeat of water, Sheila knew there was a faint pulse of something else. A feeling. A feeling she had spooned into a mason jar a long time ago and set high on a shelf in the cellar of herself. She could hear it pulse, could hear it breathe like a living thing when she let herself be silent. She leaned her head back against the couch and made herself breathe deeply.

She felt cornered and angry. He repulsed her. There was a goddamn picture of a snow blower on the fridge and a brand-new soldering gun in the basement and a router and a plane saw and an electric toothbrush set, an electric putting golf practice machine and a two-hundred-dollar hedge trimmer for the one crabapple tree they owned, which was almost dead anyway. And a car vacuum. She didn't know how to stop this, how to pull the emergency break. And even if she knew how, she didn't know whether she could. It would be heavy, she would have to pull with all her might, and she was tired. It was as if he had harnessed everything about him to her and she was lugging it around.

She sat there in the empty house, willing the silence when she breathed in to flow down her throat into her lungs, to fill her with nothing. She yearned with all her might to be filled once again with nothing. "Leave me alone," she said out loud to no one in particular, not just to her husband, her children, the whining game show host on the television program she had just turned off, not to the carpet that seemed to attract every bit of lint, the tables that stood ready for dust. She said it to them all and imagined holding the old rusted hedge trimmers that were abandoned when the electric ones were bought. She could picture their long mottled blades and their handles, could feel the strength it would take to open them and then push them shut, cutting. And then she imagined the cutting, bending down and slicing through every cord, every twine, every garbage tie, every single reason that kept her here. Sheila sat on the couch in the house alone and imagined cutting herself free from them all. Free. Finally free.

Maybe she'd try a tablecloth, she thought. It couldn't be that hard. It would be like making a series of smaller doilies, attaching them. She envisioned spreading it over the table, crisp and white, covering all the nicks and scars on the tabletop from the long years of use. The pounding of Les's fist on the table, emphatic, making his point. She'd make it bigger than the pattern called for so it would hang to the floor and cover not just the top but the table's legs, the cracked rubber caps hiding the bottom of them, the floor, the scuff marks. The thought of the tablecloth was crisp and white, it soothed her. She could crochet one easily, she thought. Easily.

Gary sat on the black bridge with his feet dangling over the edge. He sat and smoked, squinting through the smoke up to the sky. The stars were bright, peering at him intently. He could hear cars driving fast past the town on the highway. The town was to his right, over his shoulder, a giant hulking thing that breathed with chimneys and with shadow. He heard the far-off pull of train whistle, tossed his cigarette into the ditch and stood up. He wasn't going to think any more, he had been thinking the whole time he'd been running. He had been thinking of his father's eyes watching, how his father's eyes seemed to send out currents and attach to some kid in a weird electric exchange, an extension wire of desperation. He had seen his father charged by it, glowing red and hot, and it made him feel sick. It was the look on Les's face that did it, that lit up all the other times Gary remembered seeing him like that, and now he knew why. Now he remembered.

And it was his grandmother and his great-aunt telling him that he was the spitting image of his father. Look at those eyes, they'd marvel, he's got his father's eyes. He climbed down from the bridge and ran harder, running from memories of being a boy in his father's house and all the possibilities, running from the thought of looking like Les, of family resemblance and ties. He ran because underneath it all he was tired of being a coward.

He ran and thought of Grace and how much she didn't know and of his mother, who tried so hard to keep their house clean, as if her scrubbing could ever clean up the real mess of it. And then he stopped running. His breathing filled his ears and the sound of his feet on gravel walking, the rhythm of the crunching. He didn't even have to make an effort to step over the railway tie, it was just the next step. Courage, he thought, and then he kept walking, the sound of the train bullying its way into his veins until it was his pulse, the beating of his heart, the flowing of his blood, intrinsic. Courage and magic. He had everything he needed.

When he looked up at the engine, he offered himself to it without a fight. He threw back his arms and head and became weightless, filled with night air and pipe smoke and the sound of the train moving through him. For a moment Gary was alone with joy, a rush of release from being who he had been, free of it all, finally. Then he thought of his father and the thought of him kept Gary there, anchored to the tracks. He heard his father whisper *Coward* and then he was gone.

* * *

Curtis woke with a start. A train. He had heard the train in his sleep. He quickly scrambled to the window and stuck his head under his blind and watched it through the bare trees, loving it for its sound, for following its track and for coming when it always came. He waited until the red lights of its caboose were long gone and then he reluctantly slid down from the window and got out his copybook to mark it down. His bed was still warm when he climbed back in. He was asleep in minutes, happy that he hadn't missed it, that he had managed to wake up and count it, that he was doing a good job of keeping track of them all.

Lily woke him up the next morning for school. She had laid out his clothes for him at the foot of his bed and then had left to get Dellie.

He stayed there for a moment, curling and uncurling his toes. Sunshine leaked around his blind and made lines on his floor. He could hear Dellie singing a good morning song, probably to her bear, and he lay there, pushing his thin arms way over his head and getting caught up in a long stretch. This was part of his routine. He'd lie like this until he heard the early commuter train and then get up and dress before going down to eat his oatmeal or his waffles.

He waited, counting the sunspots on the ceiling. He counted all the yellow books on his shelf. He already knew how many but counted them anyway. He counted the orange ones, counted the knobs on his dresser, and then he counted the bubbles in the picture of the cat blowing bubbles that hung on his wall. Lily came back in his room, exasperated that he was still lying there.

"C'mon, Curtis, you're going to miss your bus."

"Are you sure you have the time right?"

Lily looked down at her watch and then turned it to face him. "Seven-fifteen, Curtis. You're fifteen minutes late." She walked over to the blind and gave it a quick pull. Sunshine flooded his room and jewelled everything that glittered, the shiny stickers on his posters, his jar of marbles.

"Come on, Curtis, right now." She pulled the covers off him and then waited.

Reluctantly he sat up and reached for his clothes. Satisfied he was really up, Lily went downstairs. Curtis pulled off his warm pyjamas and sat on his bed in the light. Small goose-bumps erupted all over his arms. Something was the matter, he thought. The morning train always came on time. He sullenly pulled on his cold shirt. It didn't feel right. It felt stiff and tight under his arms. This day wasn't going to be a good day, he could tell. He finished getting dressed slowly and then went downstairs to eat his breakfast, listening the whole time.

Grace went home disappointed. She hadn't known anyone at Le Bertin and Lily's house was practically in darkness. She had nowhere to go. Opening the back door, she felt as if she hadn't left the house; the same light greeted her in the kitchen, the same smell of supper. She was surprised, though, to find a cooler now at the top of the stairs to the kitchen. Her father was sitting at the kitchen table, and the entrance to the hallway and living room was blocked off by a board.

"Why are the doorways blocked?"

Les didn't answer, he just motioned with his head to the table. Confused, Grace looked at the table and then back at her father. He motioned again and she bent to look under the table this time. Sitting under one of the chairs was a tiny puppy. It cautiously walked over to her with its head low and its tail not quite wagging. She scooped it up and it sat in one of her hands, looking uncertainly at her.

"Does Mom know?"

"Yep."

"What did she say?"

"She went up to bed."

"Where did you get it?"

"I went to see a man about a dog. I figured I could use the exercise walking a dog." He watched his daughter coo at the pup and nodded, satisfied. "Yes, just like I told your mother, kids love dogs. Hell, kids need dogs. We always had a dog growing up. There was Ginger and then Pepper—wait now, Pepper came first because we got him from old Skinny McNeil down in Orford. Then Ginger and then we got Snap."

Grace wasn't listening. She was enthralled with the tiny animal. Its eyes were huge and chocolate brown. Its tongue hesitantly licked her. "What kind of dog is it?"

"Oh, she's just a mutt, a bit of shepherd in her, I think, and maybe Lab."

"Does she have a name yet?"

Les shook his head. "Nah, I just got her home."

Grace couldn't believe that her father had bought a dog and that they were going to keep it. She held the puppy close to her and breathed in the dog smell. She examined a paw, the tiny toes and claws.

"Look at the paws on her. She's going to be a big girl, aren't you?" Grace watched amazed as her dad gently scratched the puppy's head. The dog leaned into his hand gratefully. She handed the pup back to him.

"Has Gary seen her?" She looked at her father but he shook his head. "God, he's going to freak, he's always wanted a dog. He's been asking for years." They watched the puppy run to its water dish and slide into it, not knowing how to stop on the slippery kitchen floor. There was newspaper spread all along the wall and the puppy went over to it and squatted.

"See that?" Les said proudly. "She's practically trained already. I'll have her trained in a couple of weeks. I've been training dogs all my life. I could write a book about training dogs." He got up and picked up the wet paper and put more down.

Grace was astounded, watching her father. She had never seen him act so kind. She felt hopeful. Maybe he wasn't such an asshole, she thought. How could he be an asshole and be so nice to a dog? She thought having the puppy might change him and went up to bed feeling better than she had in weeks.

Sheila was lying in bed and imagining a big, panting dog lying on her chesterfield, its claws tearing the plastic and exposing the material to its fur, its fleas, its tongue. She shuddered. And her carpet. She vacuumed that carpet every other day to keep it clean, and she knew the puppy would grow up and leave the kitchen, would trot into the living room and squat. And while it peed, it would look up at her as if to say, "There is nothing you can do to stop me." And then the dog would clean itself. She turned on her side and faced the wall. He knew she didn't want a dog. He knew it and that's why he had got it. It was just another treadmill, eight-track player, metal detector. Something he'd use once and then move to the basement, already bored with it. Gary would like the dog. And just thinking of Gary made her wonder where he'd been. He hadn't slept at home for a couple of nights. Days, she should have said—he always stayed out all night. She sighed. And Grace. Grace would like the dog, but Sheila would end up taking care of the creature, she'd end up cleaning up after it. The rest of them didn't care where they lived. She closed her eyes and willed herself to fall asleep. She had to get up in the morning. She had to go to work to pay for all of this.

Rave found Gary, his head nearly severed from his body. He stood over him for a minute, thinking of Grace and how badly she had wanted to find her brother the other night. Her brother. Gary was so physically gone, so unlike himself, Rave felt stunned by sadness. He stayed still for a moment and then retreated, moved back into the bushes that grew alongside the tracks and waited against a tree for someone else to show up. He didn't want to leave Gary alone. He thought of the night he had watched Ralph block the cement pipe Gary had been sitting in, how he had to sit and wait for Ralph to go before he could help Gary out. He remembered how the metal lawn chair had felt that night, the long arm rails white like bones and cold, how he had leaned into it, grateful for the rest, despite how cold the chair made him feel. He decided to shinny up a pine nearby and watch from the tree. Once up, he extended his legs along the lower branch and waited for someone else to come and find Gary.

The new lunch monitor didn't care if their hats weren't on. She just cared about how well they cleaned up after eating. A crust left on a desk or a balled up piece of foil would make her face get really red. She didn't even know their names, she would just point and say "You." Curtis was afraid of her because she always stood over him and asked the same question about the cat getting his tongue. He wasn't sure what she meant by this and always imagined a cat with fangs pawing at his mouth. She never waited for an answer, and most days he didn't even take the time to zip his jacket all the way up so he could get outside and away from her.

Every day the kids would head to the hill at the edge of the school grounds and play king of the mountain or roll or just run up and down it. Curtis liked rolling. So many kids had run down or were pushed down the hill that there was a smooth path. If you were going to roll, the trick was to roll over at the bottom or you could end up on the sidewalk, and lunch monitor Mrs. Craig got really mad then and would blow her whistle. Curtis didn't even mind lining up and waiting for the bigger kids to have their turns. They pushed each other, jostling for a place in line, and smaller kids waited behind Curtis so he felt safe. He didn't like getting pushed into anything. He had been planning this all morning. Yesterday he had made the mistake of not lifting his feet and they had kept getting caught and slowing him down. This time he wasn't going to tuck up his legs but would roll down with them stuck straight out the way the older boys did. One boy almost made it to the street that way yesterday. Lucky, Curtis thought as he waited.

He waited until the bottom of the hill was clear before he lay down and leaned back, looking up at the sky, clear with just tiny little clouds that looked like poodles. He inched his bottom down until he was far enough onto the slope to start moving on his own and then started rolling, the cold air whistling in his ears. He could see the sky, then the grass and the houses across the street. He closed his eyes because the rolling was making him dizzy. At the bottom, he turned his body the way he'd seen the others turn but somehow managed to land on the sidewalk anyway. He stood quickly, dusting off the grass from his back, and turned to see where Mrs. Craig was. Relieved, he finally saw her at the other end of the yard. He turned to move out of the next person's way when his heart leapt to his throat.

The man from the car was standing right beside him with a little puppy on a leash. Kids were starting to come over to pet the dog, but the man was looking right at Curtis. Curtis could feel the man's eyes on him like fingers on a frosty window. He felt them burn the blades of grass left on his jacket, on his hat, like a magnifying glass in the sun. Someone called Curtis by name and he looked around in terror, wondering where he should run, but felt frozen in place. The man leaned over the group of kids and spoke directly to him, repeating the name he had just heard. Curtis watched his lips move, his breath come out foggy. He didn't know what to do. His brain screamed, and then he thought of his favourite number. Eight. He instantly felt soothed. Eight was the number of people in his family, six people and two cats. There were eight rooms in his house, not counting the bathrooms. Eight was the shape of the racetrack Jerry had left set up in the basement. The man kept talking, offering the puppy for Curtis to pet. The man's eyes, Curtis noticed, were blue, like the sky. Eight didn't have any corners to stand in. When the man leaned closer, Curtis climbed into the number, felt its smooth walls and curled around its curves the way his cats slept curled around each other. It was green inside and velvety like his mom's housecoat. He sniffed and it smelled like her housecoat too and his dad's shirts, that green smell of leaves when you tear them apart and dandelion stems that turned your fingers brown and the green smell of Jerry rolled into one.

Curtis felt a hand on his shoulder, a hand clenching his shoulder, hot. The man's face was so close to him, he could see where his whiskers were starting to grow, he could see spit in the corner of his mouth, he could see hair curling out of his ears. Curtis felt himself slide to the bottom of his lucky number and then made himself run. He ran through the schoolyard past the school and over the rutted mud in the parking lot. When he reached the street on the other side of the school, he slowed down. He'd been crying without even knowing it. His nose felt warm and wet so he wiped it with the back of his hand. He looked back but no one had followed him. His shoulder still throbbed where the man's hand had been; he could feel where each of his fingers had pressed. Curtis kept walking down the street looking for a friendly house because that's what Lily had always told him to do if he ever needed help: look for a friendly house and ring the doorbell.

At first he couldn't decide what a friendly house would look like. Maybe, he thought, a house that had Christmas lights up or still had flowerpots on the front steps from summer. Or a house that had Christmas lights and flowerpots, Christmas and summer at the same time. He finally decided on a house that had a wreath on its front door decorated with berries and pine cones. The tree in the front yard had two bird feeders and the address was 1088. Two eights. He figured this had to mean friendly. He timidly climbed the front steps and rang the doorbell. He could hear the chime on the other side of the door and then panicked. He didn't know what he was going to say. He should've just gone into his school, but the man was too close there. The door opened and a woman looked down at him.

"*Oui?*"

Curtis started to cry again and he couldn't stop his body from shivering.

"*Mais, que'est-ce qu'il y a? Entre, entre, il fait froid dehors.*"

Curtis didn't understand what she was saying. He wanted to ask her to phone his dad, to tell her that he worked at a job with trucks, but he couldn't remember the name of the place.

"Har you lost?" She tried again in English this time and spoke slowly.

Curtis shook his head.

"Do you go to dat school?" She pointed in the direction of his school down the road. He nodded this time. "Did some boys—" She shook her head, searching for the right word. "Did some boys fight on you?"

Curtis shook his head.

"Never mind, I will call the school. You come in this house and wait, yes? Do you like *chocolat chaud?*" Curtis understood the word *chocolat* and nodded.

Curtis watched the woman reach up for the tin of cocoa. The kitchen was bright and full of ceramic cows. Everywhere he looked, he could find a cow. There were two cows grazing on the kitchen table with paper napkins stuffed between them. There was a cow looking over its shoulder at him, its tail holding a pair of orange oven mitts. He tried counting them but kept losing his place. He got up to eight or twelve and then would wonder whether he had remembered the cow under the tree on the dish towel. He had never realized how exasperating cows could be.

The woman was stirring milk into a pot. He felt the cold from outside melt off him. The kitchen smelled good, smelled warm, and the furnace came on making clunky metal noises he knew well from home. The man at the school who had called him by his name, who had looked at him with eyes that were hot, eyes that made Curtis look right back and made his legs feel full of sand, that man seemed as small as his puppy now. He seemed far away. Curtis leaned his head against the back of the kitchen chair. It felt solid behind him. His shoes, he saw, were caked with dirt and chunks of mud were dropping off onto the floor. He wasn't sure if he should wipe the dirt up or not. The woman was smiling as she put down a mug in front of him. She didn't seem to mind that his shoes were dirty. Lily had been right—if you picked a friendly house, everything would be okay. He smiled back up at her and blew at the steam. She disappeared down the hall, and for a moment the noises of the house seemed to get louder. Ticking and the furnace and somewhere a radio or television set and a woman's voice singing.

Curtis took a small sip, afraid of burning his tongue. The cocoa tasted better than it smelled; it tasted so good, he wanted to chew it instead of swallowing it right away. He could feel its warmth down his throat and in his belly. He took another sip and then another. Being scared, he figured, made you hungry. He looked up and smiled to himself. He was surrounded by cows. His dad had told him once when they were out for a drive that you knew it was going to be a hot day when the cows were all lying down. He remembered standing on a wooden fence and holding out long pieces of grass for the cows. One of them came close, took the grass from him and licked his hand. Its tongue, he remembered, felt just like his cat's tongue. He liked cows. He settled back into his chair, holding his mug the way he had seen his mother hold her tea, with both hands. He could stay here all day.

The woman came back with a phone book and sat down opposite him. She was muttering to herself and flipping the pages, squinting down at the columns of names and numbers. Curtis sat up and watched her, wondering if she was going to call his father or his mother. He watched as she mouthed a number to herself, repeating it almost out loud as she walked over to the phone. She picked up the receiver and dialled the first three numbers and then had to go back and look in the book for the number again, smiling at Curtis. He smiled back.

He liked her not because of the cocoa, but because she liked being surrounded by cows. He smiled at her as she dialled and he smiled at her as he listened to her speak French into the receiver. She spoke loudly as if the person she was speaking to was outside sitting up a tree with the other end of the string and a tin can. She nodded as she listened and then hung up and faced him.

"Har you finished dat? I am going to take you to the school. They want you to go to the school."

He hadn't anticipated going back to school, he wanted to go home.

"I want to go home," he said quietly. His throat felt scratchy and his face burned. He felt as if he hadn't spoken for a long time. His voice sounded small in this kitchen. The cows chewed and watched him. She hadn't heard him; she had gone and got her coat from the closet and was doing up the buttons, winding a scarf around her neck.

"Come, I'll return you to the school." She turned to the front door before he had a chance to say anything else. He slid off the chair and looked around the room, the sun coming through the yellow curtains, the sink and the clean dishes piled on the rack, the wooden spoon and the pot still on the stove, his mug and the best part of his cocoa left. He followed her to the door and stood on the front step while she bent and locked the door. All the sweat that had dribbled and rolled down his neck, down his back, his arms, became magnets for the cold. Long slivers of sweat turned icy now, slithering down his back and making him feel shivery and cold. The sun had disappeared behind a big fluffy cloud that looked part cow and part dragon. The ground crunched under their feet as she led him back in the direction he had came from, back to the schoolyard where the hills sent kids running onto sidewalks. Curtis knew how that puppy felt, shaking and wanting to go home, the man holding onto it tightly. The way he had held Curtis's shoulder too tightly. Curtis's feet ached from being cold, his shirt was wet, and when he followed the woman into the school, he couldn't see a thing. The hall was long and dark after the light outside. He knew that morning when the train hadn't come that the day wasn't going to be a good one and he'd been right. He stumbled beside her and let her lead him to the office, let her place him in a big cushioned chair. He listened to her speak to the secretary and then he waited to see where they'd send him next.

Les had watched Curtis run, his small legs working furiously to get away. Les smiled at the boy's strength, his small legs and how muscled they must be. His hand could still feel the slender frame of shoulder in it, the cupping of it. A little man. He wondered if the boy played soccer in the summer. He chuckled to himself and then prickled warm at the thought of helping him, directing his leg to the ball, his small foot. Kick with this part of your foot, Les would say, his thumb pressing the curve of instep, his other hand on the boy's leg. He shook his head clear of the heat that was fogging it. He had lots to show him. He watched Curtis run from the school grounds, his arms pumping, gravel kicking up behind him; he watched him until he felt a tug on his sleeve. He looked down at a young girl whose hat hung undone and whose nose was running into her mouth.

"Your dog is cold. It's shaking."

Les felt the puppy in his arms. It was shaking. He'd have to get it home. He looked back down at the girl, whose mouth hung open, unhinged, while she watched him. She was missing a tooth and her cheeks and nose were covered in freckles. He took a step back, repulsed at the snot that she'd lick every once in a while. He turned without saying anything and headed back to his car.

Lily wrote *Darter* and underlined it with a red pen. Then she copied out the description that followed. *A curious aquatic bird,* she wrote. *The bill is long and straight, the neck long and slender.* She skipped the part about the eighth vertebra but did write about the special muscle that enabled the bird to make powerful thrusts with its bill for the capture of live fish. And she wrote the last two sentences, tempted to underline them as if to warn herself of something. *The darter,* she wrote, pressing hard into her copybook, *swims with its body submerged. The head and neck extending above the surface of the water present a snakelike appearance.*

Nothing, she thought, was how it appeared. She thought of Grace and her family and how, at first, she had thought they were normal and how lucky they were, but now she knew better, now she knew how much was submerged. And her family looked so eccentric, so weird, but compared to Grace's— She put her pen down and stretched her legs out under the table. The library was full of students on their lunch break, finishing homework or reading. Though it was quiet, there was a hum, a buzzing of hoarse whispers. The entries, Lily thought, were like a Book of Knowledge horoscope for her. She could gauge what kind of day she'd have by what she was writing. It took her two days to write out the dance entry, and for two days she thought about dance, felt light on her feet, gliding on air. She thought about the turkey trot, the grizzly bear, the samba. She imagined her history teacher doing the rumba as she handed back their quizzes, the cafeteria line two-stepping to the cash. But then she wrote about the dance of death and later about Daniel and his skill at interpreting dreams. The small picture of him in the lions' den stayed with her, his head bowed and balding, his hands clasped behind him, and the snarling lions, the scattered bones on the floor in front of him, the thick brick walls. The encyclopedia didn't say why he was there or whether he got out alive, and Lily was beginning to wonder if knowledge was a bottomless pit. Every entry she copied left dozens of questions unanswered. She used to feel so determined when she thought of owning her own set of encyclopedias, determined to read each word and remember what she could.

She would imagine herself brimming with facts, with knowledge of borders and populations, lifespans and mountain ranges. She had been ferociously hungry and had fed like an aphid on the pages, chewing them up slowly and digesting them, saying them out loud. *Brazil, cadmium, chestnut.* But she wasn't being filled. She felt restless and prickly and wanted to scream at the high library ceiling. "What was Daniel doing with the lions and did they eat him or not?" She was beginning to realize that her project was going to take a lot longer than she had first thought and that she'd still have questions. And she was beginning to feel tempted to skip whole entries.

Lily looked around the room to give her eyes a break from the small, even type she'd been reading for almost an hour. Everything looked so colourful, a bright red sweater over in the literature section, striped blue and orange in the reference aisle. Someone had left a book about white sharks on the table she'd been using. A whole book about white sharks, she thought. A whole book. She looked down at her handwriting. It was neat and slanted to the right as if every word was rushing to be finished. She needed a break. That was all. Anyone would get tired of writing all the time, she reasoned to herself. She thought briefly of looking up the Book of Daniel, of finding out why he was with the lions in the first place, but she needed to move, to walk and stretch. It was bottomless, this quest for knowledge; it was quicksand. The people around her seemed so vibrant after the small print and black and white photos. Their clothes looked lush, tropical. She gathered up her things and stood, deciding to go and find Grace. Talking to Grace would be good, she thought, and left the library looking for her as she went.

Les lifted the dog from the car and put it down on the driveway. Its leash was leather and weighed more than the puppy. Les had buffed the leash with Dubbin and shined its brass clasp. He had engraved the dog's name on one side of a dog tag he had bought and on the other side had engraved his name, address and phone number. Lady, he had engraved with his shaky, thin scrawl, and tried the name out loud for effect. This dog would grow up to be a fine dog, calm and obedient. She was still a pup, he told himself as he watched it squat and piss a small puddle onto the driveway, its legs wobbly, its tag jingling with the weight of the leash. She would grow into her name, he figured, with time. He coaxed the puppy to walk towards the side door, clicking his tongue and making soothing noises. He had to lift it up each stair and over the door frame. It had short legs and couldn't manage.

Once inside, the puppy walked uncertainly to its blanket, sniffed and pawed at it and then curled up into it. Les took off his coat and boots and sat on the chair closest to the blanket. As he pulled part of the blanket over the puppy, it nuzzled in closer and he watched it for a while, feeling its warm and breathing body in his throat. His eyes burned with tears. She was a fine dog and he'd take good care of her. He cursed when the doorbell rang and looked quickly down at the puppy still sleeping. He got up quickly so whoever was at the door wouldn't ring the doorbell again. Morons, he thought. Who would be ringing the doorbell in the middle of the morning except born-again Christians? He'd tell them a thing or two about the Bible, he could quote passages to them and see how they liked them apples. He opened the door to the sun and two police officers on his doorstep.

"Mr. McIntyre? Lesley McIntyre?"

Les looked them both over before answering. "Yes, I'm Mr. McIntyre and I happen to know that it's not illegal for a man to walk his dog now, is it?"

The police officers looked at each other in confusion. The older officer took a breath and continued. "Mr. McIntyre, I'm afraid I have some bad news."

Les's legs felt the way they used to feel after he had sat in the rowboat all morning with his father and stepped out onto the wharf. His legs had always buckled, and his father would hold out an oar for him to use to steady himself. Without thinking he reached for it now, his father's voice reedy with memory, coaxing him to hold on: *Steady, steady, that's it.*

His hand still glittered with fish scales and they stayed like that for a moment. He could see his father sitting in the boat on the lake, reaching out with an oar to steady his son's step, and Les, the son, standing on the wharf holding the oar held out to him, feeling his legs strengthen, and when he felt he could let go of the paddle, he looked up and realized that he was standing in his socks with nothing but a metal railing to hold onto and he had become the father.

The room was dark and drenched with the smell of smoke. A narrow blade of light cut across the jeans he had stepped out of and left on the floor, across socks rolled off from his feet, underwear still inside the jeans. Sheila stepped over plates and empty cereal bowls; she caught herself from sliding on glossy magazine covers with pictures of electric guitars and women in bikinis. She gingerly stepped around records left out of their sleeves and cans of Coke lying on their sides. She reached and pulled the blind up and stood back for a moment in the fading light of the day that managed to come in around the long grass that was growing outside her son's window. She waded back through the clothes, around heaping ashtrays, headphones, to the light switch and turned it on. The room still seemed dim.

He had wanted the room in the basement. She remembered him arguing earnestly, promising that he'd keep it clean, that he'd put in laundry for her. He was going to be down there anyway, he had said, smiling. She remembered telling him that it was too dark down there, that it wasn't healthy. The floor was cement, it was damp. He said he'd get rugs from somewhere and he'd use that old plaid sleeping bag as an extra cover. She worried that it would be like sleeping in a cave and he had joked about bears, about hibernating in the winter. She'd given in then, when he joked. He hadn't tried to make her laugh for a long time and his effort went right to her heart. She'd help him, she had said. She would pick out curtains that were sheer, that would brighten up the room. They stayed sitting after supper, after Grace had gone out, while Les was still at work, and they talked. She should have said no, should have stuck to her first instinct about the basement being too dark. It must have got to him, that darkness. It had to. Or, she thought, sitting down on his bed, he hadn't heard the train. He was walking home along the track deep in thought and didn't have time to get out of the way.

She got back up quickly at the thought of the train and straightened his bed. She stacked the empty bowls and emptied the ashtrays into the garbage can beside his night table. She dumped in all his empty cigarette packages. When he was five or six, he had hated the dark. He used to call out for her in his little boy voice and she would get up out of bed and go sit with him, tucking the blankets under his chin and singing the song he had liked about having the whole world in his hands. She bent and gathered his dirty clothes, picking up his T-shirt with a photograph of one of the bands he liked printed on it; she held it to her nose, inhaling deeply the smell of her son, the cigarette smoke, the Mennen Speedstick deodorant he used. She closed her eyes and breathed in deeper. She thought underneath the smoke, the deodorant, she could smell the boy again, the back-yard dirt, the sweat, the hot summer sun, his freckled skin, and she let herself cry, she let herself look at his room without him and for the first time she let herself think the words *without him* and wondered if he had called out for her in that voice, that thin twig of a voice, called out for her in the dark and she hadn't heard him. If she had, she would have got out of bed, she would have sung anything for him, she would have sung about all the mommies and all the babies in his hands, she would have pushed his hair back from his eyes and sung about the whole world in his hands.

*   *   *

Later she wheeled the Hoover in and vacuumed his room with hard sweeps of her arm. She vacuumed under his bed, she pulled the night table over and vacuumed where it had been, she pushed the pile of records with her feet and vacuumed around them, she closed the door and vacuumed the corners, and then she pulled the nozzle back to where she had been sitting and pushed it back and forth where her feet had been, where her tears had fallen onto the matted, rusted orange shag rug. She vacuumed the words *without him* and she vacuumed the memory of him afraid of the dark, and when the pile on the rug had been vacuumed so often that it almost looked new, she pushed the Off button with her foot, bent and unplugged the cord, gave it a quick yank and watched it slither back up into the canister. On her way out she flicked off the light and turned to look over her work. The sun had gone down and the room was left in that thin, pale light before dark. She thought briefly about how early it was getting dark. The intent faces of rock stars looked down at her from his walls. Alice Cooper, Pink Floyd hung over his bed. She turned then, yanking the hose closer, and pulled the vacuum like a wagon behind her, leaving the room to the dark. Some other boy was going to be buried in the pale blue sweater she had ordered from the Sears catalogue, some other boy, but not her boy. He'd be back, she thought, the way he always came back home, hungry and tired, and this time she'd feed him, this time she'd touch his face and tell him to get some rest. "Sweetie," she'd say, "go lie down and get some sleep."

Grace had never been in a funeral home. She let a man in a suit who spoke in a whisper take her coat and she watched him hang it, pushing the other coats aside to fit hers in. Her parents were already in the viewing room, she was told. Room number two. She looked into room number one on the way down the hall. It was crowded with well-dressed families speaking quietly, leaning into each other to listen. Between the dresses and suits, she saw the coffin against the back wall surrounded by flower arrangements. A man was kneeling in front of it, and when he stood, she briefly saw the old woman's face, her hands clasped and holding a rosary. Grace looked away quickly but the woman's face stayed with her and she was tempted to look again. The woman didn't look as if she was sleeping; she looked stiller than that and her cheeks were rouged like the faces in the "don't" photos in *Glamour* magazine. She slowed her pace down when she got closer to the room where her brother lay.

All along the hall were oil paintings of tall ships sailing on the ocean. The carpet was green and spotless. There were upholstered chairs tucked into corners with small tables beside them. On every table was a box of Kleenex. Men who worked at the funeral home slid by Grace without making a sound. They managed to move her out of their way while expressing their condolences in one small economical movement. Grace was amazed by how sympathetically they looked at her. One of them walked towards her with an older woman sobbing on his arm. He looked up and nodded with a compassion that suggested he knew how Grace was feeling and could she please step out of the way. Another came up behind her with several coats over his arm. He nodded at her and again she felt he was on her side and stepped out of his way.

The room where her brother lay was panelled in the kind of wood seen in a rec room. There were chairs and small tables similar to the ones out in the hall. As she walked into the room, she felt the pull towards the coffin without looking at it. It seemed to be the nucleus, the heart of the room, beating and beating. She turned quickly from where she thought it was and looked down at a guest book that lay open on a table by the door. There was only one signature in it. Her father had written his name in his shaky penmanship, looping his *l*s and *y*s dramatically. Beside it Les had written the date and "Rest in Peace." Her mother hadn't signed the book yet.

Grace picked up the pen, wondering what she should write.

She thought of the rhyming verses that filled her autograph book. *If all the girls lived across the sea, what a good swimmer Gary would be. By hook or by crook, I'll be the last name in your book.* She thought of the poem her teacher had read out loud to the class a couple of weeks ago, about death and the boy it had taken. Gary's eyes were brown. She gulped when she thought of him by name. The word *brother* was easier, farther away. She reminded herself to breathe. She had cried herself raw when they had told her and now she felt ragged inside, in shards, every breath ripped and snagged. She wasn't even near the stage where she would need the upholstered chair and small table with its box of Kleenex. She thought of the small iced-over puddles she came across whenever she walked to the bus stop, how she'd make her feet glide across the puddle and then stop herself abruptly when she reached the concrete again. She was at the small iced-over puddle stage, she figured. Every time she let herself think about Gary, she'd make herself glide, stop thinking until the thought passed, and then she'd walk slowly until the next puddle.

She could feel him behind her, the beating of the closed box. Glide, she thought, glide. She didn't want to turn around. She didn't want to see her father in his good suit, a matching handkerchief folded into his breast pocket, his hair slicked back and the smell of Listerine coming out in gasps of breath, crying. Or her mother, who seemed to have gone to bed as her mother but had woken up old. Grace was shocked when she saw her in the morning, her shoulders thin and stooped beneath her blouse, the sleeves ironed smooth with a line pressed down from her shoulder. Her mother, who could barely lift the orange juice pitcher from the fridge and who stood in her nyloned feet on the kitchen floor that was covered with wet newspaper, the puppy scampering around her.

And there'd be the relatives, the well-meaning aunts and uncles who would whisper the story of how her brother had stood in front of the train, how his face was skinned, torn beyond recognition. The knowing looks and opinions that they'd feel compelled to share. The cousins who would look as uncomfortable as they felt in their shirts and ties, their skirts and sweaters. Nothing about this felt right, Grace thought. She put the pen down without writing anything and left the room. Standing in a hallway with paintings of ships made her feel better. The ship hanging across from the entrance to the room where her brother lay was on calm waters. Its sails billowed breezily in a soft, salty wind. There were gulls overhead. Three, no four, she counted. And the sun wasn't painted in but only implied, its long rays warming the deck, lighting a path across the water that seemed to spill out of the frame and make its way right to her feet.

Grace stood there, her eyes closed, her back to the room where her brother lay, and breathed in deeply the smell of the ocean, the screeching of the gulls, the water lapping lazily in the sun. She tried to ignore the steady pulse of the box her brother lay in, how it was once a tree and how it now must crave wind, how her brother was once—Glide, she ordered herself, stop walking and slide over this. She looked down the hall, the hall that now seemed to go on forever, lined with paintings of ships voyaging, sailing smooth and choppy waters to the chair and small table at the end of it. The box of Kleenex, the soft upholstered arms of the chair open and inviting. She stepped towards it and then stopped. She didn't want to leave her brother yet. She couldn't. Even if she wanted to go and sit, to pluck a Kleenex and wipe the mascara from under her eyes, she couldn't. By not saying his name, she felt him everywhere. He was the ship, he was the ocean, he was the gulls reeling in the wind and he was the chair sitting at the end of the hall and inviting her to sit. He was the home she wanted to go back to. He was the room where she could just sit and not say anything. And he was the lighthouse she knew was left out of the painting, the beacon for those lost at sea, the warning and the reminder. He was the sun, the light implied and painted over the waves and sails. She owed it to him to say his name, even in her head. One thought of just him. But she couldn't yet, and she knew that somehow he knew.

Eliza and Lily let the man take their coats and then usher them into the room where Grace's brother was. There was a slow vortex of movement in the room that they became part of as soon as they stepped in. It moved them to a seated couple who Lily thought had to be Grace's parents. The woman was nearly bent over and would hardly look up when someone offered condolences, but the man, Grace's father, stood up and cried loudly each time, hoisting his pants or fixing his tie between each visit. She couldn't see Grace anywhere. Lily hoped she was all right and not alone somewhere, locked out in the way she always seemed to be. But how could she be all right now? Lily wondered, and she felt her stomach, her heart, sag, her knees bend at the thought of how enormous Grace's sadness must be. She felt her mother's hand on her arm, felt strength in the grip, and made herself breathe. Her mother moved in front of Lily and bent down to take Grace's mother's hand in her own. Lily watched her mother speak softly to Grace's mother—Gary's mother, Lily corrected herself, today she was Gary's mother. The women bent into each other, leaning forehead to forehead, both their shoulders shaking. Lily stood back and watched grief consume them, watched grief collapse them into one mother with four clasped hands.

Les cleared his throat and the vortex, the slow circle of it, moved Eliza from Sheila to Les. Lily watched her mother shake his hand and was surprised that she moved so quickly away from him. He moved his hand quickly in Lily's direction, eagerly. She felt herself step back.

"So you're Grace's friend, eh?"

"I'm sorry," Lily managed to whisper, and Les's eyes welled up with tears.

"It's not right, my son being taken from me like this. It's not right." He began to sob, great gulping sobs that seemed to shake the room around him. Lily wasn't sure what she should do. She put her hand out again and he grabbed at it, holding on to it tightly.

"What can I do now?"

Lily felt panicky and wasn't sure what to say. He was still holding her hand. He held it tighter when she tried to pull it out of his grasp. She thought of her encyclopedia entries but couldn't think of any remedy for grief. She couldn't think of one thing to say to him that would soothe him and make him let go of her, ease his sobbing. Birds came back to her, the colour of their feathers, their paths of migration, but by then Les was finished with her and was reaching for the man behind her before she could say anything.

He had held her hand long enough to have stopped the procession, and Lily realized there was a gap between her mother and herself. People were waiting behind her for their turn. She walked quickly to Eliza, relieved to get away from Les. She thought about Grace again and the way Grace lingered at Lily's house, at her front door, when it was time to go home. Les had sat down again, Lily noticed, and was tapping out small white pills into his palm, making a big show about taking them without water, throwing his head back and swallowing them. Lily looked away quickly when he turned to look at her. She stood as close to her mother as she could.

Eliza was staring intently at the coffin, her hands spread on it, moving as if soothing some kind of salve into sunburnt skin. She looked up at Lily and smiled palely. "I'm ready to go now."

The movement of the room was circular, counter-clockwise. First stopping at Grace's parents, then at Gary, and then signing the guest book and leaving. A kind of cycle, Lily thought, a cycle of grief, maybe, or of loss.

*   *   *

The path down the mountain wound around trees and stumps. The root systems of these trees reached out and clasped each other across the path, sometimes buckling above the ground. Jerry lifted his feet over these roots and listened to the branches rattle in the wind, sending needles down in clumps. The moonlight came down in shafts, lighting up the path and then leaving it in the blue light of night. He heard an owl, heard it leave its perch and fly. He looked up but could see only the underbelly of pine, of spruce, balsam. Ahead of him, off the path, was a small statue of the Virgin Mary that he made his way to. The monks went there to pray, leaving small offerings at the statue's feet. He picked up a crucifix made of branches and twine that one of the monks had left leaning against her legs. He wasn't religious, had never gone to church, but he stood now before the statue, in the same place the monks must have stood or kneeled to pray. He closed his eyes and tried to divine an echo of their prayer, a lingering plea to God that still hovered here. He wanted it, he wanted their faith and the peace that settled on their faces when he saw them pray.

He thought of the crystal his mother had hung up in the living room window, how it took in the sunlight and shot it back out into the room, prismed. Prayer had to be part light, he thought, and he could be the conduit that caught it and sent it in the direction it was most needed. He looked up at the night sky, Orion's Belt, the dipper, breathing in the clean white light of them, the green needles of the trees, the frost. All of this was important, he knew, because he would watch the monks walk through their orchard, he'd watch the old monk who tended the gardens stoop sometimes to look closely at a leaf or a bud or, once, an opaque puddle of frost textured with fine lines like feathers and fronds. The old man had peered into it as if he saw something important, and Jerry was beginning to realize it was the seeing that was important, not what was being looked at. It was the stopping, the stooping, the peering closely that seemed to him the most religious act the monks did, and he had begun to look as well. Maybe, he decided, prayer was also a wish for others to stop and look, a wish for the fronds of frost, the long shard of starlight, to become more noticeable again. Maybe prayer was a way of saying, Come back here, to this moment and help me move through it.

He thought of Grace. When his heart had stood up in the back of Ralph's car that night, when it had dived into her, part of it had stayed there. She was the silent half of every one of his thoughts. She was the person he wanted to stop with, to bend and look at the lime green moss by the rock that seemed to absorb light like a sponge. Every time he breathed in and every time he breathed out, he breathed Grace. Her voice stayed with him, her eyes, worried and intent. He couldn't imagine how she'd be feeling now, now that her brother had been found. He hoped that somehow she could feel Jerry sending out his own amateur kind of healing to her, that somehow he was soothing her a little.

His boots crunched on the ground and he saw his breath each time it left him. He turned from the statue, with her arms held out, beckoning, and headed back towards town.

The town seemed asleep. Snow had fallen, the first snow, the snow that everyone agreed wouldn't last. It covered everything, erasing the garbage, the dog shit, the garden tools left out to rust. Yard after yard seemed smooth and white, blankets pulled up tight to the glowing windows of the houses. Some kitchen windows were lit up and people moved in them from the sink to the counter, looking out into the night, not seeing him in the shadows of their yards. He walked quickly through a gate into a backyard and followed the cedars along to the next yard. He jumped over the small ditch between properties and followed a wooden fence to the next property. He walked through backyards that were neatly kept, with shed doors locked, shovels leaning at the end of cleared paths. He walked through backyards with patio furniture still out, clumps of browned plants still in clay pots at the edge of gardens, clothes still hanging, frozen and swaying stiffly on clotheslines. He moved across town through yards and driveways. He kept away from the properties with the dogs that barked, patted the dogs he had got to know, and when he reached Grace's house, he stopped and watched it, pulled his hood up and shoved his hands in his pockets. He timed each beat of his heart to her name, calling her to the window. He'd wait until he saw her, even briefly framed in the kitchen window or pulling down the blind in her bedroom. He'd wait until he saw her move, saw that she could still move. He shook the image of Gary lying on the tracks out of his head and tried replacing it with the Gary he had seen around, the Gary with the jean jacket and the Zeppelin shirts who walked with his head down as if he was always figuring something out, as if he was always walking into a hard wind. Jerry stood behind the shed and waited for just a glimpse of Grace to ease his mind. He wanted to tell her somehow that he was there, standing in the dark for her.

Lily dreamt she was helping Daedalus construct wings. She had to keep stirring a vat of wax while he made an armature with fine wire and a small set of pliers. She tried asking him who the wings were for and had he thought of the heat of the sun, but he kept shushing her, intent on weaving the wire. She looked at his work, thinking that it looked like the underside of a leaf, with the stem and small lines veining off from it. Could she have the wings, she asked him, for a friend? Lily's arm was getting sore and she looked at the big clock he had set before her, indicating how long she was to stir. The ticking of it echoed in the chamber and for the first time she looked around at where she was. The walls were brick and moss grew along the bottom of them. There were candles burning everywhere with thick, melted wax pooled at their base, and on a wooden table between her and Daedalus was a huge book with strange writing in it, pencilled-in sketches of shoulders and extended arms. Calculations of flight and velocity. Below the sketches of arms and shoulder blades was a smaller sketch that she could only see by leaning closer. It was a photograph of Daniel facing the lions. She turned quickly to Daedalus.

"Do you know Daniel? Look." She pointed to the illustration. "He's there with the lions. Do you know what happened to him? Is he all right?" The clock that had filled the room with its ticking began to ring. Lily stood back confused as she watched Daedalus hurry over and take the wooden spoon from her. The clock continued to ring and she moved slowly away from the room where wings were being constructed as if she was walking through wax, and slowly, thickly, she realized her alarm clock was ringing and that it was time to get up.

Lily's father was at the stove, plopping out oatmeal into cereal bowls he had lined up on the counter. Dellie was sitting on the floor between his legs, setting a small stuffed bear on her father's foot. Every time he moved, the bear would fall and Dellie would tsk to herself and set it upright again. When the bowls were full, Stan bent down and swooped Dellie up and put her in her chair. Then without stopping, he picked up the bear and stuck it in his sock so its head peeked out. Curtis came into the kitchen next, rubbing his eyes and yawning.

"Good morning, Curtis. Would you like some oatmeal?" Stan ruffled his son's hair as he walked by Curtis to put the bowl of brown sugar on the table. Dellie was wiggling in her chair and Stan quieted her protests by shuffling his feet and making the bear stuck down his sock dance. She clapped her hands.

"Look, Curtis, Daddy's got my bear in his sock!"

Stan put her bowl down in front of her and replaced the soother in her hand with a pink plastic spoon. She immediately dug the spoon into the cereal, intent on guiding the melted brown sugar into the milk. Curtis reached for the brown sugar and counted out two teaspoons, sprinkling them into his bowl.

"No more than two, right, Curtis?" Stan said with his back

to the table. He turned and caught his hip on an opened drawer and cursed loudly. His voice sounded harsh in the quiet morning air. The room became silent. Curtis watched him, holding his breath, afraid to say anything that might make his father turn and yell at him. He waited until his father straightened and carried Dellie's spill-proof cup and a small Batman glass filled with orange juice over to the table. "Any sign of Lily yet?"

Curtis breathed slowly out and shook his head, cautiously putting his tongue into the porridge on his spoon. Still too hot. He blew gently into his bowl, blowing the milk into the brown sugar, and watched the mixture swirl into the oatmeal. His father was humming that song he liked about being lonely and he was kicking his feet around to make Dellie's bear dance. Curtis laughed to himself. Lily came into the kitchen carrying her notebook. Her hair wasn't combed and she didn't have socks on.

"Finally, Lily. Did you sleep well?" Stan waved the bear at her feet. Lily didn't notice. "Are you still sleepy?" Stan put her bowl down in front of her and rubbed her back with his free hand. "Dellie's going down to Mrs. Sullivan's this morning. Do you think you could drop her off on your way to the corner?" He looked closely at her. "Did you manage to get any sleep at all? I know your mother tossed and turned all night." She nodded. Stan sighed and then shook his head, turning to Curtis. "You've got gym today so I put your sneakers by your bookbag. Don't forget your cheese and crackers this time, they're in the fridge. Okay, cowboy?" He looked around the room, picking up the spoon Dellie had dropped. "Okay, Lil, I'm off. You'll get Curtis off and Del over to Mrs. Sullivan's?"

Lily nodded again and her father left the kitchen. She could hear him in the hall pulling his jacket out of the closet. The same jacket he'd been wearing for years that had "Stan" embroidered on the sleeve. She waited to hear the front door and was surprised when he stuck his head in the kitchen again.

"Almost took Bear to work," he said with a grin, tossing the stuffed animal onto the table, then winked and left. There was no sound from upstairs, no stirring or steps or running water. Their mother was still sleeping. She had left a drawing leaning between the salt and pepper shakers. Lily pulled it out to look at it. It was a sketch of the three of them. Curtis was bent over a drawing. Eliza had drawn his face just the way he looked when he was working on a picture: determined and serious. Dellie was simply standing with her pyjamas on, her soother in her mouth. Lily couldn't believe how well her mother had captured Dellie's eyes, the liveliness of them, the mischief, and her hair—it almost seemed to bounce and tangle. She looked slowly at how her mother had drawn her. She was pleased at the way Eliza had framed her face loosely with her hair. Lily looked down at her hands and then at the drawing of her writing in her notebook. She had lovely hands, she thought. Her mother had shaded the space between the three figures so that they were connected, surrounded by zigzagged shading and joined by her mother's small signature on the bottom right-hand side of the sketch. She must have been watching them for a long time to have been able to draw them all so well. Lily smiled, warmed by the thought of her mother watching each of them so closely and with so much love. She handed the drawing to Curtis, who looked at it thoughtfully, picked up his binoculars and studied it even longer, and then held it out for Dellie to see.

"Hey!" Dellie exclaimed. "That's me in my jammies!"

Lily rinsed a face cloth and finger by finger began to wash her sister's hands. She moved to Dellie's face. Dellie squirmed, trying to get away from the cloth. Curtis went to the drawer and got out the tape. He looked around the kitchen at the walls and decided on the spot above the table. Carefully he pulled off two pieces of tape, put them on the top corners of the paper and pressed them to the wall. He pulled off two more pieces and stuck them to the bottom corners and then backed up to admire the drawing and the place it now hung.

"Okay, Curtis, you've got to go brush your teeth. The bus will be here in a minute."

Curtis ran up the stairs and Lily could hear him turn on the water. She went looking for Dellie to put her coat and boots on. Dellie had climbed in the front hall closet and had pulled out an old pair of Curtis's cowboy boots. She pulled them on and stood teetering in them. They went up over her knees.

"You'll have to take those off, Del, and put on your snow boots." Lily bent to find the right ones.

"No, Lily, I got to wear these boots today."

Lily looked up at her sister standing there with her small arms folded defiantly across her chest, her soother moving back and forth from the force she was sucking it with.

"It's very important to me," she added, holding out her soother and then popping it back into her mouth.

"It's important that you wear cowboy boots today?"

Dellie nodded so hard that her curls jiggled.

"All right, Del, but you need a hat and mitts because it's pretty cold out, okay?"

Dellie held her arms out and let her sister put her coat on her. She lifted her chin and let Lily tie her hat and then put her mitts on, tucking them up under her jacket cuff the way she liked. She stood in the hallway, bundled up and waiting, shuffling her feet, the heels of her boots on the hard wood floors. Curtis came down and Lily helped him find matching mitts and then helped him with his zipper. He left the house first, walking slowly down to the corner where the bus would pick him up. Lily ran upstairs and quickly brushed her teeth, grabbed a pair of socks and ran back down. It was later than she had realized. She pulled on her jacket and boots, picked up the bag her father had filled for Dellie and hurried down the hall. Dellie followed her, taking big loud steps that made the house seem even quieter when the front door closed behind them.

*   *   *

Grace didn't want to go to school. She ached all over as if she had fallen asleep in an awkward position and had woken up with kinks and cramps. The funeral had been on the weekend and the house had been full of relatives who left salads and baked hams and coleslaw that no one was eating except her father. She didn't feel the regular disgust she usually felt when she watched him eat, even when bits of cabbage stuck in the corners of his mouth or pieces of food landed back down on his plate or he began sobbing uncontrollably with his fork poised mid-air. And she didn't feel anything when she watched her mother wipe everything. Over and over she wiped the counter, the table, then moved the kettle, the toaster, and wiped under them. If she wasn't sitting, her shoulders slouched and her mouth pulled down, she was wiping and tidying, washing and drying. But Grace didn't feel impatience. She just lifted the plate someone had put in front of her, heaped with scalloped potatoes and baked beans, she just lifted it for her mother so Sheila could wipe underneath it, and then she put it back down and stared into the food for some guidance on what she should do next.

She worried at how numb she was. She listened to her aunts talk about Gary when he was younger, when he played soccer and won medals. She let her grandmother touch her face and exclaim how sad this all was, what a pity, what a tragedy, tears rolling from her watery blue eyes down her lined, sweet-smelling face into her mouth. And she didn't feel anything, didn't cry when she watched her brother's body being lowered into the ground, saw her mother's knees give out as if she'd been kicked from behind, heard her father's sobs and the sliding sound of his rosary. Grace watched as uncles led aunts to the hole in the earth and watched as they dropped single flowers onto the casket. She watched when dirt was shovelled over, and when they were being driven away, she watched out the window at the fresh mound in the cemetery for as long as she could, thinking any minute, any minute, he'd turn up and tell them all that he had been forced to pull this off, this fake death, to get Ralph off his back, and he'd grin apologetically, his hands in his pockets, touched by how much everyone was grieving.

She didn't want to go to school but she couldn't stay at home either. The puppy pranced around her, excited by the visit of feet. It nipped playfully at her toes, pulling at her sock, sitting with its effort. Grace couldn't stand the puppy. She couldn't stand how her father cradled it the way he would cradle a baby, how he cooed at it and then hissed at her mother that he had a broken heart, that he had lost his only son, and to leave him the Jesus alone. Couldn't she see? he'd ask. Couldn't she see how upset he was? And then he'd pet the puppy gently, gingerly, before setting it back onto the floor.

Grace needed to go out but she didn't know where to go.

She had put on Gary's old plaid shirt, had taken it from the hamper still smelling of him and had put it on. It was a heavy shirt, one he wore open with a T-shirt underneath. It had settled on her like smoke, as if he was standing there talking to her, waving around his cigarette, inhaling deeply and then exhaling, the smoke turning into blue and black plaid. The smell of Export A. She had found a bag of grass between his records downstairs and another bag in a jacket pocket hanging in his closet. She took them both, quickly putting them in her pocket before her mother noticed. She had a bag with her now, in the shirt pocket. She'd go somewhere and smoke the way he had smoked and let herself become blurred the way Gary had always seemed to be blurred. Grace stood for a moment holding herself in his shirt, rocking herself gently, and then bent, pulled on her boots and coat and stuck some mitts in her pocket, determined to get out.

She opened the door and left the house so quickly it looked as if she had been pushed out. She was amazed to see birds, small chickadees flitting in and out of the cedars. Sparrows. Two crows cawed back and forth, each perched on the highest branch of nearby trees. She watched the mailman walk jauntily by, the bag over his shoulder stuffed with letters and cards and bills. A car drove by and a group of small children played noisily in a yard a couple of houses down. It hadn't occurred to Grace that the rest of the town would keep living, that they'd get up and go to work as if today was just like any other day. She felt betrayed. The chickadees sounded almost joyful chick-a-dee-dee-deeing to each other, swooping and gliding and showing off. She wanted quiet, she wanted the maple at the front of the house to be bowed and the crows to be silent. She wanted them to realize that her brother was dead, and that without him she couldn't imagine writing a letter to anyone, sealing the letter, walking to a mailbox and mailing it. She wanted her street to mourn, to bow down to the sadness and just stop.

She walked slowly down the driveway, the sun hard and bright in her eyes, the kids laughing, the crows loud. She closed her eyes and thought of his face, the way he'd hold his cigarette, examining it while he talked, the way he flicked off the ash, the way his feet, his big, clumsy feet, could never stay still, his legs and feet always moving to a rhythm, a song that only he could hear. Tears filled her eyes and her nose started to run. Impatiently, she rubbed at her eyes and then opened them. The sun was still bright and hard, the crows cawed back and forth, gossiping. There she is, she imagined them saying, there is the girl who lost her brother. She walked down the driveway faster now and onto the road. The whole town would know her as the one whose brother had killed himself. She let herself follow her feet, and trusting her feet allowed her mind to wander, to close out the sounds of life carrying on the way it always had. She let her mind tend to the tiny cocoon of hope she had that it wasn't true, that her brother was somewhere now, waiting for the right time to come and tell her that he was all right.

Jerry watched her walk, his heart aching at how lost she seemed, at how she stood in the driveway with her eyes closed, her face turned away from the sun. And he followed her, keeping close behind her. He could have walked right on the street, she wouldn't have noticed, but he stayed farther back, not wanting to intrude, not wanting to get so close he'd scare her.

Grace ended up at the field behind the elementary school. Long yellowed grass moved in the wind. Long dead goldenrod, chicory. She walked through them without seeing. Hydro towers surrounded her, looking like long-legged praying mantises, grasshoppers, but she walked beneath them, stepped over their shadows and stopped finally at a boulder, the only rock visible in the expanse of field.

The highway sounded closer than it was; eighteen-wheelers thundered by, cars, buses. Behind her the recess bell had sounded and schoolyard noises wafted over to her, shrieks and yells. She didn't hear the trucks or the screeching of kids let loose out of the building or even Jerry's footsteps behind her. She placed her hand on the rock and closed her eyes, feeling its dents and sharp corners as if she could read it, as if she wanted to know how to be that solid and that alone. She wasn't surprised when Jerry touched her shoulder. She opened her eyes and looked long at him. He looked back at her, saw the sadness in her, how it had taken over everything about her; her hair seemed to sway sadly in the wind, her eyes were brimming with sadness. He didn't look away from it, wasn't embarrassed at how raw she looked, how potent and poignant it was. He embraced her with his eyes, tried pulling some of the grief from her so he could carry part of it for her. A jet flew over them, droning low and loud. They stood in its shadow for a moment, and when it was gone, the sun seemed warmer and the rock held the warmth.

"I keep thinking, maybe he's still alive." She took the bag from her pocket and opened it, selecting one of the rolled joints.

Jerry nodded and waited. It was like listening to Curtis. If he spoke too soon, Grace, like Curtis, would stop.

"He needed to get away from Ralph so maybe he set all this

up and will come back later when it's all blown over." She slid the joint into her mouth, wetting it. Baptizing it, Gary would say. She baptized it Gary and then she lit it.

Jerry waited.

"I didn't see the body, they said it would be too hard, so it could've been anyone in there." Even to her, her voice sounded shrill, desperate. She took a long drag and held the smoke; it was like having a burr in her lungs. She breathed the smoke out slowly, watched it leave her body, and then she turned back to the rock and put her hand on it, coaxing its smooth solidity into herself. Small flecks of fool's gold glittered in the sun.

If she was part tree, Jerry thought, then she was birch—birch in the way birches were in an ice storm, bent over by the weight of the weather all the way to the ground. And birch in the way they thawed, slender and straight again, supple. She was stronger than she thought. "I saw him, Grace."

She turned slowly from the rock and looked at Jerry through the smoke. "Who? Who did you see?"

"I saw Gary."

"You saw Gary?" She felt that cocoon of hope swell and open. "When did you see him? Is he all right?" It sprouted wings, fluttering around her words as if they were a light that the small moth of hope tried to get close to.

Jerry swallowed deeply. He wished he could swallow that whole night, the train, the tracks, Gary's boots, his jacket torn right off him.

"I saw his body after he had been hit."

He watched her.

She looked into his eyes. Her mouth was thin and angry, bent.

"Bullshit."

"No, Grace, I swear, I found him and stayed with him until someone else came."

"How do you know it was him? I mean, maybe he got some guy to wear his clothes—" She stopped herself. "Fuck off, it wasn't Gary." Her hope fluttered and then landed, stilled and heavy.

Jerry reached for her but she backed away.

"I'm so sorry, Grace, I am so sorry but it was Gary. He was wearing that ZoSo shirt and I saw his face." Jerry was crying. Hot tears made their way down his face and quickly turned cold. She watched him cry. And though he was crying, he didn't look away. He held her gaze.

Everything she had heard for the past three days came back to her without warning. Everything charged down the track and she heard it all again, this time knowing that it was true. Her grandmother with her watery blue eyes, sobbing that it wasn't fair, that she should have been the one who was dead. And her mother, her mother whose knees just gave out. And her brother, lying in that coffin, arms folded on his chest, and dirt being thrown over him. The pale blue crewneck sweater from the Sears catalogue, the pressed trousers her mother had sent to the funeral home, underwear, socks—"Do they need underwear?" Sheila had asked—a white shirt. Gary, she thought, silently pronouncing his name, pulling it out in two full syllables. Gary.

And then she cried, at the sound of her voice, her heart's voice, and the sound of the words *brother* and *Gary* colliding and landing dead at her feet.

Curtis's stomach started hurting while he was sitting at his desk. The kids around him were doing the math sheet Mrs. Leduc had just handed out. He was supposed to be figuring out patterns. He had done the first one. Triangle, square, circle, cylinder, triangle. He drew a square and coloured it in. The next one was numbers: 2, 4, 6, 8. When he had said *eight* to himself, he remembered rolling down the hill, his feet straight out so they wouldn't slow him down. He thought about the sidewalk and trying to stop, turning sideways, and then about standing up and that man standing there waiting for him. And his puppy, the small black dog that was sitting by the man's big boots. The man had said his name. He had put his hand, his hot hand, on Curtis's shoulder. Eight was his favourite number, he thought. Maybe they wouldn't have to go outside because it was too cold. Maybe they would all go to the gym for recess or just sit at their desks and eat their snacks. He thought of the crackers and cheese his father had made for him, that Lily had made sure he had put in his bookbag. His dad always gave him the kind of cheese he liked, the orange kind, and he always cut it thick and square and put a slice on each cracker, stacking them and then wrapping them up.

He heard the teacher clap her hands and tell the class to put their sheets in their math folders, they'd finish it later, and to please get their snacks out of their bags. The first set of tables ready, with their arms folded on their desks waiting quietly, would be the first to get up and get their coats on to go outside.

Curtis shuffled through papers in his desk long after everyone in his group was ready.

"Curtis," hissed Mandy, the girl next to him, "hurry up or we'll never get outside."

He unzipped his bag as slowly as he could and reached in, moving the crackers around inside the bag. Mandy folded her arms and glared at him.

"You are so slow, Curtis. We'll be last. It's not fair, Mrs. Leduc, Curtis is making us all wait."

Mrs. Leduc had herded two groups out; three groups were left. Curtis took out his crackers and then bent to retie his shoe. Mandy kicked at his chair impatiently. When he couldn't think of anything else to do, he sat up and folded his hands on his desk. Mrs. Leduc pointed to his group and before he could get up off his chair, the other kids had run out.

He went to his spot under the slide. He was never going to go on the hill again. The sun filled the long yellow tube with light, and he thought it would be warm against his back but it wasn't; it was cold and made him shiver. He put his crackers down on the snow and pulled out his binoculars from inside his jacket.

"Curtis, ya wanna play Scooby-Doo with us?" His friend Jeremy was prancing around him proudly. "I get to be Scooby!"

Curtis shook his head and put the binoculars up to his eyes and squinted into them. He took a long sweeping look along the far sidewalk. He went back and forth three times to make sure he hadn't missed him somehow. The man wasn't there. Just kids sliding and pushing and climbing on the hill. No man with big laced-up boots and a small black dog on a leash.

Curtis leaned against the underside of the slide in spite of the cold. He took a big breath and felt his stomach unclench. He remembered his snack and unwrapped it. His teeth, he imagined, were sharp as a dinosaur's, as a sabre-toothed lion's. He bit into the cheese and crackers and chewed ferociously.

Jerry held open the back door of his house for Grace. She found herself standing in the kitchen and could see the table was set for two. Something smelled good on the stove and there were two sandwiches on plates. Jerry's mother had her back to them at the sink. She was filling the kettle. The teapot was on the counter, its lid off. Grace looked at Jerry, not sure what to do. He smiled and motioned for her to go in. Eliza turned to greet her son, smiling, and when she saw Grace, her smile deepened and she pulled out the second chair, indicating that she should sit. Grace handed her jacket to Jerry, who hung it on a peg, and then she sat. Eliza put her hand on Grace's shoulder and gently rubbed her for a moment. Nothing had been said. The fridge hummed. Jerry and his mother moved as if lunch had been choreographed. Jerry sat in the other chair, his mother put down two bowls of steaming soup, the kettle began to hiss and when it boiled, she unplugged it, pouring the water into the teapot, clinking the lid into place and carrying it to the table as well, setting it down between them. Then she left. On her way out she touched her son's head and touched Grace's back. They heard her climb the stairs and then walk over their heads. Music started to play. Some man sang deeply, sadly, of the green, green grass of home.

Grace wanted to ask if Jerry came home a lot and if Lily knew, but it didn't seem important. She looked around. There was a drawing of Lily and Curtis and Dellie on the wall. She smiled at Dellie's face and at Lily so immersed in the big book on her lap. The room was filled with sun, dishes were stacked around the sink and on the floor were two bowls with fish painted on the sides. For the cats, she thought, and then realized that Jerry was waiting for her before he started eating, so she picked up the spoon and dipped it into her bowl. The soup was homemade, she thought, full of cut-up vegetables and spiralled noodles. She brought the spoon to her mouth and sipped the broth. It was delicious—tomatoes and onions, carrots, celery. She ate it hungrily and then without stopping moved on to the sandwich. When they both had finished, Jerry poured them each a mug of tea. And they sat in each other's company, Grace not even aware of the silence. The numbness that had filled her had shrunk a little and she was going over what had happened during the last few days. She was plucking memories from the murkiness and was polishing them until they were clear. She had started a small collection of moments before and after her brother Gary's death. Somewhere she knew that she'd want these memories, that they'd be there when she needed them, so she was selective, ignoring the ones that still were too hard to touch.

"Are you tired?"

His voice startled her. She was tired. More than tired. She nodded.

"Come lie down for a few minutes. My mother will wake us up when we've got to go." He led her into the living room. Knitted blankets were folded on every chair, on the couch. Drawings lined the walls and there was a stereo in the corner with records leaning against it. She had never been in the living room before and was comforted instantly by how at home she felt, how she could sense Lily's presence even without her being here. She felt herself recline into the feeling of it.

"You take the couch." He waited for her to lie down and then covered her with a dark green afghan. The cat hair on it made her nose itch. She watched him sit in the chair across from her, watched him pull a blanket down over his shoulders. He smiled at her and she smiled back. He was the reason, she realized, why she was so relaxed, why she felt so at home. He felt more like home to her than her own house did. Upstairs the man's voice was crooning. It sounded like he was saying *quando*. When, he was asking. The fridge hummed off and the furnace rumbled. She could hear the wind outside and the sun got caught in a small crystal and a piece of stained glass hanging in the window and reflected in dark red and blue on the wall above Jerry. She closed her eyes and fell asleep almost instantly. A deep sleep, the kind she needed.

Jerry woke briefly when his mother pulled another blanket over his legs. As she covered up Grace, he fell back to sleep. Eliza stood and watched her son. His dark eyelashes fanned his cheeks. And Grace, Lily's friend. She had met the girl's parents at the funeral home, had looked into her mother's eyes and looked into her father's eyes as well. Pulling a sketch pad from under the chair, she drew Grace's hand holding onto the blanket. It was a hand that was almost a woman's hand, Eliza thought, but still had something of a child in it. She sketched quickly, the curve of fingers, the clench of them with the wool blanket fisted inside. The shape of Grace's hand made her ache. She concentrated on the sadness that seemed to radiate from Grace's face and drew it into her fingernails, into the thin piece of skin she had chewed, the nails bitten ragged. She drew her wrist, the bend in her fine slender wrist, its dark veins and white knuckles. Nothing about Grace was easy; she was holding on to the blanket so tightly that the crescent moons of her cuticles had disappeared. Eliza drew them in, and with the sadness she sketched an ease that Grace was hungry for, starved for. And then she left them both to sleep, exhausted herself. She'd wake them in an hour, before Dellie would be dropped off and Curtis would get home. She climbed the stairs silently, careful not to disturb them.

"How can you talk about money with me now?" Les sat at the kitchen table in his bathrobe. His hair stood on end from his hand raking through it. No father, he thought, should have to go through what he was going through, the pain he was feeling, the anguish. He felt for his rosary in his pocket and pulled it out, then pulled out his handkerchief, coughed up and spat into it, and stuffed it back into his pocket. He was an old man, he thought to himself, a poor, broken man with a heart problem, and his son had been taken from him. There was a heaviness in him now. He wondered briefly if he could sue the train company. The conductor must have been drinking on the job or was half-blind not to have seen his son walking on the track in the glare of the headlights. There had to be some explanation.

Sheila had slid the bill from the funeral home onto the table in front of him. She had listened to his refrain about losing his first-born so often, she didn't hear it any more. She just saw him red-eyed, red-eared, bawling pathetically. She waited with her arms folded.

"Why are you looking at me like that? Have you no sympathy? My heart is broken, it feels like I could have a heart attack or something. My left arm feels numb and I have a sharp pain here, in my ribs. I don't want to pay those bastards. What a racket. I could've made a better box. Did you see the workmanship on it? Those corners didn't even meet. I would've used tongue-and-groove. I'm not paying for that piece of crap. They're nothing but shysters, out to get money. Those greedy bastards. I've paid enough already." He pushed the puppy away with his foot. He couldn't look Sheila in the eye.

"You need to go back to work. We are digging ourselves into a hole and I'm not going to borrow more money." She glared at him, her anger thinning her lips and narrowing her eyes. It was as if she was seeing him for the first time. Pathetic, she thought, he was pathetic.

"Work! I can't work. My God, I lost my son. Doesn't that say anything to you?" He began to cry again, rubbing his chest. The puppy sitting at his feet wagged its tail. "Would you leave me the hell alone? You always want something from me. You want money?" He stood up and looked at his wife, turning the pockets of his bathrobe inside out. "Here, take what I have." His handkerchief fell to the floor and the puppy pounced on it, shaking it in its mouth. Sheila felt her stomach heave. The sight of her husband in his terry cloth bathrobe, the lining of his pockets hanging limply at his sides, his nose and eyes running, made her feel sick. She had no idea how she was going to pay for Gary's funeral.

Every day Sheila would wake up before her alarm went off and she'd lie there thinking about her son. Only then would she allow herself to do this. She'd think of his face, not of how he looked before he died, but his face when he was thirteen, when it bordered between the adult he grew into and the boy he was. She remembered the time he had wanted to eat outside, and remembered making him lunch and carrying it out for him. She had worried about the dish and told him to be careful. He was so clumsy then, banging into walls, shouldering into doorways. She kept remembering that lunch because she had hesitated when he had asked her to sit down with him. "Sit down in the sun, Mom, it's really warm," he had said, and she had thought about it for a minute. But the seat of the picnic table was rotting, the wood black and splintered, and she shook her head no. She had a sink full of dishes to do, the laundry was piled on the basement floor, the bathroom needed to be scrubbed and all the sun shining into the house had made everything look dusty. No, she had said, I've got so many things to do. And he had nodded. He knew there were dishes, he always complained when his jeans hadn't been washed, he knew the work she had to do. But these past few mornings Sheila would wake up wishing that she had sat down, wondering if everything would have been different if she had. And that thought would lead to a whole parade of thoughts that marched through her head, and she'd whip back the blankets and get out of bed to silence them. She'd take hours with an old toothbrush, scouring the grout around the bathtub. She'd use Q-Tips to clean around the faucets. She'd spend entire days tidying up her grief, polishing it, sponge-mopping it, and when that didn't do the job, she'd get down on her knees and scrub it, scrub it until it shone and she could see herself, her red and sweaty face reflected back up to her from the floor.

They had given her three weeks off at work. Three weeks. At the end of the first she had taken apart the spice rack, cleaned the wood and each jar and then put it back together, the jars in alphabetical order. She had dusted everywhere and had used an old recipe her mother had given her to wash the walls with, ammonia and lemon and vinegar. She'd scrubbed the kitchen walls and then the hallways, used newspaper and vinegar and washed everything shiny in her house. And when she vacuumed, she used every nozzle. She'd take the plastic slipcovers from the couch and chairs and vacuum them and then recover them. She'd drag the long, narrow nozzle along the baseboards and around the door frames. She washed and dried the curtains, wiping down the rods that had held them. She soaked and then hand-washed all her doilies, dried them laid out flat on tea towels on the kitchen table and counters. And Les watched her from his chair, dressed always in his pyjamas and terry bathrobe, leaving dishes for her to pick up, handkerchiefs hard with snot and spit to wash, and every day that passed she hated him more.

And he had forgotten all about the puppy in his grief, and the puppy became something else she had to take care of, feeding it and standing outside the back door in her nightgown and coat while it peed. It had been left to her to take it to the vet for its shot, to hold its small, trembling body afterwards. It was her money that had paid for the shot and bought more dog food when none was left. She cleaned up after it when it threw up, a twist-tie or, once, a button in the middle of the mess. And she hated the puppy because it was his, because it had a name tag, its name etched with his fancy electric etcher, because of its heavy leather leash.

The more she hated Les, the more he seemed to be around her. It made her nervous. He was prickly and quick-tempered. He had tried kissing her one night, smacking his lips in her ear, and she had pushed him away. He'd left the house then and hadn't come back for hours, and when he did, he was different, jovial almost. He had joked with Grace about the newfangled music she was listening to.

Sheila just wanted to go back to work, to walk down the driveway to the bus stop and get on the bus that would take her away from her house, away from the carpet that showed every bit of lint and away from the basement and Gary's huge Keep Out sign that reminded her every time she passed it that even if she had sat down that day and shared a piece of his sandwich with him, he would still be dead. She wanted to get the hell away from them all. She hoarded her unhappiness, and in its own way it kept her busy, occupied, and made the time pass somewhat more easily. It gave her a sense of purpose, balancing it all like a cheque book: withdrawal, withdrawal, payment, payment, mortgage, insurance, withdrawal. She was in overdraft, she was broke, she was empty and she had no energy to do anything about it.

Les lifted his feet so Sheila could vacuum. He moved his glass so she could dust underneath it. He waited for her to clean off the television screen even though that young boy from Lachine was talking and Les was aching to go out, prickled and hot and pacing inside, to walk off the heat he was feeling. Just to the store, he bargained with himself, even a man in mourning needed pipe tobacco.

"I'm going to the store," he announced to his wife's back. She turned and faced him, her rag poised, ready to wipe him away. One day, he thought, she's going to dust me like one of her goddamn lamps.

"I'm going to the store," he said, this time more forcefully. "The store," he repeated more slowly as if talking to someone who needed time to think what a store was.

"For what?" she asked, alarmed. "What are you going to buy now?"

He looked at her for a moment, measuring the panic in her voice. "I was going to get some pipe tobacco, but I think maybe I'll go browse around Canadian Tire, see if my buddy the district manager is there."

"For God's sake, Les, don't spend any more money." She was wiping the top of the television set rhythmically, hypnotically dusting around each small knob: Bright, Tint, Colour.

"Don't tell me what I can or cannot do. If I want to spend money, I will spend money. My son has been taken from me, for whatever reason the Almighty might have, and what good is money now? It can't bring him back. Money is useless. Who needs it?"

She looked at him coldly, holding the rag clenched in her fist, her knuckles white and bony. He didn't even see her. In his mind he was already out walking; the sounds of kids playing in the late afternoon light pulled at him and made him ache. He took the stairs two at a time, peeled off his pyjamas and quickly put on a sweatsuit that was folded in his bottom drawer. Then he thundered down the stairs like a kid who didn't want to miss anything. Every one of his movements, putting on his shoes, zipping up his jacket, said "Wait for me, wait for me." He didn't see the small dog at his feet, excited and thinking it was going out, didn't feel his wife glaring at him. But when he turned before leaving to check the time, to calculate how much light was left in the day, their eyes met and held.

"Don't get into any trouble."

Les felt rage replace the sweet tension that had tightened his limbs. He glared at her a moment, watched her pick at something on the wall, and then left the house.

The train tracks ran from one end of the country to the other. Through large cities and small towns. Children would run beside the train, waving at the driver or the engineer in the caboose. They'd cheer if they waved back. Pennies were put on the tracks and retrieved after the train had passed, flattened with the copper coaxed out to shine. Drivers would hit their steering wheels, would grumble when the railroad crossing sign flashed red and the long barrier slowly moved down, stopping traffic. The train would be a small dot down the tracks like some drawing exercise on perspective that got closer and louder until it whooshed past the line of waiting cars, the tracks clinking metal, clouds of dirt and small stones whipping around, frenzied and the drivers would sit, stuck, and read CN or CP on the side of the rust-coloured cars as they passed. Freight cars from as far away as British Columbia and they'd shake their heads while drumming the dash with their fingers, impatient, impatient to get on with their day.

The train that passed Beaumont either came from Montreal and was heading east to Nova Scotia or came from the east and was heading west. Passenger trains used the tracks as well as freight trains. There was a commuter train to Bonaventure, downtown Montreal, that stopped at the small railroad station on the outskirts of Beaumont and came back from the city at night, the passengers disembarking looking tired, their suits, their skirts, crumpled, newspapers read and rolled to throw away.

Whatever kind of train passed, it always let out a long, mournful whistle, and the long pull of it was a kind of semaphor of sound. Each whistle, long or short, meant something, a signal for speed or track or distance. The sound was so frequent, it became part of the landscape. The long wheat, the goldenrod, or in winter the stiff twigs and branches, moved with the sound as if it was the voice of wind. At night the sound moved in the curtains, slid across the ceiling like headlights driving by. It was an accompaniment to the days and the nights of the town, a sound that kept the people verging on nostalgia, missing something they couldn't even name.

The train whistle also gave their days a rhythm and an escape route. No matter how badly things were going—all three kids with the chicken pox or the mortgage payment bouncing or fifty men laid off or the Habs losing to the Nordiques—no matter how badly the day or night was going, the train whistle reminded them that there were tracks outside of town heading in either direction, east to one coast and west to the other. And that knowledge gave them room in their lives for hope because if life got worse there was always a way out.

Winter was like the train. Inevitable. The people trudged through the season, pulling on salt-stained boots, shovelling narrow, crooked paths to their cars and then clearing their driveways while their cars sputtered exhaust. Daily they wrapped themselves up with scarves, gloves, mitts, and left for work or school in the dark violet of morning and came home in the dark violet of night. Nightly they heard the wind and rubbed their hands together before getting into beds that were cold, their feet finding each other or other feet to rub against and warm.

The cold, the snow, were conditions they didn't really think about. They shovelled, they salted and sanded their way out of their homes and made their way back, cursing the plows that sealed them out or in with the even pile of snow blocking their driveways.

They had different shovels for different snow. Aluminum shovels for the heavier, wet snow that would begin to melt and then would freeze up again; wider, plastic shovels for the light snow, the kind that jewelled in the sun and blew in drifts against doorways, creeping up to doorknobs and windowsills. Winter was a season of days they shovelled out from, trying not to remember as they made their way out to their lives, shovelful by shovelful, how much energy it took, how much time, to clear away something that would end up just melting anyway.

The sky in winter was something they noticed. The sunrises as they cleared off their cars or walked dogs. The long streaks of light emerging on the horizon from behind trees or the houses across the street would fill them with something: hope, maybe, the way light does. And then they'd get into their cars, tug at the leashes of their dogs and go back to their days, the short winter days. If anything, it was the light they'd savour, they'd bring with them. The memory of the first slant of sun, the brilliant blue of morning, and how too soon, too soon, dusk would compress the light until it was once again a narrow band on the horizon, brilliant in its fading. The days were growing smaller, the nights longer. Unbalanced. Light became something they looked for, something they'd switch on and bask in, something they began to miss.

They got used to the daily doses of cold and snow until one day the weather seemed different somehow, warmer. Then they noticed it, how dirty the snow had become, then they complained of the lack of light in their lives. They began pacing inside, anxious for the weather to get better so they could go outside without jackets or toques, so the morning would come sooner, the evening later, so the sky would finally be lighter.

*   *   *

Curtis marked a thin line in his copybook before he went to bed. He had heard the train as he brushed his teeth. He flipped through the pages already filled with rows and rows of lines, of trains he had heard. There were already twenty-six lines on this page. Soon, he thought, he'd need a new notebook. He flipped to the last page and looked at the row of small, dangerous-looking cars. Nine. Nine dangerous-looking cars. The last car had pointier teeth than the others, with drops of blood dripping from each point, fangs. That was when the man had brought the puppy and had called Curtis by name. The day the man had touched his shoulder. Curtis tried to remember how long ago that was. The car hadn't been at the school for a long time. At first he spent all his recesses under the slide with his binoculars scanning the street where it was usually parked. When it didn't turn up, he thought about it all the time, imagining he'd see it at the grocery store or on his street, but when he didn't, he slowly began to think about it less and less. Lately he'd been playing Scooby-Doo or dinosaurs with Jeremy at recess. He liked playing dinosaurs better because triceratops didn't talk and no one yelled at him to say what they had told him to say the way they did when he was supposed to be Shaggy or Scooby-Doo. They had played dinosaurs or Scooby-Doo right through winter, even on the days they stayed in. A whole season had passed while they growled tyrannosaurus growls or ran around pretending to be solving the mysteries of the schoolyard.

He put his notebook in the drawer of the night table beside his bed and waited for his dad to come and tuck him in. While he waited, he lifted the blind above his bed and looked up at the sky. There were no rain clouds and the branches of the trees close to his house looked pink in the porch light. Soon leaves would be getting ready to open, he thought. He wondered where Jerry was. He hadn't seen him in a few nights.

Stan strode across his son's room in three big steps, got down on his knees and leaned on his bed.

"Sweet dreams, Curtis. Mommy will be here in a minute, after she's through with Del, okay?"

Curtis nodded, smiling, and watched his father get up and leave. Small waves of happiness made him feel warm and wobbly. He heard Dellie call out good night and knew his mother was on her way to him.

"Hello, Curtis." She moved softer than his dad, he thought, like a whisper. She sat down on his bed, careful not to sit on his feet. "Are these your toes?" She squeezed his feet and he giggled. "You are getting so big, you'll need another bed soon!" She pushed his hair from his face and looked into his eyes. "My Curtis." He wiggled closer to her, to smell her and to hear every word. "Do you want a song?"

"Yes, please."

She smiled, surprised that he had spoken so happily, but continued as if he spoke that way every day. "What would you like? We've got Engelbert, Tom Jones and Elvis Presley. Today's special is 'Love Me Tender.'"

He shook his head.

"The Beatles."

"Okay, one Beatles coming up. Do you want the one I always sing for you—?"

Again he nodded and nestled his head deeper into the pillow, closing his eyes and waiting for her voice to wash over him, to sing about the world being round.

He fell asleep with his mother's voice wrapped around him like a blanket. His thumb made its way to his mouth and Eliza smiled down at him while he slept. He was such a little boy, she thought, such a sweet little boy. She leaned down and kissed the top of his head, breathing in his sweaty scalp smell, and then she left.

When Curtis woke, he was confused. It was still dark. The night light in his room was still on. No one had called him for school. He didn't have to pee. His hair was stuck to his head and sweat ran down the back of his neck. He peered around his darkened room and jumped when he saw Jerry sitting in his chair, asleep.

He got out of bed and tiptoed up to his brother, putting his hand on Jerry's knee. His jeans felt cold and hard. Curtis tapped his finger on his brother's leg. Softly but insistently. Jerry stirred, then woke up.

"Are you all right, Jerry?"

"Curtis—" Jerry stopped and stretched out his legs, yawning.

Curtis looked up into his older brother's mouth. He had way more molars than Curtis did. Jerry closed his mouth again before Curtis had a chance to count them.

"Did I wake you up? Sorry, I tried to be quiet. I came for a visit but you were already sleeping. I must've dozed off."

Curtis breathed in the smell of his brother, the smell of cold sidewalk, the outside-at-night smell that surrounded him. It was metal smelling, like handlebars, he thought, or the underneath of one of his Hot Wheels cars. That had to be what woke him up. The outside smell inside his room.

"You feel cold." Curtis had laid his hand flat on his brother's leg.

"Yeah, it's been a weird night. I needed to come in for a while."

"You can share my bed if you want. Mommy says I'm getting bigger than my bed but that's just a saying. My toes don't even reach the end. You could sleep with me, Jerry, my bed is really warm."

Jerry looked at his brother, his tousled hair, his pyjamas buttoned all the way up, cowboys and cactus strewn in a tumbleweed kind of pattern all over them. He still looked warm and sleepy.

"Are you sure I wouldn't keep you awake?"

"I'm sure. It would be like a sleepover, like camping." Curtis smiled up at him.

"Okay. You get back into bed, you have school in the morning."

Curtis went to the bed, looking back to make sure that Jerry was following him. He climbed up and held the cover for his brother.

"You move over to the wall. I'll sleep on the edge, okay?"

Curtis nodded. His bed had gotten cold while he was up. And Jerry's arms and legs felt chilly, as if his brother was still outside; the night air hung over him like a cloud. Curtis pulled his blankets up to his chin.

"Go back to sleep or you'll be tired in the morning," Jerry urged and then sneezed. Curtis closed his eyes and then opened them.

"Bless you."

"Thanks. Good night, Curtis. Now go back to sleep or I'll have to leave. You've got to get up in the morning."

"Okay. Good night, Jerry." Curtis closed his eyes and willed himself to sleep. He tried not to think about Jerry beside him, about telling Jerry that his tooth had finally fallen out, telling him about the story he wrote in school that morning, about Jeremy's stitches and the way Matthew still had chicken pox all over him like polka dots. He tried to ignore his brother's deep breathing, the length of his long body sagging the bed towards him. He opened his eyes and looked at Jerry. The night light at the foot of the bed cast an orange glow on his brother's face. Even as he slept, he looked tired, Curtis thought. His hand was against his chin as if he had to hold his head up in his sleep. Curtis looked at his brother's knuckles, at the scrapes and cuts across them. He looked at his hair, at how black it was, so black that it looked blue in places. And how long it was. He let himself look at Jerry's ears, the deep cleft on his chin. Tentatively, he put his finger in it, the way he used to when he was younger. Jerry didn't wake but stirred in his sleep and turned over on his back. Curtis continued to watch his brother sleep, memorizing each feature of his face as if it were a letter in a word he was studying for spelling. *House*, he thought, he could spell *house* now and *sister* and *brother* and *mother* and *father* and *dog* and *cat*. He closed his eyes and Jerry's face was before him in his mind's eye, his brother's lashes curved to his cheeks, his ears still red from being outside. He could spell Jerry's face, he thought, and in his mind he put his finger in the cleft again and finally fell asleep, curled up to the length of his brother.

Eliza had heard the sneeze. She was still awake, reading. She waited to hear another. It hadn't sounded like Lily or Curtis. She read until she finished the chapter and then got up and went in to check on her children.

Dellie had kicked off her blankets and was lying on her back, her arms stuck straight up over her head. Supergirl, Eliza thought, and pulled the blankets up over her youngest child's body. Dellie's soother was hanging out the corner of her mouth and the movement of blankets made her pull it back into her mouth and suck on it. Her hair curled around her face. Eliza watched her for a moment, in her bed, stuffed bears and dogs surrounding her, each in its own special place. She backed away softly, not wanting to wake Dellie.

Lily had fallen asleep with the light on again. Eliza picked up the copybook that was lying still open on the bed. The heavy encyclopedia had slid off and was on the floor. Carefully Eliza unhinged Lily's glasses from behind her ears and folded their arms, putting them on the night table where she could find them first thing in the morning. Without her glasses on, Lily's eyes took over her face. Even closed they were beautiful, long dark lashes and fine sculpted eyebrows. Eliza bent and turned off the light, smoothing the bedspread over her daughter as the moonlight lined the floor in long slants. Eliza stepped through it, moving quietly, slowly, into Curtis's room.

At first she was puzzled by the shape in his bed but as she moved closer, she realized both her sons were sleeping in it. She stood for a moment over them, amazed at how alike they looked. She could see a young Jerry in Curtis's face, all excited about the salamanders he had found, needing a container to keep them in. And in Jerry's face she could see her Curtis grown up, his features heavier, more defined. This had been Jerry's room. She looked around; the walls had pictures of cats and mice and dinosaurs. They had painted the room when Curtis moved into it and Jerry had moved down to the basement. She wondered if this room still felt like home to him and how often he returned without her even knowing he had. Out in the hallway Eliza got a blanket from the linen closet and went back and covered Jerry. He looked cold to her. And as she thought that, he sneezed again and she tucked the blanket around him closer.

The night after he was born, she remembered standing in her hospital room alone, looking out at the snow-covered city. Montreal looked magical in snow, and she had tried to make out the different buildings she could see. The blinking lights, the glow. Stan had left for their apartment in the north end and it was late. Jerry was sleeping, a wizened little baby wrapped tightly in a receiving blanket the way the nurse had shown her, lying on his side. Keep switching sides, the nurse had told Eliza, or his head will be an uneven shape, pointy. She remembered feeling how so much of his life depended on her and that she didn't know what she was doing. She would try nursing him, burping him, changing him every time he cried. She worried frantically about being responsible for his growing up with a pointed head. She had felt overwhelmed by everything she didn't know and was in charge of. The day nurse had given her a plastic ring—a donut, she had called it—to sit on when she peed. She was sore; each breast seemed to weigh more than Jerry.

Eliza remembered watching the city from her window, thinking how each light represented a life and she had just added another, when out of the corner of her eye she saw movement, a woman a few windows from hers swan-dive onto the roof below, her nightgown billowing behind her, the amber parking lot light making her look otherworldly, golden. Her body landed, sinking into the snow, leaving a desperate imprint of a snow angel, arms flung out and moving. Eliza's nurse came rushing in and moved her gently from the window. Behind her, an urgent-sounding voice called out a code on the intercom system and the corridor filled with the sound of running feet, of shouts. Hormones, the nurse had whispered to Eliza, don't worry, she'll be fine. But Eliza knew then that the terror, the fear she'd been feeling was real and that she was alone with it, that everyone was. Alone. She let herself be led back to bed, let the nurse cover her, waited while she checked the clipboard at the foot of Eliza's bed, waited while the nurse pulled the curtains over with an efficient swipe of her hand, waited until the heavy door slowly swung closed to the outside noises of the hallway and then she let herself cry. She wanted to go home, not to the apartment off St. Zotique Street but back to a time she had already left, before everything, when she couldn't even imagine that kind of terror, back when she hadn't even known that she was alone, that she'd always be alone, back when she had felt safe and taken care of. Surrounded.

She looked down at her son now, whiskered and muscled, his feet hanging over the end of the bed, and knew that he must have already felt that longing for home, intense and aching, and how he must also have realized by now the impossibility of returning to how it once was. It made her ache that he knew this, that he knew he was alone. He was grown now. His head was beautifully shaped. She used to bite his fingernails instead of clipping them and she'd take him in the bath with her and wash him as he'd frog-kick furiously, lying on her belly. She could kiss it all better then, tickle him slowly up his belly to under his chin until he couldn't help but laugh. She watched him sleep for a few moments longer before she left him, left them both quietly, went back to her book, to her bed, to Stan sleeping on his back, his mouth slightly open. He turned to her when she lay back down, putting his arm across her stomach, and in his sleep he pressed his lips to her arm and kissed her, staying close to her like that all night. Alone, she thought. And surrounded.

Spring

It had been unseasonably warm for April. Almost every backyard had clotheslines full of sheets and towels. The birds flew rollickingly from tree to tree. Cardinals flitted in the cedars, startling red, and the robins were plump, landing on front lawns as if they knew their arrival heralded spring, and they'd stay perched long enough for someone to see them, to point at them and exclaim that spring had indeed come. Victory, victory, they sang, winter had finally been beaten. The town came out in twos and threes as if the beast of the season had fallen and it was safe to come out of hiding. There was snow only along the curbs, dirty snow with gravel embedded in it, and pale, waterlogged litter blew limply along the street. The sewers ran loudly and eavestroughs dripped. The sound of water was beneath all other sounds, running, dripping, melting ice. Children went to school without hats or mitts, without snow pants or boots. Some of them had their jackets open, some didn't wear a jacket or coat at all. Unseasonably warm. It was April, and April had that way about it, persuading people out onto their driveways with their cups of tea after supper. It stayed lighter longer. The sounds of children playing, bicycle bells ringing, hung over the town. Gardeners looked for the tips of daffodils and tulips, for crocuses that had begun to break through the earth like teeth. They knew it was too early, that there would still be frost and snow. They knew it, but everyone else had fallen for the pull of April. Unseasonably warm. Lighter.

They were tired of shovelling, of leaving and coming home in the dark. They had missed the light, had craved it, and opened their windows to it now and gladly believed any warm wind. Any ray of sunlight could convince them that finally, finally, winter was gone, that they were heading for the day when light would be balanced with darkness, and beyond that when light would be even longer. They breathed in deeply this warmth. They believed it.

Ralph got Mike to drive past Grace's house again. He was bored. Slowly, he had said, drive slowly. The Impala crept along the street as if following a scent, nose close to the ground. He looked up to where he knew Grace's bedroom was, but the blind was pulled and he couldn't tell whether she was there or not. They had been up all night, cruising. It hadn't gone well. And Gary—it still bothered him that Gary had got out of paying him back. Gary had cost him. Ralph calculated that Gary must have smoked all of the ounces he was supposed to cut up and sell as dime bags or joints. What a fucking coward, he thought, killing himself like that. Ralph had given Gary lots of favours, fronting him a bag now and then, overlooking missed payments at the beginning. But fuck, that guy was just an asshole. A dead asshole who thought he had got away from Ralph. But there was always his sister.

"Do you want me to circle around and drive by again, Ralph?"

Ralph sneered at Mike's high, whiny voice. Asshole, he thought. "No, fuck-up, I do not want you to circle around and drive by again. Take me the fuck home. I'm burnt." He looked nonchalantly into the side mirror and watched Rave step out into view. Ralph sneered. This must be driving him crazy, he thought, having to guard her almost every night. He must be exhausted.

Mike whinnied a shrill, nasal laugh and continued driving, rolling through the stop sign at the corner and steering the car across town.

"What are you going to do to her?" Mike's voice slithered

and ended with another nervous laugh. His eyes were intent, though; he wanted to know.

"Why? You want a piece of her, don't you?" Ralph smirked at Mike's obvious excitement. "She fucking turns you on, doesn't she?"

Mike rocked back and forth in the driver's seat. His hands rubbed the steering wheel.

"Oh yeah, she's fucking hot, man."

Ralph watched him for a moment, noticing how wound up Mike got talking about her. He hadn't realized Mike was all twisted over Grace and thought he may as well play.

"You know that bitch owes me big time. She inherited Gary's stash and that means she inherited his debt. She's not going to fucking get away with it either."

Ralph roughly pushed in the cigarette lighter, and when it popped back out, held it to the joint hanging in his mouth. It was all so fucking boring, he thought, inhaling deeply. The grass was raunchy and the smoke scratched his throat. Bogus, he thought, looking at the joint. Homegrown shit. He felt Mike watching him and took his time taking another toke, holding the joint while he exhaled slowly. "You want a toke?" he asked, knowing that Mike was desperate, already reaching for the joint. Ralph held it out of his reach until Mike took his eyes off the road and looked at Ralph.

"C'mon, man, just a toke, Ralph."

Ralph took another drag and then handed it over to Mike, watching him inhale, the veins on his neck bulging, his eyes watering, until he finally let the smoke go, coughing it up. Ralph nudged his arm and Mike inhaled again quickly before handing the joint back.

"What are you going to do to her? You'll let me have a go with her, eh, Ralphie? And that fucker. That fucker stabbed me. I want my time with him too." Mike gave a stoned staccato laugh. Feral. He was cockier now, he was revved, licking his lips slowly, planning, savouring the thought of Grace, the taste of her.

Ralph looked out the window. The sun was up and there was more traffic on the roads. The grass had made him tired and dried out his mouth. That was all it ever did any more. He flicked the roach out the window, ignoring Mike's protest. That fucker would smoke anything, Ralph thought as he watched his house getting closer. He wanted to blow this town, this small fucked-up town with its small fucked-up people. He looked over at Mike, who was driving hunched over the wheel like an old lady, and grimaced. The car had barely stopped when he got out of it without saying anything, without looking back, and Mike drove off slowly, leaving a grey trail of exhaust behind him.

Jerry had watched the car in front of Grace's house. He had been poised, coiled behind a shed in a yard across the street, ready if the car doors opened, if Grace had come out of her house. He knew Ralph wouldn't let go easily.

When she finally did come out of the house, he hurried down the driveway to meet her, his heart thundering and melting at the same time.

"Hi." She looked over at him shyly, blushing. "Here, I brought you a muffin and some carrot sticks. Breakfast. Have you eaten?"

He shook his head, taking the food and managing a quick "Thanks." She still took his breath away.

He'd been walking her to her bus stop for a few weeks now. Before he had got up the nerve, he had just stayed hidden and watched her from across the street. He realized, though, that he didn't have very much to talk about. He had tried, the first morning, to tell her about the mountain but ended up sounding like some weird tree-loving freak, and so shut up and let her talk. The walk to the bus stop was only a few minutes, but she always got him talking by the third driveway.

"So the cat was yours and Lily's?"

He nodded. "They got the other one for Curtis. It's kind of cool the way the cats get along."

"I had guppies. We've got a dog now, but when I was growing up I had guppies."

He waited for her to continue. Each of her stories was like a different kind of weather that showed who she was in a different light. It was like his tree, he thought, and how the sun made it look different, or rain or clouds. He still marvelled at how the same tree could look different every day, how he could still notice something he hadn't seen before. Like Grace, he thought. Getting to know her was seeing her in all of her weather.

"They had babies. It was really amazing, all those tiny fish. But no one knew that the babies had to be separated from the mother and by the time I got up the next morning, she had eaten them all. Every one of them." She kicked at a rock and paused to kick it again. Jerry waited, watching her. She was wearing a black turtleneck and had written her name on her jeans.

"My mother cleaned the tank with Windex and killed her off as well." She looked over at him, smiling. "And that's the end of my fish story." Sometimes when she smiled, he'd noticed, her eyes didn't catch up with her mouth. They'd be left behind, serious and sad. Today, though, she was smiling all the way, infectiously. He found himself smiling back.

He waited at the bus stop with her and watched her get on when it drove up. And when it drove off, after she had waved to him and he had waved back, he stood there and watched the bus until it turned onto another street and he couldn't see her any more.

Lily watched Curtis run down the street to the bus stop. She had let him wear his new spring jacket; his winter one was getting too small anyway. She hated the way his wrists were always bare. She breathed in the smell of soggy grass and mud. The sun had been out earlier while they were eating breakfast, but now the sky was overcast and felt damp. She went back into the hallway and packed her notebook and the encyclopedia that the librarian had let her take home. Dellie was sitting with their mother on the couch, pulling thin strands of hair out of her mother's bun. They were both wrapped in a blanket and looked as if they were going to fall back asleep.

"Bye, Mom, bye, Dellie."

"Have a good day, Lil," her mother replied.

"Bye, Lily, see ya tomorrow."

"Not tomorrow, later today, Dellie."

Lily left the house as her mother was trying to explain the length of a day to her sister. Breakfast, she was saying, then there's lunch, then nap time. Lily slowly walked to her bus stop thinking how some days slid by and others hobbled, minute by minute, as if they were hanging onto a banister and pulling themselves up. Her feet crunched over the small pieces of pavement that had broken loose over the winter.

Every spring, she thought, the roads came undone, splitting long cracks or erupting into potholes as if whatever was beneath the town could barely be contained any longer and threatened to let loose. The wilderness that had been paved over pushed against the roads, the sidewalks, to break free of its constraints, to erupt into the town. Underneath everything was always something else. A darter. Already a construction crew was out at the end of the street, spreading tar and setting up pylons. It must be a continual job, she imagined, keeping things paved over, smoothed.

Later, when she got to school, Grace was already waiting at her locker.

"Hey, Lily."

Lily picked up her combination lock and turned the dial twice around to the right. She had dreamt several times that she had forgotten the combination and couldn't get into her locker.

"Hi, Grace." She stopped turning her lock and looked at her

friend. Grace looked different; her skin was glowing. She looked happy. Lily watched her pick at a sticker on the locker next to hers. She opened her locker and shoved her knapsack in, looking at the schedule taped inside the locker door.

"Math. What do you have?"

Grace shrugged.

"I don't know. I think I'll go to Nicole's for a coffee. Wanna come?"

"No, I can't."

The bell rang then and the locker bay swarmed with students rushing to their lockers or hurrying to class holding Duo-Tangs to their chests, calling out to each other. Lily moved with the flow of bodies heading towards the hall where her math class was. She looked back to wave at Grace, but she had lost sight of her in the crowd.

By the time the recess bell rang, the temperature had dropped and flakes of snow were falling onto the schoolyard. Not the big downy flakes of a first snow but the small icy flakes that could easily turn into freezing rain. The end-of-winter snow kind of flakes.

The sky was grey now without a hint of sun, a solid grey, metal.

Curtis ran outside onto the playground looking for Jeremy. He ran to the swings where they usually played. It was hard for Curtis to find his friend because Jeremy was wearing another coat too. Curtis knew that Jeremy's winter coat was blue with red stripes on the sleeves, but he didn't know what his friend looked like in his other jacket, his new, lighter one. He looked around, putting his hands in his pockets. It was cold. His nose had started to run and the tips of his ears hurt. He looked up at the top of the slide and walked around the swings to the monkey bars, then looked over at the field where the older kids were playing soccer. Maybe Jeremy was playing soccer.

The wind, caught in the space between the swings and the

slide, gusted around him, sending shivers down his back and raising goosebumps on his arms. He watched the kids play soccer and was about to turn when he began to watch the ball instead, kicked up higher than usual, white against the low grey sky. He followed its arc to the ground, where it landed near the sidewalk. Curtis took a step back when he realized that it had landed near the man's feet.

The wind whipped tears from his eyes; his hands were small knots of cold in his pockets. He ran clumsily into the wind back to the building and stood with his back to the wall as far away as he could be from the car, which he saw now was parked where it hadn't been parked for months; as far away as he could be from the man who had stood on the sidewalk and watched him and was now bending for the ball, talking to a couple of the boys who had run to kick it back into the game. He remembered the man had touched his shoulder and he could feel now where his hand had been. Each memory of fingertip pulsed on him, burned.

Curtis finally spotted Jeremy lying on his back near the slide. He looked over at the man talking to the boys playing soccer and then back at Jeremy. He ran to his friend, looking over at the man every few seconds.

"Jeremy, get up, the bell is going to ring. Come wait with me at the wall."

Jeremy opened an eye and peered up at his friend.

"Shh, Curtis, I'm dead, I can't move. Robert M. shot me twice."

Curtis felt panicky. He didn't like to be standing in the open where the man could see him, but he didn't want the man to see his friend either.

"C'mon Jeremy."

Jeremy sat up, exasperated. "Curtis, I'm dead. I can't go over to the wall if I'm dead."

Curtis stood by him for as long as he could, then ran back to the safety of the school wall and as far away as he could be from the man and his car.

By the time recess was over and the bell rang Curtis was cold all the way through. The snow was whirling around him, the wind whistling up his sleeves, into his ears. He got in line, turning his back to the street, and climbed the concrete stairs into the building, where he sat at his desk and coloured in a barn with grinning chicks and ducks and he shivered so hard, he coloured outside of the lines like a baby.

Les held the soccer ball up to his chest and watched the boys' eyes follow it. He held it there as he spoke.

"Pretty good kick. Which one of you fellas kicked the ball so hard?" He grinned congenially. Charmingly. Get them talking about themselves, he thought, talking about their interests. He lowered the ball and felt the heat of their gaze in his groin.

"Mitchell kicked it. Can we have our ball back, mister?"

Les looked down at the boy who had answered him. The boy looked back at him defiantly. Too old, Les thought, and tossed the idea of him back overboard like a fish that was too small, a sunfish not worth cleaning. He looked at the other two boys in front of him while he rolled the ball slowly across himself.

"Can we have our ball back?" The boy looked at him even more brazenly this time.

The cheeky little bugger, Les said to himself, and ignored him.

"Do you fellas like soccer? Have you ever heard of Pelé? I used to coach soccer myself, I could show you a few tricks. I used to be pretty handy with the old soccer ball." Les bounced the ball off his arm and tried to head it but missed. The older boy scoffed and grabbed the ball mid-air, then turned and ran back to the game. The other two boys followed.

Les watched them run. They were wearing thin spring coats and their shoes squelched in the mud. He closed his eyes for a moment, oblivious to the snow landing on his face, in his hair, his lashes. Soon, he thought, it would be warm and there'd be no school. He opened his eyes and watched them all run towards the building when the bell rang. Soon there'd be no bell to lure them all away from him.

He walked back to his car warmed by the prickled heat of impatience. If that older boy hadn't been with them— He let himself wander through what might have happened, how he could've shown the young fellas where to kick the ball, holding their feet and helping them balance on one leg. He thought about their legs. He looked at himself in the rear-view mirror and smiled serenely. He could wait. And there was always that younger one, the one he had touched. Les had pressed his fingers into the boy until he had felt the smooth curve of his bone. He had left his mark. He had written Les McIntyre just by touching him. There was always him, he thought, Curtis.

Les drove into his driveway. Lady barked. The dog was tied up in the backyard and had wound the rope around the crabapple tree in the yard so tightly that it was lying down near the trunk.

"Useless dog," Les muttered, and its tail thumped happily. He walked heavily into the backyard, carefully navigating around the dog shit. He yanked Lady up by the collar and started pulling her around the tree. The dog backed away from him and he raised his hand as if to hit it. It blinked and looked up at him from the corners of its eyes, and he continued to pull it, dragging the dog and lifting it and cursing it around the tree until the rope was untangled and it was free. It sat looking up at him, its tail thumping, until he left it there and went into the house.

The dog barked when it heard the door close and then found something on the ground to paw and sniff at. It walked around the tree, sniffing at the base, and continued walking until the rope was wound tightly around the trunk again. It lay back down on the ground, its head next to the trunk, chewing something it had nosed up, and it waited, watching the house, the side door, for movement.

*　　*　　*

Les went into the living room and turned on the TV. He watched a game show for a while but got up restlessly, pacing back and forth in front of the television set. He felt coiled and irritated. The phone rang and he went into the kitchen, glad for the distraction.

"Hello." He listened. "No, I'm not interested." He paused again. "Listen, buddy, I told you, I'm not interested." He scowled as he listened and then barked into the phone: "Don't you tell me about driveway sealers, I know more about sealers than you could learn in a lifetime." His face reddened and he began to pace the short distance that the phone cord allowed him. "I don't care if my driveway cracks, I'll fix the goddamn thing myself. I used to seal driveways for a living, and I could tell you a thing or two about the business, so don't try to con me with that bullshit. You picked the wrong number to dial!" Les hung up the phone so hard that the plastic memo board hanging beside it fell to the floor. He kicked it out of his way and went back in to the living room.

Jerry let himself in the back door of his house. His mother and Dellie were sleeping on the couch, so he stood quietly by the sink in the kitchen, eating a slice of bread and a banana. When he had finished, he leaned over the sink and looked up at the morning sky through the window. The sun through the trees looked pale and the clouds he could see were grey, heavy. Snow, he thought. He opened the fridge and took out the carton of milk, poured it straight into his mouth and then closed the fridge door quietly. He sat and laced up his boots and took down his parka, which was hanging on one of the hooks by the door, and went back out.

When Grace got home after school, the dog was still outside, still wound around the tree. It blinked fast when Grace reached down to undo the clasp of the rope. She walked to the house, hunched down, holding onto the dog, urging it to go with her. The dog scrabbled to its place under the kitchen table and dolefully watched Grace take off her shoes and hang up her jacket. The loud, tinny sound of her father's big band music blared from the living room, and Grace went in, shouting over it for him to turn it down.

"Jesus Christ, you've gone and wrecked the tape on me." Les was sitting in front of the stereo with his records strewn around him and a small microphone masking-taped to its stand on the coffee table. He lifted the arm on the record player and the music stopped.

"I was on the last song too, and you had to clodhopper your way in here and ruin the whole goddamn thing."

Grace looked at her father incredulously. "What are you doing?"

"For your information, missy, this here is a technological age and your dad is keeping up with the times. I bought myself this little tape recorder and I'm taping all of my records so I'll have them on audio cassette as well. Right now I'm taping"—he leaned over and picked up the record cover, squinting to read it—"'the Big Band Sound of The Rolling Stones.' See, I'm not the square you thought I was, am I? And that number you just ruined was called"—he scanned the list of songs—"'Paint It Black.'" He looked over at the cassette player by his knees, ran his finger over the play and record buttons and then looked back at Grace. "This little microphone picks up everything, so would you mind piping down so I can finish this recording?"

Grace watched him press the rewind button, leaning over the machine, his tongue out, looking to see the counter in the top right-hand corner. He pressed the stop button forcibly and then pressed play and sat back, impressed. The music that started playing sounded muffled and far away. Les pressed rewind again and again until he found the end of the last song. He rearranged the microphone, straightening the wire, and then with two fingers and his thumb ceremoniously pressed the play and record and pause buttons. He looked up at Grace smugly. "Didn't think your old man had what it takes, did you?"

After supper she went back up to her room and took out a small plastic bag from her pocket. She unwrapped and then swallowed a small blue pill and waited, studying her wallpaper, the columns of flowers and the poems she had copied and taped onto her wall. A small blue pill that contained all the suitcases she'd need, her boarding pass, her ticket to get away. She straightened her legs and stretched her arms over her head. The guy she had bought the acid from this morning had said it would be a really mellow trip. She didn't care what kind of trip it would be; a trip meant leaving and that's all she wanted now. Even Gary had figured out that much.

She had never done acid, had been afraid to before, but now she had nothing to lose. Her mother was always cleaning or sitting slouched in her chair watching TV and crocheting. Her father spent most of his time in his workshop pounding away at a cabinet he'd been making forever. Now his tape recorder would be plugged in and blaring "Satisfaction."

Grace felt herself shudder when she thought about Les, his incessant sobbing and then abrupt anger. Today was the first time he had seemed interested in something other than being the grieving father. The wailing, simpering father. The tool. His two latest diversions were the tape recorder and the snow blower, which he had bought last week and now sat in the shed covered in plastic. He read the weather reports with a passion, panting for snow so he could show all those French buggers what he was made of, they wouldn't look down their snouts at him any more, not once they got a load of his ten-horsepower machine with its serrated auger and steel chute. They'd all want to know him then, he had told Grace, with their driveways full of snow, shovelling half the day, having heart attacks left, right and centre while he sat inside watching TV, nice and warm and relaxed.

She had held the blue pill up to the ceiling and had toasted snow blowers and Mr. Clean and tape recorders and doilies before swallowing it. Her life was fucked. She knew this. Jerry was the one small light she had of hope. Her parents were fucked. Her mother had used so much bleach in the past few weeks, it was a miracle she wasn't bleached to the bone. Her father slobbered that he was a broken man. Whether he was beseeching God for all the troubles that had been sent his way or was cursing Canadian Tire for the pathetic job it did at writing instructions, Les slobbered. Grace closed her eyes. She could hear him cough downstairs. He always coughed as if his lungs were banging on his chest to get out, then he'd clear his throat and get up and gob in the toilet or into his handkerchief. Grace shook her head. She had to get out.

She looked around her room again, testing her vision for hallucinations, for the straight lines of the windowsill and blind to curve the way she had heard that lines moved. Nothing. Maybe she'd been ripped off.

She took the stairs two at a time and went by the living room without slowing down.

"Where do you think you're going?" Les leaned out of his chair.

"Out." She hadn't heard him come up from the basement and looked quickly at him, at his grey sweatsuit and plaid slippers, his hair full of sawdust.

"Do you have any idea what time it is? No daughter of mine is going to go out at all hours of the night." Les leaned back into his chair as if the matter was settled. The theme music for "Hawaii Five-O" was playing loudly on the television and strangely it gave Grace courage.

"I'll go out if I want to." She felt a brazen surge of release like a wave and surfed it, feeling like Jack Lord with a mystery to solve and the whole island of Hawaii before her. Fuck you, she almost said out loud.

Les lunged out of his chair, red-faced and choking. His arm was raised as if he was going to backhand her.

"Oh, so now you're going to hit me? You are such a fucking loser." Book 'em, Danno, Grace almost added, and giggled to herself. She went into the kitchen and grabbed her jacket from the hook. The dog's tail was wagging, hitting the kitchen floor under the table rhythmically. A snare-drum beat, Grace thought as she slammed the door behind her, a jazzy swish that said *leave, leave, leave,* so she did. She didn't slow down on the driveway, didn't turn back to see if her father was going to chase after her, but walked to the street and turned down it, facing the parked cars and weeping willows. The light that fell from the lamp posts fell in diamonds, shards of glass that shined iridescent. She wanted to paste them to her skin like jewels, gems of street light glittering on her body. The theme song from the television show had come outside with her and made her walk with determination as if she had a mission, a dead body to see and the whole Pacific Ocean behind her. Book 'em, Danno, she thought again, book 'em all, and then she surfed the street. When she looked up at a street light, the halo of light was revolving like a disco ball. "*Bon voyage,*" she whispered to herself and headed to the centre of town, to the McDonald's and the clumps of French kids who would see her shimmering with street light. They'd notice her, they'd whisper, *C'est qui, cette fille là?* and she would pretend that she didn't hear them and would walk through the town as if she belonged to it, as if it was hers. Her town. She'd sit down on a bench and when one of the French kids finally got up the courage to sit with her, Grace would speak French fluently. *Je suis bilingue,* she'd announce. *Je me souviens.*

Rave had been walking, hands in pockets, legs stretching out as far as they could go. He was thinking about his muscles, how he wished he was made of them. He jumped over a narrow garden that bordered the yard he was walking through. He had to stick to backyards now. Ralph was out and had followed him for a while. That's all he had been doing lately. Following Rave, staying close behind and following him. Relentless. Or he'd park in front of Grace's, waiting. Rave wished Ralph would just get out of the car and face him once and for all. He had turned and looked at Ralph, a look, he had thought, that would get Ralph out of the car and onto the road, but Ralph had just stared and said something to the guy who drove him around. Rave watched them laugh and then he left the road for backyards.

He slipped between a metal shed and a fence, jumped a hedge and was soon in Grace's neighbourhood. He had the sense that she was something wild. That if he got too close too fast, she'd bolt. And there was a current of anger below her surface that he could see in her eyes, but only for seconds, like when the stream ran clear and he could see each rock, each pebble and weed. Then she'd cloud over; her eyes would change and the anger would be gone. She was wild in those moments, though. He knew she would do anything when she was feeling that way.

She had told him about getting lost, how she used to get lost once a week in Miracle Mart when she was younger. She had used the department signs hanging from the ceiling the same way he used backyards and trees to figure out his way around. She could always find her father, she had said, in the aisle that bordered the tool and toy departments. She told him later of getting lost in Saint-Hubert, of hitchhiking because she had wanted to run away. The driver who had picked her up spoke French and finally dropped her off at a Dunkin' Donuts, where she sat and drank coffee and watched a plow clear the parking lot. Lost, she had said, turning to him, I've been lost a lot.

He wished he had said then what was in his heart, that he'd always be her compass if she wanted him to be, that he'd be the one thing she could count on, the one thing that would stay in its place, that she could use as a landmark. Constant. He'd be her tree so that she could gauge how far away she was and how much farther she had to go. He knew the whole town inside out, he had a mountain where he knew she'd feel at home, but she hadn't given him a chance. She had changed the subject quickly and asked him about Curtis and how often Jerry visited him, and he had told her, looking into her eyes, hoping she'd know anyway, that she'd feel what was radiating from him whenever she came close.

Rave had been right about the snow and was glad he had his parka. He jumped over the small hedge beside Grace's yard and stood in her backyard, then knelt to pat the dog that was caught around the tree. The dog cowered and wagged its tail. Rave coaxed it around the tree, whispering that it was a good dog. When it was free, the dog ran clumsily around and then back to Rave. It sat for a while, head cocked, watching him, and then began to dig. Grace's window was dark. The whole back of the house was dark except for a light in the kitchen. Maybe she was sleeping, he thought, and watched for a while, the dog pulling at the bottom of his jeans. He bent and patted it again and then walked away, turning to look back at the house every few steps.

Grace stared across the street at the McDonald's sign. The large yellow M was oozing and pulsing and no one else seemed to notice. Lots of kids were out walking but they were all hunched over, talking to each other urgently as if something was about to happen, something big. She was afraid to cross the street. Headlights of the passing cars left light streaming behind. She heard a hum from the street lights. The electric charge of hydro poles and street lights must be like an electric fence, keeping the whole town corralled in, she thought. That's why she couldn't leave Beaumont if she wanted to. She needed to talk, to warn everyone of the hum she heard. She thought of Jerry and then of Lily and Curtis and Dellie. They were worth saving. She turned and began walking to their house. The sidewalk reared up once in a while like waves. And she couldn't cross any streets so she had to plan a route using the same side of the road. Her jaws were clenched and her heart hammered quickly. When she finally turned onto their street, she had to walk to the end of the cul-de-sac to get on the right side of their road.

The house was in darkness. Grace's legs felt wooden. She sat down on the fender of the car that was still up on blocks and rolled up one leg of her jeans and poked herself. Flesh. Her finger sent bolts of lightning up her leg. Lightning. She sat up quickly. Gary. She thought of how her brother used to poke her in the back seat of the car when they were young, and the time in the car he had to hold a curtain rod on the way home, crying quietly during a thunderstorm. Their father had cursed them, telling them that they were safe from the lightning because they were in the car. She had been seven so Gary must have been ten or eleven. The curtain rod was much way too long and stretched from the back seat out the front window. Gary was in charge of holding them up. The metal poles rested beside his neck, on his shoulder. The thunder was the loudest she had ever heard, and by the time they got home, they were both hysterical. Cowards, Les had called them and had left them there in the car on the driveway, fed up with them and their goddamn fear of death, he had said.

She looked behind her as if she could see through Lily's house, past the backyard and woods to the winding train tracks. She could hear her eyes focus and opened her mouth, realizing that she had been holding her breath. Fucking Les. Those rods extended way past where the curtains ended. He would end up, he had hollered, his face red, spit spraying from his mouth, with a family that only sees that the rod is too long and not that the curtains are too small.

It must have been close to here. Jerry had said that he had found Gary on the way to his house. She stood up, her jeans still rolled on one leg, and walked up the path that led around the house. The backyard was dark and green. She could taste the pine trees and the air seemed cooler. There was a body she'd been sent to investigate, like Jack Lord. She had a mission. There was a way into the woods, a path that Jerry never had any trouble finding. "You never know you're on it until you're on it," he had said. She whispered his words, hoping they'd be a flashlight, a small beacon showing her the way through the woods to the tracks. And then she was standing a few feet into the brush with a crooked, narrow path before her, winding its way into the trees. She followed it, not afraid of the darkness. The roots and branches seemed more embracing than menacing, and the humming had stopped. This is the way, she thought, this is the way to escape the town. She walked through the trees, warmed by their creaking, their movement in the night air. She felt like part of them, the same species. She raised her arms and stopped for a moment. She wanted to blend in.

Too soon the woods ended. Sounds from the highway outside of town broke through her thoughts. Cars drove by fast. There was more litter on the ground now as well. She kicked through chip bags and yellowed newspapers and long, brittle grass until she was standing in the brief clearing between the woods and the tracks. She knew that she'd have to walk down them, would have to use the tracks as a channel to her brother's spirit. She didn't think that the guy who had sold her the blue pill was right, that it was mellow acid. She didn't even think "acid" any more. She was beyond that. The dry protest of breaking grass, the long, thin sound of cars and the scar of train tracks, was real, more real than they actually were. Emblematic. Magic. And like someone on a pilgrimage, she accepted her path, she went forth on her mission that was at once holy and absurd. She went forth with the pounding music of a cop show set in Hawaii and her brother drumming on her heart. She went forth wanting to see her brother.

*   *   *

The night sky held some light from a city miles away and the strand of light posts were lit along the highway. Grace looked up. Above her the sky was dark but its edges were a pale purple. The colour that suited all the bare-limbed trees the best, she decided, and breathed the night in deeply. Briefly she wondered what the weather had been like the night Gary walked these tracks. She believed weather was a talisman on birthdays, a prediction of how the year ahead would be. Some-one told her when she was younger, someone at a birthday party, that if the weather was bad, you weren't meant to be born. At the time she had scoffed at the idea, but it had stayed with her. It had rained on her last three birthdays.

She began walking east on the track, towards Le Bertin. Gary was probably coming home from the bar that night, she figured, and she concentrated on calling him, beckoning his spirit the way she used to during seances at sleepovers in grade school. "Gary," she called quietly, "come to me." And at first she felt as if she was back in the fifth grade, sitting around with her friends, eyes closed and whispering urgently, but then something changed, her voice left her lips and blossomed into wings. She watched it fly the unhurried flight of a bird gaining sky. And in its wake, a stillness. She could hear everything then, the soft earth clasping at reeds, the reeds silver and wispy. She heard herself breathe and felt her feet solid on the ground. Slowly she began to walk the tracks, not calling her brother, not even needing to form his name in her mind. He was here, she felt. He was part night, part earth and part grass, surround-ing her. She didn't realize she was crying until the air hit the trails her tears had made. She stepped on each railroad tie, walking slowly, and each time she touched the track, she knew she was getting closer.

It was as if she had boarded a train, had picked her seat next to a window, taken her book from her bag and her sweater. It was as if she had covered her knees with her cardigan and sunk back into the upholstered train seat with a good story in her hands and a one-way ticket. She didn't have to think about where she was going, didn't have to plan the destination time—she just had to travel. So Grace walked towards the purple edge of sky, readying herself for what she'd see, how she'd feel, who'd be there to meet her.

She followed the track as it curved with the land. On her right, a creek, an embankment and then the highway; on her left, the woods. This seemed right to her. She held her hands out, cupped to both, traffic and trees. She thought of a picture of St. Francis, with his outstretched hands, his birds, on one of the prayer cards left behind, and walked more slowly now. Around the bend she stopped. Before her was Le Bertin. She could make out the building, its neon martini glass sign. Between her and the bar was the black bridge. She looked over to the highway and saw traffic lights, a car stopped signalling a turn; she looked left at the woods and saw that the trees had stopped and there was only brush. All these were signs, all these were solemn and dignified to Grace. The bushes were thorned, adorned with old plastic bags and paper. The bridge was made up of black metal and rivets, formal and serious in the street light. She watched the car turn and leave the highway, drive over the bridge and slowly head into town. She felt her knees give and fell to them, bent her forehead to the tracks and then turned her head, pressing her ear to the ground to listen. And she thought she could hear the heaving of earth beneath her, the settling noises it must make at night. She listened for her brother, for what he wanted to tell her. That he had to do what he did, that he hadn't meant to hurt her, to leave her alone. She felt herself melt into an enormous ear, each finger splayed on the metal tracks, a device, a receptor. Her knees bent, her legs all poised to receive. Slowly the sounds of traffic, the rubbing sound of the dead bulrushes, left her. She was bowed before the bridge that led into town and out of town and all she could hear was her own heart beating. It was making its way into her outflung arms, cradled into the ear that was pressed into the ground. She could feel its pulse behind her closed eyes. And that was all she could hear, that was all the track was willing to give her. Her own heart beating her name: *Grace, Grace, Grace*. All it gave her was what she already had. Herself.

She slowly opened her eyes and rolled over onto her back, exhausted. One by one stars twinkled at her until the whole sky seemed to be looking kindly down at her lying there on the railway tracks. Like a fairy godmother, she thought. She got up and faced the bridge one more time, reverently and then she turned and headed back to town the long way, the way she had come. Alone.

Lily stared down at the encyclopedia on her bed. She didn't want to open it. She pushed her glasses up and pulled her pillow up between her and her bedroom wall. She took the cap off her pen and then recapped it. She was disturbed by how her dreams were becoming alphabetical, how the entries she copied during the day trailed after her in her sleep. She gloomily opened the book to the page she had marked. She had never realized how many things started with the letter *D*. *Dunbar; Duncan—See Macbeth*. Entries like *See Macbeth* thrilled Lily. She was slowing down, she should have been on *F* by now. She had even started making up cross-references herself: *Duncan, Isadora—See Dance*.

That was what it felt like now, gathering all this information. Everything relied on something else to be defined, and she was starting to believe she'd never know anything, that she had started a wild goose chase and didn't know how to end it. Sometimes she skipped entries altogether, entries she knew that no one would ever need, people long dead or industrial terms. She squinted down at the page she was on. Duncan, Isadora (1877–1927). She quickly did the math. She'd been fifty when she died. Lily stopped when she read about the dancer's scarf getting caught in the wheel of her car and strangling her. It struck Lily as being both a glamorous and a tragic way to die. She wondered where Isadora was driving to, whom she was meeting. She imagined her speeding with the urgency of desperately wanting to see whoever was waiting for her, whoever made her feel glorious enough to recklessly throw her scarf over her shoulder the way Lily knew she had. Glamorous. Lily felt her own neck and then pushed her slipped glasses back up and leaned on her pillow. Isadora Duncan. The name sounded so luxurious. Isadora. She stretched it out, wanting to be called Isadora. Just once. Isadora Duncan. The name danced, pliéd across Lily's mind wrapped in sheer white tulle. It pirouetted and stretched gracefully from her tongue. Isadora.

"Lily," her father called from the hallway. "It's getting late."

She grunted. Lily. Lily Duncan. Lily Isadora Duncan Evans. Tragic. She sighed and looked at the next entry. *Duncan, John Charles. Astronomer.* She looked up to her ceiling for a moment and then wrote *See Sky*. Next was *Duncan, city.* She didn't hesitate this time and wrote *See Oklahoma.* That was the trick, she thought, go to the source.

"Lily, turn out your light, it's too late for you to be up." Her father opened her door. "C'mon, Lil, give your brain a rest. Get some sleep." He strode over and marked her place before closing the encyclopedia, then put it and her notebook and pen on her night table. He leaned over and kissed her on the forehead. "G'night, Lil. Pleasant dreams."

"Good night." She took off her glasses and laid them carefully on her night table, then turned and faced the wall. "Where's Mom?"

Stan looked back at his daughter from the doorway and sighed. "She's trying to finish a drawing she started. Doesn't want the idea to get away from her. She'll be up later to tuck you all in."

"Oh. Goodnight."

Lily heard her father close the door quietly behind him. She closed her eyes and tried picturing herself in a sports car driving fast and hard, her scarf whipping in her face. Who was she driving to? Who was she running red lights and stop signs for? She never did anything but copy from the encyclopedia. It had taken over her life alphabetically. Lily opened her eyes. Her room was dark. She could make out the window and the small desk under it. She knew by heart what was on her wall. A drawing her mother had done of her when she was ten. She had liked herself in it, the way she was looking. Feisty, her mother had said. Beside it, a poster of dolphins and a poster of a sunset with a poem about setting something you love free and how it might come back and how it might not.

Lily didn't dream of Isadora that night the way she had hoped to. Instead the dancer stayed offstage. Even while Lily dreamt about climbing stairs, of the endless hallway at the top of them and all the doors she knew she had to open, she had the feeling that something was missing, and the more she felt that, the more agitated she became in her dream. She felt herself sweat at the exertion of climbing the stairs, of opening each door quickly, hoping to catch a glimpse of whatever it was that was just ahead of her. She woke up the next morning feeling as if someone had leaned over her bed all night and whispered *thirst* into her ear and *heat*, and she wasn't sure what she was really thirsty for or how she could be quenched. Reading about something wasn't enough, she was beginning to realize.

All over town the tight-fisted buds on branches began to unclasp. Birdsong began early in the morning and was at a fever pitch by the time the sun was fully up. Lawns began to look green, and on the weekends people began to come outside and walk their properties, looking for what damage winter might have caused.

Potholes and large cracks tore up the town's streets, and town workers in their orange uniforms drove around now with a truck full of tar and pylons to direct traffic around them while they worked, patching up, smoothing out winter from the roads. Street cleaners drove close to curbs, their huge brushes turning mightily, sweeping up dirt and litter, leaving a clean trail that children filled, following the slow-moving truck on their bicycles as if it was the beginning of some sort of town parade heralding the coming of spring. Squirrels ran fearlessly across the tops of fences, tightroping their way into the trees with the bird feeders. They'd watch the town slowly move more outdoors and their cheeks would bulge with seed intended for chickadees, cardinals and finches. Occasionally someone would catch a squirrel boldly scooping the seed from a feeder and would run outside in slippers, waving a broom at it to frighten it away. Then that person would stand outside in wonder, the broom and squirrel forgotten, amazed at the warmth of the sun, the clean smell of green growth, and feel more cheerful, sympathetic even to the small squirrel's antics, and decide to put peanuts on the grocery list to feed it.

Kids were outside early, turning over rocks for startled salamanders, riding their bikes over the long worms that lay ribboned on driveways and sidewalks, hollering for each other to come play. *"Come play!"* they'd yell up into the sky. *"Viens jouer!"*

The town workers busied themselves with paving over winter, cleaning the streets, and when that was done they'd work on getting ready for summer. They'd turn over the earth in the blocks of gardens dug into the medians of land that divided the main streets into two. Barrels would be rolled out of storage and soon be filled with geraniums and petunias and placed on street corners. There were hanging baskets to be filled and hung from street lights, and picnic tables to be hauled out and put in front of the small café and the ice cream shop. Soon they'd drive big-barrelled garbage cans up to the first clearing on the foot of the mountain and they'd hammer together a small stage. St. Jean Baptiste Day in June. A day when the whole town would walk up to the mountain, get fleurs-de-lys painted on their cheeks, eat corn on the cob and sit on blankets. The teenagers would cart cases of beer and hide them behind trees. By the time the fireworks went off, they'd be drunk, paired up with someone English or French. It didn't matter, Molson or Labatts had a way of translating language into hips and hands, into lips, into nonverbal *yes*es, into understood *oui*s.

The town workers' job was to keep the town running as each season moved through it. Their job was a routine; each fall was the same, each spring. The men considered themselves a team and had nicknames for each other. *Le vieux. L'anglais.* They knew the town the way they knew their cars, how some sewers would back up with too much rain, which trees were dying, and they took care of the town as if it was theirs.

Curtis loved his bike. His father had bought it from someone at work and had brought it home a few nights ago. Curtis had watched his dad take off the training wheels and replace the old split seat with a brand-new sparkly banana seat. He watched him clamp a bicycle bell onto the handlebars and felt the bell's trill in his tummy when his dad tried it out. The bike was red. Curtis loved the colour red. He had just switched his favourite colour from green to red only days before his dad had brought the bike home. He followed his dad outside, waited for him to check the air in the tires, and then swung up onto it. The handlebars gleamed and caught the reflection of his dad bending over him, smiling. Curtis shyly pulled the bell back and let it ring. His feet felt for the pedals and he pushed down and started gliding down the driveway with his dad jogging behind, holding him and then letting him go. He fell and tried again. He rode, balanced for a moment, teetered and then fell. He rode into the memory of what it had felt like to stay upright for that moment, and soon that moment grew. Pedal, he urged his feet, steering into what it had felt like. He coasted, wobbled and then he fell. After several attempts with his father running behind him, Curtis turned onto the street and pedalled hard, riding through puddles. The wheels made a whirring sound that seemed to say *faster, faster.* He rode to the end of the cul-de-sac, passing the few houses between his and the woods. He wobbled and steered his way through every puddle, and when he got to the end of the street where the pavement melted into grass, he realized he couldn't stop and drove right into the brush and fell over.

Stan showed his son how the brakes worked, how to move the pedals backwards to stop the bike, and Curtis could do it when the bike was still, when he sat on it to show his father he understood. But when he was pedalling, when the wind lifted his hair from his ears and whistled *hurry, hurry* to him and his legs were pumping and his eyes were full of windy speed and passing driveways, he couldn't do it and always ended up turning too abruptly and falling over or riding past where he wanted to go, trapped until the bike exhausted itself. When Curtis was riding, he just couldn't stop.

Dellie liked following him. She'd ride the old tricycle, her feet sometimes sliding off the pedals, and would wail when he got too far ahead of her: "Wait for me, Curtis, you got to wait for me."

Curtis heard these words fleetingly. They lingered briefly and then floated up with the crows that flew into the woods and then back into town. Curtis couldn't wait for her if he tried. He pedalled hard and would coast off the road onto the grass, sometimes slowing to a stop before the edge of trees and sometimes falling over. Once he rode right into a tree.

Another sign of spring besides the road crew truck and the street cleaning truck was the ice cream truck—Monsieur Cornet and the seductive chimes he would play driving slowly through neighbourhoods coaxing children from backyards and games of tag. Follow me, the music from his truck would persuade, ice cream, *crème glacée.* The truck sounded like the soft swirls he'd wind onto a cone. Painted on its panel were giant cones covered in dripping hot fudge or rainbow sprinkles. Lists of sundae toppings were printed in French: *ananas, cerise, chocolat.* The words would elicit pangs of hunger in the children old enough to read them, and crowds of younger children listened to the list, enraptured by the sounds of it. Please, they'd beg their parents, please can I buy ice cream? and would break down into tears of desperation at the sound of the truck leaving.

If they were lucky, they'd come back out of their houses holding onto quarters that their dads had fished out of pockets, their mothers had dumped out of change purses, and then they'd run as fast as they could, their younger siblings behind them at their mercy, hoping they'd split the money fairly. There was always a line, queuing from the front of the truck to the grumbling exhaust in the back where Monsieur Cornet stood, stooped, serving soft ice cream through the doors that opened halfway up, the lower parts of the door forming a sort of counter.

Monsieur Cornet was everything ice cream wasn't. He was hairy and cranky and the hand that he held out cupped for the money was a short and knuckled hand with thick gold rings and dirty nails. He was always sweaty and looked more like ice cream that had been dropped, picked up and cried over, bits of gravel and grass and dirt embedded in it, inedible.

And he didn't speak English. Or he didn't like speaking English and would serve the English kids with distaste, not looking at them or offering any help when they tried stammering out their order. Sometimes he wouldn't stop his truck, would just drive through his route quickly, not even slowing down.

Curtis was terrified of him. He'd hear the alluring tinkle announcing the truck and would pedal home, fall over in his driveway, get up and run into his house to beg, cajole, plead for money for ice cream, just like every other kid on the street. He wasn't very good at begging so he'd wait for Dellie to do the talking and then his mother or Lily or his dad would ask if he wanted some ice cream too. Then he'd stand in his driveway, the coins already hot in his hand, and try to get his nerve up to approach the truck.

Monsieur Cornet had hair hanging from his nostrils, curling around his ear. It was as if he was stuffed with hair and it was poking out everywhere. But the ice cream was so creamy and sweet, the cone soggy with melted ice cream pooled in its base.

"C'mon Curtis, let's get some ice cream, this is really important to me." Dellie pulled at his shirt impatiently. He looked down at his sister and thought hard. If he brought Dellie with him, he might feel safer, and he started walking down his driveway with Dellie clumping in his old cowboy boots behind him. They were the last in line. Dellie pranced up and down, singing, "Ice cream, ice cream, I'm going to get some ice cream." Older kids laughed at her and pointed to her boots, but she didn't notice. She ran to the beginning of the line and then back to Curtis.

"We're going to get some ice cream, aren't we, Curtis?"

Curtis glumly nodded. Monsieur Cornet had just chased some kids away who didn't have enough money. *"Va-t-en!"* he had yelled, shaking an empty cone at them. The line moved forward and Curtis stalled, then stepped up when Dellie pushed him. He wished he was on his bike, pedalling hard down the street, the sound of loose gravel and dirt crunching under his tire. The line moved again. He turned back and looked at his bike leaning on its stand in the driveway, the sun glinting speedily off its fenders. He moved again with the line to the truck. Dellie had parked her tricycle beside his bike. She had turned it on its side so it leaned the same way his did. Dellie was such a copycat, Curtis thought.

He looked up; they were next in line. His empty hand could almost imagine the cold curve of handlebar, the round top of his bell. Dellie pushed him forward when it was their turn, and Curtis looked up into Monsieur Cornet's nose and froze. Dellie looked at her brother and back up at the man in the truck and then yelled: "We want some ice cream!" And then she peeled back Curtis's fingers from the coins he was clenching and handed them up to the man. Curtis stayed spellbound, frozen at the sight of Monsieur Cornet's scowl, and felt the same way he had felt when he was riding right towards the tree, right before he hit it and then fell off his bike. Dellie handed him his cone, took hers and then pulled Curtis away from the truck.

"That's good ice cream, eh, Curtis?" She slurped at her cone, her lips and cheeks covered in soft ice cream.

Curtis put his tongue to the cone. It tasted cold and sweet. Creamy. He began to lick it earnestly and followed his little sister home.

Sheila stood at the kitchen sink waiting for it to fill. She looked out the window, wondering why the shed doors were open and where Les might be. The grass in the other yards was getting green and she noticed that the spot under the tree where the dog was tied was now bare dirt. Their yard always seemed the last to turn green. A stubborn mound of blackened snow had sat in the middle of the front yard until only a couple of weeks ago; the last snow on the entire street and it had been at her house.

She used to have a garden when they first moved in. Gladioli and lilies and annuals she bought in town. Four-packs of petunias, impatiens, pansies. Gary had been only about ten and he had wanted tomatoes and green beans, a vegetable garden he could help with. And Grace had planted sunflowers in the corner.

It was all lawn now. The flowers had lasted for two summers until Les had traded in the old lawn mower they had brought with them for a new, more powerful, hungrier model. Sheila shook her head, remembering how she would run out of the kitchen waving her tea towel at him to get his attention, to get him to stop pushing the mower right into her flowers. The long stalks of her glads at his feet, the stem of buds, blushed and promising with colour, and his look of defiance.

She wanted him to mow the lawn, didn't she? The flowers, he had claimed, were in his way.

She didn't want flowers any more anyway. They were such a bother and she had too much to do to worry about weeding or watering. She had enough on her shoulders keeping Les out of trouble. As long as she could see him, they'd be all right, she thought, gathering the glasses and mugs and slipping them into the water and scrubbing them.

Every year Les adjusted the blades on the mower and every year he mowed the lawn too close to the ground, leaving swirled blade marks and patches of brown, dried grass until their whole yard was a dull brown that he'd water, adjusting the sprinkler and cursing when it fanned onto him. She'd watch him sometimes from an upstairs window, pushing the sprinkler over, then getting caught in its rain, swearing and backing up out of its reach. Then he'd stand, polishing his glasses, and glare at the sprinkler as if it was the reason the grass was brown, as if it wasn't doing what it should be doing. It usually took him all summer to get the lawn back to being green and then the green lasted only a few weeks before the grass got caught up in the season and began to brown again. A losing battle, she thought.

Sheila pulled up the plug. She opened the window over the sink while she waited for the water to drain. The air from outside smelled sweet; the sounds of children playing, of crows and dogs, came breezily in. For a moment Sheila listened to the birds. She closed her eyes and counted three different birdsongs until a loud, grating sound interrupted her. She opened her eyes and watched her husband wheel out his snow blower from the shed, pushing it heavily into the backyard. The noise was overwhelming. It chugged out black smoke and sputtered, making Les brace his feet before taking another step. The dog was crouched and pulling on its chain, worriedly trying to dig its claws in and pull free from the noise. Sheila could tell Les was pushing the snow blower with all of his strength, pushing it onto the lawn as if he could muscle his way through the birdsong and warm air back to winter. She slammed the window shut and busied herself with rinsing out the sink. He was completely out of sync with the time of year, she thought. He was still stuck in winter.

Grace stirred upstairs. The sound of something, the vacuum maybe, made its way under her door like wake-up gas. She sat up, immediately angry. Why couldn't her mother have waited to vacuum until Grace was up? She threw open her door and stomped downstairs. The living room and hallway were empty. She went into the kitchen. Her mother was at the sink.

"What's that noise?"

"Your father." Sheila gestured to the window with her head. Grace stood next to her, and they both watched Les turn the machine at the end of the yard and push it forward again as if he were clearing paths of high white snow and the whole backyard was a driveway.

Upstairs again, Grace tried to go back to sleep but couldn't. The drone of the snow blower kept plowing its way into her thoughts. It was the end of April, Grace wanted to scream down at him, there was no snow in the yard. She lay back on her bed and then turned to the pile of books next to it. She could read. She leaned over and read the titles: *To Kill a Mockingbird, A Tree Grows in Brooklyn, Nancy Drew*. Books she'd had forever, her small collection of favourites. A collection, she realized now, not of stories but of fathers. Atticus, Francie Nolan's dad, Johnnie, Carson Drew and his pipe and gentle teasing. Outside the snow blower stopped and silence rushed in to fill the big space the noise had left. Grace remembered racing through the parts about Jem and Dill, about Boo Radley, to get to Scout and Atticus on the porch, at the supper table. Then she would read slowly, savouring Atticus's lap, his newspaper, and Scout's sounding out the words until she could read. The solved mysteries were never as satisfying as when Carson Drew came home from work, calling out for his daughter Nancy, Johnnie Nolan's whistling up the stairs and Francie knowing her dad was home and rushing out into the hallway to greet him.

Grace knelt on her bed and moved over to the window, pulling up the blind so she could look down into the backyard. Her father was lugging a red gas canister back to the shed. She flinched, thinking of how he had laughed at her, mimicking her voice, asking: "Are you my mother?" She'd only been little, she thought, looking down at him. Was he her father? She felt her stomach sink. He was her father. *Restez calme.* She watched him set down the canister and pull out his handkerchief and blow his nose, then wipe his forehead with his sleeve. He had on a new track suit that Grace had never seen before. If she hadn't known him, if she'd been seeing him for the first time, she would have thought he looked regular enough. He had glasses and shortish hair. Nothing outlandish, nothing eccentric about the way he looked. She watched him return to the snow blower, unzip the pocket of his new windbreaker and pull out a key on a long leather key chain. She watched him put it in the ignition and turn it, starting up the snow blower again. Dirt flew up out of it and he pulled up goggles he was wearing around his neck, the big, square plastic goggles he used in his workshop. Then she watched him turn the snow blower and push it, digging in his heels at the weight of it. The dog had wound itself tightly around the tree and was now slouched down, watching Les miserably. The sun glinted off the red shininess of the snow blower; even the windowpane felt warm. The kids in the next yard over were blowing bubbles and chasing them. They were wearing shorts. She looked back down at her father making his way across the yard and then pulled down her blind. She decided to get some breakfast and then go out, go anywhere rather than stay here in this house. A house surrounded by drifts of blowing snow that only her asshole father could see.

Her mother's head was in the oven, and the smell of oven cleaner burnt Grace's nose when she went into the kitchen. She stood and watched her mother scrub, the back end of her body, the pale pink sweatpants and slippers, shaking with the effort. Grace couldn't bear the smell and the sight of her mother half in the oven, her thin legs in the bleach-splattered pants, the effort she was using to scrub. She hurried past her, hoping Sheila wouldn't hear her, and grabbed a banana on her way downstairs.

Quietly she opened the door to Gary's room, looked inside and then closed it. It didn't smell the same any more; it smelled of pine cleaner and room freshener. The trouble with the kind of trips Gary always took was that they had return tickets, they were two-way. They got him stoned enough to forget but then he had to wake up. Except for the last one, she thought, the last trip he took he hadn't looked back. But she didn't want to leave that way. She was moving her hope, dismantling it into small pieces and carrying them to Lily's house, holding them out to Jerry. And Jerry seemed to be a nest where she could store things. She told him things and he took them from her, kept them safe for her. She liked the way he looked at her, as if she was worth looking at. She wanted him to be her destination; she wanted to leave with a one-way ticket but she wanted to keep leaving, daily, and daily she wanted to arrive.

She took off the shirt of Gary's that she'd been wearing, let it slide off her body like water and pool around her feet, and then she stepped out from it. It wasn't hers to wear.

She went into the furnace room, over to her father's workbench. There was a small wooden cabinet with tiny drawers. Grace pulled one out. Each drawer was filled with feathers meticulously sorted. She thought of Lily and that entry about

Daedalus and his wings, how he had escaped his island. She pulled out a long beige feather with a turquoise tip. Les had used these when he used to tie flies. The feathers were lures. Bait. He used to tell her about all the fish he had caught in his day, the fight they had given him and how he had eventually pulled them out of the water and into his boat. He'd show her his *Field & Stream* medals pinned to an old hat. Each pin represented a fight, and each fight, a death. He'd brag about killing ducks, stalking deer in the woods and shooting them. He told her once that he had been chased by a bear and had outsmarted it. But feathers were things of hope too, she thought. There was something miraculous about flight, the effortless soaring of birds, the lifting from trees, the leaving.

Grace took out a few more feathers and put them in the pocket of the cardigan she was wearing. Later, she thought, she'd wear them in her hair. Lures for hope.

There were baby food jars of nails, of screws and nuts and bolts. He had put a pegboard on the wall and hung his tools. He had built them a coffee table with a cribbage game drilled into it. Her mother hated it because dust clogged the holes and it took her forever to clean them out with a toothpick. He was going to make a lot of money, he said, once people saw the craftsmanship of his work. When he was cutting the wood for the stereo cabinet he'd been working on, he had sliced off the top of three of his fingers on the table saw. He had come rushing upstairs holding his hand, blood spurting everywhere. No one else was home and Grace had to turn on the water and stand with him until he stopped bleeding, she had to bandage his hand up for him while he barked orders on how to wrap his fingers. Jesus Christ, he had screamed at her when she had dropped the gauze, what the hell do they teach you now at that goddamn school? What the hell are you good for? he had yelled.

Her mother had found bloodstains on every stair and had spent the night with a toothbrush and a bucket of water and bleach, scrubbing.

Grace nudged an upholstered chair leaning against his work table, a chair he had found on someone's lawn on garbage day, though he wouldn't admit that he had picked it out of the trash. It wobbled and nearly fell over. She leaned it back up. He insisted it had been put out for someone to take and there wasn't a damn thing wrong with it except that it didn't stand upright. Grace bent to look at the legs. He had attached three more on so now there were seven legs octopussing out from underneath the chair. It still didn't stand.

He had chisels and saws. A welding gun and all kinds of tapes. It was his workshop. He had a special vacuum for sawdust and water, he had a drill press. And everything had his name on it, that same spidery scrawl that was on everything upstairs as well. Les McIntyre, everything belonged to Les McIntyre. Grace took a few more feathers and left. Fuck Les McIntyre.

Eliza could hear Curtis and Dellie outside. Their voices rose above and around the other outdoor sounds that wafted through the open window. The house was filling with the smell of brownies baking. Stan was in the kitchen with Lily mixing icing for them. He was making up his own words to the songs on the radio that Lily had turned on, and Lily was hiccuping, she was laughing so hard. Eliza smiled and picked up the paper Stan had left by the chair. She had stopped reading newspapers and listening to the news reports on television when Dellie was born. They made her too upset. World hunger, poverty. They always left her feeling helpless and small. She glanced briefly at the headlines and felt that familiar clutch of worry in her stomach, so she put the paper back down and sat back. She could do laundry or she could finish that drawing she had started of the crocuses Curtis had brought in yesterday. If she waited too long, the petals would droop. Already the flowers would look different from the way they had looked last night, when she had begun to draw them. The laundry could wait, she figured.

There was something about the two crocuses and the way they fit in the old glass baby bottle. Their stems looked thick and sturdy through the glass. They didn't know they'd been cut from their bulb and were still doing their job of holding the blossoms up and feeding them. There were small air bubbles along the side of one stem and the word *Gerber* was caught in the green of them. She wanted to catch how the crocuses were opening, the movement of light through water, the texture of the glass and how it contained the water, the green of the stems. Maybe she'd need to paint them. Watercolour. Each of her sketches was a failure, coming close to her idea and then falling short. The failure kept her drawing, attempting over and over to capture what she saw, what those flowers were, what her children contained. She worked hard at it. It seemed important; it was required of her.

She heard Curtis's voice, his cry, and quickly got up, upsetting the bottle and sloshing water on the table. She rushed to the hall and out the front door. He was lying in the driveway, his bike on top of him. Eliza ran over and helped him untangle himself from the pedals.

"Are you okay, sweetie?"

He nodded and then examined his knees. Dellie rode up to them on her tricycle.

"It's 'cause Curtis doesn't know how to stop, Mommy. He falls down all day."

Eliza looked at her son. He had torn his jeans at the knee.

"Is that true, Curtis? Are you having a hard time stopping?"

Curtis nodded.

"I used to have the same problem. You want to know how I figured it out?"

Curtis looked up at his mother and nodded again.

"I just put my feet down. Have you tried that? My mom used to complain about how scuffed my shoes got, but I didn't fall down any more. You give it a try. I'd rather your shoes got scuffed up than your knees. Do you want to get back on and try?" Eliza held the bike for her son. Slowly he got on and started pedalling down the driveway and then put his feet down when he got to the road.

"Watch me, Mommy, I can ride my bike really fast, like this." Dellie put her head down low to her handlebars and started pumping her legs furiously. She stopped and looked back at her mother. Eliza gave her a thumbs-up and watched them both for a little while, riding up and down the road, and then went back inside to the crocuses.

Something she had seen in the newspaper stayed with Eliza. The headline that had asked, French or English signs? She quickly sketched in the shading around the vase, tried to translate the lush, dark purple of the petals and then went to the bookshelf in the corner of the living room and returned to her chair with a French/English dictionary that had been Jerry's. She flipped to the English words at the back and looked up *flower,* then copied *fleur* under her drawing. She wrote *flower* under that, then tore the sketch from her pad and set it against the jar. *Fleur.*

They'll all need to know both words now, she thought.

Grace headed to the mountain. She needed to see Jerry. He had a way of looking at her and calming her down. She didn't need to make him laugh, didn't have to worry about sounding fucked up. She could just tell him that she needed to get out, her father was snow blowing the backyard and her mother was cleaning the oven again, and the sunlight, the way it slanted in their living room, was shining on every piece of plastic draped on the furniture and around the lampshades, making the surfaces look like water and the doilies like lily pads. For a moment she had thought the living room looked lovely, but then her mother had come in and asked Grace what she was doing in there, she had just cleaned, and the water on the couch had glistened and frozen back up into plastic, the doilies had stiffened into winter, and could he just hold her again, the way he had at the rock.

She walked by driveways filled with chalk drawings. Hopscotch squares and drawings of long, crooked people. Kids were outside. One boy had coloured his driveway in with white chalk and was now standing at the curb looking up at it when she walked by. He held a hockey stick and eyed the goalie net at the far end with intent. Spring. It seemed an impossible season after Gary's death. She couldn't believe that the trees would remember their leaves, that the grass would turn green. It seemed as if everything had stalled in winter when he had died; nothing could turn over, nothing could start moving out of the season's icy, dismal grip. She had resigned herself to the whole season of it, as if her grieving came in snow and wind and early darkness, had believed that facing winter, bracing herself against the cold, the harsh winds, was the least she could do for Gary. It had turned her sadness into something that required effort, determination. She didn't want to leave him yet, leave behind the feeling of being part of his loss and the daily reminder of it in temperature and bare trees. His death had become part of the season, and now spring, with its warmth, the birds, was forcing her to leave him behind. The season when the dark had been the longest and now this sunlight, the small flowers, this season with its equinox, its balance of day and night, its light overwhelmed her. The crows, loud and circling, seemed to take strands of Gary from her and forced her to look up at them, tricked her into following their flight until they'd disappear, fading from view and leaving her staring at the expanse of blue sky, empty. She felt a kinship with the boy who had coloured his driveway white: ice. She wasn't ready yet for leaves and flowers either. She unzipped her winter jacket and turned from the streets, the houses and manicured lawns, the shrubs, sculpted but still mostly bare, a pale new green at their tips, and started up the mountain.

* * *

Jerry heard Grace before he saw her. He'd been walking along the stream that ran from the highest lake on the mountain down the hillside, connecting the other smaller lakes on its way to the town in the form of gulleys and creeks. It had been running for days now, freed from ice and loud. Running water. The sound of it, Jerry realized, was always beneath everything else: birdsong, branches, the scolding of the chipmunks, the crows. Like a heartbeat, he thought, a pulse.

Someone had left the path. He heard branches snap and last year's leaves shuffling dryly. He stepped to a thick-trunked pine and pressed his body to it. He thought of Ralph and quickly felt for his knife and then saw Grace walking towards the summit. The fear that had been kicked up, the small dry leaf of it being Ralph, settled again. He felt himself smile, relieved. He was all smile, he thought; just the sight of her made his heart clamour for a closer look. He had never felt anything like it. He whistled but she continued walking, her head down, her jacket opened and snagging on trees as she went by.

"Grace." His voice sounded strange to him. He hardly ever heard himself speak outside in the woods. She turned and peered through the brush.

"Jerry?" She began to make her way to him. "I was looking for you." She had twigs in her hair and feathers. He reached out to touch one and she blushed.

"Those are my father's. I mean, I took them from his work-shop." Jerry reached for her hand, which had flown up to her hair, and smoothed its skin with his thumb. She looked at him and breathed deeply. "My father is snow-blowing the back-yard. My mother is half in the oven, the living room is covered in plastic, there is a seven-legged chair in the basement that won't stand up and there's a cabinet full of these." She fingered one of the feathers, pulling it in front of her face so she could see it. "He has all kinds of them and hooks and sinkers and knives to gut fish." Jerry pulled her hand to him and the rest of her followed. He stood holding her, listening to her cry quietly. She wanted to say that winter was going, that

Gary was back there, still in snow and hard, cold breaths, that the trees, the grass, everything was going on without him, had started to change, and there was nothing she could do to stop it. Even the landscape of her loss was deserting her. "I just want to go home," she said faintly into his chest, not really knowing what she meant.

To tell her he loved her would be like telling her the water was running hard, the creek was finally unobstructed, free to flow as it should. The sound of it was all around them, fiercely obvious. It was in his veins, hot and sweet, it was in his eyes, and when she looked, he knew she saw it. The words he thought of using were too small, but something needed to be said. It was time for a threshold, some frame, a structure they could pass through and emerge changed somehow, different on the other side, different but together. He remembered the look on his father's face when he once told Jerry of seeing a flock of starlings on his way home from work, over a year ago now, of the unexpected turquoise bird in the centre of the flock, feeding with them on the expanse of lawn near the dépanneur. A budgie, he had exclaimed, hitting his knee, his face, his eyes, transformed. The flock had adopted an escaped budgie. Jerry thought of telling Grace that he was speckled dark and grey, a plain bird, nothing out of the ordinary, and she was the unexpected turquoise, the escaped bird, and that there was hope and that hope showed itself in unexpected places and in unexpected ways: in escaped budgies in the middle of starlings, in the joy it had given his father. He wanted to open his arms wider, to hold her closer to the whole flock of him, turn everything over to her, so he led her to the toolshed at the edge of the orchard where the monks left sweet-smelling wood for him to burn and blankets, where the budding apple trees still had snow around the base of their trunks. He wanted to take her to the one place he knew where the seasons still teetered between each other and they could stay safe for as long as they wanted, balanced.

*   *   *

The fire was hungry and devoured the kindling Jerry fed it. Logs snapped, crackling warmth into the small toolshed. He had cleared a spot in front of the wood stove and laid down their jackets and then the blankets. They both dropped to their knees wordlessly and faced each other, the fire flickering on them, lighting them up, then leaving them in small darknesses. There were no words, he realized, kissing her slowly, his hand slipping to the first button of her shirt. She moved him, shifted him in a geological way. Seams and stones, granite, boulders, the face of mountains that filled him, that contained him burst open now and moved. She mined the hard rock of him, lit the caves he slept in, and he could only touch her, respond in silent welcomes. His tongue pushed through the first buttonhole, tasting the small button of her flesh. Her skin was warm and sweet, peppered. He undid the next button, his tongue in the buttonhole until he could hear her under the crackling fire, hear her under the snow melting, the water running, her voice slow and urgent at once. He tasted her until she was completely undone. Then he pulled her on him, her jeans and his jeans tangled, the empty legs of them, her bare legs wrapping tightly around his waist, her head thrown back, neck bare, and they moved into it, the threshold, the frame leading them to the other side of home. They rocked themselves with the inevitability, the certainty, the intent of it part flesh, part touch and taste, part mouth and part feather. The gesture of it was hope flexed, beyond verb into muscle, straining leg against leg and sweating. Hope exerted itself then between the two of them, joining them closer than they thought they could be.

Beyond the shed, lines of trees were beginning to blossom. Winter was receding. They had no choice; the home Jerry and Grace had both lost and now craved was in sight in each other and they headed there slowly, surely, like the trees, a whole season of themselves moving into their own.

* * *

The sun was beginning to lower when Jerry left Grace near her house. His fingers felt in his pockets for the feathers she had given him. Two feathers. One in his jacket pocket was for Curtis's collection. And one, she had said, placing it over her bare breast, was for him. He had put that one in his shirt pocket, where she had first leaned into. He felt that small stream pulse through his veins now, pushing joy and strands of her hair, her voice, through him. He breathed in deeply the memory of the smell of her, the warmth of her neck below her shirt, her shoulders. She had a constellation of freckles on her back that looked like a heart. You're wearing your heart on your back, he had told her, and she had smiled and leaned into him.

Later, when the sun was long gone, the moon in its first quarter, sliced thin and sharp, Jerry let himself into his house and silently crept upstairs, leaving the feather on Curtis's night table. The feather that had come from the workbench surrounded by all the unfinished projects, the drawers full of other feathers like it, lures to be tied together, swung out and set in the water, to entice fish to come closer, to bait.

It had been Grace's feather. Jerry left Curtis a feather from Grace, a gift. And then he went downstairs and lay down on the couch, and he slept.

"It is the fourth time in as many months. What the hell are you thinking? And don't tell me it's the boys following you around like some Pied Piper." Sheila looked at her husband with disgust and wondered when he had slipped out of her sight, when he had got away to get into trouble again.

"Don't you use that tone of voice with me." Les sat at the kitchen table. He was fixing a small motor. Its parts lay all over, oily and loose. Sheila couldn't bear to look at them on her table.

"You have a workbench downstairs."

Les looked up at her and then sat up, rubbing his chest with a greasy hand. "Oh Jesus, my heart."

"Don't pull that. There's nothing wrong with your heart and you know it." They both looked up at Grace, who had just come in.

"What's going on?" She looked at both her parents. She could hear the snow blower's grating engine between them; the smell of oven cleaner hovered.

"Your father is having a heart attack because the police phoned."

"The police? Why would the police phone? Is it something about Gary?"

Sheila looked at Les, who was trying to screw something onto the greasy mess in front of him. He sat back and rubbed his hand across his chest.

"I feel like there's a solid band of steel across my chest. Jesus." He bent and picked up a bolt that had fallen at his feet.

"Why did the police phone?" Grace asked again. She and her mother watched Les pick up a small screwdriver and peer at the parts before him. He tried fitting it into the head of a small screw but it kept sliding off, his hand knocking the pieces of the motor all over the floor.

"What do you mean, boys follow him around?" Grace felt her own heart gallop.

Sheila rushed to the phone and scrubbed at some mark she had seen on the receiver, a fingerprint or smear.

"Would someone tell me what is going on?" Grace looked at her mother in alarm and suddenly thought of the warning label on the cleaning powders and liquids that had surrounded her all her life. Her mother stood now in the kitchen, a towel over her shoulder, her hands chapped and sore-looking, and all Grace could see was that warning, that label of the skeletal hand. She stood in front of Sheila and could see her mother's bones, could see what was beneath her, right under her all this time. There wasn't much.

She watched her father's hand, shaking and full of grease as he handled the pieces of the broken motor. She knew something else in the house was broken, something that couldn't be fixed. She just couldn't name it. Her father breathed laboriously, squinting at the tiny parts. He wouldn't be able to fix it, Grace thought. There were too many pieces, it was too complicated, and she felt lost once again, a little girl wandering the aisles of Miracle Mart, following the signs hanging from the ceiling, hopeless. Shoes, Children's Wear, Stationery. She remembered stopping at Tools and Toys, the aisle that bordered both, the aisle with bikes on one side, hanging by their front tires, and long, toothy saws on the other, wooden handled, plastic. She stopped in the aisle that bordered tools and toys because she had always found her father there. He had written her name and his on a card and safety-pinned it to her snowsuit. She realized with the clarity of all those Thursdays in Miracle Mart clanging into place like empty shopping carts that he had known then that she would continue to get lost, continue to wander off on her own, because he wasn't going to take care of her. He was too busy looking after himself.

"You knew something was wrong." Grace was looking now at the bones that made up her mother and her mother couldn't look back at her. She busied herself straightening the chairs around the table.

"You knew all this time." Grace's head filled with the snow blower, with the dog tied up to the tree outside, the bare dirt it kept digging up, the piles of dog shit no one cleaned up at the side of the house. Her head filled with the thundering noise of a train. *Restez calme* in an emergency, *restez calme*. What was the next step, the next thing to do? "Did Gary know too? Did Gary know?" Neither of her parents would look at her. "Answer me!" she screamed. Her rage came from a deep place; it grated and snarled and hissed at being let out after being held in for so long.

"Don't you talk to your mother that way, missy. You show some respect."

"Respect!" Grace looked incredulously at Les, who busied himself with the screwdriver, trying to twist something out. Her mother had wet the tip of the towel and was cleaning around the edge of the sink. The dog's whining from the back-yard filled the space between them. No one heard it any more but Grace. Her parents could eat a meal, look out the window at the dog and still not hear its whines. Grace pulled on her shoes, grabbed the leash and stormed out. Fuck them, she thought. Fuck them because they had fucked her.

The chain was heavy and rusted now from being outside all winter. The dog didn't stand up when she got close but thumped its tail a few times and looked up at her, waiting to see what she was going to do. Grace unclipped the chain and attached the leash instead to its collar. The dog got up, its legs wobbly at first, and then it sat down and scratched. Grace tried to coax it on its feet again, thinking that she'd take it for a walk to clear her head. The dog looked at her suspiciously.

"C'mon, Lady. C'mon, pup." Grace spoke in a high voice and rubbed her fingers together. The dog got up slowly, all legs and ears, and walked over to sniff at her fingers. When it found nothing to eat, it sat back down again and chased an itch with its snout. Grace pulled the leash taut. The dog's collar rode up its neck and made its face bulge, its tongue hang out.

"C'mon, we'll go for a walk. Wanna go for a walk?" She emphasized the word *walk*. Just hearing the word used to send the dog into a frenzy. It would chase its tail and run up and nudge her hand with its wet nose, but now it barely looked up. Grace ran on the spot, thinking that the movement would get the dog excited. She slipped the leash around her wrist and clapped her hands. She whistled. Finally the dog, curious at all the commotion, stood up again. Grace slowly walked back-wards down the driveway, urging the dog to follow her. It walked slowly, its head low, its tail curled close to its hind legs. On the street it looked around nervously and walked carefully around sewers. Grace finally gave up and sat down on the curb next to it. It sat right against her leg and panted up into her face. Her father's dog, she thought, cupping its head in her hands. She touched noses with it, looking deep into its brown eyes, and the dog looked back quietly blinking, waiting for its head to be let go. When she let it go, the dog quickly looked away.

How often had she been getting lost, she thought to herself. And how often had her father tried to lose her, to lock her out? And Gary? Had he known? No one could look her in the eye. No one would tell her the truth. She looked back at her house. A shutter had loosened over the winter and now hung askew, making the house look off-kilter, tilted somehow. The hedge between the yards looked small and dead; even the crabapple was slow at getting its leaves. The last pile of snow on their front lawn had slowly melted, shrinking in diameter and getting dirtier and dirtier until it looked like coal, or asphalt, a black hole that all of winter drained into, staying under their house. Finally the snow had disappeared, leaving their lawn browner than any other on the street, with dead leaves from last fall still clumped around the curb. The front door was painted the colour of rusty blood or scab. Her house, it seemed, wasn't in sync with the other houses, with spring. She pulled the dog closer and could feel it trembling as it nervously eyed a manhole cover. It probably felt safe only when it was under the kitchen table or wrapped tightly around the tree, Grace thought. Even the dog was messed up.

Curtis woke up and saw the feather on his night table and quickly looked around for Jerry. When he saw that his brother wasn't in the room, he looked back at the feather Jerry had left him. It was a pale brown with turquoise at its edge. He wondered what kind of bird it came from and put it to his nose to smell it. It smelled dusty and nearly made him sneeze. He looked at it carefully, holding it up to the light that was seeping around the window blind, and then placed it on his blanket before he reached for his binoculars, which he had dropped on the floor beside his bed last night. Looking at the feather through them, he saw that there wasn't just turquoise along its edge but black as well. He examined where each strand of feather met. He looked at the sharp end of it, the end that had been in the bird, and wondered why the feather had fallen out and whether it hurt to have feathers poking in you like that.

He got out his box where he kept all the treasures Jerry had brought him and opened it, placing the feather in it carefully. He had six feathers now. He turned his head and sneezed into his sleeve. Once he had sneezed without thinking while he was looking in his box, and his sneeze had sent his feather collection whooshing all over the floor. Every time he had moved to pick one up, the others had danced around his feet. It had taken him a long time to pick them all up.

He was the first one awake this morning. It was the weekend so his dad was sleeping in. Curtis went down the stairs slowly, trying to step over the creaks. His dad got mad when he was woken up too early on days he could sleep in. The cats met him at the bottom of the stairs and wound around his legs, purring. He sat for a minute and scratched them under their chins and on the tops of their heads. They liked that and kept bumping into his hand for more.

When he remembered how hungry he was, he got up and went into the kitchen with the cats following him. He wanted some cereal. His dad had bought some Apple Jacks for a treat and Curtis had gone to bed thinking about opening the box, eating a big bowl of them.

There were small sketches propped up all over the kitchen. Curtis looked at the one leaning against the cup that was on the table. His mother had drawn the cup with its little flowers and bumble bee and then had written a word he had never seen before. He knew the letters, though. There was a *t* and an *a* and two *s*'s and an *e*. Under that was the word *cup*. Cup, he repeated to himself. He could read that.

There were other drawings in the kitchen. She had drawn the toaster, the sink, the stove and had written words under them. Curtis couldn't read most of the words. He could read *cat* under the drawing of a cat his mother had propped against the cats' water bowl, but he couldn't read the word above it. *C, h, a, t.* He fed the cats and then got out the cereal and milk, moving a drawing from his bowl.

Carefully, he carried his cereal to the living room to watch cartoons. The living room had drawings propped up all over as well, with words printed under the drawings. He peeled off the drawing of the television taped on the screen and stuck it on the side of the set and then turned it on. This was his favourite time. The living room was still dark but the hallway was lit up from the sun in the kitchen. And he was alone with his whole family above him, sleeping. Except Jerry, he reminded himself, and thought of his feather, happily crunching his cereal before the milk made it too soggy.

"Spiderman" was on. It was really early, he realized. He usually missed seeing "Spiderman." The cats circled him before settling on either side of him. He stuck his finger in the milk in his bowl and held it out to each cat. They licked him, their tongues scratchy, and then they fell asleep, purring and keeping his legs warm. Later, he thought, he'd go out and ride his bike.

Les stood in his workshop. He wheeled his golf clubs out of the way so he could get at his varnish. He was finally going to finish the television and stereo cabinet he'd been working on for years. He ran his hand over the top of the cabinet, still warm from the sanding he had done all morning. He had designed it himself, making a space for records and a drawer to hold eight-tracks. He had measured the speakers he had bought last year and built compartments they would fit into. His fingers felt for the nails he had covered over with filler. He closed his eyes and still couldn't feel them. Yes siree, he thought, leaning on the cabinet with his arms folded, he hadn't made straight As in his woodworking class for nothing. He looked at all the tools he had hung up on his wall and put away on shelves. A drill press, an electric sander, a router, a chisel set, every type of screwdriver there was, clamps bolted down to the bench. Briefly he thought of his father and his father's workbench, the tobacco cans filled with nails, the old-fashioned tools he had bought second-hand and the birdhouses he used to make. His mother had hated them, the birds in the yard all the time, the dead birds on the porch that the cat dragged home. A present, his father would exclaim. His mother, worried about germs, would hold Les back from taking a good look.

He opened the tin with an old screwdriver and stuck in a paintbrush. He sopped the finish onto the wood, not caring that it splashed all over the floor, the golf cart, the Shop-Vac. He was envisioning moving the old television stand and putting the set up on the new cabinet, hooking the wires to the speakers and running the wires along the wall. Mrs. High-and-Mighty wouldn't like it a bit, this new addition to the living room. It would drive her crazy. The more Les thought of how his wife would hate the cabinet, the more he smiled. She'd get used to it.

While he was waiting for it to dry, he took down the smallest chisel and carved out his name, the date and his memorized social insurance number on the back of the cabinet. Let someone try to steal this, he thought, admiring his handiwork. "Sheila?" he hollered to the ceiling. "When are you going to make lunch? I'm starving." The kitchen clock ticked in response. Les waited and then, cursing to himself, went upstairs and opened the breadbox, and found some leftover meat in the fridge. The dog sulked into the room at the sound of the fridge opening.

"What do you want?" Les asked, shoving a piece of pale pink ham into his mouth. "Go lie down." The dog put its head down and looked up, trying one more time for a piece of ham. "Go on, get." He shoved the animal away with his foot. He picked up his sandwich and went into the living room to watch TV.

The only thing on worth watching was a soccer match. Les

settled into his recliner and took a bite of his sandwich. A commercial about a carwash kit got his attention. It's spring, the ad announced, and time to get your car spruced up. Les chuckled. He could picture his neighbour coming over and asking Les how he had managed to get his car so shiny. He'd drive over to Canadian Tire and get himself one of those kits, the deluxe one that came with the special soap that wouldn't scratch the finish on the car. His car, he thought, reaching for the keys, was going to be so clean and shiny, he'd have a whole crowd of neighbours in his driveway.

After the front door had closed, the dog waited and then jumped up into the chair and wolfed down the half sandwich Les had left. Then it flopped down heavily into the seat and waited.

Sheila heard her husband leave. She was scrubbing the bathtub and thought someone called her and then decided it was probably the television. She got the hamper and collected the clothes he had left on the chair near his bed. She looked quickly at his night table, the crucifix he had tied with blessed palm leaves and the small bowl that held his rosary beads. There was a pile of dirty underwear and rolled socks on the floor where he had taken them off. Holy, holy, holy, she thought to herself and picked them up.

The dog was waiting for her at the bottom of the stairs and followed her. "Will you get out of my way?" she said, almost tripping over it in the kitchen. She looked at the counter where Les had left out the mayonnaise and ham. The breadbox was open and so was the cupboard where he had taken down a plate. She had been upstairs for an hour, just an hour, and the kitchen was a mess again. Wearily, she opened the door to the basement with her foot and went down to put the wash in.

Once she turned on the light in the laundry room, she saw that she couldn't get to her washing machine. Les had pulled that blasted cabinet he'd been making into the middle of the room and she couldn't possibly fit around it. His golf clubs were against the dryer and there was sawdust all over the floor in front of his workbench. She felt scoured inside. Nothing she could say would change him. He was the way he was in spite of her. She had laundry to do, she wanted to scream, she had beds to strip and dishcloths to bleach. She slammed the hamper onto the top of his so-called entertainment unit and went upstairs to clean the kitchen again.

The dog followed her from the sink to the counter, from the counter to the garbage. "What is your problem?" she asked it, annoyed that it kept slowing her down. It sat down and looked at her, and Sheila suddenly realized that it might be hungry. She was the one who usually fed the dog, and now that she thought about it, she couldn't remember the last time she had. She opened the pantry and scooped out a cup of its food and poured it into its bowl. The dog began to eat before she had emptied the cup. Sheila filled the water bowl as well, and when the dog was finished, it sloshed thirstily into its water. Sheila wiped up the water on the floor and the dog sat watching her, still licking its lips, and then it started heaving and threw it all back up, the dog food, the ham sandwich, a small piece of tinfoil still shiny and chewed in the middle of the heap on Sheila's clean kitchen floor.

The trees around the lake were mostly willows, leaning down so close to the water that their branches touched and mirrored back slim strands of budding leaves. Ducks busily swam along the shore, nosing into the long grass and dunking their heads into water. Dandelions bloomed yellow among the rocks. Spring. It was a man-made lake. A dog ran down to the water, barking at the ducks, and someone from one of the benches called it back. One time a dog had run into the lake after its ball and had come down with rabies the next day. Stolen bikes were rolled into the lake, pushed through the sludge. They would stand upright for moments before falling over into the water, and then they'd be buoyant again for what seemed an unnaturally long time. Rocks would be thrown at them, pinging off the metal frames until slowly they sank out of view.

Wedding parties drove down to the lake's shores and posed with the sun diamonding off its small waves. Small children tried to sail boats on the water. Mostly things sank in it. Slowly.

Although it was dusk, the benches around the lake were filled. Frogs croaked loudly from the marsh and birds roosted noisily. Someone had turned on a car radio. Grace walked slowly by each bench, trying to see who was sitting. She had Gary's stash in her pocket and had just smoked one of his joints. She'd smoke anything she could find to get away from her house. Parsley, oregano. She remembered walking into the kitchen once and finding Gary sitting in front of the oven with the door open, watching something cook. He had pulled out a cookie tray of something dark brown and shrivelled. Banana peels, he had said, they're supposed to be a great trip. She understood his desperation now, how he had needed to turn everything around him into an ingredient of escape. He probably hadn't even seen her, hadn't even realized that she was stuck right there along with him. He'd been too busy saving himself. Grace felt just as desperate. She had lit the joint while she was still in the driveway, smoking it hard on the way to the lake and letting it burn all the way down to her fingers. Her mouth felt pasty now and dry, as if she'd have to pry her tongue off if she had to speak. Below the frogs and birds, below Led Zeppelin pumping from the radio, she could hear the whispers, her brother's name, the word *death* trailing behind her. She felt the weight of *suicide* and *train* hitched to her, slowing her down. "You'd kill yourself too if you had to live where he lived" was what she wanted to say, but she couldn't talk any more and she didn't really want to.

"Gracie, what a surprise."

Grace looked up, squinting into the dark. Ralph inhaled his cigarette deeply, its orange glow lighting his face. He smiled at her and blew a long, steady stream of smoke through his teeth and out of his nostrils. Grace's thoughts began running uphill, slowly picking themselves up from being stoned and dusting themselves off.

"How are things?"

She licked her lips before answering, cleared her throat. "Fine." She tried to sound as offhand as she could, tried to keep her knocking knees from jarring her voice.

"Did Gary ever mention the money he owed me?" Ralph's voice hissed with smoke. This time he blew it directly in her face. For a moment she sagged, hearing Gary's name out loud, fear filling her, but quickly she made herself freeze, sealing in all the panic, the dread deep within her. She looked back at him with the disgust she'd been feeling all day towards her father, with the disdain she'd been feeling for her mother, the anger.

"No, he never mentioned you at all." And then she kept walking.

As soon as she rounded the bend and was swallowed by the willows bent over the path to the water, she began to run. She ran all the way around the lake, thinking that if he decided to follow her, he would expect her to walk back out onto the road. She didn't stop until she could see his bench across the lake. Then she let the panic, the smoke of his voice, choke her. She stood among the slim birches and rocks, trying to see if he was still sitting there.

"Hey, *qu'est-ce qui se passe?*"

Grace looked around. She saw a bunch of guys sitting on the rocks around her. One of them held a brown paper bag. When he saw her looking at it, he grinned and held it out.

"*Veux-tu du cidre?*"

She shook her head and looked back out across the lake.

"*C'est quoi ton nom?*"

Someone stood up from the bench Ralph had been sitting on. The person looked like him, but it was getting dark and she couldn't be sure.

"*Comment t'appelles-tu? Parles-tu français?* You speak English?"

Grace turned back to the rocks. She wished she hadn't

smoked; she couldn't think fast enough to be out here alone. She tried gathering her thoughts as if they were a wide crinoline, a skirt she had to fold around her in order to get through a doorway, in order to return to the sixth seat in the third row where she sat for French class.

"Je m'appelle Grace." There, she thought triumphantly, she had remembered.

"Salut, Grace. Je m'appelle Guillaume. Ça c'est Réjean, Sylvain et Philippe."

Grace nodded at them all. *"Salut."*

"Cherches-tu quelqu'un?"

Grace slowly dissected his question. *Tu* is you, she thought. *Quelqu'un* is someone. Looking for someone, maybe, she thought.

"Non. Je ne veux pas voir un guy." The guy who was holding the bag passed it to the guy beside him and then joined her at the edge of the water. He peered out to see who she was looking at.

"Qui?"

"Umm, *le guy là-bas."* She motioned with her arms that he was big.

"Il est gros?" Guillaume looked back across the water. Grace looked with him. She had never been on this side of the lake. The English side looked paved, she thought. There were benches and flagpoles and a wide path. This side was wilder, the path was mud and there were no benches, just big rocks that jutted out over the water. The trees were denser. Easier to hide, she thought.

Just then Ralph got up and began walking down the path in the direction she had gone. There was no mistaking him. He walked slowly, purposefully. Someone got up quickly to follow him. Mike, Grace thought, and watched him run after Ralph.

"Him. *Lui. C'est lui que je n'aime pas."*

Guillaume looked where her finger was pointing.

"Tu n'aimes pas Ralph? Mais je comprend, il est fou. C'est vrai, guys? Ralph est capoté?"

The others nodded in agreement. Sylvain took a long swig

of cider and passed it on. She watched Ralph stop at the last bench and then continue walking. She felt the panic rise in her throat again. Ralph had seen her walk around the lake, he knew where she was. She looked at the path. She had no idea where she'd end up if she followed it.

"C'est correct. Restes ici avec nous. On va t'aider. We going to help you. Philippe, *donne Grace ton jacket, et tiens—"* He pulled a toque out of his back pocket. *"Prends ça.* Take that."

She put the jacket on and pulled the toque down close to her eyes. Sylvain and the guy next to him made room for her on the rock they were sitting on. It was the darkest spot and she instantly felt warmed sitting between them.

"Dis rien. Don't talk," Guillaume ordered. Grace nodded. The guy across from her held out the brown bag. She took a swig from it and felt the cider roll down her throat. No one spoke. She watched their cigarettes float to their mouths and light up, then float back down. They heard Ralph and Mike long before they saw them.

"Hey, Guillaume." Ralph made the name sound as English as he could, pronouncing each letter derisively.

"Salut, Ralph."

"Did you see a chick walk by here a few minutes ago?"

"Une chick, ça dit quoi, une chick?" Guillaume looked around at his friends; a few of them shrugged. Grace made herself breathe slowly, tried to slow her heart, which was drumming up into her throat. Her heart, she thought, was going to give her away.

"Have you seen a girl, a girl?" Ralph spoke slowly, patronizingly. "Don't tell me you don't know what a girl is, you fucking frog."

"A girl?" Guillaume asked doubtfully.

"Fuck you, shit for brains." Ralph stomped past them. "You wouldn't know your ass from your elbow." Mike followed him, ducking from the branches that were whipping back into place after Ralph passed.

They waited for what seemed hours. Grace could hear the

music over the water. Ralph's and Mike's footsteps had long gone.

"Hey, shit for brains, don't you know what a girl is?" The guy beside Grace spoke softly to Guillaume and then they all laughed and began talking at once.

"Elbow." Sylvain pointed to his ass. "And asshole," he said, pointing to his elbow.

Grace pulled off the toque and tossed it back to Guillaume.

"*Merci.* Thank you." She fished a couple of joints out of the plastic bag she had stashed in her pocket and held them out. "*Merci beaucoup.*"

Sylvain whooped and took them from her.

"*Salut,* boys."

"*Salut,* girl." Guillaume pulled his toque on and smiled at her.

She waved and headed back where she had come from. This time, she thought, she'd take the street and head to Lily's. The thought of going home made her feel more dismal than Ralph did. She knew it wasn't even home any more, it couldn't be. It would be a place to sleep until she could figure out what to do. In the meantime she'd go to Lily's.

The path was darkest halfway between the benches. She stopped for a minute and listened to the blend of music and low croaking of frogs and Sylvain's loud laugh from the trees and then hurried on, her feet squelching through mud and wet grass. She followed the path that went up to the street and was soon beneath street lights again. She slipped up the nearest driveway and into the backyard. She'd head to Lily's the way Rave would. It would be safer.

Lily held the feather up while Curtis wound the string tightly around the barb of it. He had picked his three favourite feathers from his box and wanted to wear them around his neck. He could already picture himself riding his bike with them on. They'd lift in the wind as he went. He might even fly. He knew he wouldn't really, he was just pretending, but the thought of it made him wind the string around faster. He couldn't wait until tomorrow, he thought. After school he'd race home and get his bike out. He wished he didn't have to go to bed and could go out right now.

"Whatchya doing, Lily?" Dellie came in still wet from the bath. She was wearing a pair of shorts and her new cowboy hat with a plastic whistle attached to its cord. She whistled now, after she spoke. She had given up her soother.

"I'm helping Curtis put his feathers on a string so he can wear them around his neck."

Dellie came closer and picked up the string that Curtis was using.

"Can I help Curtis too?" She gave a short whistle. Curtis shook his head forcibly.

"No thanks, Del. We're okay but you can watch if you like."

Curtis looked up dismayed at Lily. He didn't want Dellie watching. She ruined everything. And she whistled every time she talked. It was loud and annoying. Even their dad had asked her to stop at supper. It was making him jumpy, he had said. She got her hat back at dessert. Curtis wished they had just thrown it out. It was too noisy. At least her soother had plugged her up and usually kept her from saying everything she wanted.

"Where did Curtis get those feathers anyway?" Dellie whistled.

Both his sisters looked at him. Dellie would ask that dumb question, Curtis thought. Lily hadn't. She had just agreed to help. He shrugged.

"Did he find those feathers from a bird?"

"I don't know where he got the feathers, Del." Lily helped Curtis untangle the knot Dellie had made in the end of his string and then she carefully double-knotted the string around the last feather he had attached. She helped him put the string over his head and turned him around to tie the ends together. "Is this long enough?"

Curtis nodded. It was perfect. The feathers hung just where he wanted them to hang, right above his belly button. He carefully pulled the string over his head and held it, admiring the feathers. He had picked the last one that Jerry had left, a blue jay's feather and a long dark feather with a white tip.

"Can I have a try with those feathers for a little minute, Curtis?" Dellie blew twice on her whistle hopefully.

Curtis shook his head. They were his special feathers and he didn't want to share them.

"C'mon, Del, I bet we can find you a cowgirl top to wear with those shorts so you won't be cold in bed," Lily said.

"Do I have a cowgirl top?" Dellie asked incredulously.

Curtis listened to her whistle happily down the hall. His sister sure was loud. His finger followed the edge of each feather and then he placed the necklace on his night table so he'd see it first thing in the morning.

"Grace's here," their father called up from the bottom of the stairs.

"Oh. Send her up." Lily heard Grace say something to her father and then come up the stairs.

"Hi. It isn't too late, is it? To come over, I mean."

"Oh, no. I was just helping Dellie find a cowgirl shirt to sleep in. If you want, you can wait in my room."

Dellie came out holding up a T-shirt.

"This is the shirt I want to wear, Lily." She whistled and pranced up to Grace. "Hi, Grace. Look at my shirt. It's a cowgirl's shirt, see the little doggie on it? Hello, little doggie." Dellie held the shirt to her mouth and kissed the dog.

Grace smiled and Dellie whistled.

"I won't be long," Lily said and herded her sister into her room.

"You've got to take off the hat to put on your shirt, Del."

"I don't want to take off my hat, Lily. It's very important to me."

Lily sighed and leaned back on her heels, looking at her little sister. Dellie stuck her belly out.

"Tickle me, Lily."

"Only if you take off the hat so I can help you put on your shirt."

"Then you'll tickle me?"

Lily nodded.

"You promise?"

"I promise. Cross my heart and hope to die. Stick a needle in my eye."

Dellie looked at her older sister dubiously. "You'll do all of that, you'll do that needle thing?"

Lily nodded again and watched Dellie take off her hat and carefully put it on the floor. Then she stooped again and picked up the whistle and blew in it before coming over to Lily with the shirt.

Lily took the T-shirt from her sister and started pulling it over Dellie's head, then pulled the little girl onto her lap and tickled her under her arms. Dellie had a deep, raucous laugh for a little girl. Lily found herself laughing along and even Grace came to the doorway to watch, laughing at the two of them. Dellie poked her head through her shirt, her face red, her hair mussed and electric.

"Stop now, Lily, stop." She hiccuped and then laughed some more.

Lily reached over for Dellie's hat and plopped it on her sister's head. Dellie put the whistle in her mouth and chirped into it.

"You go see Daddy now and tell him you're ready for bed."

Dellie got up and jauntily walked by Grace, nodding and whistling at her.

Lily led Grace into her bedroom. She waited until her friend was in before she closed the door.

"Is everything okay?"

"Oh yeah, everything is fine. I just had to walk and was in the neighbourhood, that's all."

Lily looked carefully at her friend. Grace's eyes were red and her lips dry and cracked. Her hands, which had been picking at Lily's bedspread, looked dry and cold and her nails were chewed down.

"Are you sure?"

Grace nodded. "So what letter are you on now?" she asked, still looking down at her hands.

"Letter? Oh, I've slowed down, I'm still on D. Isadora Duncan. She was a dancer and got killed when she was driving. Her scarf got caught in her car or something."

Grace looked up, interested. "Her scarf?"

Lily nodded, sorry now that she even mentioned it. She flinched for Grace whenever she heard the words *death* or *killed*. They didn't seem to bother Grace though.

"Did she have kids?"

"I don't know. That's the thing with encyclopedias, they just give you a bit of information. Not enough to answer all the questions. It's not going as well as I thought it would." She looked at Grace. "Are you sure you're okay?"

Grace nodded again. She couldn't imagine giving voice to what she'd been thinking about. All day, small connections had kept leaping at her. The dog, the long walks. And Gary. He must have known. It was funny, she thought, how the truth moved backwards and forwards at the same time. She knew that from now on things would be different, but she hadn't counted on losing the people who she thought had made up her family. Somehow they had shape-shifted, replaced themselves with strangers. Her whole life had been a kind of lie. And the thought of others knowing, people who lived in Beaumont, policemen, parents, kids she went to school with, made her burn with shame.

Each new realization was like a hundred-watt light bulb that lit up all the dark places within her and made her feel unbearably exposed. She wondered how much Lily could actually see and then began to panic.

She stood up.

"I should go. I'll see you tomorrow."

"Yeah, all right." Lily got up and followed her down to the front door. "See you tomorrow."

"Goodbye, Grace, see you another day," Dellie hollered from the kitchen and ran out into the hallway, waving and whistling like the leader of a parade.

"Bye, Dellie." The goodbye parade, Grace thought sadly. She made her way down the front walk and across the street. When she looked back at the house, Lily and Dellie had gone inside.

Les smiled and nimbly walked into the house. He picked up the guitar bought for Grace and strummed it, putting a foot up on a chair. "Oh my darling, oh my darling," Les sang to the dishes, to the table and the empty carwash kit. He held the word *darling* for a couple of extra notes, strummed and then looked around the room at his imaginary fans. The dog had reluctantly made its way from under the table and was watching him sing, its head cocked curiously, not sure what it all meant. Les put the guitar back on the table and went downstairs to finish his stereo cabinet. He was having a good day, he thought as he pulled the light bulb chain in his workshop. The small, persistent thoughts of his wife, of Grace, of calls from the police, were like horseflies that he swatted away. Buggers, he said, mentally flapping at them. He wasn't going to let them ruin his day.

The hamper full of dirty clothes that Sheila had put down on the cabinet was now stuck. Les couldn't budge it. She must have set the hamper down while the varnish was still tacky, he thought, cursing her stupidity. He threw the underwear, the socks and the undershirts behind him and tried wrenching the empty hamper off. He got down his metal ruler and tried sliding it between the hamper and the wood but the light was poor at that angle and he couldn't see where he could fit it in. He turned and faced his pegboard of tools and then the shelves beside them. He bent and pulled out his crowbar and jammed it at the bottom of the hamper, cursing his wife as he pushed it forcibly. The hamper came unstuck easily and then fell off the cabinet. Les kicked it out of his way. The crowbar had made a long gouge on the surface of the wood.

"Sheila!" Les roared to the ceiling. All his work, his craftsmanship, the long dowels he had glued in to keep the records in place. Three sections, he had thought. The small hook he had painstakingly screwed in place to hang the headphones on. He took another deep breath and felt his blood churn. "Sheila! Get down here!" Finally he heard her footsteps descending the stairs. He waited, hitting the hamper with the crowbar, keeping beat to the sound of her steps as they approached.

"What?"

He didn't answer but held the silence as if it were his and he would ladle it out in portions of his own choosing. He motioned with his head to the top of the cabinet.

"What?"

He waited and then pointed to the gouge with the crowbar.

"You called me all the way down for that?" She looked around and saw the underwear, her bras, socks strewn over boxes marked "Christmas," over the Shop-Vac, the cross-country skis and golf clubs. "What did you do with all the dirty clothes?" She looked at the hamper and went to pick it up, to gather the clothes back into it. Les stepped on it and continued glaring at her. She looked away from him, down at the fingernail she had just torn cleaning out the windowsills. He slowly took a deep breath and waited until she looked back up.

"What do you have in that head of yours?" He spoke each word in a measured tone. It was like a performance. *Oh my darling.* "What do you have between those two ears?" He tapped the cabinet with the bar. "If I were to hazard a guess, I would have to say nothing. You've got nothing in that head of yours." He waited for the words to sink in. His eyes were slits, his lips curled back. "Why don't you ever think?" He tapped these words out with the bar against the wood. "Use what little brain you have and think." He looked at his wife as she picked at her hands, smoothed out her shirt, and he smiled. Then he moved beside her abruptly and tapped her forehead with his finger. "You have to use what's in there, Sheila, and think before you do something stupid." Each word was a thump now. She had closed her eyes and was taking small steps backwards with each poke. "Like putting your goddamn hamper on my cabinet and ruining all the goddamn work I've done." He stood back, warmed by his voice, the direction it was going. He knew where he was now, he was back in familiar territory.

"I worked on this cabinet for three years of my life, with my own two hands." He held up his hands to show her. "I drew up the plans, I measured out the wood. I nearly lost a finger cutting the wood." He held out his left index finger, which had a jagged scar around the nail. "Blood, sweat and tears were shed over this piece of carpentry, Sheila"—Les put his hand on the cabinet possessively—"and you ruined it by not thinking, by not using your brain." He liked the sound of his own words, the intelligence of them. He admired how he was keeping his cool and trying to reason with her. He spoke more cajolingly now, trying to get his wife to see how foolish she had been. She just stared back at him as if he was crazy.

"Don't you look at me like that. Here I am being reasonable, trying to reason with you, and you're glaring at me like I'm the one to blame. I didn't leave a goddamn hamper on varnish that was still wet, did I?" He could feel the motor of his anger spark and hum, fuelled by his wife's smirk. He pushed the throttle all the way, pushed the pedal to the floor.

"Don't you look at me like that. This is my goddamn house and you have no bloody right looking at me like that." He waited to see if his words had any effect on her. She just stood with her arms folded.

"I've got things to do, Les, and you're wasting my time. I'm sorry I put the hamper on your cabinet. There, feel better? But who in their right mind would use a crowbar? Use your own brains, Les. A crowbar will always leave marks."

He shrugged off what she was saying and walked over to the far end of the cabinet.

"Help me bring it upstairs."

"What? I can't lift that."

"You don't have to lift it, just guide it. I'll do all the lifting." Les had already positioned his hands and crouched to get his weight behind the push. He motioned to his wife to hold the other end.

"Now pull when I say." He took a deep breath. "Okay."

Sheila pulled.

"Not yet, wait until I say *pull*. Jesus. You're not totally useless, are you?" He hunkered down again. "Okay, pull."

She pulled and he pushed the cabinet a couple of inches and then stopped, his face red with the effort.

"Okay, again."

"I can't, Les, it's too heavy. We'll never get it up the stairs."

"Would you just pull the goddamn thing and let me worry about the stairs?" He got back in his crouched position. "Okay, pull." He used his shoulder this time and slowly the cabinet edged to the door.

"It won't go through the doorway. It's too wide for the doorway. And aren't you worried about your heart?"

"What do you mean, it won't go through the doorway? Let me over there." He pushed his wife out of the way so he could see, then turned to her as he passed, their faces inches apart. "Don't you worry about my goddamn heart. My heart is no business of yours." He looked at the doorway for a minute and then back at his cabinet. "It'll go through, we just have to push it at an angle."

"Les, it's too wide for the doorway. You built it too wide. Did you even measure the doorway when you were drawing up the plans?"

"Would you shut up! How am I supposed to think with you

yammering on like that? Give me some peace and quiet and I'll figure this out."

"Well, I'll be upstairs. Let me know when you figure it all out."

Les glared at the triumph in her voice and then got his measuring tape.

He measured the width of the cabinet and wrote it down. Three feet, seven inches. He wrote the numbers in a small notebook he kept in his back pocket that he had bought specifically for his calculations. The cost of the wood, the length of it, the number of nails, their size. Then he measured the doorway. Two feet, six inches. He carefully recorded that measurement and got his calculator. The cabinet was one foot and one inch wider than her goddamn doorway. He shook his head. She would pick a house with narrow doorways. Any other house would have wider doorways but not the one she wanted to buy. No sir, she had wanted the house with the goddamn small doorways. He kicked the cabinet and felt for his pipe. He'd have a smoke and go for a walk and figure something out. Sheila was in the kitchen piling dishes back into the sink. She turned when she heard Les at the door.

"Did you figure it out? Did you figure out that you built that thing too big?"

Les finished tying his runners. He had bought them because the salesman had told him they were quiet and good for walking. He looked coolly at his wife.

"Well, you're the one who wanted to buy a house with non-standard doorways."

"What are you talking about?"

"Every other house on this street has wider doorways," Les said, sounding authoritative. "I've read books about building bylaws, Sheila. Doorways have to be a certain width and this house doesn't meet those requirements." He filled his pipe with tobacco, pressing it down with a special knife he had bought in a smoke shop. Sheila looked at him in disbelief as he held his lighter to the pipe bowl, taking small breaths that he puffed out until the tobacco was lit.

"I hope you're happy," he said icily, and without waiting for her to answer, he left.

She stood there speechless. The smell of his Old Port tobacco hung between her and the side door like a ghost that had stayed to haunt her, to remind her of him. She opened the cupboard under the sink and grabbed the Lysol spray, aiming it at the place where he had just been standing. She held the nozzle down and disinfected the space her husband had taken up, got rid of his germs with the spray, got rid of his absurd statement, the lingering smell of him.

*   *   *   *

Lily sat in the library at lunch with the encyclopedia opened to *dung beetle*. She couldn't concentrate though, couldn't convince herself that knowing a dung beetle feeds on dung and has handsome, metallic tints would ever be useful. She leaned back and watched students mill in and out, holding hands, laughing. She imagined herself being held, being whispered to, and having nothing to whisper back except that a dung beetle rolled these lumps of dung a fair distance before sometimes burying them.

Her Hilroy copybook lay open and waiting. She was on a new page, the right-hand side where the paper was whiter, more inviting. She put her pen to the paper, the first thin blue line next to the thin red vertical line running down the left side of the page, and she wrote *Grace* without knowing why, and then she stood up and returned the encyclopedia to its place and slid out volume *S*. Lily was worried about Grace. She had looked so wild the night before, so thin and tired and sad. Lily opened the book, flipping the pages until she got to *suicide*. Maybe there'd be a cure for what Grace was holding inside her, Lily thought, maybe it had everything to do with her brother, Gary. She wrote *suicide* next to *Grace* and then read the entry:

"Deliberate act of terminating one's own life." Nothing about the sadness that was radiating from her friend, no suggestions on how to dissolve the grief that was clouding her eyes. Lily sat back and looked down at the table. What a waste of time, she thought, what a waste of paper. She thought of all her notebooks neatly stacked in her closet at home, the hours she'd spent recording information she thought would help her. And now, when she needed help, these books held nothing but small black and white photos of dead generals and cross-sections of internal organs. And Isadora Duncan, she reminded herself. And damselfly and bird and cyclone. But they were just words, and what was happening around her was real. Words, she thought, sometimes fail, miss the mark. Sometimes they don't even come close.

She closed the book and rolled up her copybook, shoving it into her knapsack. There was still time for a walk, she thought, maybe she'd find Grace and they could go outside before the bell rang. Lily pushed her chair back and left the library. The noise of the rest of the school was like cold water at first, but she got used to it and slowly started looking around, smiled when a girl in her English class said hi. She felt different; her knapsack felt lighter without a heavy encyclopedia in it. She could walk faster, without the book's corners digging into the small of her back. The pages of entries that once lay ahead of her, winding the alphabet into weeks and months, disappeared and before her now were only hallways. She pushed up her glasses and looked around. She had fifteen minutes, fifteen minutes to just look. "Ha," she said out loud and went looking for Grace.

Stan turned off the kitchen light and for a moment stood in the silence. The night slid into the room through the window, the darkness that was almost a deep blue, tinged with the slivered moon. The strip of stainless steel along the edge of the fridge joined the shard of moonlight, the kettle, the rings around the burners on the stove, everything stainless glistening like stars, a constellation, he thought, of home, his home. He felt his wife behind him. She slid her arms around his waist and put her mouth to his back and blew. He felt the heat of her breath through his shirt and took her hands and brought them to his lips, kissing the place where her fingers met her palm. She pressed her legs into his, her knees bent with his and slowly he turned to face her.

Holding her had always made him want to sing, croon some sweet nothings song he'd make up for her about her freckles or her eyes. His mouth kissed its way down her head to her ear and whispered in his deep Elvis voice the words she'd been leaving all over the house, the French words for everything around them. *Tasse*, he sang, pushing his lips into the soft fold of her ear lobe. *Cuiller et fenêtre, la lune, l'amour, beurre,* he breathed. She brought her hands down to his hips and pulled them to hers, swaying to his song, fitting herself to the shape of him. They slowly moved around the kitchen, his hands undoing her braid, her hands pulling his shirt from his pants and finding their way to his back.

Poêle, he crooned, following her into the hallway. *Chaud, l'amour, porte, des fleurs,* and up the stairs, *l'escalier, les bras, les cheveux, les chats, la lumière, le lit, la chemise.* They fell onto the unmade bed. He pulled her sketch pad out from under her shoulder and put it on the night table. *Tes jambes, tes oreilles, ta bouche.* He stopped with his mouth above her breast, not knowing its word in French. He looked at her and she smiled, pulling his head to her, closer, her fingers feeling his hair, his ears, tracing their shape to remember for later. *L'oreille,* she thought, *cheveux, bouche. Et la bouche. La bouche.*

The wind picked up during the night. Stan slept on his back, one arm around Eliza, who was snoring softly on her side, pressed close to him.

Curtis had kicked his feet free of the blankets and was lying half covered, his hair wet with sweat, matted to his head. His thumb glistened, still wet from sliding out of his mouth. His binoculars and his string of feathers were coiled side by side on his night table. He had smoothed the feathers out so that they lay flat.

In the room next to his, Dellie's mouth moved as though she still had her soother, and her arms were stuck straight over her head. She had lined up her stuffed animals along the wall and they all watched her now, their beaded eyes, their felt tongues panting. Outside the wind whipped the trees, the hydro lines shook.

Lily's hair was tangled on her pillow, her glasses folded neatly on her dresser. She lay cocooned in her quilt. The two cats were curled around each other at the bottom of her bed. One of them woke when the wind whistled hard along the eaves and something hit the side of the house. The cat yawned and lazily licked at its chest, then curled back up and fell asleep. The wind pushed at the windows, funnelled down through trees, and the people in the house slept, their beds warm and soft.

The wind pushed trash that had clogged the gullies out of the murky water and whipped it around in small cyclones. It rattled the speed limit and crosswalk signs into a cacophony of stuttering metal. Oak leaves that had been hanging on all through winter got snagged in the wind and were sent cartwheeling crazily down streets. A garbage lid skidded by, followed by its empty can, which rolled dizzily down hills, stopping at curbs, until it was pushed back out into the road. The few cars on the streets swerved around the objects that were blown onto the road, not sure what they were. The drivers drove hunched over their steering wheels, peering out into the dark night, uncertain what would blow across the street next.

Phone and power lines swayed like loosely strung guitars; the wires to houses slapped at siding. Lights turned on in some upstairs windows, revealing silhouettes of people roused by the gusts of wind. The drafts, eager and hungry, made their way into warm houses and snuck into dreams, blowing them restless. People would wake in the morning feeling more tired than they had when they went to bed. Their yards would look different, moved around, lawn chairs turned over, branches scrawling over the lawn. The wind preyed on the trees that were dying or dead already; it swiped at the weakest of branches. It was akin to a forest fire, scouring through town and leaving the living holding on more tightly, resolutely, in its wake. It patrolled the edges of the town, blowing along the highway, pacing, prowling. It whipped around the dead leaves from last fall, stirring them up and sending them into the brush, the woods, erasing the last trace of them, eliminating the evidence that they had ever been there.

Jerry walked hunched into the wind, letting it plaster his hair to his head and whip tears from his eyes. Sandblasted, he thought, cleansed. He wanted to go up the mountain and hear the creek, follow it up to the lake he considered his, the lake surrounded by pines. After that he'd go back home and sleep. He needed to sleep, he thought. He felt worn, as if he was coming down with something.

He looked up, expecting to be closer to the path than he actually was. The wind, he thought, was like a hand pushing him back, away from the mountain, shoving him in the opposite direction instead, back towards his home. He walked on, more determined to get there. He could imagine the sound of the water after the rain and now with the wind. And the lake. He'd sit on his rock and watch it. Not for too long though. If the wind was a hand, then it had fingers, and its fingers were making their way into his jacket. He zipped it up to his chin and shoved his hands into his pockets. The wind roared in his ears and he couldn't hear anything else. It had become an ocean of noise, the whole Atlantic pushing into the air and filling the night with itself. It roared, a high tide of wind turning everything to rock, to sea wall, until nothing else was audible, not the shed door in the yard Jerry was going through, banging open and then slamming shut, not the whistling of the wires slapping, not the stop sign that jackhammered against the pole and not the low growl of the Impala driving slowly behind him. Ralph watched him intently, determined not to let him out of his sight.

The creek was how Jerry had imagined it would be. It rushed and gurgled over rocks, swerving and cavorting over the roots of trees that grew into it. And the trees overhead whispered together and then in a gust collided, branches scissoring and falling around him. The wind whipped up the smell of forest as well and Jerry breathed deeply, smelling the combination of moss and pine needles and bark and earth and mushrooms. He stood still for a moment with his eyes closed, listening to the dead trees, brittle and clinking like knitting needles, like knives being sharpened. The wind rushed down hollow stumps and moaned low. Farther off in town he heard the thin train whistle, and closer by a dog howled in response, a long, woeful moan. Jerry shivered and looked quickly behind him. He had never felt spooked in the woods before; it had never even occurred to him to feel frightened. Of what? he asked himself and continued, this time more quickly, to the lake.

Ralph watched him disappear into the trees and waited a moment before motioning to Mike to pull over and park. He rubbed his hands together and then cracked his knuckles. This, he thought, was going to be too easy.

The rock was damp so Jerry pulled his jacket down and sat on it, pulling his knees to his chest, and looked out at the water. His rock was in a grove of pines and jutted out over the lake where the sun would reach it and warm it for him. Not tonight; not even the moon when it untangled itself from the clouds scurrying by could find its way to the rock. Jerry sat in darkness as the pines overhead bristled and fretted. He waited for the feeling that came when he sat before water, the feeling that seeped into him and convinced him that he was part of the lake, the rock, even part of the trees. He waited and looked nervously around him. The wind moaned mockingly. Poor Jerry, it seemed to whine, and when he looked behind him again, he wasn't surprised to see Ralph this time, to see Mike standing there, with their arms folded, watching him, sneering. The moment slipped into place, into the vault where expected moments, inevitable moments, were kept. Rave slowly stood up on his rock, the lake behind him, the trees, and then he jumped down to face them.

He tried opening his eyes but couldn't yet. He moved his arm. He heard Ralph's voice come closer and smelled the liquor on his breath, cigarette smoke.

"Don't fucking mess with me again," he hissed into Jerry's ear and then kicked him hard in the ribs. Jerry heard Mike's high squealing laugh and then he passed out.

He came to, tasting the metal of his blood in his mouth. His hand clumsily made its way to his face and he felt his lips, swollen and cracked. His tongue felt for missing teeth. Only two moved when he probed them. His eyes. His fingers gently moved over the lids that were bulged shut. He tried opening them and slowly they widened, and he saw through the slit of them the clouds still skidding over him and the sky now the purple-blue colour of the approaching dawn. He shut them again, exhausted.

The wind continued bullying its way bossily through the night and into the day. Grace sat at the breakfast table and listened to it howl. Her mother had just left for work, the door slamming behind her. Les had come down in his housecoat, sleep making his hair stand on end.

"Jesus, that's some wind. Kept me up all night." He opened the fridge and peered into it. "Did she get any eggs?"

Grace chewed her toast faster, feeling repulsed by him, his plaid slippers, his striped pyjamas, the way his hair was sticking up. She couldn't believe he had the audacity to talk to her as if nothing had changed.

"I said, did she buy any eggs?" He turned to her expectantly.

Grace shrugged and continued chewing. She had already left, in her head. She had packed a suitcase, folded her clothes, pressed down her books, wrapped up her toothbrush, her makeup. In her mind she had already sat down on all the years she'd been fooled and had pushed the latches in on them, turned the small key and locked them away.

The dog, hearing their voices, trotted in and then flopped down between them, looking back and forth at each face.

"You will speak when you're spoken to, Grace. I asked you if she bought eggs."

Grace shrugged again. She was empty when she was home. He could knock till the cows came home, ring the doorbell, talk until he was blue in the face. She wasn't going to answer him again. He couldn't make her talk. Les slammed the refrigerator door and took a step towards the table. The dog quickly got up and out of his way. Grace finished her toast, and without looking at her father, picked up her plate and carried it to the counter. He blocked her way up to her room.

"I said you will speak when you are spoken to. Did she or didn't she buy any eggs." He spoke low and so forcibly that his spit sputtered out of him. She wiped her cheek and looked up at him.

"If you're going to be that way," he told her, "I will personally take that guitar of yours and break it over my knee."

They looked at each other, the kitchen clock ticking loudly, slowing the moment that hung between them to a stop. It stayed there between them, a solid and hard moment. She took a step towards him but he didn't budge.

"Did she buy the eggs I asked her to or not."

She saw his hand move up to her face but didn't feel it. *Restez calme,* she thought.

"You start showing some respect around here. You're just like your goddamn mother." He hiccuped a sob. "It's not my fault, Gracie, I swear it's not my fault. The police don't know what they're talking about." He was crying hard now, his eyes and ears bright red. She turned her head away.

He sat down heavily on the chair closest to him. She moved quickly into the hallway, not wanting him to see that she was crying as well. Hearing him call her Gracie had melted her into being five years old again when that was what he had called her. His Gracie. She took the stairs two at a time, trying hard to get away from the sound of his sobbing.

All day at school Curtis watched the playground out the window. He watched the chip bags, the candy wrappers, lift into the wind and swirl around the yard, dancing and flying, whirling. He couldn't wait to get home to ride his bike and wear his feathers. He listened to his teacher talk about the planets. He looked up at the sky and could still see the moon. It looked as if someone had coloured it in with white chalk. She called him to return to his desk and he sat obediently colouring where he was supposed to colour, writing his name on the line where he should. He put away the books when the teacher asked him to and got out his math sheet as he was told. He did everything she asked, wishing the day would go as fast as it could. He wanted to ride his bike, he wanted to wear his feathers.

Curtis, the teacher told the class before the bell, was going to get that week's star for being such a good student. The rest of the class clapped and watched him as she wrote his name in blue on the blackboard and then drew a big star under it. She gave him a gold star sticker and wrote that he was the class star in his homework notebook so his parents would know. That made him happy, but he still counted the minutes before the bell rang. He was the first one out, had his jacket on while kids were still stuffing their bookbags with their homework, and he was the first kid on the bus. He sat by the window watching hats being blown off and chased and he waited, kicking his feet impatiently against the seat in front of him. That wind would make him go really fast.

Dellie was riding her tricycle around in circles on the driveway waiting for him. She blew into her whistle when she saw him getting off the bus. He saw her yelling something but the wind scooped up her voice and threw it up into the sky. He ran down his street as fast as he could, using his muscles to run against the wind.

"Curtis, it's so blowy out! Look, I don't even have to pedal." Dellie lifted her feet from the pedals and the wind pushed her forward. She grinned. "C'mon, get your bike. It's fun, Curtis."

Curtis ran into the house, dropping his backpack by the front door. He went into the living room where his mother was drawing. He looked at her sketchbook. She was drawing an ear. He put his arms around her neck and kissed her.

"Hi, sweetie. Did you have a good day?"

"Yes," he answered softly. "Is it okay if I go outside and ride my bike now?"

"Of course you can go outside and ride your bike. Stay on the street with Dellie, okay?"

He nodded and ran up the stairs to his room, to his binoculars and his feathers.

He tried putting the binoculars on first and then the feathers but the cords got tangled, so he tried the putting the feathers on first and still the cords tangled. He didn't want them to get all knotted up. He had to choose. He put the binoculars up to his eyes and looked down at his bedspread. He could see how all the threads were woven together to make his blanket. He looked at his hand, his fingernails. He always wore his binoculars. But then he looked at his feathers. He should give them a try. He could imagine them getting caught in the wind and flying crazily around him. Curtis carefully took the binoculars off and placed them back on the table. He'd wear the feathers today. He wouldn't look at anything up close until after.

Dellie was right, he didn't have to pedal very hard to go fast. His feathers whipped around his neck, twirling gleefully. The faster he rode, the wilder they flew. He pedalled hard to the corner of his street.

"Curtis," Dellie screamed, whistling to get his attention. "We're not allowed to go down there. Don't go down there, Curtis." She whistled again.

He looked down the next street. Leaves were dancing along the curb, a garbage bag was doing somersaults along the sidewalk. This street was even windier than his because it had all those trees beside it, he thought, trees and hardly any houses. Trees must catch the wind, bounce it back and forth between them. He'd ride on it for only a minute and then he'd go back to his street, he reasoned to himself. He was the class star, he was really good at listening. He just wanted to try this wind, on this street. Just for a minute, he told himself, and then turned his bike and pedalled up onto the sidewalk. His feathers bobbed behind him. He heard the sound of Dellie's whistle but ignored it and pedalled faster.

The wind curled up into Curtis's ears, whispering *faster, faster.* He gripped the handlebars and felt the muscles of his legs get stronger. The wind was behind him now, pushing him farther from his street. He looked down at the feathers that Jerry had left him one by one on his night table. They twirled on their string around his neck. He looked up quickly, his tire hit a rock and he fell.

His knee felt hot and burnt. He sat up and examined his leg.

His jeans were torn at the knee and he could see the bright red of his blood.

"Do you need some help there, young fella?"

Curtis looked up, shocked that someone was so close and he hadn't even seen anyone. For a moment he wished he had picked his binoculars to wear instead of the feathers that hung limply now around his neck. He looked at the man's shoes and slowly worked his way up to looking at his face.

For a moment the wind stopped. The leaves that had been whipped around, the branches and garbage, the street signs that stammered against their poles, were silenced. Everything seemed to breathe a deep sigh of relief. In this stillness Curtis looked up at the man who was offering to help. It was the same man he'd been watching at the school. In that instant the wind picked up again so loudly, so intensely, that Curtis couldn't hear his heart pounding hard in his throat.

"Curtis, come back." Dellie threw her head back and wailed up into the sky. Her brother wasn't supposed to leave her. He wasn't supposed to ride his bike off their street.

Les looked down at the boy at his feet. He noticed his small nose, his fingers and dirty nails. And then he saw the feathers. They moved enticingly in the wind as if they were in water. Mesmerizing. He could see why fish would swim to them. He watched them slide across the young body of the boy at his feet, caught by them, hooked by their movement. He reached for them, already knowing how they'd feel to his touch. How soft he'd be, how giving. The lake was smooth, without a ripple, the boy small and so afraid he was still, so afraid that he was frozen. Les warmed him with his touch, let his fingers thaw out the small parts of him. And he melted, Les could feel him give in to it. He let his fingers undo the boy's pants and felt himself stiffen. The boy was really too small a fish, too fine. His hair glinted in the sun, his lips were parted, panting. Les knew he had to throw him back. He thought of all those sunfish from long ago, the iridescence of them awakening a longing in him to keep them, to turn them on their side and catch the sun on their scales, to light them up. He pulled the boy's pants down, the lake was clear and empty, he turned him on his side and watched the sun catch the blue of his eyes, the fine hair of his arms, of his legs. Les could taste the lake of him, could see how the boy knew he was caught, knew it was all up to Les to let him go. Les held onto him even tighter then, pressed up against him and slid his finger in his mouth.

Curtis's brain screamed at him to run, to count the steps from this moment to his front door. His brain ordered him to put his bike away, to be the class star and do as he was told.

He could only think about beetles. And caterpillars. And wish with all his might that he could turn into one, or into a turtle. Pull his legs up into his shell and sit on the sidewalk encased in hard armour. His knee was burning, his skin where the man was touching, squeezing. He shouldn't be touching there, Curtis thought. He'd have to give back his star, he realized sadly, he wasn't being good any more. He thought about hiding, of going under his covers and staying as still as he could, he thought about the dark, about being in it and no one being able to see him. He let the dark ooze into his head, a black crayon that could colour over everything if he pressed hard enough.

Curtis thought at first that his brain was screaming until he realized that it was Dellie's whistle. He opened his eyes and watched the man straighten up quickly, fiddling with his belt, his zipper. Curtis reached down and hoisted up his pants. He was surprised to find that his pants had been pulled down. Dellie came up to them, dragging her tricycle behind her.

"Curtis, you're going to be in really bad trouble." She put her whistle in her mouth and then spat it back out, eyeing the man who had been bent over her brother.

"You're not a policeman," she said accusingly and then looked back at Curtis. "Curtis, you know we're only supposed to talk to policemen." She whistled shrilly and the man took a step back.

"Well, now that your friend is here to help, you don't need me any more." The man moved backwards quickly and then turned and hurried down the street.

"I'm not his friend," Dellie shouted to his back. "I'm his sister." She looked back down at her brother, who had begun to cry quietly, and squatted next to him. "Did you hurt yourself, Curtis? Do you want me to help you?"

Curtis nodded, crying harder now. He pulled the string of feathers off his head and dropped it. The wind snatched the feathers up and scurried away with them, hoarding them, then sending them up and down along the curb. The string and feathers were tangled now and limp.

Dellie stood in front of him and helped pull him up.

"Does your knee hurt?" she asked, looking into his face, worried. He shook his head. "Was that a bad man, Curtis? Was that a bad guy?" Curtis looked at her and started to sob. His shoulders shook and the wind whipped his tears off his cheeks and into his ears. All those cars he had drawn crashed into his stomach like the bumper cars at La Ronde, came smashing into his stomach and near his heart. He was having a hard time catching his breath. Everywhere the man had touched had left burns on him; his arms, his legs, felt as if they were on fire. Dellie watched and began to cry as well.

"Oh, Curtis, did you lose your binoculars?" She sobbed harder than he did and tried standing his bike up. He helped her and they turned their bikes around and headed back to their street, Dellie's cowgirl hat slung down her back now, her whistle tight against her throat.

*   *   *

Dellie pulled her brother through the front door and then shouldered the door closed behind them. The wind howled on the other side of it. They could hear it rattle their mailbox, shake the porch light.

"Wait here, Curtis," she whispered hoarsely. "I'll get Mommy." She took a step into the hallway and then hollered into the house. "Mommy, Curtis is crying."

Curtis slumped at the sight of his mother, of her rushing to him.

And Eliza, when she saw her son, his face streaked with tears, his shoulders and chest jerking with sobs, fell to her knees before him and cupped his small face in her hands. He hardly ever cried. Even as a baby. She used to lay him in the small infant seat and he would look up solemnly and watch her move around him, intent on not losing sight of her.

She pulled her sleeve over her hand and gently wiped his eyes, looking into them.

"What's the matter, Curtis? Where are you hurt?" She felt Dellie prance behind her and then stop, putting her small hot hand on Eliza's back.

"Curtis fell off his bike, Mommy."

Eliza looked at her son.

"Did you have a hard time stopping again? Was that what happened, Curtis?"

Curtis's eyes welled up with fresh tears.

"And," Dellie twirled now and breathlessly continued, "a really bad guy came and took Curtis's binoculars and then ran away."

Eliza heard her daughter walk down the hallway, her cowboy boots clunking on the hardwood floor. She hadn't taken her eyes off Curtis. He blinked heavily, releasing more tears that quickly rolled down his face and dropped off onto her bent knees. She felt her heart swerve from its regular beating. She breathed deeply, willing the fear that was spidering up her throat away from her voice.

"Did a man talk to you, Curtis?"

The house creaked behind them. Curtis looked over his mother's shoulder down the hallway and into the kitchen. The wind was knocking at every window. He'd have to give back his gold, shiny sticker, his teacher would erase his name, his name that had been written in big blue letters, from the blackboard. She'd scratch out the words *class star* from his homework notebook.

He had never been the class star before, he thought sadly. Melinda D. had been the class star twice. Even Jeremy had been the class star. And no one in his class had ever had to return their sticker or get their name erased after the first day. Just him.

Hot tears sprang from his eyes. He couldn't look at his mother. If he had worn his binoculars, he would've seen that the wind was the same up close as the wind on his street. The feathers had fooled him.

"Curtis." Her voice was softer now. She brushed his hair back from his face with her fingers, smoothing it behind his ears. She straightened his jacket collar and wiped his nose again. He had lost his front tooth weeks ago and the space in his mouth was still empty. Her hands slid down his arms to his hands. She spread his hand against hers. He had always liked doing that, always liked how big she'd say he was getting. Soon, she always said, his hands would be bigger than hers. And he'd smile, pleased at the thought of bigger than.

His fingers barely reached where her fingers started. It was such a little boy's hand, she thought, chubby and grimy and small. Really, she thought, fighting back her own tears, really so very small. She smiled at him and pressed his palm to her mouth, kissing it, and waited for him to speak.

"Here, Curtis, I brought you some crackers." Dellie shoved a handful of crackers at him, her own mouth stuffed with some. "Crackers will make you feel better." Crumbs blew from her full mouth onto her mother's arm. Curtis reached out and took the crackers and then let his hand fall back to his side.

"Eat 'em, Curtis," Dellie urged. "They'll make your tummy

feel good." She shoved another one in her mouth as if to prove to him that she was right. Eliza smiled at her daughter and then looked back at Curtis. She noticed his knee for the first time, his torn jeans and the blood that had stained the material.

"Come sit down, sweetie. I'll clean that knee up for you." She led her son to the closest chair in the living room and gently helped him sit in it. He squirmed his way to the back of the chair and let himself lean into it. His legs stuck straight out. Again Eliza thought how small he truly was and wanted to pick him up and just hold him, to rock him the way she used to every night, the weight of him reassuring on her lap, his head in the crook of her arm, his eyes watching.

The cats came into the room and both jumped up and circled on either side of him. He offered the crackers that were hot in his hand to the cat closest to them and it licked at them. He heard Dellie's whistle upstairs and then heard her running hard down the stairs.

"Curtis, Curtis," she yelled breathlessly. "Look what I found! I found them, Curtis." She came rushing into the living room holding out his binoculars triumphantly. "I found you these." She hurried over to her brother and stood up on her toes to put them over his head. He let her, feeling safer as soon as he felt their familiar weight clunk against his chest. No one could sneak up on him when he had his binoculars.

"Now you can see again." She twirled around in front of him, banging into the coffee table. She stopped and dizzily took a couple of steps towards him, the whistle in her mouth again, tooting her accomplishment.

He put them up to his eyes and looked down at his cats. He liked the way their whiskers grew and the fine hair that curled around the inside of their ears. He looked over at his mother's sketch pad that she had left on the arm of the chair in her hurry to come to him in the hall. It was the drawing of the ear she'd been working on when he had come home. She had filled in the head around it. It was his father's head. His father's ear. The ear that Curtis whispered good night into every night.

The ear that always listened. He began to cry again, softer cries, cries he felt leave his stomach and work their way past his heart and into his throat like the feathers he had let go of, burning, as if the feathers had been set on fire. Maybe his dad wouldn't get too mad at him. Maybe once when he was a little boy, he'd left his street too. Maybe a man had touched him too.

"Okay, darling. I'm going to roll up your pant leg and clean that scrape." His mother put a bowl of water down beside her. She gently rolled up his jeans and dipped the corner of the cloth into the bowl, dabbing the cut carefully, cleaning out the small stones and dirt that were stuck to his skin. And then she dried it and covered it with bandages that Curtis had never seen before. Not the peel-off kind but the kind she had to cut with scissors. Even Dellie was watching quietly. It was a really big bandage.

"Can I have one too?" Dellie asked softly, eyeing her brother's knee enviously. Eliza smiled and cut off a square for Dellie. Dellie held out her hand and watched her mother eagerly, then danced around, holding her hand up.

"I got a bandage, I got a bandage," she sang, running up to the cats and singing to their faces. They opened their eyes sleepily and then closed them again.

"Look, Curtis, I got a bandage just like yours."

Curtis nodded, already engrossed in looking at his knee with his binoculars. The skin around the bandage was red.

Eliza watched him for a moment, waiting to see if he wanted to talk, slowly gathering up the cloth and scissors. They all looked up when the front door opened.

"Lily, Lily! Curtis was crying and a man took his binoculars, a very bad man, but I got them back for him and I even got a bandage, look." Dellie lifted her hand up for Lily to look at and then whistled shrilly around her sister.

Lily took off her jacket and came into the living room, looking at Curtis, who was still in the chair, too engrossed with watching one of the cats clean its paw to notice her or the tears that were still streaming from his eyes. She looked at her mother, who sighed and smiled at her. She went over and sat on the arm of the chair beside her brother, moving her mother's sketch pad out of the way.

"Hi, Curtis."

He swung his binoculars up to her face.

"Did you hurt your knee?"

"And a very, very bad man talked to Curtis but I told him to leave him alone. Leave him alone, I am that boy's sister, I said to him." Dellie blew hard into her whistle and then spat it out indignantly, her hands on her hips.

Lily looked back down at her brother.

"What happened, Curtis?" Lily saw that Eliza was watching her son, concern furrowing her brow. She looked at Lily, a look that passed the concern to her as well, and they both watched Curtis and waited for him to talk.

They all busied themselves around Curtis, waiting. Eliza picked up her sketch pad and began drawing him, coaxing his voice to paper, drawing his head, his neck, the ring of T-shirt around it, as if everything about him shone with the current of his voice right below the surface. With every line she drew, every shadow she filled, she silently urged her son to speak, to tell her what he was holding onto that was making him cry softly and steadily. She drew in his lips, imagining them moving. "Mommy," he'd say, and she'd wait and listen.

Dellie was winding a piece of string slowly around her legs. The cats had watched from the chair and then pounced down at her. They swatted at it with their paws and the smaller cat followed the string under her legs and around her feet, making Dellie squeal with laughter. She got up and pulled the string slowly, tantalizingly, behind her and the cats followed, galloping up to it and flicking at it. Then they'd stop to clean their paws, their faces, until she jerked the string close enough to them, left a trail of it off the coffee table, shaking it to get their attention.

Lily watched her sister and the cats. The definition of cyclone came back to her. A system of winds. A system of cats. And a system of waiting, each of them joined and cycloning gently around Curtis.

Without an encyclopedia to copy from, without the whole set of volumes lined up ahead of her, she had nothing to write in her notebook. She turned to the next blank page and wrote down the date and then looked at her brother, who was studying the arm of the chair, his binoculars close to the upholstery. Once in a while he'd sniff and wipe his face with his free hand. He was still crying. She looked at her mother, who was drawing, and at Dellie getting chased by the cats. She uncapped her pen and wrote the word *Waiting* and then closed her eyes. If she came across the word *waiting* in the encyclopedia, she wondered how it would be described. *A state of being poised. On the edge. When one is filled with anticipation. Related to longing and to wishing. A room full of family and a small boy crying quietly, not speaking. Each member of the family is a finger, together a hand holding the small boy, who has not yet spoken. The family soothing the boy with their presence. Waiting. See patience and impatience. See worry.*

All four of them looked up at the sound of the door opening. They heard Stan humming to himself, occasionally breaking into song about having to be free. He came into the hallway carrying his lunchbox and sweater and then stopped at the entrance to the living room.

"Well, look at you all sitting in here." He smiled, looking around the room, and then stopped at the sight of Curtis intently watching him. "Hey, cowboy."

Dellie rushed over to her father, the cats stampeding behind her still chasing the string she was holding. She ran into her father's legs and pressed her face into them.

"Daddy, Curtis talked to a bad man and then the wind blew all his favourite feathers away and now he is very sad." She spoke muffled, her face still pressed against her father's leg. He heard the words *Curtis* and *bad man* and dropped everything, his sweater, his lunchbox, dropped even the rage that had filled him first, gently moved Dellie from his legs and with two big strides was before his son, bending his face close to his.

"Curtis? Are you all right, cowboy?"

He watched his son lower his binoculars and nod, without looking up. Stan looked over at Eliza.

"I was going to phone but you were already on your way home."

He nodded and looked back at Curtis, whose head was still down. His hair had been parted and pushed behind his ears. Eliza must have been stroking his head, he thought, Curtis's hair was never parted, never behind his ears. Stan put his hand, still dirty from work, smelling of exhaust and factory and cigarettes, under his son's chin and gently lifted it so he could look into Curtis's eyes. Stan was surprised at how red they were. He'd been crying for a long time. Curtis never cried, he thought.

"What is it, cowboy? What happened to you?"

His son looked away, his lip quivering, and Stan put his forehead against Curtis's, looking deep into his eyes, their noses touching.

"You can tell me anything."

Curtis cried then, harder than he had been, sobs that hiccuped and shook his shoulders. Stan felt his son's body shake with tears and felt his own eyes water. Curtis. He closed his eyes and waited, rocking their heads back and forth like a pendulum measuring the beat of this sadness, trying to absorb it for Curtis, trying to coax it out of his son so he could carry it for him. He'd do that easily, without hesitation. Curtis's breath slowed and Stan felt his son's arms move around his neck. He straightened slowly holding Curtis's body to his, feeling the little boy's legs wrap around his waist, his head burrow into his neck. Stan walked slowly to the rocking chair and lowered himself into it, careful not to bang Curtis's bandaged knee on the wooden arm of the chair.

He rocked them slowly, soothing the wrinkles from his son's T-shirt. He felt for Curtis's hair and smoothed that down as well. He felt his son's head turn, felt his breath, hot, into his own hair. His whisper tickled Stan's ear.

"I got a star today."

"What's that, Curtis?" Stan asked softly. "You got a star?"

Curtis nodded and dug into his jeans pocket, fishing out a small gold star, the tips folded, the centre creased. He held it out for his father to see, watching his face closely.

"You can have it," he whispered.

"Oh, Curtis, that's your star, buddy. You keep it."

Curtis shook his head vehemently and buried his face back in his father's shoulder. Stan looked around the living room at Eliza and Lily, who'd been watching him rock Curtis. Waiting. He felt for the arm of the chair and rose from it slowly, holding onto his son.

"What do you say we make some supper, cowboy? How does that sound?"

"Can I help you make some supper too, Daddy?"

"Sure, Del, you can help us." He smiled weakly at his wife and then went into the kitchen, Curtis's arms clinging around his neck so tightly that it hurt. He didn't know what else to do but wash his hands, pour a bag of frozen fries on a baking sheet and wait while the oven got hot. He offered a fry to Dellie and Curtis. Curtis shook his head but watched Dellie take one and bite into it, squealing at how cold it was. Stan felt his son watch him cut open the package of hot dogs and dump them into a pot of water. Curtis's legs tightened around his stomach when Stan reached into the fridge for the ketchup and mustard. Dellie set the table, putting out spoons and knives. She got out plastic bowls from the corner cupboard and placed a bowl at each place.

"We're going to eat our fries and hot dogs out of bowls, Del?"

Dellie nodded.

"Sounds good to me, sweet pea. What do you think, Curtis? Bowls okay with you?"

Curtis nodded into his father's shoulder.

"Fries in bowls is tonight's special then." He filled the sink and put the dishes that had accumulated all day into the soapy water. Every once in a while he'd rub his son's back or smooth down his hair and would kiss his small shoulder or bare arm. Waiting. By the time the water for the hot dogs was boiling, he felt Curtis's hold slacken. He peered down at his son's face to make sure. His eyes were closed, his breathing was slower. He had stopped crying although his body still shook.

Stan went into the living room and sat back down in the rocking chair. Eliza and Lily got up and finished making supper and Stan rocked slowly to the sounds of them eating, of Dellie's high little voice talking and Eliza's low murmur responding to her. He leaned back into the chair, grateful for its support. Curtis was pressed hard against him, a film of sweat where their bodies touched. He was heavier than Stan remembered him being as if whatever had happened to him had weighed him down. He looked at his son's sleeping face, his mouth open, parted, as if he were about to say something. Stan would wait for as long as it took. He hummed a lullaby into Curtis's hair, not knowing what else he could do.

Grace walked until she could hardly move her feet. When she came home, the house was empty. The dog had pulled everything out of the garbage and had spread it all over the floor. Eggshells, coffee grounds, orange peels, bread and milk bags were strewn in piles everywhere. The dog looked up from a bacon wrapper guiltily, skulking into the corner with its tail between its legs. She must've been hungry, Grace thought, and began picking up the mess Lady had made. The dog watched, thumping its tail whenever Grace looked over. I should be feeding her, Grace thought, no one else bothers to. She swept up the coffee and leftover rice and dumped it all back into the garbage can, then snapped her fingers.

"Come here, Lady." The dog came over timidly, its head down, its eyes watching Grace.

"That's a good dog." The dog immediately lay down and turned over on its back, its paws up in the air. Grace scratched its belly for a while and then got up. The dog scrambled up and sat watching her open the fridge for something to eat. It watched the apple move from Grace's mouth and then down, up and then down, not taking its eyes off the fruit. The dog looked away when Grace turned to it. She threw it a small piece and it gobbled the apple up, licking its lips appreciatively.

The dog watched Grace look out the window, and every time Grace looked back down at it, it thumped its tail. Grace went to the pantry and scooped out some dog food. The dog pranced behind her, circling her legs excitedly. It began eating from its bowl before Grace had a chance to dump in all the food, and its tail wagged when Grace patted its head.

Les came in without making much noise. Grace looked up in surprise and then quickly looked back down. Her father seemed different. He was flushed and happy.

"Hello, Grace, hey there, Lady." He squatted down and called the dog over. It approached him slowly, its tail wagging cautiously. Les patted the dog and rubbed its chest; the dog looked up at him adoringly. Then it ran into the kitchen and came back with a bread bag, playfully swinging it into the air.

"Were you eating garbage?" The dog thumped in response. "We can't have that, can we?" He went over to the pantry and scooped out some dog food. He scratched the dog's side and its tongue lolled out.

Grace watched her father talk to the dog and the dog wag and follow him to the dish. She couldn't figure out what was different about him. His cheeks looked flushed and he seemed excited about something, happy. She watched him fill a glass and slosh some water in the dog's water dish as well.

She watched him get down on the floor and play with the

dog. He laughed when the dog licked his ear. He never laughed, Grace thought. The dog was gleeful, excited by all the attention. Les let it lick his face, his neck and ears. Grace looked away. Les was slapping at the floor and the dog was hunched, pawing at his hands.

She wondered where her father had been just now. Toys and tools. She knew she could just go upstairs, just grab some cookies and go upstairs, but something was different about him, and if she pressed, she might find out what it was. She could hardly breathe any more when she was around him, could hardly swallow. She felt as if her mother's words were sitting in her throat like rocks. The police had phoned. Boys.

"Where were you?"

"You mind your p's and q's. I don't have to answer to you. I don't have to tell you my whereabouts, missy." He pushed the dog away from his face and the dog tried again to lick him. Les laughed and grabbed at its paw. The dog yelped.

"You're hurting her!"

"Jesus Christ, Grace, I didn't mean to hurt her. Would you quit nagging at me?"

Grace felt the anger that had grown so familiar lately rise in her.

"I'm not nagging you, I'm just asking where you were."

Les looked at his daughter, his eyes narrow, his lips drawn thin and pale.

"You never mind where I've been, Grace." He stood now, shoving the dog away with his leg. "It is none of your goddamn business where I was, so leave me the hell alone."

"You were out walking, weren't you? Looking for boys?" She knew she should stop, she knew by the colour of his face, the way he was facing her, his hands clenching and unclenching, that she should stop. But even if she wanted to, she couldn't. Something in her had changed gears and now whirred faster. She needed to know if what her mother had said was true. She watched herself press him, rewind, stop, play, push him into admitting it.

He took a step towards her, his arm raised threateningly.

"Don't you talk that way to me. You have no business accusing me of anything."

She felt hypnotized, as if she couldn't look away from him until he said it himself. She felt bewitched, and watched herself facing him as if from far away. Everything she had heard came hurtling into place.

"Is it true?"

Part of her wanted him to stand there and tell her calmly, to walk back from the Les he'd become to the Les she wished he was. Part of her wanted to see him gesturing at her with his pipe, wearing a cardigan, the newspaper tucked under his arm. "Honey," she imagined him saying, "of course it's not true. How could it be? They've caught the guy they were looking for. It was just a case of mistaken identity." Part of her willed him to step from their kitchen that still smelled of garbage and into this spell, to transform into Atticus or Carson or Johnnie and to comfort her, to hold and soothe her. To be the father she had always craved.

"It's those kids who are the perverts, Grace, not me. They're the little hooligans looking for trouble. I'm just an innocent bystander."

Grace watched each father leave. "Goodbye," they said to her in turn at the door on their way to work, on their way to the corner store for ice cream. "Goodbye," they each said. And she said goodbye back to them, knowing that they were leaving and would never come back.

Les started coughing so hard, he held onto the chair for support. When he stopped, he cleared his throat and pulled out his handkerchief, spat into it and then shoved it back into his pocket. He looked at her.

Goodbye, she thought, ignoring him. Goodbye. Goodbye. Goodbye to the cardigans and the crossword puzzles, the gentle teasing and the crinkly smiles. And hello to the tool man, hello to the man who admits every day that he has a bad heart.

* * *

Les watched his dog sleep. It lay on its side and moved its paws as if running. It whimpered and its lip twitched. He bent and patted it, made soothing noises when it cried out. "There, there," he said to the dog. "It's going to be all right." The dog grew still and slept fitfully. Les waited, hand poised, ready to calm it down, to ease its whimpers but it slept soundly. He straightened and then left the kitchen. Lady was a good dog, he thought, submissive and whiny but good. He felt a wave of satisfaction move through him. It had been a good day. He thought of the boy's bike, how its front tire turned and how he had watched the boy fall, his small cries, his knee. Les rubbed his fingers, thinking of the boy's feathers hanging around his neck. The dog slept deeply now, not moving at all.

Without his help, without Les coming along when he did, that kid would still be lying there. That boy had needed him today on the sidewalk. There were fishermen and there were fish. The dog's nails scratched at the linoleum. It whimpered. Les went into the living room and sat down in his chair, pulling the lever that made it recline. He closed his eyes and put himself on that street again. The wind had been at his back, pushing him to walk faster, getting him there just in time. He smiled. Just in time.

Before he fell asleep, Les took inventory of everything that was good in his life. He listed the new router he had bought and the palm sander. The snow blower, he reminded himself, ten-horsepower hungry for a driveway full of snow. He pushed aside the thought of the spring, the summer and fall between now and a snowfall. It would wait, he thought, the snow blower would wait. He thought of the gospel music eight-track he had just bought and that kit he got at Radio Shack to tape telephone calls. Just let those cops call him again, accusing him. He'd press charges and he'd have proof. He smiled smugly. He thought of the pen he had bought the last time he went into the tobacco store. And the extra cartridges that had come with it, that fit snugly in the velvet case that snapped shut, sounding efficient and important. He loved that pen and could see himself signing papers at the bank with it, in the general manager's office. Yes siree, he'd whip out that pale blue velvet case and sign his name on every line he needed to. A class act, they'd all think, noticing his cufflinks, his twenty-year tie pin they had given him at work.

What else, he thought sleepily, what else was making him happy? He mentally walked through his house, noting his things, holding them up and measuring their worth. His stereo, his eight-track player, his cassette player, his shoe polish kit. They were all good but something was bobbing, humming, just on the tip of his tongue and then it came to Les. Curtis. How could he forget Curtis? He let the image of the boy, crying and looking up at Les gratefully, smiling through his tears, wash all over him, showering him with detail: his torn jeans, his missing tooth. He let the thought of the boy, his name, whirr, purr its way through his veins, his fingers, his stomach and then settle. Curtis. Les fell asleep with the boy's name on his tongue, the feel of him etched into his hands, his fingers curled around the memory of him. Curtis. He slept deeply, quickly, his mouth open and breathing in more, it seemed, than he was breathing out.

"A very, very bad man," Dellie told her parents solemnly, look-ing at each of them sitting on her bed. "So bad that he had big scary teeth and horns this tall." She used her own head to show them how big his horns were. "Really big horns." She nodded sadly.

"Did he talk to Curtis, Del? Did the man talk to Curtis?" Stan watched his daughter squirm, reminding himself to be patient as she grabbed one of the stuffed dogs and kissed it good night. He tried to keep his heart that was beating to get out from reaching his voice. He didn't want to scare her.

"He talked a little, he growled like this." She growled evilly at her father. Stan felt Eliza breathe deeply beside him. Curtis had gone to bed, exhausted. The only thing he had talked about was his star and how he wanted someone else to have it. His gold star sticker. Stan had read out loud that Curtis had been chosen as the class star but it had only made his son cry again.

"Dellie, did the man touch Curtis? Did you see the man touch Curtis?" Eliza asked this quietly and the tone of her voice stilled the little girl. She thought before answering, pulling at her hair.

"Curtis and the man were talking about those feathers, I think. I had to pull my bike because I'm not allowed to ride it on that street, so I pulled my bike and it's so heavy. I was tired. I was sweating even. I got muscles now. Look at my muscles." She flexed her arm and each parent took a turn feeling her muscle.

"Okay, sweet pea, time for bed." Stan stood up and pulled the blankets around his daughter. He bent and kissed her and she held onto him until he tickled her and then she let go.

"Good night, Dellie." Eliza kissed her forehead and then both cheeks.

"Don't forget my nose, you forgot to kiss my nose!"

Eliza smiled and bent and kissed her nose. "You were very brave whistling at that man. I'm very proud of you, Del. But you and Curtis have to stay close to the house, okay? That's the deal. You can't leave our street, okay?"

Dellie nodded. They both left her room, leaving her door open a little. Her shouted good nights followed them all the way downstairs.

Lily heard her parents in with Dellie. She'd been sitting on her bed with her notebook opened on her lap. She uncapped her pen and printed the word *worry* under her entry for *wait*. And then she looked up at her ceiling. Worry, she thought and then wrote: *twisted, clenched thoughts. Thinking of all the things that could go wrong. The worst scenario. Parents looking at each other grimly and not talking. Pacing. Stomach aches. A folded gold paper star. Burned french fries. Second cousin to* waiting, watching. *Sister to* hope. *Population varies though each person worries alone. See* uneasiness *and* premonition. And then she put her pen down.

These entries would be more useful than dung beetles and dandelions, she thought. They'd all be able to use them. She lay on her bed for a long time before falling asleep and just listened to the sounds of the house. The wind had died down, only gusting occasionally. She heard her mother's music faintly playing downstairs and the water running somewhere. Something had changed in the house; it didn't seem easy and rumbling into sleep with the rest of them. Her father wasn't singing along with Tom Jones the way he always did. Lily could just hear the record, Tom Jones singing by himself, as if he were asking a question and everyone in the house was quiet as if waiting for the answer.

Jerry moved stiffly through the woods. His ribs still ached and his eyes were still swollen. He had spent the day staying away from where Grace might find him. After everything that had happened with Ralph, she might want to go after him herself and Jerry didn't want that. He just wanted it all to be done.

He made his way to the creek and lowered himself to its bank. The water was clear and moved quickly over the rocks and roots. He could make out the small pebbles and grasses that grew beneath its surface, and then closed his eyes and listened to the sound of the water, thirsty for movement, its current small and feisty, splashing and gurgling. Jerry felt himself grow calm. All he hoped now was that Ralph would leave them alone, that the beating had evened the score, that Ralph was convinced again that he was the strongest, the toughest, and that Jerry and Grace weren't real threats. Ralph had caught him and Jerry hadn't put up a fight, he hadn't even really defended himself, and he knew that Ralph despised him for it. He felt the contempt when Ralph had let him go, dropped him to the ground disgusted, and let Mike have his turn kicking. Jerry had made it too easy.

Jerry opened his eyes and watched a squirrel scurry down a tree and dig at the pine needles and dead leaves on the ground. It sat up on its hind legs, chewing busily and staring back at him, its small hands always moving, rubbing and fretting, scavenging. He hardly could see the squirrel against the tree, its fur and the pine needles and tree bark blended and joined. It had its own Ralphs, Jerry thought, throwing small stones into the water. There were Ralphs everywhere, and as if he had spoken it out loud, a crow responded, cawing loudly, bobbing vehemently with each caw. Jerry looked up at it perched on the highest, thinnest branch and watched when it took flight, climbing the sky higher and higher, swooping great circles over Jerry's head, swooning. Jerry's heart clamoured the way it did for Grace and he wondered about that, about love and bird and how they must be related. He wanted to go and find her now. It was always so effortless when he was with her, his heart, the ease of its flight, the swooning. She was like standing in that light at dusk, the light between sun and moon when every tree seemed to be more itself, each branch held out, basking. He stood up, his heart still clamouring.

His jaw hurt, his ribs. What was he doing, he wondered, without her? How could he not be drawn to that kind of light? Each branch, her arms, her neck, her head leaning against him, both of them overcome and easy. A place to take flight from, a place to land. How often had he watched birds, gulls, crows, the occasional hawk just swerve and swoop, joyous while he watched, his breath nearly taken away? Like when he was with Grace, he thought, looking for the feather she had given him: part bird, part branch, part button, part buttonhole. She undid him until he was bare and even more of who he was. Clamouring. Swooning.

He found a stick and began fishing out the garbage the wind had blown into the water as he walked along its edge. A shopping bag was snagged on a stone, cigarette packs, gum wrappers floated by soggy and pale. He had to leave the water at the end of the path, where it changed directions and disappeared into a backyard. From this height he could see most of the town, its street lights coming on, the light from living rooms and kitchens almost golden. Jerry zipped up his jacket and walked quickly across the street and up into the yard with the German shepherd. He bent to pet it and then hurdled the white fence into the next yard, and then the next yard. He had gotten to know the yards to her house the way he knew the trees to the lakes. Swimming pool, blue shed, rock garden, road. Broken clothesline, rusted wheelbarrow, road. Bird feeders, wooden gate, patio with flowerpots, garden path. Each stone named Grace, each fence, each gate, Grace, each house, each garden, Grace.

Grace took the key for the shed off the hook and went out to get her bike. She wanted to go to Lily's, to the house where she could feel Jerry. She'd tell Lily she was locked out again, which she was in a way, locked out of her house, locked out of her family. She opened the shed door and peered inside. The musty smell of dead grass filled her nose, her mouth. The snow blower took up most of the space. Her father had covered it with a special plastic cover he had bought specifically with the shed in mind. She noticed he had used a black marker to write his name on it. Les McIntyre. His printing got smaller with each letter, less convinced, she thought, of who he really was.

Her bike was trapped, pinned behind his snow blower. She wouldn't be able to get it out. Everything in the shed was stuck behind it, the rakes, the watering can, the lawn chairs, everything. The thought of her bike pinned behind his snow blower enraged her. She left the shed door swinging open behind her and stomped back into the house. Her father had gone up to lie down, yawning sleepily when he had told her, contentedly.

"Bastard," she muttered, opening the side door and marching into the living room still in her boots, her boots muddied from the backyard. The dog followed her jubilantly, sniffing at the footprints she left, marking her mother's carpet.

The living room glistened like an ice rink, the plastic on the sofa shiny and hard. The sound of birds squawking, of kids screeching outside, made its way and was stopped by the sheers that hung in the window, the spotless panes of glass. The room was still. Motes of dust floated through the air she had just walked through, disturbed and then settling again as if she were in one of those miniature winter settings that had been turned upside down and shaken. A blizzard. Somewhere a clock ticked. The end tables, the coffee tables, shone like concrete in January, parking lots undisturbed, a whole night reflected frozen. Doilies snowflaked on the back of the furniture, under lamps. December, December. Grace strode over to the window and flipped up the curtains. She pulled the window open and stood in the fresh, cool air that came pooling in, the sounds of outside louder now, inside.

It all came off more easily than she thought it would. Long strips of plastic, some of it yellowed from the sun, lay in heaps at her feet. She threw the doilies on top of it until the plastic was covered in white. A snowdrift in the middle of the living room. Winter. Her mother had worked so hard at protecting the furniture, Grace thought, picking up the pile in her arms. The couch still looked the way it did the day it was delivered. The armchairs were immaculate. Gary. She stopped for a moment. He'd understand, wouldn't he? He'd understand that she had to leave this house caught up in the right season. A car drove by outside, its wheels crunching. The curtains billowed and the dog sat by them, its snout in the air, sniffing. Part of her didn't care whether Gary understood or not. She realized she was angry at him as well. He could've warned her, she thought, let her in on the big family secret.

She hoisted the bundle of plastic and doilies higher, surprised at how light it was for its size, and made her way back outside, the dog following her expectantly. It cowered at the door, not sure what to do. Grace closed the door gently. "I'll be right back for you, pup." The dog wagged its tail and cocked its head.

She made her way back to the shed and kicked the door open, letting the plastic, the doilies, fall onto the snow blower, surprised at how they stayed perched there. He finally got the snow he'd been wishing for. A dream come true, an unexpected melt in the living room.

She closed the door on the heap, leaving it to the dark, spider-webbed shed. The latch slipped into place and she hooked the lock onto it, pushing it firmly closed. The key was small and silver. There was a piece of white tape across it that said *shed* in Les's shaky handwriting. She went back into the living room and squatted behind the television set. The key made a scratching sound against his social insurance number. It gnawed at the number until it erased him from the set, from the stereo. It left long lines on the barometer. Grace used the small shed key to unlock all of his possessions, to set them free, and then she went back outside. The ground was hard, worn to dark dirt and last year's stubborn brown ragweed. Under the tree the dog had dug up a hole. Grace dropped the key into it and covered it over with dirt. She stamped down on the mound until it was even with the rest of the yard. And then she went back to the house and let the dog out on its chain, closing the door behind her.

She breathed in deeply the smells of soggy grass and earth. The sun was beginning to drop behind the maples across the street. She looked back only once, raised her hand to the dog, who had stopped digging to watch her. It would dig up the key to winter, she thought. The dog would dig up the key. She smiled. And then the dog would swallow it.

Lily's hand was sore, her wrist throbbing. Just one more, she'd only write one more entry. After so much worry: *shy, cautious but inevitable. Drenched still by worry, wet and shivery. Long-limbed, knock-kneed and unsteady. Rotates inward, swirling together. Standing, then stepping forward. Curtis's voice, soft and serious, finally, asking for more pudding. "Please," he remembered after, with an even smaller smile, and then reached for the black crayon, pressing it hard onto his piece of paper. Later, the sun in the kitchen at suppertime. The lift in her mother's voice: look how light it still is at this hour! Eating in the light of it, together. The metered click of spoon and teacup stirring sugar and milk. The chickadees at the feeder. A glimpse of Jerry in the trees. Grace. All of these a system, a gentle cyclone, a bright, sunlit hurricane of hope. Hope,* Lily wrote again, underlining it a couple of times. The word that would begin these entries and the word that would end them.

The wind finally stopped. The last of it had whistled through the trees the night before, climbing up branches, panting and out of breath. It had blown the remnants of winter around the town, scoured the gutters and yards of dead leaves and whipped them across streets and sidewalks. It had bellowed and moaned and slammed doors shut. Then it had left, wheezing and gasping, in a huff, leaving broken trees in its wake, bent and bruised grasses. Slowly the sounds of the town began to sprout, to bud and open, filling the silence with bulbs and seeds planted last fall. Perennials. The train whistle, long like the willow branches, each leaf small and pale green reaching for the water. The slender shoots of children calling across yards to each other. Dogs barked, doors and windows opened. The light began to last moments longer each day. It lingered, fingering the new leaves, picking up and putting down the long familiar branches, examining the small details of each day the way only light can, up close and with reverence. Slowly, lumberingly, the town itself blossomed into spring, the days coaxed into unfurling, lighter and longer, and lured into summer.

Acknowledgements

I am incredibly grateful for the time spent by both my agent, Dean Cooke, and my editor, Iris Tupholme, on this story. They are both responsible for coaxing the shine out. I'm also grateful to Rebecca Vogan and Suzanne Brandreth.

I'd also like to extend deep love and gratitude to my two children, Ryan and Robyn, who ate breakfast for supper so often they became pale and pasty, for leaving me alone, for listening to the same CDs over and over again, for writing their names in the dust of the house with smiley faces and hearts.

I'd like to dedicate the hope in this story, the long light, all the good feathers, to Helen Humphreys. And to Joanne Page, for her shovel and stone, I dedicate the paths made easy, that just appear. The moonlight, every silver sliver of it, is for Gayle Upton. And the orchard, its shed, the red and yellow leaves of autumn, the trees, are for Tim Quick.

The daily weather of the writing was made brighter by so many people: Debbie Bourque, Peggy Snook, Marie Murphy, Maggie Armitage, Lynn Davies, Deannie Sullivan, Kelley Aitken, my continuing education classes at the Mount, Grant Patriquin, Virginia Hickey, Eleonore Schönmaier, Teresa Giovannetti, Scott Murphy, the baker, the butcher and the guitar player at the market, and finally, for his light touch, Steve the tattooist.

I am grateful to Jane Buss, Mary Jo Anderson (and Frog Hollow, one of my favourite bookstores) and Brian DesBlois for reading so closely and so wisely.

My thanks go also to Heather Gibson and her miracle computer at the Word on the Street office, as well as to Joanne Merriam and the Writers' Federation of Nova Scotia for support and encouragement.

Thanks to the Canada Council and the Nova Scotia Arts Council for their financial support.

Finally I wish to thank Don McKay, Jan Zwicky and Tim Lilburn, and the Nature Writing and Wilderness Thought Colloquium participants, and Rachel Wyatt and the Banff Writing Studio where this story started as poems. Really bad poems.